One Last Shot

A Second Chance Sports Romance

Julia Connors

To the women who fix other women's crowns
without telling the world they were crooked . . .
I see you. Keep building each other up.

Chapter One

PETRA

14 Years Ago
Innsbruck, Austria

"It's time," Papa says from the doorway of my bedroom. I look up from my laptop where I've been preparing for the upcoming season by rewatching video footage of my ski racing from last winter.

Behind my father, an old picture of Mama hangs above my desk. She's standing on the balcony of a little hotel overlooking Lake Hallstatt with her hands on her hips and a smile so bright that looking at it is equal parts beauty and pain. Her long dark hair frames her heart-shaped face, but her heavily lidded eyes look at me like they know I'm doing something wrong.

What would you have me do, Mama?

I take a fortifying breath, praying that I'm not making a deal with the devil. I may only be sixteen, but one thing I

1

know for sure is that when things seem too good to be true, they generally are.

"Let's go, *Zaichik*." Papa still calls me Bunny, the nickname from my childhood that will not die.

As I follow Papa down the narrow staircase to the first floor, I take in the mismatched frames full of family pictures that still hang in the stairwell. They haven't been updated since the horrific car crash that took Mama and my brother, Viktor, from us three years ago. In them, my mother is still young and vibrant. Viktor is still a high schooler who loved to torment his little sister.

As I do every day that I pass them, I wonder who they'd be today. Who we'd be—Papa and me—if they were still alive.

"Be grateful," Papa reminds me as we leave the comfort of our small caretaker's cottage to head down the path to the lawn that will lead us to the big house.

"I am." I don't mention the other emotions—the fear, worry, and regret.

I breathe in the flowers that line the path behind the big house. Above them, the imposing stucco walls of Whitehall glow in the fading light of the golden hour. For most of my life I've curled up on the cushioned window seat of my tiny bedroom, gazing across the lawn at Whitehall as the sun sets, watching the lights come on and the family inside come alive.

Those two boisterous boys were like cousins to me—until Mama and Viktor died. Through that tragedy Sasha and I grew impossibly close, but now he and his older brother, Nikolai, are grown and gone most of the time. Niko spent the summer in London for an internship and is now back at university for his senior year. Sasha has been living in St. Petersburg and traveling all over Russia and Europe, playing professionally in the Kontinental Hockey League for the last year.

Having him home for the summer has been both torturous and heavenly. My feelings for him have been blossoming for years, but this summer it's starting to feel like maybe it's mutual. The shared glances, the whispered secrets, the way he often can't take his eyes off me. It's like we're sliding into new territory that I can't quite name but am desperate to get to. But tomorrow he's leaving to go back to his team and who knows how long it'll be until I see him again.

From the patio, Papa opens the door that leads into the kitchen of Whitehall, rather than one of the many glass doors that lead into the grand sitting room at the back of the house.

Last year, when Sasha graduated from high school, Mr. Ivanov had a fancy party to celebrate. Even though we were guests that night, Papa still refused to enter the house through those glass doors that were cast wide open. Sasha had been insistent that I come in the same way as all the other guests, telling me that I was more important to him than anyone else who was there. But Papa claimed that the only doors the property's caretaker should use are the garage door and the kitchen door. Old habits die hard.

We head through the kitchen and dining room, then into the massive two-story entryway. At the far end, we climb the wide wooden staircase up to the mezzanine, which we follow until we reach the doors of the library.

Mr. Ivanov sits at the ornately carved wooden desk like a king on a throne. Mama once told me never to trust a man like Mr. Ivanov—"duplicitous devil" was how she'd described him. I'm not sure why I shouldn't trust him, he's never done anything but try to help my family. Still, the warning hangs there over his head, reminding me to be alert.

"Petra, Leo. Come in." Mr. Ivanov manages to direct one of his smooth smiles at me and Papa, but like always, the smile doesn't quite reach his eyes.

I feel Sasha's presence as he ambles in behind us—a warmth spreads throughout my body and just as I'm about to turn around and smile at him, the look on Mr. Ivanov's face stops me. His voice is about ten degrees cooler as he greets his son with a curt "Aleksandr."

I've never understood Sasha's relationship with his father, how the two of them are so detached from each other. Papa and I aren't super close either, but that's because I was always Mama's shadow and Papa spent more time with Viktor. But Sasha's only ever had his father, and I've long wondered if Mr. Ivanov resents his youngest son because his wife died during Sasha's birth. Even though Sasha is my closest friend, I've never had the guts to ask his opinion on the matter.

"The paperwork is all ready?" my father asks.

"Yes, we just need to sign these two sheets here. You and I, with our children as our witnesses. I'll have Gerta translate and notarize it in the morning." He looks over at me, "Then you'll be off to Switzerland for school. Are you excited?"

"Beyond excited," I tell him. I swallow down all my concerns about being so far from home, about how this takes me even farther away from Sasha. But he's going to be back in Russia again this year anyway, so I can't let him factor into my decision. Instead, I tell his father, "I can't thank you enough."

"It's nothing," he says, waving his hand in the air. To him, it probably is nothing—a tiny drop in the bucket that is his fortune.

"To me, it's everything. Please, know how grateful I am." I feel the heat creep into my cheeks because I can tell when Sasha's eyes are boring into me, even when I can't see him.

"You are very welcome," Mr. Ivanov says smoothly. "Make us proud."

"I will, sir."

I hate pandering to his father like this when their relationship is so strained—it feels like a betrayal to Sasha—but this boarding school and the ski training it will provide me are my last hope at making the Austrian National Ski Team. I have two more years of high school, if I don't make the team by the time I graduate, it's unlikely I ever will. My high school coaches are good, but not good enough. The coach for the national team has told me as much. He said I am a promising skier but need more training. So I'm headed to the best school with the best ski training program I could get into.

I don't know how my father will ever repay Mr. Ivanov, though Papa insists it's doable. He says all I should worry about is my skiing and my academics, and leave the rest to him. As if I will be able to do that.

My father clears his throat and holds his hand out for the pen. There are two papers on the desk, and he bends to sign on the line above his name on both pages, and then hands me the pen to do the same. The Russian letters swim together, and I'm frustrated that I can't read them. I speak four languages, but only read and write the three I've studied in school—German, French, and English. Still, I recognize my name and sign where I'm supposed to on both pages.

Before I push away from the desk, my eyes track to Sasha

where he stands off to my side, but his eyes don't meet mine. They're too focused on the space where my denim miniskirt meets the back of my upper thighs. I'd give him shit for that if I wasn't so thrilled and both our fathers weren't here.

There was a time I worried he'd only ever think of me like a little sister, and then this summer happened. There have been so many moments like this one that have given me hope. And the longer his eyes are locked in place, the more that hope grows. Eventually he looks up, sees me noticing him staring, and quickly looks away.

Behind his desk, Mr. Ivanov takes the papers back. "Aleksandr," he snaps as he holds the pen out to his son. If he's embarrassed his father just caught him staring at my ass, he doesn't show it.

Instead, he steps confidently up to the desk and the back of his left hand brushes against my hip as he passes me. I slow my breathing to calm my racing heart as I debate whether that was an accident or whether it was intentional. Sasha signs both papers, and Mr. Ivanov quickly pulls them out from under his son's hand and signs them himself. He shuffles them together, opens a folder, and sets them inside.

Mr. Ivanov stands, and it's obvious where Sasha gets his height, though it's always amused me that the resemblance ends there. Whereas they both have fair skin, Sasha's got eyes the color of steel and hair that's nearly black like mine, while his father's blond hair is graying with age and his blue eyes are so pale they're almost lifeless. Both Niko and Sasha must take after their mother.

"I wish you the best at school, Petra," Mr. Ivanov says and holds his hand out to shake mine.

"Thank you. I'll work my hardest." I sound like an idiot,

but I'm not sure what else to say to this man with the eyes that refuse to thaw. Even his well wishes sound forced, like he doesn't know how to show genuine emotion—which has me wondering why he's helping me at all.

I want to feel the thrill of excitement from this amazing opportunity I've been given, but there's a worry wriggling around in the deep recesses of my mind. I pray Papa hasn't gotten in too deep.

Papa and I leave the library and head back toward the stairs. I glance over my shoulder once we're in the hallway and find Sasha watching me walk away. I don't have time to consider what that means because as we descend the stairs Papa tells me, "I have to go check in with Felix about a delivery of some fruit trees he's ordered."

The mention of our new gardener, who just started this summer, gives me pause. He's in his twenties and stupidly attractive. I may have spent some of the early summer flirting with him—more out of boredom than anything—but I've been keeping my distance since Sasha's been home. When he's here, Sasha occupies all the space in my mind.

I've spent the last few years wishing I didn't care about Sasha quite so much. He's never seen me like I wanted him to —I was like a little sister or a best friend, but never more— until, I hope, now. Each time we've touched accidentally and not pulled away immediately in response, the way he looks at me sometimes, his eyes lingering on my body in a way they didn't before. Or maybe they did, and he's just not as good at hiding it this summer? Maybe at sixteen I'm finally old enough that he doesn't need to hide it?

"All right," I say to my father as we walk out the door. "I'll see you back at the cottage, then."

7

Papa turns right, toward the greenhouse, and I head down the crushed stone path between boxwood hedges that will lead back to our cottage. I've walked for less than a minute before the sound of crunching gravel behind me has me stopping. I turn to find Sasha.

The boy is a man now, he just keeps growing. He seems to have topped out at six foot three, but he has more muscle every time I see him. He stalks toward me, never as graceful on his feet as he is on his skates. His huge frame should be intimidating. I rarely feel safe around men, but Sasha has always been a protector. My protector.

He steps into my space, a hair too close to be considered polite distance, and those gray eyes are practically black in the fading light.

"I'm leaving tomorrow," he says, as if I haven't been dreading the day he returns to Russia and his hockey team.

"I know, I've been counting down the days."

"Because you can't wait to be rid of me?"

I consider being coy. I think about telling him I can't wait for him to finally leave, then reaching out and sliding my hand down his chest. My entire body tingles at the thought, at how he might react to my mixed message. But I can't do that to him. He doesn't need teasing. Sasha needs unconditional love more than he needs anything else, even if he doesn't know it yet.

"Because I hate it when you leave." I can feel my lips turning down at the corners.

"Hey," he says, reaching out and tilting my chin up so I'm looking at him instead of at my sandals. "I'm still very much here."

"Yeah, for like twelve more hours." I don't know if this

crushing sense of disappointment is just because he's leaving, or because he's leaving and I still don't know if he feels the same way about me.

"I bet you're not even going to miss me. You'll be away at boarding school anyway," he says with a small smile. "You're going to love it."

"I hope so." So far, high school has been hell. The girls all hate me, and the guys pay way too much attention to me.

"Most importantly," he says, "you're going to be skiing all the time. This is your chance, Petra. Keep your eyes on the prize and don't let anything distract you from your goals. You're so close."

I love skiing, but I do worry that getting to do it every day still won't be enough to fill all the lonely voids in my life. "I know. I don't do anything halfway. I'm one hundred percent committed."

My eyes are focused on his face and I wonder if he knows I'm talking about him, too. The way his Adam's apple bobs as he swallows, he must.

He shifts his weight back and forth between his feet—he seems edgy or nervous around me lately. Then he takes a step closer. He's only a breath away, and I reach up to rest my hand on his chest. I'm amazed at how solid he is, how beneath my hand his pecs feel like stone that's been sitting in the sun all day. The man's all muscle and radiates heat. But despite the way my body craves his, I still see the boy I've loved for years.

My eyes are locked on his, and his ragged breath meets my face in shuddering waves. His eyes do that thing they sometimes do where it looks like his irises are changing color —a swirling riot of different shades of gray—as they skim over my face and land on my lips. Then he extends one of his strong, capable hands and rests it on my hip, his calloused fingertips caressing a soft patch of bare skin above my waistband.

"I have something for you. A going away gift, of sorts." He pulls away, just a small step. But his voice is a low, soft caress and the sound of it brings goose bumps to my skin in the same way I imagine it would if he trailed his lips along my neck. "Meet me at the treehouse in an hour?"

Our secret meeting spot is a treehouse that Mr. Ivanov had built for his boys when they were little. Back then, my brother Viktor was welcome there, but they always pulled the rope ladder up so I couldn't join them. When they outgrew it, abandoning climbing trees in favor of organized sports, the treehouse became my hiding spot. The place I could find solitude for hours with snacks and a good book. The place I could cry when the girls at school were especially mean. The place I could plan out a future where I didn't have to pretend I didn't care what people thought about me.

It's also where I went, despite the snow and freezing temperatures, when I first learned about the car crash. It was there that Sasha found me and held me while we both cried. It was the beginning of our friendship, where we turned the corner from neighbors to people who truly cared about each other. Over the years, we've continued to meet there frequently. It's a refuge from a world that can often be too harsh.

His hand is still on my hip, the pads of his fingers resting on the skin of my lower back and his thumb gently stroking my stomach. "Yes," I agree. "The treehouse at nine."

"I'll see you then," he says and steps away. I turn and rush back to my house, knowing with utter certainty: *Everything is about to change.*

———

My hands are shaking from the anticipation and excitement as I scurry up the rope. The straw bag I've looped over my shoulder swings back and forth, continuously sliding forward and hitting my knees as I climb. When I'm close enough to the top, I use one hand to lift the bag onto the floor of the treehouse and climb in behind it. I only have a few minutes to get everything set up before Sasha gets here.

I spread the patchwork quilt over the dusty floor and take the candles out of the bottom of the bag. With only two small windows looking out into the leafy branches, the inside of the treehouse is pitch-black even though there's still a little light in the sky. Not only will the candles be necessary if we want to see each other, I'm hoping to create a romantic atmosphere for our goodbye tonight.

This feels like our last chance.

If we leave this summer without acting on these feelings growing between us, we might never have the opportunity. He might meet someone in Russia, or I'll meet someone at school. Our lives are already heading in opposite directions. If there's nothing more than friendship to bind us together, I'm afraid he'll just drift away from me. And I've lost too many people already, so I'm planning to hold on to him with the strength and love he deserves.

His head pops up through the hole in the floor as I'm on my hands and knees lighting the third and final candle.

"What's this?" He looks around with one of his unreadable expressions stitched across his face.

I push up so I'm standing on my knees, and I know my skirt is bunched up around my thighs because his eyes pause there for a moment, just like they lingered earlier. Then they move to my belly, focusing on that sliver of skin between the waistband of my denim skirt and the tight button-down sweater I'm wearing. I hope this is a good sign—with Sasha, it can be hard to tell.

"I wanted to be able to see you in this dark, old place."

His half smile is a rare, hard- won victory. A relieved sigh escapes my lips.

"Well, are you coming in or just going to hang out on the ladder all night?" I ask.

The muscles in his arms flex as he plants his hands on the floor and pulls himself up into our secret room. The space is far too small for either of us to stand up in now that we're fully grown, so he sits cross-legged on the blanket, facing me. I sit back on my heels, which puts us at eye level despite our height difference.

For a minute we just stare at each other, that awkward-ness that didn't used to exist suspended in the air between us. Then he reaches behind him. "Here." The word is gruff, and he shoves a book I hadn't noticed him arrive with into my hands. "I found it for you."

I glance down at the book in question even though I know by his statement, by the pride in his voice, what it'll be. "Oh my gosh, Sasha!" I gasp. "I can't believe it."

"Why would you even want a first edition of *War and Peace* in Russian? You don't know how to read it."

"I told you, it was my mother's favorite book." I glance at

the slightly worn hardback cover again. "Mama had one just like this and she lost count of how many times she'd read it. It was practically falling apart. I don't know what happened to it after she died. It's like it disappeared off our bookshelf."

His left eye twitches, which only happens when he's lying about something. He pauses a beat too long. "Well, now you have your own copy."

"Thank you," I say as I hug the book to my chest and try to ignore my curiosity about whatever it is he's hiding from me. Then I reach to the side and set it down at the edge of the blanket. When I turn back toward him, his eyes are focused on my body again. Somehow I don't mind, even though I hate it when the boys at school ogle me like this. I wait for his eyes to drift up to my face.

His lips part like he's going to say something, but no words come out. The look on his face is something akin to pain.

"What's wrong?" I ask.

He swallows again. "Nothing." His left eye twitches.

I scoot forward on my knees so we're only a foot apart. "Sasha, you're my best friend and I need you to stop lying to me." There's a palpable tension in the air, something electric that is snaking its way around us. If I reach out and touch him now, sparks will fly and we'll both burst into flames. I want that—the thrill of touching him, the fire that would erupt between us—more than I've ever wanted anything. And it feels possible, within my grasp for the first time ever, because finally he seems to see me the same way I see him.

"What's wrong?" I ask again, leaning in close enough to feel the heat radiating from his body. I'm torn between wanting him so badly it hurts, and wanting to understand why he doesn't even look like himself. He's good at staying calm, wearing that mask that hides all his feelings. But this isn't his normal mask. This is something else entirely.

He takes in the limited amount of space between us, his eyes sliding down and back up to my face. "Petra," he says my name like he's choking on the word, "nothing can happen between us."

I'm so surprised by his response that I just blink at him, my lips parting slightly as I try to catch my breath. His eyes are on my mouth, just like they were in the garden earlier. His forehead is creased and his eyes crinkle at the corners. If that isn't a look of longing, then I don't know what is.

"Why are you doing this, Sasha?" I ask. He's fighting something that is so obviously right.

"You're a child." The condescending tone hits me like a spray of ice water to my face. "I don't see you like that."

"Bullshit," I say. The attraction that's been growing while he's been home this summer is clear as day, painted across his face, embedded in that hungry gaze. I know he loves me, and I know he could be *in love* with me if he let himself.

"I don't feel that way about you, and if you don't realize that, you're a fool."

His words don't just sting, they crush. Sasha is *trying* to hurt me and I don't understand why he, of all people, would do this. Especially when I can tell that he doesn't mean it. His words are at odds with everything else . . . his body, his face, the emotion I see in his eyes. He's in pain too.

"Why are you saying these things?" I whisper, trying to hold back the tears that are clouding my vision.

"Because you need to hear them. You're playing a dangerous game, flirting with every man around you. You're sixteen, but you look a lot older, and you're going to get yourself into trouble one of these days."

"You sound like all the jealous, catty girls at school. Is that what you are, Aleksandr? Jealous and catty?" When he doesn't respond, I say, "I can't help what I look like."

"You need to be careful," he says, his eyes bouncing all over my face like he's cataloging every last detail.

"Oh." The word is an icicle dancing between us. "You're one of *those*."

"One of what?"

"One of those people who thinks that instead of teaching boys to respect girls, we need to teach girls to be careful not to attract too much attention from boys."

"No, I'm just someone who used to be your friend, but I don't think we should be friends anymore."

A literal knife piercing my pounding heart would do less damage than these words. He's left a gaping hole in my chest, a wound so deep and fresh I can barely utter, "What?"

"You heard me." There's no expression on his face, his eyes are placid, his lips are flat. "This is goodbye."

"Sasha." The words are a whispered plea floating off my lips and falling on deaf ears. "No. I can't lose you too." This doesn't even make sense.

Not once did I envision tonight ending this way. I would have done anything to keep his friendship, because there is *no one* in this world more important to me than him. I don't understand why he's doing this to us.

"You have no choice," he says, and he's never sounded more like his father in his life.

When he descends the ladder, I don't for a second believe this is really the end, that this is really goodbye forever. We're too close for that. He's my best friend, and even if he doesn't want anything more than that, he would never end our friendship like this.

Over nothing.

Would he?

Chapter Two

PETRA

Present Day

I stand at the window in the living area of the hotel suite, sipping my coffee as I take in the view of the southeast corner of Central Park. I can see across The Pond to the Nature Sanctuary, and beyond that, the buildings of the Upper West Side rising above the opposite edge of Central Park.

When my coffee is half gone, I hear the sound I've been waiting for—the rustling of the sheets. I pick up the second cup of coffee off the windowsill and head back into the hotel bedroom.

He's propped up on one elbow and his muscles bunch up in ripples across his abdomen. Yep, he's as fit as he felt in the dark last night.

"Wow," he says, sleep clinging to his voice as he looks me up and down. I'm in nothing but a T-shirt, and I've spent the past twenty minutes fixing my curls from their post-sex messiness.

"I made you coffee," I tell him as I hold up the to-go cup. "To have on your way home."

"Ouch. I was ready for round two. You kicking me out already?" His voice is teasing, like he thinks I'm going to say *Oh, round two? Yeah, let's go for that.*

"I don't do this whole next-day thing," I say, picking up his dress shirt off the floor and tossing it to him. The only reason I didn't kick him out last night was because I fell asleep, exhausted from a day of travel between Park City, Utah and New York City, combined with some pretty decent sex. It wasn't a terrible way to end my day, but waking up with a stranger in my bed is never my favorite way to start a new one.

His face is screwed up into a mask of confusion as he catches the shirt, but he slips it on. As his fingers work at the buttons, he says, "Just so you know, usually I'm the one gently ushering someone out the door the next morning."

I hold in my *Not this time* comment, because there's no reason to rub salt in the wound. Instead, I say, "I had fun last night."

"Me too," he says, swiping his pants off the floor at the edge of the bed. He slides his legs into them as he stands and looks at me while he zips and buttons them. "Maybe we can do it again tonight."

"I've already got plans tonight," I lie.

"It was worth a shot," he says. I wait while he gets his socks and shoes on, then I head to the hotel room door, which I hold open for him to indicate it's time to go. I hand him the to-go cup of coffee on his way out, shut the door behind me, and lean against it, relieved to have the space to myself. I have a lot to do to get ready for this meeting today.

W ith a courtesy smile for the doorman, I step out the hotel doors and let the crisp, April air wrap itself around me. The bright midday sun hits the buildings and reflects off the windows and limestone, making it feel like the city is lit by a spotlight. People stream past me, muttering their frustration as I stand on the wide sidewalk and take in my favorite city. As much as I've tried to ignore and deny it, I have missed New York more than I imagined I would.

I walk along the concrete, my heels pounding the pavement as I head toward the restaurant Emily picked out. It's only four blocks from my hotel, a luxurious building on Fifth Avenue. I'll have to figure out who booked my hotel room and thank them.

Emily is waiting outside the restaurant when I arrive, her hair piled on top of her head in a messy bun, and the loose pieces framing her face blow freely in the breeze. With her perfectly peachy skin and matte pink lips, she looks like she's shooting a makeup ad—which makes sense given that she's currently the face of one of the leading makeup brands in the country. Every single person who passes gives her a second glance, like they're trying to figure out how they know her.

She opens her arms wide when she sees me and gives me a kiss on the cheek as she pulls me close. "I've missed you. It's been way too long."

"I know," I sigh, pulling back and getting a good look at her. I promised I wouldn't be that girl who moved away and never visited. "It's just harder to get back here as often as I planned."

"I know, and I understand." She pulls open the restaurant door and ushers me inside.

As soon as the waiter has taken our drink order, Emily says, "So tell me everything. Why are you here? And how long are you staying?"

"I don't actually know," I tell her as I slide my cream wool jacket off and hang it over the back of my chair.

Her brows furrow. "What do you mean, you don't know?"

"My assistant, Morgan, got a call about a week ago from a lawyer here. His client is interested in hiring me for a big event, and wanted to meet with me privately to discuss it. But I don't know who the client is."

"You flew across the country for this meeting and you don't even know who it's with? That doesn't sound like you." Emily furrows her brows as she takes a sip of her water.

She's right on a hundred different levels. Walking into any situation where I don't have control of all the moving parts is akin to walking into a pit of snakes.

"According to Morgan, what they're willing to pay will make it worth it. Besides, a trip to New York was long overdue. It's all on them, and I get to see you. Win-win. So, I'm headed to that meeting this afternoon."

"I thought events planned by Petra Volkova were booked a year or more in advance."

"Usually that's true. But I had a high-profile society wedding in Park City planned in a month, and the whole thing fell through. I have other smaller events scheduled here and there, but that was the big thing we were working on, and so now I have some room in my schedule." I consider this a win because I kept the deposit money so if I fill that time with another event, it'll be like getting paid twice.

"I'm not at all surprised that event planning has turned out to be the right fit for you." Emily's smile is the small, private kind—not the dazzling one she flashes for the camera. "If you ever did want to get back into modeling though, let me know. My agent is taking on new clients."

I shake my head immediately. "There is no way that will happen."

"She's not like Ryan," Emily assures me. The sound of that man's name is like someone dragging a razor blade down my spine. "She's wonderful. Supportive of her clients, tough as nails when it comes to negotiating a contract."

"I'm so happy for you," I assure her. "But my modeling days are long past. It's been five years. No one gets back into modeling when they're thirty."

"Things have changed," Emily says. "There are so many more avenues into modeling now. It's not all catwalks and photoshoots. I make as much money on social media as I do in my official modeling gigs—I only do those to stay relevant."

"I prefer working behind the scenes. Give me a big fashion show to plan, and I'm your girl. Walking in that show, however . . . those days are over."

"You belong in front of the camera," Emily says, shaking her head. "A face and a body like yours? They deserve to be seen."

"And they are. But only by the people I choose to see them." Since leaving New York, I've built myself a small army of supporters—friends who are like family, employees who would protect and defend me at any cost. However, that small security blanket will get ripped off when I report to LA in a month. But I can't tell her that because the show I'll be hosting won't be announced until we're well into filming, and according to my contract, I can't tell anyone about it other than immediate family. In other words, I can't tell *anyone*.

After the waiter delivers our drinks and takes our lunch order, Emily holds up her glass. "Well, here's to you building a new life you love."

I raise my glass to her toast, even though it's odd to hear her refer to this as my "new life." I only modeled for a couple years, then left to do event planning here in New York. After visiting my friend Jackson in Park City during the Sundance Film Festival, I started looking into the event planning market there and recognized a good business opportunity when I saw one. I moved there four years ago to start my own company and have never looked back. It wasn't the first time I'd reinvented myself, and it won't be the last.

"And to you," I tell her. "For sticking with the thing you love, and being even more successful at thirty than you were in your twenties!"

Emily blushes, her cheeks pinking just the perfect amount. "Sometimes it still doesn't feel real. I thought I'd be irrelevant by now. A suburban housewife looking back on the glory days, you know?"

I laugh. "No. I've never even pictured myself married, much less as a suburban housewife." I tilt my glass to hers. "Here's to not letting men define us."

She tilts her glass toward mine before we both take a sip of our drinks, but her lips pull down at the sides.

"What is that look?"

"Hmm?" she asks, looking up at me as if she's not really seeing me.

"Why do you look sad?"

"How could I be sad, Petra? I have everything I've ever wanted."

I pause and take in her expertly highlighted brown hair; the big brown eyes, thickly arched eyebrows, long lashes, and the high cheekbones that have made her face perfect for modeling; the elegant column of her neck and the slope of her slim shoulders. "What's missing?" I ask.

The quick intake of breath flares her nostrils—the only indication that I've hit on something she doesn't want to talk about. She doesn't reply.

"I'm here if you want to talk, okay?" I tell her.

"Everything is fine." She shrugs and gives me a small smile. "But thank you."

I wonder what she's not telling me, but then I think of all the things I haven't told her. This woman I lived with for years when I first moved here, someone who was like a sister to me, is almost a stranger now. And that's mostly my fault.

"I'm here for at least a few more days," I tell her. "One lunch is not going to be enough time for us to catch up. What other plans are we making?"

Her face lights up, and I realize she's missed me more than she's let me know. And given that I've always prioritized my friendships with my girlfriends over everything else, I wonder how I let her down so badly—and what I can do to make it up to her.

————

"I'm Petra Volkova," I tell the receptionist as I step up to the desk in the lobby of the lawyer's office. "I'm here to see Tom Shepherd."

"Oh, yes," the receptionist says. She stands at the wooden desk she shares with the two other receptionists. I glance behind her where *Callahan, MacDonald, Reardon & Shepherd* is written across the frosted glass wall in gold lettering. "Mr. Shepherd is expecting you. Follow me."

She waits for me to step up next to her before she turns and leads me around the glass wall that separates the reception area and the rest of the office. I tower above her as we walk down the aisle between desks. My goal with high-profile clients is to give off the vibe of professional power, and nothing makes me feel more powerful than a well-fitted dress and sky high heels.

Leaning toward me with a conspiratorial grin, she tells me, "I'm probably not supposed to say this, but I've just been temping here, so whatever," she waves her hand in the air like she's brushing away the stigma around whatever it is she's about to say. "All the girls in the office are in quite a tizzy today. We always are when *he* comes in. We've all been dying to see who he and Mr. Shepherd are meeting with."

This type of inane chatter is exactly why I could never work in an office. And though I'm still not sure who *he* is, I'm guessing that whoever Tom Shepherd called me here to meet is extraordinary in his own right.

"I can't say that I see what the big deal is," I shrug, feigning nonchalance while hoping she tells me who I'm meeting with.

She gasps. "Okay, maybe you're not a hockey fan, but

you're *clearly* a woman. You can't possibly be immune to a guy that looks like he does."

I'm sure my face conveys exactly how unimpressed I am. I know next to nothing about US hockey and care about it even less. I've never loved the sport, and Sasha ruined it for me like he ruined so many other things.

"Hockey players don't impress me," I tell her as we come to the end of the rows of desks that sit outside the offices lining the wide hallway we just traversed. In front of us is a wall of glass windows looking out over Midtown Manhattan. "There's something very—" I pause as I search for the word. "—brutal about the sport . . . and the men who play it."

I've actively avoided hockey for the past fourteen years so it's not like, even if she'd told me his name, I'd have ever heard of this mystery man.

"Brutal, sure." She shrugs and adds, "But he's hot as hell."

She takes a left and I follow her down a hallway of conference rooms with frosted glass doors. When we come to the end of the hallway, an executive assistant sits alone at a desk with her back to another bank of windows. Across from her is a small but elegant waiting area with comfortable chairs, a marble table with a variety of magazines, and an elegantly simple chandelier lighting the space. It feels cozy and graceful and not at all like the waiting area of a high-rise office building.

The assistant stands when we approach. Her light brown hair is coiled on top of her head in a loose but tidy bun, and her tortoiseshell glasses are a brand I wouldn't think she could afford on an admin's salary. A smattering of freckles across the tops of her cheeks and the bridge of her nose make her look even younger than she probably is. She nods to the receptionist, dismissing her, then reaches her hand across her desk toward me. "Hello, Ms. Volkova. I'm Avery Parker, Mr. Shepherd's assistant."

"Hi, Avery," I say, shaking her hand. "Please, call me Petra."

"Right this way, Petra." She steps around her desk and walks toward the door where the hallway ends. *Thomas Shepherd* is written across that door in modern raised letters reminiscent of the lettering on the glass wall in the reception area. Inside the office, we can hear raised voices.

She glances at me, obviously not expecting arguing behind the door. She knocks twice and there's dead silence in there as she pushes the door open for me.

My stomach gives a small lurch as the door swings in, but I make sure I exude confidence on the outside as I take in the imposing space. Natural light from the two adjoining walls of floor-to-ceiling windows floods the far end of this corner office, with dark finishes everywhere else—navy walls, and a sitting area immediately off to the side.

Past that sits a dark walnut desk, the man behind it is presumably Tom Shepherd. He stands as I walk toward him, saying, "Ms. Volkova, welcome. Please, have a seat." He gestures to one of the two mid-century modern walnut chairs with leather seats that face his desk. The one that's empty.

The man in the other chair hasn't moved since the door opened. He sits there like a hulking beast, his tall and muscular frame barely fitting in the seat. I can tell by the tense lines of his thick neck that there's raw power beneath an otherwise calm exterior. As I come up behind him, I feel like I'm approaching an animal who could turn and over-power me with no effort at all. Despite my own stature, I feel uncommonly vulnerable as I step up behind that empty chair.

I pull it out and as I prepare to take my seat, and glance down at the man in question right as he glances up at me. Those eyes, the color of steel. That razor sharp jawline, apparent even under the facial hair. Those cheekbones that run along the top edge of the neatly trimmed beard. The permanent scowl. His dark hair is longer than I've ever seen it and the lines at the corner of his eyes are new, but I'd still recognize him anywhere.

"Sasha?" My voice is full of wonder, because I'm not sure how he is here after all this time. Fourteen years of no contact has that sense of wonder turning to anger in the pit of my stomach.

His deep voice is a husky growl, achingly familiar even as the man who sits in front of me is so different from the one who left me years ago. "Hello, Petra."

Chapter Three

ALEKSANDR

Her look of astonishment is replaced immediately by confusion.

"What are you doing here?"

I can barely follow her question because my brain is going haywire, looking at her for the first time in so long. She's more beautiful than ever.

"Ms. Volkova." Tom's voice fills the space, but Petra's eyes never leave my face. "My client, Alex Ivanov, recently discovered some legal documents that concern you. We thought it best to inform you in person."

"You tricked me into coming here?" she asks, looking straight at me. She waits a beat, then says, "I don't care what documents you've found, at this point I want *nothing* to do with you."

It's not what I expected her to say, but it's not a surprise either. Fourteen years without any contact. Of course she's pissed. She starts to turn, and I'm afraid she's going to walk out that door and I'll never see her again.

"Petra." Her name comes out harsher than I intended,

but succeeds in getting her to stop. I say the one thing I hope will get her to stay. "We're married."

That tight blue knee-length dress she's wearing skims across her body as she staggers forward a few steps in her heels.

I want to get up, go to her, hold her, and tell her we'll figure this out together. But I can't. My end goal is unfortunately more important than her feelings. More important than mine too.

"I can see this is quite the shock," Tom says, his voice all polished finesse that couldn't sound more different from the man I've gotten to know on the squash court. He is the only person in the world who I would actually call a friend.

Petra's eyes flit to Tom as she turns to face us, and the look on her face asks why he's even speaking. Then she levels those bright blue eyes right back at me. "What. The. Hell?"

Tom and I agreed it would be better if he were the one to explain things to her. There's too much at stake for me to stick my foot in my mouth and piss her off. But I can't sit by silently and ignore her like I have for the past fourteen years. She has always deserved better than that.

"Alex," Tom draws my name out as a warning, like he knows I'm about to go rogue and is reminding me what we'd agreed to.

I ignore him and turn my attention to Petra. Nothing has changed—the attraction I didn't want to feel then and don't want to feel now is still there.

"When my father gave yours the money for your boarding school, that wasn't an agreement for an exchange of funds. That was a marriage contract."

Her eyes widen. "Did you know that's what it was when we both signed it?"

I'm relieved she still trusts me enough to ask this question. "Of course not."

"Even if we signed a marriage contract, that doesn't mean we're actually married," she insists. "I went back to Austria for my cousin Natasha's wedding a few years ago. And I distinctly remember her and Mathéo having to go to the vital statistics office *in person* to apply for their marriage license, and then return there for the civil ceremony. And since we didn't appear in person to apply for a marriage license, nor did we return to get married there, we can't be married."

My lips turn down at the corners before I say, "I consulted with a lawyer in Austria already, but the paper trail is airtight. Every single thing points to us having applied for a marriage license and taken part in a civil ceremony, both in person. And even though *we know* that we didn't, the lawyer insisted that no judge is going to believe us fourteen years after the fact."

"You did all of that before even telling me?" Is that hurt I see in the way she narrows her eyes at me? "How long have you known?" She sets her bag on the chair and rests both her hands on the back of it. She's not sitting, and with the way she's braced herself on those nude stilettos with the gold studs along the straps, she seems poised to leave if she decides she doesn't like my answer.

"That's hardly relevant to the issue—" Tom starts.

"Like hell it's not," Petra interrupts him, never taking her eyes off me. "How long have you known, Sasha?"

"Who the hell is Sasha?" Tom mumbles, more to himself

30

than to either of us. I'll have to explain how Russian nicknames work later.

"I found out about three months ago when my father died."

I see her expression change when I mention his death, like she's internally at war with what she wants to say next. "I hope it was a good death?"

"It was," I tell her, but it's a lie. My father died of a heart attack, alone in his mansion after he'd ostracized everyone who ever cared about him. In Russian culture, we'd call that a 'bad death.' But I don't want her to feel sorry for the man who gave her father money in exchange for wedding vows, especially since that wasn't even the worst thing he did to her or her family.

"Good." Her face softens a bit as she looks at me like she's trying to determine how I feel about my father's passing. It was no secret that we had a contentious relationship at best.

"I went through the same thought processes you're going through when I found the marriage license and the marriage certificate among my father's papers," I say before she can ask any more questions about my father. "So whoever our fathers had to pay off to make this happen, they did."

An acerbic laugh breaks through her pursed lips. "As if my father had enough money to pay someone off to fake marry me to his employer's son."

"Petra—"

She hears the pity in my voice and interrupts me before I can say more. "So why? *Why* would they do this?"

I shrug. I have no answer I can share with her.

"So if you found out about this months ago, why are you just telling me now?"

"I was hoping I could figure a way out of this for us."

"Oh, you were going to figure a way out for *us*?" Her voice is rising—no longer low and raspy—she doesn't even sound like herself. "You can't just go around making decisions on my behalf without consulting me! Especially not after all these years."

"Petra." Her name rolls off my tongue like a caress. "Of course I was going to consult you—once I had more details. Which is *now*."

We look at each other in silence for a moment before Tom clears his throat, trying to move this conversation along. We haven't even gotten to the reason we're here. We both look at him, which he seems to take as an indication that he should take over from here.

Now that I've seen her again, I really wish I'd set this up differently. It should be just the two of us having this conversation.

"Given this new information, my client would like to propose a solution that we think will be amenable to both parties."

"Oh, I'm *all* ears." That raspy voice of hers escapes through tight lips, sarcasm dripping from each word.

"My client needs US citizenship. You have your Austrian citizenship via your birth, but given that your mother was a US citizen, you've also retained your citizenship here."

Petra raises her eyebrows. "Yes, I understand my own citizenship status."

"And given that you have legally been married to my client for the past fourteen years," Tom continues, "and you have both resided here in the United States for at least the past three years, that would qualify him to apply for citizenship."

"What does any of this have to do with me, then?" she asks.

"Well, there is a hiccup. US Immigration requires that you must have been living in *marital union* with your spouse for at least three years before the application for naturalization is submitted."

"We obviously haven't done that," Petra says. "And besides, what makes you think I'd want to help *Alex* here?" She spits out my name like it's a lie, and I guess in her world it is. Never in my life was I called Alex until I made the NHL and my agent decided a more Americanized name would be easier for fans to remember. Before that, I was always Sasha. And why *would* she want to help me after the way we left things?

"Alex is prepared to make this endeavor worth your while," Tom responds. "After he receives his citizenship, he'll grant you a divorce with enough alimony that you'll never need to work again."

"Oh, he'll *grant* me a divorce, will he?" Though her words are for Tom, her eyes are back on mine. Behind those blue irises, a Petra-level storm is brewing, and I'm almost looking forward to watching it break. Tom has no idea what he's in for as she turns toward him. "Unfortunately for him, I *like* working. I love the company I've built and I'm proud of the work I do. And no man is going to walk into my life and act like he's granting me some sort of salvation, when really what he needs is my blessing and my assistance."

Tom sputters, clearly not expecting that reaction. A

typical lawyer, he thinks everything can be solved with enough paperwork and money.

"How do I even know that marriage was legal?" she asks me. "I was a minor."

"You were sixteen," I tell her, "which is the age of consent for marriage in Austria, as long as a parent signs off on the union. Which your father did. And as long as the other party is over eighteen, which I was."

As the realization that her own father betrayed her seeps in, the small crack in her armor shows me just how much this hurts her. "And so now you're trying to buy me off? Use me to get what you want, then send me on my way with a divorce and money. How quintessentially Ivanov is that?" Her low, rumbling laugh is bitter.

"You're right about my family." That is exactly how my father handled problems—throw enough money at it and the problem goes away. "But that's also not what I'm trying to do here."

"Oh? Then what the actual hell *are* you trying to do here?" The color rises in her cheeks, a flood of red-hot anger she can't hide.

"I need US citizenship, and I'm willing to do whatever I have to do to get it."

"Why the sudden need? You've legally been living and working in New York for . . . how many years now?"

"Eight."

I see a momentary flash of realization in her eyes. Eight years. When she lived in New York I was here too, which she didn't know then, but I did. And I never contacted her.

"So why the change now?"

"Alex is about to retire," Tom provides the lie we agreed

on. "His P-1 Visa is dependent on him playing hockey, which he won't be doing after the end of this season. That could be as early as this month, depending on how the playoffs go."

Petra looks back and forth between us. "You've had eight years to apply for citizenship. Why didn't you think to do this sooner?" Her eyes fly between me and Tom as she tries to figure this out. "I feel like there's a missing part of this situation that you're not sharing with me."

"Let's just talk about this like rational adults." I know immediately that I've said the wrong thing. Why did I suggest she's not being rational when I'm the one who sprung this on her?

"You ambush me in a lawyer's office with news that we're married, threaten me with divorce, and offer to buy me off with future alimony. You have a plan and paperwork, and you've consulted me on exactly *none* of this. I don't even know who you are anymore." There's a note of sadness mixed in with the anger.

"I know this is a lot of information being thrown at you. I should have handled things differently—" I glance over at Tom quickly, hoping he receives my *I told you this was the wrong way to go about this* message loud and clear, before I turn back to Petra. "But please, let's talk about this. Come over to my place tonight and we'll sort this out."

"You abandoned me fourteen years ago," Petra says. "I can't imagine why you think I'd help you now."

"Just think about it this afternoon. I know you have more questions. Meet me tonight and I'll answer them as best I can." My voice shakes the slightest bit even while I try to maintain my composure. "I really need your help, Petra."

"I need time to think about this," Petra says, shaking her head.

"Alex, I'm not sure—" Tom warns, but I hold up one hand, stopping him from saying anything more.

I should have done this differently in the first place. I was a coward to have Tom be part of this conversation, and it's backfired badly. I need to rebuild Petra's trust in me, and it won't happen through Tom.

"Just come over tonight," I say, my eyes still locked on hers. "I'll text you the details."

Out of the corner of my eye, Tom crosses his arms over his chest and leans back in his chair, shaking his head.

"How do you have my number?" she asks.

"I got you here, didn't I?"

"You're unreal," she spits out as she grabs her leather bag off the chair where she'd set it when she first came in, then spins and stalks out of the room.

"Sasha, huh?" Tom says the minute the door to his office slams.

"Of all the things that just happened, that's what you lead with?" I shake my head, then lean forward and set my elbows on my knees so I can rest my forehead on the palms of my hands. I have a sudden tension headache.

"Okay . . . that went well."

I press my lips together, so the frustrated growl rattles around in the back of my throat rather than escaping my mouth. His legal advice might have been the "safer" approach, but it has made this whole situation so much more difficult. I should have known better.

"I'll take over from here," I tell him. There's no room for disagreement in my statement, but still Tom argues with me.

I guess that's what you get when your only friend is a lawyer.

"I think that's a mistake."

"Of course you do. But you have no idea who we're dealing with here."

"You think you're going to change her mind?"

"I think the only way to get Petra to do anything she doesn't want to do is by being honest. Right now, she doesn't trust me. I have to fix that. She needs all the info."

"You're going to tell her about Stella?" he asks, both eyebrows shooting higher.

I lean back in my seat and cross my ankle over my knee. "Doesn't seem like I have much of a choice."

———

I push myself back against the wall, wishing I could blend in a bit better among the cadre of nannies here to pick up their little ballerinas. On the other side of the glass, the dance teacher corrals the six-year-olds into a circle where they put their hands on each other's shoulders and practice sliding one foot forward and pointing their toe. Or at least, that's what it looks like they're doing. I can't claim to know the first thing about ballet. And neither did Stella until a month ago when her best friend Harper asked if they could take lessons together. Now it's all she talks about.

"Do you think they'll be done soon?" Harper's mom, Sofia, asks as she slides into the space between the end of the waiting room chairs and where I'm standing against the wall. She glances at her watch. "I need to get back to Benjamin soon."

Sofia is the only one of Stella's friends' parents I know. Her other friends seem to spend their every waking hour with their nannies. In my experience, that's the norm among the Upper East Side families that have chosen The Buckingham School, where Stella is in first grade. The fact that Sofia is so involved in parenting Harper and Benjamin is half of why I trust her so much. That, and she was my sister-in-law Colette's best friend.

"I think they're wrapping up," I say, glancing up from my phone. Stella loves Miss Peggy's ballet classes, but our nanny, Natasha, has warned me that the woman is not known for her timeliness.

"I'm surprised to see you here," Sofia says. I know I stand out like a giant among the women here waiting for ballet to end. "Is Natasha already gone?"

"Yeah. She left yesterday." We are just entering playoff season, so my nanny could not have picked a less convenient time to leave. But her one-year contract was up and she understandably wanted to get back to her fiancé in St. Petersburg.

"When's the new one start?"

"Not soon enough." It's unfortunate I couldn't get her to start this week, but she's finishing up a contract with another family. "She's coming over for a bit on Friday to spend some time with Stella, then she starts on Monday."

"Well, if you need any help in the meantime, let me know. Harper always loves spending time with Stella."

I glance at the girls in question, who are holding hands as they practice moving across the floor in what looks like skipping with straight legs, some ballet move that I'm sure has an official French name. "The feeling is mutual."

"God, every year they are more adorable together," Sofia says, her hand over her heart.

I'm relieved that Sofia and her family were already in Stella's life when my brother and his wife died. I don't know how I would have gotten through the first couple months of being Stella's guardian without Sofia's help. Stella's nanny, Natasha, moved with Stella from my brother's place into mine. And while she did most of the day-to-day childcare, it was Sofia who taught me how to be a dad—a role I was not prepared for, and at the time wasn't sure I wanted.

On the other side of the big glass wall, Miss Peggy tells them class time is over. When Stella and Harper weave through the maze of dancers and rush up to us, I bend down to scoop Stella into my arms and hear Harper ask Sofia, "Did you ask him yet, Mommy?"

Sofia gives her daughter a soft chuckle. "Not yet. Why don't you do the honors."

Harper looks up at me, her head so far back I'm afraid she'll fall over. "Mr. Ivanov, can Stella spend the night this weekend?"

"Please, *Dyadya*," Stella begs. From her perch on my hip, she grabs my face with both hands, giving me an angelic pout. "Please?"

I swallow. For reasons I can't articulate in front of her, the thought of Stella spending the night anywhere but my place makes me deeply uncomfortable. It's not that I don't trust Harper's family. It's that I don't have total control over their home and what happens there.

"I need to check on our weekend plans," I tell Stella, then I turn to Sofia. "Okay if I get back to you about that later?"

"Sure," she says, but by the tone of her voice she already

knows that my answer is no, even if the six-year-olds haven't figured it out yet.

———

"I wouldn't have to go to bed early if you'd let me stay at Harper's," Stella complains as she stomps her foot on the bathroom rug. It's hard to take her seriously in her fuzzy pink bathrobe with her wet curls hanging heavy around her face.

"Harper invited you to spend the night this weekend, not tonight. Besides, you're not going to bed early," I say again. "You're going to bed at the exact time you always do."

"But you're making me go to bed before your company comes over. That's not fair. I want to meet her. You let me stay up late and say 'hi' when Mr. Shepherd comes over."

"That's different," I say as I hang her towel on the back of the door. "Do you want braids tonight?"

"No, I want to meet your friend who is going to help us. If she was your best friend when you were little, did she know my papa too?"

Stella is much more comfortable talking about her parents than I am. Growing up, my big brother was my idol. As adults, he was my best friend. And not having him around now makes it hard to talk about him through the lump in my throat every time he comes up in conversation. "I don't know if she's going to help us yet, Stella. That's what I'm going to talk to her about. And yes, your dad knew Petra too."

"Then I should get to meet her." Stella presses her lips together as she waits for my response. Someday, this kid is going to be a ruthless CEO.

"Maybe another time," I say. With any luck, Petra will agree to my ruse and will be around for a while.

"At least tell me what she looks like. Is she beautiful?" Stella grabs a comb and two rubber bands from the top drawer of the bathroom vanity and casually hands them to me like she didn't just tell me she didn't want braids.

"Yes, she's very beautiful." There's no point in lying about Petra's beauty. She was gorgeous when she was a teenager, and if it's possible, she's gotten even more gorgeous over time. Now, she has the look of a woman who knows what she wants and how to get it, and this is my favorite version of Petra that I've seen.

Stella climbs up on the counter of the vanity and sits cross-legged with her back to me, but she's studying me carefully in the mirror. "Why was your best friend a girl?"

Why am I having this conversation with a child?

"I don't know, she just was," I say as I use the comb to part her hair down the middle and brush half of it to one side. "She lived in a little house in my backyard called the caretaker's cottage."

"Why was it a little house? Is she small like a fairy?"

I can't help but laugh at the inner workings of the six-year-old mind. "No, it was a normal house, just small compared to mine, I guess. Her dad took care of my family's property and her mom was a teacher at the school your dad and I went to. Petra went to school there too."

"Was she your age, or Papa's age?"

"Neither. She's three years younger than me, so she was five years younger than your dad."

Her eyebrows scrunch up and her nose twitches, a classic Stella thinking face. I divide the hair into three equal-sized

41

sections and then begin braiding them as I watch her think about this.

"But why was she your best friend if she was so much younger?" she asks. "That would be like my best friend being a three-year-old."

"Good subtraction." We've been working on extra math lately. "But she wasn't my best friend when I was your age," I say, considering how much to tell her.

"Why not?"

"I was good friends with her older brother. We played hockey together."

As I tie the elastic around the end of her first braid, she looks at me in the mirror like I haven't answered her question at all—which I haven't. Petra's family's story is riddled with tragedy, and I'm not sure how much is appropriate to share with someone Stella's age who has her own family trauma.

"But then, why did you become friends with her?" She is nothing if not persistent.

I move to the other side of her head and divide that hair into three. "Her brother and mom died in a car accident," I tell her. "She and I became closer when that happened."

"Like how my mom and dad died?" she asks, and I nod. "If she's your best friend, how come I haven't met her before?"

"She was my best friend when I was a kid. Sometimes you grow apart from people as you get older."

"Does that mean Harper and I won't be friends when we're older?"

I groan internally. This parenting thing is hard work. Constantly worrying about the right way to explain things, trying to help shape this little person into a strong and resilient young woman. Why did I think I could do this? Not that there was another choice, but I worry that I'm failing her every day.

"No, not necessarily. Look at your mom and Harper's mom. They were friends since they were kids, and maybe you and Harper will be too."

Stella's smile is huge and hopeful. "We will be. I can tell."

"I hope so," I say as I finish up her second braid. "Now, let's get you in your pajamas and in bed."

Chapter Four

PETRA

I glance at the text again as the driver turns up Park Avenue to travel north toward Sasha's Fifth Avenue penthouse.

ALEKSANDR

I'll send my car for you at 8 p.m.

So presumptuous.

Yet here I am, because I have a million questions and there's only one person who can give me the answers. And because, if there really is a marriage contract, I have to figure out how to get out of it.

I sit back against the supple leather in the back seat of his luxurious Jaguar with a heavy sigh. The driver's eyes immediately track to the rearview mirror, but I glance out the window because I have no desire for him to see me flustered or to report my current state back to his boss.

I switch over to the web browser on my phone, where I have about fifteen different tabs open—all of them a result of my numerous Google searches for Alex Ivanov. He already told me he has been playing hockey in New York for eight years, which—now that I've had time to process it—means that the entire time I was living here, he was here too. What he hadn't mentioned was how damn good he is.

As I'd read article after article about him, I couldn't help but feel so unbelievably proud of him. He'd done it. He'd accomplished everything I'd watched him work so hard for as a teenager. All those years of before sunrise practices, traveling constantly for hockey tournaments, giving up college to go pro in Russia's Kontinental Hockey League. He ended up exactly where he always said he would—dominating the NHL.

Why didn't I know?

I close my eyes and take a deep breath, trying hard not to think about the night he left me for the last time. I've had plenty of loss in my life, but there was nothing I could do about the car crash that stole Mama and Viktor from me when I was thirteen. There was nothing I could do about Papa dying when I was in my early twenties. But Sasha leaving, that was personal. A big, huge F You to our friendship, to the space I held for him inside my heart. I lost my best friend that night, and in a way, I lost a piece of myself too.

I didn't know because I made sure I never found out. I never looked him up, never asked about him. I avoided hockey like the plague. The only way I got through it was by pretending like there was no Aleksandr Ivanov out in this world.

"We're here, miss," the driver says. Those dozens of city blocks went much faster than I was prepared for, and I'm feeling emotionally off-kilter—unbalanced—as I reach for the door. "The doorman is expecting you. He'll show you the way."

"Thank you."

The car door is opened for me. "Ms. Volkova, I'm Martin. I'll show you to Mr. Ivanov's floor."

The man dressed in a green-and-black livery who extends his hand to me has friendly eyes with enough wrinkles around the edges to know he's spent a lifetime smiling. His white hair is closely cut, and the way his white mustache moves when he talks is an amusement to behold. I like him instantly, and I'm an exceptionally good judge of character.

I follow Martin through a double set of glass doors and up a few time-worn marble steps to a posh lobby in a prewar building that reeks of old money. Enormous slabs of marble tile and deeply pigmented Oriental rugs line the floors, the walls are all gleaming white stone, and several gold and crystal chandeliers drip from the high arched ceilings. I've been in plenty of posh New York residential buildings, but there's something extra special about this one.

Martin leads me past the concierge's desk and pushes the call button in front of the second elevator on the right side. Around us, gilded mirrors veined with age glow from the light of the lobby like mercury glass. "This elevator will open into the entryway of his apartment. He'll meet you there."

The thought of being alone with Aleksandr sends my stomach plummeting and my intestines threatening to give out. I have ended up with my mother's nervous stomach, which she'd always threatened when I teased her about it as a kid. It's not the part of her I would have wished to keep, but at least I have her smile too.

The elevator doors open and Martin uses his arm to hold

them for me while I step in. He then reaches his arm in, sticks a plastic key card into a slot in the bank of buttons, presses the button for the sixteenth floor, and sends me on my way with a small nod and a salute.

I swallow down my nerves and my fear, instead putting on the air of indifference that I'll need in order to deal with my ex-best friend, the man who is now a perfect stranger I'm allegedly married to.

When the elevator comes to a stop, the doors open into a grand entryway. The floors are a warm wood laid in a herringbone pattern, the walls are white-on-white with ornate baseboards and thick art deco crown molding that tops every wall. Framed art hangs in regular intervals around the room, and the curved glass ceiling with thin black steel framing the large pieces of glass sits like a crown above the space. In the center of the room, in jeans and a sweatshirt and bare feet, stands Sasha. In his casual state surrounded by the elegant space, he looks so much like the teenager I once loved that it squeezes my heart painfully.

"Hello, Aleksandr," I say as I step from the elevator. He winces slightly at my use of his given name rather than his childhood nickname.

He stares without saying anything, those intense gray eyes raking over me until I'm shifting uncomfortably. Ordinarily, I'd make a crack about him not being able to take his eyes off me, because I've always found that keeping things light and flirtatious is the best way to maintain the upper hand in any given situation. But not with him. We have to deal with legal issues together—there's nothing to be won by flirting with him.

He shakes his head like he's trying to clear it. "I can't believe you're here, in my apartment."

I almost scoff at the term "apartment" and the way people on the Upper East Side throw that word around when they're talking about twenty million dollar co-ops.

"You invited me."

"I didn't think you'd come," he says, and I'm struck by the wonder in his voice.

"I need answers, and you didn't exactly give me another choice."

"You always do what you're told?" He runs a hand through his hair and looks away, so it's hard to know if he's legitimately asking or if the question is meant flirtatiously.

"Actually, I usually give the orders." I eye the living room through the eight-foot doorway to his right and the dining room I can see behind him. "Are you going to invite me in, or should we have this conversation standing in your entryway?"

"Sorry," he mutters, gesturing toward the living room with its pristine carved wood walls. He walks into the room and heads toward an open door on the far side. I follow him into a much smaller sitting area, a room dominated by floor-to-ceiling glass doors along two walls and a fire burning in the fireplace along a third wall.

It's hard not to gush about the city lights on the other side of all that glass. Instead, I silently walk over, observing the twenty-foot wide terrace with views of Central Park beyond the trees that line Fifth Avenue, and the Upper West Side lit up on the opposite side of all that green space. It's like having a view of the NYC skyline from within New York.

"The view is even better during the day," he says from

behind me. He's close enough that his breath tickles the side of my neck and a shiver runs through me.

"I'll take your word for it," I say, turning with my arms crossed under my chest. I stumble for a second over my next words because I'm not prepared for how much space he takes up, how he seems to tower over me even though in these heels I'm at least six feet tall. "That was a huge bomb you dropped on me in your lawyer's office today."

"I shouldn't have surprised you like I did." Aleksandr turns and sits on a large sling-style chair with a gunmetal frame and thick tobacco-colored leather cushions, and gestures to the long ivory couch next to it.

Instead, I take the chair that matches his on the far side of the coffee table. This seat gives me the perfect view of him. I can watch his face for the telltale signs I know—his left eye twitching when he lies, his lips turning down at the corners when he doesn't like what he's hearing—without having to be too close to him. Over here, I feel like I can breathe.

"Tell me how this happened," I say.

He sighs and runs his hand through that thick black hair again. "I already told you. What we thought was a contract about my dad loaning yours money was actually a marriage contract."

It's hard not to be embarrassed, even all these years later, that my dad couldn't afford the training I needed to make the Austrian ski team, and that Sasha's dad "lent" it to him even though there was no way he could repay it. I'd promised myself then that I would pay him back myself. After years of skiing followed by a couple years modeling, I'd saved enough.

"I saw your dad years ago," I tell Sasha. "I tried to pay him back, only to be told that the debt had already been repaid. I have no idea how my father could have managed to pay him back, and your father wouldn't share any details, only insisting that I owed him nothing." That money became the seed money to eventually start my own event planning company, and so in a way I feel like I owe Mr. Ivanov for my financial independence too. "He didn't mention being my father-in-law."

"Like he would." Sasha rolls his eyes as he sinks further into his chair.

"And you really didn't know a thing about this until your father passed away?"

The eye twitches when he says *no*, just like it did in his lawyer's office when he told me he had the same questions I did about our father's intent.

"I know all your tells, Aleksandr. Which means I know you're lying to me. What aren't you telling me?"

"I've told you everything I know," he says, and this time his eye doesn't twitch. Well, what the hell does *that* mean? I don't know what to believe.

I pick at a piece of nonexistent lint on my black wide-leg trousers just to have something to do, some way to channel all the energy that's ricocheting around inside me. Finally, I look across the table at him. "Why would they marry us off to each other and not tell us? It makes no sense at all. And what if one of us had wanted to get married in the meantime?"

"That's never even been close to being an issue," he says. "Has it for you?"

"No, but that's beside the point. My father's been gone for six years. What if in that time I had wanted to marry someone else? Was anyone going to tell me I was already married?"

"I don't know the answer to that, either," he says.

I jump to my feet, too frustrated to keep still, and use the space behind my chair to pace along the wall of glass doors. The view from behind the chair looks directly across Central Park to the Upper West Side, but from this angle I'm looking north, toward the heavily wooded area. The buildings beyond the trees emit a glow that emanates above the North Woods.

The chunky heels of my black open-toed booties click noisily across the brick tiles as I pace. I have a sinking suspicion that he knows why our fathers agreed to this marriage and he isn't telling me. With both of them in their graves, he is my only hope of discovering the truth. The frustration is evident in my voice when I say, "I came here for answers. If you aren't going to give me any, why am I here?"

He stands and makes his way toward a low cabinet I didn't even notice on our way in. "Here, let me get you a drink."

"Don't you dare open a bottle!" It is a Russian custom that once you pour from a bottle of alcohol, you finish the entire thing. It's bad luck not to. And I'm not sitting around drinking an entire bottle of vodka with him tonight. I have too much to accomplish tomorrow, and I already lost too much time today looking into marriage laws in Austria and citizenship laws in the US.

He turns toward me, a flash of annoyance in his eyes. In our culture, it is very bad form to turn down something your host offers you, and we both know it. I'm being both rude and petulant, but I couldn't care less if I offend him at this moment.

"You are impossible, as always!" His voice, which is usually so level and controlled, is a loud growl. I find that I like that as much as I did when I was a teenager. I lived to rattle him, to see that carefully crafted layer of self-control begin to crack.

"Why are you guys yelling?" a small voice asks.

Both our heads spin toward the open doorway, where a little girl with an angelic face and dark brown hair in two braids stands in her light pink pajamas.

What the actual hell is happening right now?

Aleksandr is at her feet in half a second, kneeling in front of her so they are face-to-face. "Remember how we talked about you going to bed early tonight?" he asks. His voice is soothing, not reprimanding like I'd have expected.

He has a freaking daughter?

"But I heard yelling," she says.

"Sorry, we didn't mean to be so loud."

"But, *Dyadya*," the little girl—his niece, I assume, since she just called him Uncle—says. Then she looks at me, lowers her voice, and says to him, "She's even more beautiful than you said."

The air is sucked from my lungs—maybe from the whole room, based on how I can't seem to catch a breath. Aleksandr told his niece I was beautiful?

He glances over his shoulder at me for a fraction of a second, then back to his niece. "Okay, time to get you back to bed."

"I want Petra to put me to bed." She looks directly at me. *How does she know my name? They've obviously talked about me, but why? Does she know we're married, too?*

"How about I just put you to bed, Stella?" he says, standing.

"I'll do it." The words are out of my mouth before I can

stop them. I don't even know what makes me offer. But I need a moment away from him to collect my thoughts, and maybe a conversation with Stella will help me figure out what's going on here. She seems more likely to tell me the truth than Aleksandr.

She bounces on the balls of her feet, a beautiful and victorious smile spreading across her lips. Before Aleksandr can express any objection, she rushes over to me and takes my hand in her little one, pulling me toward the door.

I'm led back through the living room to the entryway, then down a long hallway. Her room is the first one on the left, and when we enter and I see the big windows out to the terrace, I realize that her bedroom probably shares a wall with the sitting room we were in.

She climbs in her bed, then pulls the covers up and pats the space next to her. I've never spent time around a child this age before. Holding my friend Lauren's twin daughters, who aren't even one yet, is the only experience I have with children.

I sit on her bed next to her, and she immediately grabs my hand in both of hers, holding it to her chest. "*Dyadya* said we need you to help us."

I have no idea what she is talking about. This must be Nikolai's daughter, but why is she here in Aleksandr's apartment in a bedroom clearly designed for her? Does she stay with him sometimes? Does this mean Nikolai lives in New York too?

"Tell me how I can help," I say, because I don't know what else I can do.

"Dada said maybe you can help him adopt me."

I give her a small smile, hoping it hides the way my entire

body is reacting to these two pieces of information—the fact that she is using *Dyadya*, which means uncle in Russian, interchangeably with Dada, and the fact that he is trying to adopt her, which means something has happened to Nikolai. My heart breaks for her in this moment, so young and apparently orphaned.

This also means Aleksandr is being even less honest with me than I initially thought and he's somehow put Niko's daughter in the middle of this, which infuriates me.

I give her little hands, which fit perfectly in my palm, a squeeze. "I need to talk to your uncle about all this."

She sits up quickly and wraps her hands around my waist and presses her head into my chest as she squeezes me into a hug. "Thank you!"

I don't know what to do, so I pat her back in response. When she lies back down I tell her, "Okay, time for bed, for real. Should I turn out this light?" I nod toward the pink lamp on the dresser next to her bed.

"Yes. I have a special nightlight that keeps all the bad dreams away, so I don't need the light on anymore."

A knife twists in my stomach. What has happened to her that's causing bad dreams? What happened to her parents?

I turn off the light and brush my palm across her forehead as I whisper goodnight. When I shut her bedroom door behind me, I stand in the hallways with my back to the wall and rest my head against it as I stare up at the high ceiling.

What have I gotten myself into?

There's movement in the corner of my eye, and I turn my head to see Sasha standing in the entryway. His face is anguished, like the pain is seeping out through cracks in his tough exterior. I've seen this look once before, when Mama and Viktor were in a fatal car accident. The day he climbed up into my treehouse to comfort me through his own pain. We'd cried together that night, and it was the beginning of the three years where he was my best friend.

It's easier than I would have imagined to put the anger and resentment aside in the face of his unimaginable loss. I don't know exactly what he's been through, but I can see in his eyes that he needs me like I once needed him.

My steps are quick and sure as I rush down the hall to him. I wrap him in my arms, and though his sharp intake of breath alerts me to his surprise, he wraps his thick arms around me in response. We stand there for a minute until he says, "What did she tell you?" His cheek moves against the top of my head as his words drift down my hair.

"She said I need to help you adopt her."

The sound that leaves his mouth is half sigh, half groan. "I wouldn't be asking if I didn't really need you."

That stings a bit. I wish he'd come to me as a friend, not out of desperation because I was his last resort "You going to be honest with me now?" I ask, without letting go.

"I was always going to be honest with you. I was just going to get a couple drinks in you to take the edge off first."

I laugh into that space between his neck and his shoulder, and for a second I think maybe things will be okay.

Chapter Five

ALEKSANDR

Why does she have to be so fucking beautiful?

She should come with a warning: Nearness may cause distractibility and lapses in judgment. Proceed with Caution.

We settle back into the sitting room and she takes me up on the drink offer when I tell her I have some cans of premixed cocktails, thus there's no need to drink until we're stupid. But as the first drinks go down and we move on to the second, it occurs to me that if there's one person in this world who I want to get drunk with, it's Petra. She's both easy to talk to and incredibly guarded. I've only ever seen her drink one time, and I am curious if she's the same happy, bubbly drunk who will tell you anything like she was back then.

After two drinks, she's not even a little tipsy. Instead, she drills into me like I'm on trial and she's leading the prosecution.

"You damn well should have told me everything upfront," she says. "Niko's *child*, Aleksandr? How could you not mention that he'd *died*, and he left behind a child you were responsible for? *Why* would you not mention that?" She emphasizes a different word in each sentence and slaps her hand against the metal arm of the chair she's sitting in with each one.

She's shed her coat and sits there in a sleeveless black turtleneck that does way too much to emphasize the curve of her breasts above her tiny waist. *Do not look at her boobs*, I have to remind myself. I'd forgotten about these internal dialogues I require when I'm around Petra. I'd thought that fourteen years of distance would have dulled the inappropriate attraction I'd felt toward her back then. Instead, it's not only still there, but my reasons for keeping her at a distance back then seem less important now that we're both adults. *Except you know a truth about her family that even she doesn't know—and it's one she could never forgive you for.*

It's a hurdle in our relationship I'll never be able to get around.

"Honestly, almost no one knows about Stella. Somehow, Tom managed to keep the news of Niko and Colette's death and my application for guardianship out of the papers."

"Why are you trying to keep her a secret?" she asks, her brows raised as she fiddles with the metal tab on top of the can and awaits my answer.

"I'm not trying to keep her a secret. I just don't want to flaunt her in the face of Colette's sister and her husband," I say. "They filed for guardianship of Stella at the same time I did, even though the will named me as guardian and Colette's best friend Sofia as backup guardian. Colette's sister, CeCe, was not only *not* mentioned in the will, but Niko and Colette met with both me and Sofia separately when they created their will a couple years ago to emphasize how imperative it was that CeCe and her husband never get custody of Stella."

She leans forward in the chair, sizing me up. "So the court gave you guardianship in accordance with the will, and now you need citizenship because you're afraid . . .?" She trails off, but I don't jump in with a response. Instead, I wait to see if she'll come to the same conclusion I have. "You're afraid that if something happens to you, they'll give guardianship to Stella's aunt because she's next of kin?"

"Exactly. Even though the will named Sofia as the backup guardian in case I wasn't able, I'm worried that keeping Stella with family will override her dead parents' wishes. I can't adopt her unless I'm a US citizen, but if I was able to adopt her, I could create a new will that echoes her parents' wishes of naming Sofia as Stella's guardian if anything should happen to me. With two wills saying the same thing, I imagine the court would side with Sofia, no matter how much money Stella's aunt and uncle were willing to spend to litigate this."

"Why are you worried that something will happen to you?"

"Accidents happen. I travel a lot for hockey. What if something happened to me while I was gone? What if I hit my head so hard in a game that I was incapacitated as a result? Failing to prepare for these possibilities is the epitome of bad parenting," I say, as if I have any idea what good parenting looks like. Luckily, I have Sofia to guide me, and I can take everything I experienced from my own father and flip it, doing the opposite as he would have done.

"Okay, so it makes sense to prepare. But I still can't believe you brought me to New York just to lie to me. That you've known we were married for months and you didn't tell me sooner. That you were just trying to use me to get what you wanted."

The hurt in her voice twists the guilt into a knot in my stomach, especially since I still haven't told her a crucial piece of information—that I found out about the marriage contract right after we signed it. I thought I'd taken care of the issue back then, only to find out that my father lied to me when he said he would make sure it didn't go through. But I can't tell her that—ever. There are too many family secrets locked into that story, and knowing any of them would inevitably cause her more pain, with nothing to gain from the knowledge.

"I'm sorry," I say. "I wasn't trying to hurt you, but I am very protective of Stella. I'll do whatever it takes to keep her safe, happy, and healthy."

"But how in the world did you think that I wouldn't find out about her?"

"I didn't. I listened to Tom's advice even when I didn't agree with it," I shrug. I understand why Tom thinks the less Petra knows, the better. But I don't know why I thought for a second that she'd show up and sign the paperwork, going along with his plan without knowing everything, then just head back to her life in Park City.

"I guess I still don't understand why you can't just apply for citizenship the normal way. Why do you need to be fake married to me to make it happen?"

"Because I haven't been a permanent resident for five years yet."

"How's that possible? You've lived here for eight, right?"

"Yes, but for tax reasons, I didn't apply for permanent

residency until last year, when I bought this place. If I could go back and trade a few years of higher taxes for permanent resident status so I could apply for citizenship now, I'd pay it tenfold. But I can't. So I'd have to wait four more years before I could apply." I paused, letting her absorb this. "But if I can prove we're already married and that we've lived together, even off and on, for three years, I'd be free to apply for citizenship immediately."

"How in the world would we prove that? I haven't been back to New York since I moved to Park City *more* than three years ago. You haven't been to Park City, that I know of. How would we possibly make it look like we lived together during that time?"

"I think there are ways—"

"Yeah," she interrupts. "Ways that involve lying to the federal government. No thanks."

"Petra, we'd only move forward if we were sure we had a convincing story. But you are my last hope. I can't let any more time go by without being able to adopt Stella."

"I don't even know what would happen if we were caught lying to the government about this, Sasha. Federal prison? For sure, you'd lose guardianship and be sent back to Austria, at the minimum. I'm not sure it's worth that risk." She leans forward and sets her drink on the table. "This is a lot to think about. I should head back to the hotel."

"Wait." The word is out of my mouth before I can stop it, and she looks at me with a small degree of surprise. "I never got the chance to talk to you about the event I'm hoping you can plan."

"There's actually an event? That wasn't just a ploy to get me here and spring a fake marriage on me?"

I may have created an event just so this whole interaction, this transaction, isn't so one-sided. But now that she's here, I find I want to keep her near me as long as possible. Some things haven't changed—will probably never change.

"I'm hoping you can plan an end of season event for my team in a month. Whether we win or lose in the playoffs, I'd like to have one last get together with them."

"Wait, so you really *are* planning to retire?"

"Not exactly. My contract is up, and I'm not sure if I'll stay in New York or end up somewhere else. My agent is still working on that." In fact, Jameson is getting offers left and right. But New York is refusing to negotiate until after the playoffs are over, undoubtedly to see if I can lead the team to another Stanley Cup. If I can, the offer will be more competitive.

"Okay. Why don't you send me an email with all the details and I'll start looking into it. But be forewarned, the options for what I can pull together in that time frame are going to be *very* limited." She slides her jacket on and stands.

There's nothing else I can say to keep her here without sounding desperate. So as much as I want her to stay, I have to let her go—for now.

———

"But you said I could bring a friend," Stella says as she pushes her lunch plate away from her. She has a distinctly pissed-off look that I didn't know someone her age could have already mastered.

"I meant Harper, or another friend from school."

"But I want to bring Petra." Stella's lower lip trembles and I know she's about to lose it.

"Sweetie, Petra isn't your friend," I say the words kindly to soften the blow. "She's someone I was friends with back when I was a kid."

"She's my friend now. She tucked me into bed last night. You wouldn't let someone tuck me into bed if they weren't a friend, would you?"

It's hard to argue with her logic, and yet Petra is *not* her friend. "I'm not calling Petra and inviting her to go to the Orchid Show with no notice, in the middle of the day when she's probably working."

"We won't know if she's working unless we call and ask," Stella says.

I put both my hands on the small table and level my glare at her. "I'm not calling her."

"I'll call her," Stella says and holds out her hand for my phone.

"I don't think we should interrupt her while she's working."

Stella's arm is still extended, waiting for me to place my phone in her hand. "If she can't go, she'll tell us."

"There is no *us*. If you're going to ask her, you tell her *you* wanted her to come. Don't say anything about me."

"Okay," she says, calling my bluff. The girl has the confidence of a twenty-six-year-old who knows exactly who she is and how to get what she wants. It makes parenting her extremely difficult at times, but I never want her to lose that spark.

I pull up Petra's contact on my phone and hand it to Stella. She doesn't even hesitate for a second before she hits the icon to place the call. I watch her expressive face, noting the way she raises her eyebrows every time the phone rings, like she just knows this is the ring where Petra will answer. Finally, on the fourth ring, her patience is rewarded.

"Hello?" Petra's low, throaty voice carries across the table to me, even though Stella's holding the phone up to her ear.

"Hi, Petra, it's Stella. Stella Ivanova," she adds, in case Petra couldn't figure out which Stella might be calling her from my number.

"Hello, Stella. What's up?" I can't tell if her voice is amused that a six-year-old is calling her, or concerned.

"*Dyadya* is taking me to the New York Orchid Show this afternoon, and he said I could bring a friend. Will you come with me?"

Petra's laugh is low and throaty, just like her voice. "Don't you have school today?"

"Yes, but we got out early because the teachers have a meeting."

Early release days at Stella's private school mean the kids are out before lunch, which begs the question, why even go in at all?

"Okay, can I talk to your uncle about these plans?"

"So you'll come?" In her excitement, Stella's voice sounds like the high-pitched scream of a teakettle.

"I will if the timing works. That's why I need to talk about the details with your uncle."

With a victorious look, Stella hands me the phone.

"Hi."

"You know," she says, "if you'd wanted me to come, you could have asked me yourself. You don't need to have the kid do your dirty work for you."

I reward her flirtation with a chuckle. "She is very insistent that you are the friend she wants to bring. I tried to tell her you were probably working."

"I just wrapped up a conference call with my team. And the only thing I planned to work on this afternoon is scouting a location for your post-season party. So it's your choice, I can work on your event, or I can go look at flowers with you and Stella."

I glance at Stella's hopeful face, and there's only one answer. "Flowers it is."

"I have dinner plans with my friend Emily tonight. Will we be back in time?"

"Yeah, definitely. We actually have to be back by six anyway."

"Plenty of time, then," she agrees. I doubt her dinner plans are before eight or nine. Mine never were back when I was childless.

"We're leaving in an hour. Where should we pick you up?"

"I'll be back at the hotel, which is perfect, by the way. Who do I have to thank for that? You?"

"Indirectly, yes. Tom's assistant Avery made the arrangements, though."

"Ah," Petra says, but doesn't elaborate. "I'll see you in an hour, then."

As I hang up and see the triumphant look on Stella's face, I can't help but feel like we both just got played by a kid.

———

"Of course not," Petra laughs. I'm not even sure what Stella asked her. I'm too focused on the way they are walking in sync, each holding an ice cream with one hand while their free hands are linked together. I'm trailing behind them, irrelevant to their conversation. It's been like this since the moment we got here. It's been a long time since I've seen Stella this relaxed and happy.

Maybe I shouldn't be surprised. As a teenager, Petra was open and honest. She didn't hold her punches, either—she had a way of knowing what advice people needed to hear and when they needed to hear it, and she delivered it whether you were ready or not. I loved that about her, but I think it could rub some people the wrong way. Not Stella, though. She's clearly enamored.

Petra looks back over her shoulder and winks at me. I step closer so I can figure out what they're talking about.

"So if I can't punch him, what can I do instead?" Stella asks.

"Okay, so here's what I'd do," Petra replies. "I'd say 'Jason, if you're so desperate to be around me, maybe try being nice for a change.'"

Ah, Jason. Stella's nemesis. I've unsuccessfully been coaching her on how to deal with the daily conflict he brings into her life. And Petra's advice sounds pretty good to me too.

"But he'll just say 'I don't want to be around you!'" Stella counters.

"So then you just say 'The feeling is mutual. So go away already!'"

"What's mutual mean?" Stella asks, looking up at her as she licks her ice cream cone. Her dark brown curls frame her face and hang past her shoulders, and in that moment it looks like a six-year-old version of Petra standing with the adult version. I'd never noticed how much she resembles Petra at that age. Hell, I only ever focused on teenage Petra. I almost forgot she was a little girl who grew up on a country estate with three older boys, and that Viktor, Niko, and I wanted nothing to do with her back then.

"Um," Petra stalls as she tries to think of a way to explain *mutual*. "It means you both feel the same way. So instead you could say 'I don't want to be around you either, so go away!'"

"Okay," Stella says, "I'll try that. *Dyadya* keeps telling me that Jason is just being mean because he likes me."

"He might be right," she tells Stella, "but you need to stand up for yourself and teach him that you won't be treated like that. Boys need to learn more appropriate ways to get girls' attention than tormenting them."

"I think so too." Stella beams up at Petra, then stops to look up at the arch of orchids we're walking through on our way toward the exit. "I want orchids like this in my bedroom," Stella says.

"While that would be beautiful," I speak up from behind them, "it is also impractical. Orchids don't grow in arches like this naturally. This is a thousand plants together, carefully tended by master gardeners."

"What if I just got a few plants?" she asks.

"I don't think there's time to stop at the Botanical Store on the way out, but maybe another time," I tell her.

By the way Stella frowns, I'm afraid we're heading for an argument. Stopping at any museum gift store as you leave is a must with kids, but we really don't have time if we're going to make it back into the city for her piano lesson. Instead, Petra distracts her with some questions about school and we make it out of the Botanical Gardens without an issue.

In the car, we all sit in the back seat as my driver, Daniel, navigates us through stop-and-go traffic. I glance at my watch, wondering if the rush hour traffic will result in her missing her lesson. Again. For the third week in a row.

"We aren't having dinner with Aunt CeCe and Uncle Tony tonight, right?" Stella asks, looking up at me from her booster seat between Petra and me. I see the worry etched there and my heart constricts. The thought of her ever ending up with people she so clearly doesn't feel comfortable around is the main driver of my determination to adopt her.

"No, that's tomorrow night," I tell her.

"Hey," Petra says softly as she rests her hand on Stella's knee and gives it a little squeeze. "Why aren't you excited to see your aunt and uncle?"

I've never asked Stella that question. I've never wanted to be the one to pit her against the other side of her family.

"They just make me feel . . . icky," Stella says.

"Icky?" Petra asks.

"Yeah. I just don't like being around them. I don't like when they come over for dinner."

Petra looks at me, her eyes opening wide and her eyebrows raising. I give her a small shrug in return, because I don't know what Stella means any more than she does.

"They can't be that bad," Petra says. She's not dismissing Stella's comment, she's clearly trying to get her to better explain the issue.

"Can you come to dinner tomorrow night too?" Stella asks. "Then you can see what I mean."

Petra stills. Across the back seat of the car I watch her placid face, wondering what's going on beneath the surface.

"It's probably a good idea for you to meet them and see what we're up against," I suggest.

She glances over at me, and in her eyes I can see the push and pull—not wanting to get involved, but already involved nonetheless.

"Okay," she says.

"Thank you!" Stella says, launching herself at Petra as much as her seatbelt will allow. Stella wraps her arms around Petra's waist, and though she looks a little uncomfortable with the affection, Petra lifts her arm and wraps it around Stella's back, holding my niece to her side.

"Six thirty tomorrow night, my place," I tell her.

She closes her eyes and gives me a quick nod. I wish I could read her thoughts. How does she feel about getting involved in my niece's life like this? And most importantly, is she willing to help me get citizenship so I can adopt Stella? She'll give me those answers when she's good and ready, but for the first time, it occurs to me that the wait might damn near kill me.

Chapter Six

PETRA

"Twice in one week," Emily smiles as she slips into the seat next to me. "I haven't seen this much of you since I visited you in Park City, what was it, three years ago?"

"That sounds right," I say, taking a sip of my sangria.

"Are you drinking wine?" Emily laughs. "With fruit in it?"

I tend to like my alcohol neat, the way I grew up seeing my Russian family and friends drink it. Beer and wine are a last resort, and don't even get me started on fruity cocktails.

I roll my eyes. "I know. This is such a Sierra drink." This tapas bar Emily recommended only serves beer, wine, and sangria, so I went with the house specialty since they're supposedly known for it. My best friend Sierra loves drinks like this, and I constantly give her shit about it.

"How's Sierra doing?" Emily asks, fondness softening her voice. She and Sierra have very similar personalities—extremely sweet and constantly wanting to think the best of everyone. Emily likes Jackson and Lauren too, but I think Sierra is her favorite.

"She's off traveling the world with her boyfriend."

"Wait, what? I thought Sierra was engaged?"

"Long story. But her fiancé cheated on her and now she is dating Jackson's younger brother." I tell her a bit about how that all happened.

"Wow, that sounds so unlike Sierra," Emily says, and she could not be more right.

"Yes, and I've honestly never known her to be happier. It's like once she accepted that not everything goes according to plan, she was able to really start living her life, and she's loving it."

"And Jackson is back in New Hampshire now?" Emily asks. Jackson is my oldest and best friend. We met when we were twenty and both competing on the World Cup alpine skiing circuit. She raced for the US and I raced for Austria, and despite being each other's competition, we became fast friends. In fact, she's the only one from my ski days that I still keep in touch with. The only one from any previous part of my life, except Emily, actually.

"Yep, back in New Hampshire, married, and running her own ski resort. Well, her and her husband's."

"Oh yes, I remember that delicious hottie from the photos you posted from their wedding. You were a stunning brides-maid, by the way."

"Thank you."

"So Jackson moved back to New Hampshire and got married, Lauren's married with twins, right?" she asks and I nod. "And Sierra's traveling the world with her boyfriend. Are you all alone in Park City?"

"Of course I'm not all alone," I scoff, even though it does sometimes feel like that. "I mean, Lauren's still there, but yeah, the twins keep her kind of busy. But work keeps me plenty busy too."

Besides, Jackson and Nate will be in Park City this weekend for a ski getaway now that their resort is closed for the season. And she was just out for Sierra's birthday a few months ago, so it's not like I don't see her.

"Petra, *work is not life*," she slowly repeats the mantra she's always held dear.

"You know me." I shrug, lifting the wine glass toward my lips.

There's nothing I want more in life than to let my successes prove all the naysayers wrong. All those times I finished in the top three and stood on a World Cup podium holding my skis up—that was a big screw you to all the annoying boys who said I'd never be fast enough. And the years I modeled, every magazine I was in and every runway I walked down—that was for the girls in my high school who told me my lips were too big and eyes were too wide for my face, and called me a gazelle because of my skinny legs, and made fun of my chest because I was already a D cup by freshman year. When I left New York to start my own event planning company, that was to prove to my mentor Patrice—who said I would never make it without her company's name backing my work—that I could succeed in this business beyond her wildest dreams. This TV show I'm set to start filming next month, this is for the scared teenager I once was, who couldn't imagine surviving without her mom, much less envision herself thriving the way I am now.

I. Don't. Rest.

"I worry about you, you know," she says as she takes her glass of sangria from the bartender.

"Then you're wasting your time and energy. I'm doing something I love and I'm wildly successful at it. I'm happy, Emily. You don't need to worry."

She tilts her head slightly, appraising me. I don't crack under her gaze. Am I really happy? Sure, I'm happy enough. Am I satisfied with my life? Yes, absolutely. Is something missing? That's a question I refuse to consider.

"If you say so," she says. "So, how much longer are you in town?"

"A couple more days, max. I was supposed to leave today, actually. But that supersecret client I was telling you about hired me to plan a party for him and I needed to stay a few more days to find a venue."

"Can you tell me who he is?" Emily asks, one eyebrow raised slightly.

"I don't think it's so top secret anymore," I say cautiously. Is there any reason to hide this from her? "How well do you know hockey?"

"Oh my God, please tell me it's Alex Ivanov. Please!"

Her request catches me so off guard I can't be responsible for what my face does in response. "Why?"

"Because he's unbelievably hot and entirely single. If you're planning a party for him, I want to be on that guest list." Her brown eyes darken with longing, her lips part slightly as she sighs.

My mind is at war with itself, reviewing all the reasons I should tell her I'm married to him, and then countering with all the reasons that it's better if no one knows. In the end, discretion wins out.

"I'll see what I can do," I say, sipping my sangria. I'm enjoying it more than I thought I would, not that I'd ever admit it.

"So it *is* him?" Her voice is a girlish squeal, something distinctly like what would come out of Stella's mouth. I nod to let her know she's guessed correctly. "He's doing something public?" she continues. "That's so unlike him. I don't know why he's so reclusive, but it only adds to his appeal."

"He's just a really private person," I say, and by the way her eyes flare, I know I've said too much.

"You know him? Like you already knew him before he hired you to plan this event?"

"He's a friend from childhood."

Her eyebrows knit together, and I'm reminded how much Emily converses with her face. "How? Isn't he from Russia?"

"No. His family is originally from Russia, but like mine, they lived in Austria. Growing up, my family lived on his family's estate." I don't mention that since my dad didn't speak German, he couldn't find a job as an engineer, which had been his career back in Russia, and instead found work as the caretaker for Sasha's family's estate.

"If you've known him your whole life, why didn't you ever say anything?"

"I didn't know he was here, honestly. We had a falling out when we were teenagers and I haven't spoken to him since. Last I knew, he was playing in the KHL, the Russian and European hockey league."

"But you had to have heard his name," she says. "How did you not put two and two together?"

"I haven't followed hockey since I was a teenager." Quite intentionally avoided it, is more like it. "And his name isn't

Alex. It's Aleksandr, or Sasha. Ivanov is literally the most common Russian last name. Like a huge percentage of the population is named Ivanov, so if I ever heard the name 'Alex Ivanov' it didn't register that he was the same Sasha Ivanov I grew up with."

Emily spears a garlic-coated shrimp from one of the plates of tapas the waiter slides on the table between us, then eyes me skeptically. "You haven't ever looked him up since you were kids?"

"Nope," I say, taking a few different tapas and adding them to my plate.

"There's obviously a story there, and you're obviously not going to tell me." She pauses, before adding, "That must have taken superhuman willpower."

"Not really," I say as I pick up a garlic-coated shrimp with my fork. "I like to leave the past in the past."

"No doubt," Emily says. "Kind of like how you left New York behind."

Her honesty catches me off guard for the second time in the same conversation. Clearly I'm off my game.

"Em . . .I didn't mean to hurt you."

"You left and you haven't been great about keeping in touch," she tells me. "If it weren't for my trip out to visit you a few years ago, I wouldn't have seen you since you moved."

"I'll be better about keeping in touch," I promise. "And I'll be back out for this event in a few weeks, so we'll make sure to see each other then."

"When people find out Alex Ivanov is hosting this, they are going to be banging down your door for an invitation."

"I'll warn Morgan," I say, making a mental note to do just that.

"Well, even if you're clearly hiding things from me, I'm glad that you're here and even happier that you'll be back again soon."

"I'm not hiding things from you, Em," I tell her, but it's a lie and we both know it. What I really mean is, I'm only hiding the things I hide from everyone—it's not personal. "I'm just a private person. You know that about me."

"And I love you anyway."

"So tell me what's going on with you." The redirection works and as she launches into more of an update than I got the other day at lunch, I'm relieved to not have to talk about Aleksandr, to not explain our connection, and most importantly, to not admit how much his niece Stella has already stolen my cold, frozen heart.

———

"You wouldn't believe the gossip going around in the office," Morgan says. Over the video call, I can see she's in my private office and I'm sure she's got my sound-proof door shut, so no one else in the very open loft-style office space we rent in downtown Park City will hear her. I only have three employees, but we're a tight-knit group.

"Really? What about?"

"You." Morgan pushes her blue light filtering glasses up her cute turned up nose. Her blond hair is in a ponytail with a three braids running from the front of her head to the elastic, and I'm reminded there's almost nothing cute like that I can do with my curly hair.

"And why are people gossiping about me?" I ask in that voice I've perfected, the *I couldn't care less, but you might as well tell me anyway* one that hides how desperately I always want to know what people are saying about me. Not because I like being the subject of gossip, but because knowledge is power and without it, you can't control the narrative. And if there's anything I want, it's to be in control of my own life— make my own damn decisions, influence the way people think and talk about me, define success on my own terms. I need complete autonomy over my triumphs and failures.

"Because you were supposed to be on a plane back here yesterday and instead, you called a virtual meeting to tell us about a new event we're planning for arguably the hottest and most successful hockey player in the NHL. How'd you pull that one off?"

"You think Alex is hot?" I ask, trying not to stumble over the Americanized name.

"Duh," Morgan says, rolling her eyes, and I'm reminded how our six-year age gap feels like more sometimes. She's my friend Lauren's cousin who needed a job out of college, right as I was looking for an assistant. She was organized and flexible and willing to relocate, so I hired her. And she's been a great assistant. But she's so much younger at twenty-four than I was then, and sometimes it makes me wish I'd been that carefree. *You were never carefree,* I remind myself, *not even before the accident, before everything else that happened to you.*

"But . . ." I say, and realize I have nothing, no argument to invoke. Sasha's not hot in the traditional sense. He's too big, too raw. His flat, smooth forehead is just the right size between his black hair and thick, nearly straight eyebrows. The bridge of his nose is wide and flat, except for the small bump where he broke it when he was fifteen. He has a perfectly square jaw with a cleft in his chin that you can't see through the short beard he sports now, and a neck wrapped in thick, corded muscle that leads to the rest of his powerful body. "I guess I just don't see him that way," I tell Morgan. *Lies.* "I've known him since we were kids. Grew up with him, actually."

"Are you serious?" she squeals. "That's so cool."

"Not really. Anyway, I was already here, so extending the trip a few days to try to nail down a location for the party just makes sense." I glance up at the coffee shop I've made into my office today. I stopped here for breakfast, stayed for a midmorning coffee, and just finished lunch before my call with Morgan. "Were you able to make those calls I asked about yesterday?"

"Yes," she says, and shares her screen with me so she can walk me through her detailed notes on the various location possibilities for each type of space I'm looking into: rooftop patios where we can bring in real furniture, empty lofts that can be totally redecorated, or outdoor garden spaces. Anyone can throw a party at a hotel, restaurant, or bar, but I'm looking to do something unique—something worthy of my name being attached to it. People don't pay me obscene amounts of money to throw lame events that any event planner could arrange.

We decide on four locations that make sense for me to try to see while I'm here. "I've got until 6 p.m. tonight, any time tomorrow, or I could even do Saturday morning before I leave."

My phone vibrates as a text comes in, and I glance down on the table to see Aleksandr's name. I snatch it up so quickly I almost drop it.

"What is that look?" Morgan asks, her voice taking on a singsong quality like she's caught me in the act of something I shouldn't be doing.

"I don't know what you're talking about," I say, casually glancing back at my computer screen.

"Sure you do. Your face just got all dreamy, and you never look like that at work."

Dreamy—pfft. It's Aleksandr, not some guy I'm going to sleep with.

"Give me a sec, I need to respond to this."

"Sure," she says, and sits back in my office chair while I read Aleksandr's message.

ALEKSANDR

> I just finished practice and was thinking about dinner tonight. How the hell are we going to explain who you are to Colette's sister?

PETRA

> We could just say that I'm a childhood friend who's in town for the week.

ALEKSANDR

> You make it sound so simple. How do we explain why you're at a family dinner?

PETRA

> Tell the truth. Stella invited me and I couldn't say no to Her Royal Cuteness.

ALEKSANDR

> You don't think they'll suspect that there's more to that story?

PETRA

> Not unless you or Stella tell them there is.

ALEKSANDR

Okay. I'll talk to Stella about that. Thanks.
I'll see you at 6:30.

PETRA

See you then.

"So you're definitely coming home Saturday?" Morgan asks when I set my phone down and glance back up at the video call on my laptop.

"Sunday is closing day. No way I'm missing the last day of skiing this year." In fact, this trip really put a damper on my end of season spring skiing. Normally I hit the mountain every weekday, when it's least crowded, for a few runs. Not to mention that now I'll only get one day with Jackson before she and Nate leave Park City to head home.

"You booked your own flight?" Morgan sounds hurt, like I've taken away some of her job responsibilities for no reason.

"When I canceled my last one, yes."

"Okay, I'm going to start making these calls," she tells me. "I'll put any appointments on your calendar, and I'll get you transportation for each one. All details will be in the calendar invites."

"Thanks, Morgan. You're the best assistant I've ever had."

"I'm the only assistant you've ever had."

"Same difference. Talk soon." I disconnect the video call and take my earbuds out.

"So, you're a skier?" I hear from the table next to me. I glance over at the blond guy sitting there with his laptop in front of him. He's in a lightweight, tailored blue wool suit, his hair styled and his face clean shaven. That face exudes charm, and his Patek Philippe watch exudes wealth.

"So, you're an eavesdropper?" I rest my elbows on the table as I turn my head fully toward him.

"Touché. But you have the sexiest voice I've ever heard. I couldn't exactly tune you out."

"Fair." Honestly, I'd much rather him comment on my voice—which is low and raspy for no reason other than that's how it developed—than on my face or body, which is what everyone seems to notice about me first. "Yes, I'm a skier. You?"

"I have a place in Vermont, I try to get away as often as I can during the winter. Where do you ski?"

"Park City."

"Is that where you grew up?"

"No," I give him a smile, but don't offer any more details.

"Are you going to make me guess?" he asks, leaning toward me and resting his elbow on his table, mimicking my position.

"You'll never guess, and I don't have all day to wait while you try." I reach up and shut my laptop without taking my eyes off him.

"Because you have plans?"

I give him the smile I reserve for guys I'm flirting with. "Because I have a life."

"Does that life include having a drink with me tonight?" His voice is smooth and deep, like a caress. This is exactly my type of guy—persistent without being pushy. I can tell he's looking for one thing, the same thing I'm looking for when I hit on a guy: intense, short-term attraction.

"I have dinner plans tonight."

"So do I," he says. "Drinks after dinner would be the perfect way to end the day, don't you think?"

Oh, I do. But I don't know how long tonight's dinner will last or if Sasha will need me once his sister-in-law is gone. "That does sound lovely, but I'm not sure how long my dinner will last."

"Why don't I give you my number and if you're free after dinner, send me a text."

"Okay," I agree.

"Where are you staying?" he asks as he types his name and number into my phone.

"Upper East Side."

"Perfect, that's where I live. I have a great bar in mind." He hands me back my phone. "Are you going to at least tell me your name, so I know who you are when you call?"

"You won't recognize me by my voice?" I tease.

"I will," he says, "but I'd still like to know your name."

"Petra," I say, holding my hand out to him.

"Sam," he says in return as he shakes my hand.

"Maybe I'll be seeing you tonight, Sam." I take my laptop and slide it into my bag.

"I certainly hope so," he says, a small smile playing on his lips as he watches me add the rest of my things to my bag

I strut out of that coffee shop high on the notion that even if tonight's dinner is a shit show, I can retreat right into Sam's willing arms when it's over.

Chapter Seven

PETRA

When I arrive at Aleksandr's building, Martin holds the door open with a flourish, saying, "Welcome back, Ms. Volkova. Do you want help with your bags?"

I glance down at the two bags I'm carrying, one with wine bottles and the other with a layered sponge cake with sliced strawberries and whipped cream. "I'm good, thank you."

His white caterpillar-like mustache dances above his lips as they curve into a smile. "Right this way."

He leads me through the lobby once again, and it feels less intimidating this time, now that I'm not taking it all in for the first time. Now, it's almost cozy. The low leather chairs sitting on those Oriental rugs, the mirrored coffee table in the middle of them, the gilded chandeliers—it's the perfect, elegant place to sit with a book and people watch.

When we get to the elevator, Martin inserts his key card for me, and the lift rises to the sixteenth floor so quickly that I've barely had time to collect my thoughts before the door is opening and I'm stepping into the empty entryway.

Well, this feels intrusive. I'm already uncomfortable coming to a family dinner when I'm not family, and now I'm standing here alone, not sure what to do with myself. I listen for some indication that the space isn't actually empty, and I can hear faint voices coming from the opposite end of the apartment, a part I've never been in. I step into the dining room and the voices grow louder, so I follow the sound through a swinging door into a butler's pantry that's as big as my kitchen and twice as nice, then through another swinging door into a kitchen. In typical New York fashion it's a galley-style because even in apartments this big, space is still at a premium. Everything in here looks original—painted white cabinets, white subway tiles that have so many hairline cracks in them they look intentionally aged, and worn soapstone countertops with a big soapstone farmhouse sink. People pay astronomical prices to remodel their kitchens to look like this, and here's an original.

And at the end of it, standing around a little peninsula with a stand mixer on top, are Stella and Sasha. Covered in cake batter. It's all over Sasha's T-shirt, but even on her step stool Stella only comes up to his armpits, so she's got much more on her: it's on her face, in her hair, splattered across her dress. And they're both laughing like it's the funniest thing that's ever happened. They probably haven't noticed it on the walls yet.

"Petra!" Stella says, her face lighting up when she sees me.

Sasha's laugh stills when he notices me standing there. "Hey, I didn't realize you were here already." He sounds happy to see me, but his face is expressionless, so I can't tell for sure. He clasps Stella's shoulder when she tries to step off the step stool toward me. "You're covered in cake batter," he reminds her softly.

"Can people always get in this easily without you knowing?" I ask as I set the bag with the cake on the counter, then use both hands to set the bag of wine on the counter next to it so I can make sure neither bottle falls over.

He uses a dish towel to wipe some of the cake batter off Stella's face, but she swats his hand away because she's clearly enjoying licking all the batter she can reach with her little tongue. "I have a list of people who the front door staff know can access the apartment any time they want, which is why you were let up." He wipes the towel slowly along the counter, but his voice is defensive, which means he doesn't realize I was teasing. And also—*what?*—why am I on this list of his?

"Who else is on your list?" I lean my hip against the counter and cross my arms under my chest, keeping my voice teasing and my pose casual.

"The nanny will be when she starts next week."

"So I'm the only one?"

My eyebrows knit together. He eyes me, then glances down at Stella. "Do you want to go take a quick shower before CeCe and Tony get here?"

Stella nods and hops off the stool.

"Do you need help?" he asks.

"No, I can take a shower myself," she assures him. "I'll be right back for my hug," she tells me as she runs past me on her way out of the room.

Sasha looks down at his shirt, then glances around at the mess. "So much for dessert."

"Lucky for you, I brought some." I reach into the bag and take out the box so he can see the cake through the cellophane wall on the front and top.

"And you picked Stella's favorite bakery. She's going to be very happy."

"Need help cleaning this up?" I ask as I glance around, trying to figure out how many surfaces are covered in cake batter.

He looks at the sleeveless shirtdress I'm wearing with a pair of wedges. "I don't want you to get batter all over yourself too," he says. He reaches behind his neck and pulls his T-shirt over his head effortlessly.

There is about half a second where I'm so captivated by his body—by the ridges and valleys of each muscle stretching and contracting as he drags his shirt up and over his head, by the sheer size of his powerful abdomen, chest, and shoulders —that I stop breathing. I forget who I'm looking at.

But then the shirt crests his head and I see his face and I remember: the loss, the devastation, the desolation. I feel it all like it was yesterday, and I remember how I promised myself I'd never let him, or any man, make me feel that way again. I am who I am, and how I am, because men like him exist.

"Can you hand me that towel," he gestures opposite me. I tear my eyes from his body to see another dish towel hanging on the bar of his eight-burner Wolf range and oven combo. Grabbing it, I take opposite corners in each hand and spin the fabric around itself until I have a long rope of towel. He eyes me warily. "Don't you dare."

For so many reasons, I should heed those words and keep my distance. Instead, I take another step toward him.

"But it was always so funny when it was you chasing me around the big kitchen at Whitehall." I can't help but smile at the memory of us as kids, and how the Ivanov's cook would always chase us out of the kitchen threatening to butcher us and serve us for dinner if we didn't learn to behave ourselves. "Not as funny if you're on the receiving end?" I walk toward him slowly, each step measured so I can retreat if needed.

"You realize I have a dish towel right here," he says, nodding toward the towel he used to wipe Stella's face and then the counter. It's covered in cake batter, which makes this game twice as risky because I don't have anything to change into if he decides to whack me with that dirty towel. *He wouldn't dare.*

"You wouldn't get me covered in cake batter before your sister-in-law shows up," I remind him. "I'm counting on you to be a gentleman."

"I am so many things," he says, his voice low and steady, "but a gentleman is not one of them."

He covers the space between us in two huge steps and a fraction of a second. For a man of his size, he moves with remarkable speed and before I know what's happening, he's directly in front of me, ripping the towel out of my hands.

"You always were terrible at this game," he says, looking down at me. His voice has that growly quality that competition always brings out in him, but it's the heat in his eyes as his body holds mine in place against the cabinets that startles me most. It seems impossible, but it's like his pupils are molten—liquid steel churning over and over.

"Maybe I was never trying to win," I say, my voice barely

audible. It feels like the most vulnerable thing I've said in a long time. I watch him process this information—is it a revelation to him? Because losing at this game is not just getting whipped with the towel, but getting caught.

Is that what I wanted? To be caught by Sasha, not just temporarily in the game, but for good?

He tilts his head to the side, studying me, and I watch those molten steel orbs as they skim across my face—assessing, questioning, affirming. He opens his mouth to say something when there's a bloodcurdling shriek somewhere in the apartment.

He's through the door so fast I only see his back for a second before the door swings shut behind him. I follow, heading through the dining room, into the entryway, and then down the hallway where I hear his footsteps. The door to Stella's room is open, and by the time I catch up, he stands in the doorway with a sobbing six-year-old plastered to his legs.

He looks over at me and mouths *spider*, rolling his eyes so hard that it makes me laugh. I cover my mouth just in time, so the laugh is inaudible. I'd never want Stella to think I was laughing at her expense.

I approach slowly, ignoring the way Stella's death grip on Sasha's leg has his jeans riding low on his hips and the waistband of his briefs standing out against the deep grooves of his abdomen. I sink down so I'm sitting on my heels with my arms wrapped around my knees.

"Hey," I say to her, and she looks at me with enormous tears spilling over her eyelids. "What's going on?"

"There's a spider in my bathroom."

"I don't like spiders either," I tell her. "You know what I like to do when I find them in my apartment?"

Her eyes get even wider. "What?"

"I like to catch them in a cup. Then I slide a piece of paper under them so they are trapped. Sometimes I let them crawl around in there for a couple hours thinking about the error of their ways." Above us, Sasha's chest shakes with silent laughter. "But then, because I'm benevolent, I take them outside and let them go so they can eat all the bad bugs."

"What's benevolent mean?" she asks, perking up as the tears stop falling.

"It means I try to use my powers for good."

"Even to help"—her lower lip is practically trembling at the word—"spiders?"

"Spiders don't want anything to do with us. They're just looking for bugs to eat. So if I put them outside, they can eat bugs, like mosquitos, that might bite me and then they're actually working for *me*, right?"

"Do you want to catch the spider on the wall by my shower?" she asks.

"Sure thing," I tell her. "You know, girls need to know how to catch bugs."

"Why?" The word is part curiosity, part revulsion.

"Well, what if when you're older there's a spider in your room and there isn't someone else around to catch it for you? It's important to know how to do these things for ourselves."

Her face manages to perk up a bit while still looking skeptical. I slide my eyes up to Aleksandr, who looks at me with that same mask he wore when I first entered his kitchen.

Gone are the eyes that were burning as they slid across my face.

"How about if I show you how I do it so you'll know how next time?" I say as I hold my hand out to Stella.

"Okay." The word is fear and bravery wrapped inexorably together.

I glance up at Sasha. "Could you get me a glass and a piece of paper? Or something stiff like an envelope?"

"Sure," he says. Now that Stella has released her hold on his legs, he steps around me and hurries down the hall.

I take her hand and say, "Why don't you show me where this spider is, and then I'll explain how I'm going to catch it."

She follows me to the bathroom door but stops on the threshold and won't come in. Instead, she points her hand up toward the glass door of her shower. There on the wall is a light brown spider, smaller than a dime. "Okay, so what I'm going to do is put a glass over it. Then, I'll lift one side of the glass ever so slightly and slide a folded piece of paper or an envelope under it. Once the spider is on the paper or glass, the trickiest part is getting your hand under the paper so you can carry the spider in the glass outside, without the spider getting out."

"But when you put the cup over it, won't it jump or run around?" she asks. I notice that she's looking at the spider with some degree of curiosity. At least she doesn't seem petrified anymore.

"Maybe. But spiders can't jump or run through glass, or through plastic if we use a plastic cup. And even if the spider gets away somehow, believe me, it's trying to run away from you, not toward you."

She takes a small step into the bathroom so she's standing next to me.

"What makes you so scared of them?" I ask.

"They move so fast."

"Think how fast you could run if you had eight legs," I say. *Where the hell is Sasha with the glass?* I don't like spiders any more than the next person, but I do want her to know that it's important that she learn to do things like this for herself. As a rich kid growing up on the Upper East Side, it would be too easy to end up spoiled and entitled and unable to do anything for herself.

I never had anyone teach me how to be independent, how to take care of myself, or how to advocate for myself. My parents did everything for me when I was a kid, then my mom died and my dad became what I generously call 'emotionally mute.' I had to learn how to be an adult overnight, and I had to figure everything out myself because my dad was so wrapped up in his grief he was utterly useless as a father.

"Here you go." Sasha's voice startles me. He stands in the doorway, his hand extended with the glass. At least he has a shirt on now.

"For someone so large, you move remarkably quickly and quietly," I say as I take the glass. I try to ignore the shock of his skin on mine when our fingers touch, but I bobble the glass and he has to catch it and hand it back to me again.

"You've seen what I can do on skates. This should not be a surprise."

Still, how does a two hundred-pound man not make a sound when he walks?

I show Stella how quickly and easily a spider can be caught, then I leave the bathroom with the offending arachnid. Aleksandr tells her to take a very quick shower and shuts the door behind him.

He eyes the way I'm holding the spider between the glass in one hand and the folded piece of paper in the other. "How mad would you be if I tickled you right now?" A sly smile barely cracks his lips enough for me to see his teeth.

"How mad would you be if there was shattered glass all over Stella's floor and a spider loose in her room?"

"You play dirty, Volkova. Always have," he mutters.

"Sometimes winning is dirty work," I say, throwing the words he always used during our childhood right back at him. He never apologized when we were kids and he tripped me or knocked me out of the way during a game. Back then, he'd win at any cost. I wonder if the same is true today?

Our eyes size each other up in a mini staring contest, both of us, I'm sure, remembering our competitive childhood relationship that turned to deep friendship before his betrayal.

"Can you show me where to let this thing out?" I say, not wanting to dwell on the past I thought I'd left far behind me until he showed up in a lawyer's office two days ago.

He leads me back through the living room and opens one of the glass doors. I follow him through it and onto the terrace. The sound that leaves my mouth when the spectacular view of Central Park hits me is almost a grunt of pain. The view I saw the other night was amazing, but he was right, it is even better in the daylight, especially now that I can see this terrace. We stand on travertine tiles laid in a diamond pattern, and there's a low stone wall that runs along the perimeter with a short glass wall above it—high enough that you can't accidentally fall over the edge, but low enough that it doesn't interfere with the view. A large wrought iron table and chairs sit near one wall, and lush planters full of small trees, shrubs, and flowers surround us. I follow the length of the terrace with my eyes. "Is that a . . ." I search for the word but can't find it.

"It's a solarium," he says. The glass walls and ceiling easily soar twelve feet from the floor to the peaked roof, and it runs to the end of the terrace. Inside it's loaded with plants and another table and chairs.

I take a few steps closer to the solarium so I can better see the inside. "This is magical," I say, because I cannot for the life of me think of another word for this space.

"The solarium is another thing that sold me on the space." His breath falls against my neck, which leads to the same tingling in my spine I felt when he had me backed into the cabinet in the kitchen. "My bedroom has glass doors that lead out to it," his arm extends past me, pointing to the end of the terrace. "So does the guest room."

"Wow, to wake up in a place like that." My sigh is laced with appreciation for this life he's built for himself.

"It would make a lot of sense for you to stay here, Petra. In the guest room," he quickly adds, as if I might have thought he meant in his room. "If you're willing to help me and Stella, we'll need to find a way to live together, at least some of the time."

My spine stiffens. "I have a life, and a career. I can't just walk away from them. Even if I wanted to help you, I can't move to New York, and it's unfair of you to ask me to."

I glance over at him and there's a flash of pain in his eyes. *I do want to help you*, I almost say. But I bite my tongue instead, because I don't know how to help him without hurting myself.

"I know this is a big ask . . ."

"A big ask is 'Hey, can you watch my kid for a week while I go on vacation.' This is life-changing. A fake marriage that needs to be real? A kid to adopt? Getting you US citizenship? You're not talking about helping you out. You're talking about me changing everything, giving up much of what I've worked for over the past few years, relocating . . ."

"Petra, I don't know what else to do. The thought of Stella ever ending up with her aunt and uncle . . ." He trails off as his body visibly shudders.

And as if they knew we were talking about them, a doorbell sound chimes inside the apartment.

Aleksandr rolls his eyes skyward. "That's Martin letting me know they're here."

I quickly set the spider trap on the ground, lift the glass, and then pick up the paper after the small spider scurries away. When I stand, I feel like I'm going to face a firing squad —I don't even know these people, I'm not sure why I am involved, or why I care what they think.

"Can you get Stella and I'll entertain them? I don't want you to be stuck with them while I get her."

Even though I still don't think they can be as bad as he's making them out to be, it sounds like he's giving me the better end of the bargain. "No problem," I tell him.

He opens the door to the solarium. "First door on the right leads to the guest bedroom. When you come out in the hall, Stella's room is to the right." With that, he turns and heads back through the door to the sitting room and is gone.

Chapter Eight

ALEKSANDR

The ten minutes of small talk with CeCe and Tony are excruciating.

A socialite, a businessman, and an athlete walk into a dinner party . . . it's like the beginning of a bad joke. They're only here to see Stella, and I can tell they don't want to be talking to me any more than I want to be talking to them.

"Maybe I should go check on Stella," CeCe suggests when we get tired of staring at each other.

"I'm sure Petra has it under control."

I can practically see her proverbial ears perk up under all those blond hair extensions. "Oh, your new nanny has started already?"

"No. Petra's a childhood friend of mine and Niko's, and she's in town this week." I do worry that if Petra decides to go along with this plan, having introduced her as a friend rather than as my wife will have been a mistake. But it's what I agreed to, so here we are.

"Oh, how delightful." CeCe's words couldn't be more at odds with the look on her face.

Petra's husky laugh carries into the living room from the entryway as she and Stella make their way toward us. The sound of her voice does uncomfortable things to the knot in the pit of my stomach. Having her here is both a relief and a worry—a contradiction, just like the woman herself.

I'm still looking at CeCe when they enter the room behind me, and I see the way her eyes bulge and her mouth hangs open in shock. She's never flustered, so I turn my head to see what she's gaping at.

"Cecelia?" Petra says, every bit as in shock as CeCe.

"Oh my God, Petra!" CeCe says as she rushes out of her seat.

They give each other a kiss on each cheek, but Petra's look is one of cool detachment. Even as I wonder how they know each other, I can tell she doesn't like CeCe one bit. I don't think CeCe can tell though, because she always assumes everyone adores her. I glance back at her husband Tony, who's still in his seat next to the one she vacated, sipping his scotch. His eyes do light up when he looks over at Stella, who CeCe has not yet even acknowledged, though she stands next to Petra holding her hand. As if she senses Tony's eyes on her, Stella scurries over to me and curls up into my lap, resting her head on my chest.

"You're Stella's aunt?" Petra says, practically stupefied. If she's anything like the teenager I once knew, she's hard to rattle. What is it about CeCe that has her so on edge?

"Yes, my older sister Colette . . ." CeCe trails off, as if it's too painful for her to continue. In reality, Colette was five years older, they ran in different social circles, and hardly saw or spoke to each other. Neither Colette nor Niko ever told me what had happened between her and her sister, but I knew it was bad enough that Colette didn't want her sister anywhere near her child.

"I'm so sorry about Colette and Niko," Petra says, "I can't imagine how hard that must be for you."

"Well, at least we still have little Stella to remind us of her," CeCe says, then glances around, looking for the girl who's allegedly the object of her affection but whom she hasn't deigned to notice until it suits her storyline.

"She's a jewel, for sure," Petra says, offering Stella the only sincere smile she's seen since her aunt and uncle arrived.

From my lap, Stella glows. I hope I'm not making a horrible mistake bringing Petra into our life. Stella adores her. If Petra refuses to help us, even after getting to know Stella, my niece will be crushed. And I don't know how much more loss she can handle.

Petra takes a seat in the chair next to mine, opposite the couch Tony is seated on, and CeCe returns to join him. The conversation is less awkward than before Petra showed up, because she can talk to anyone about anything, and make it seem like she cares. It's either a gift or a practiced skill, because there's no way she's actually interested in all the gossip CeCe is spewing about people they both know—I can tell by the way her face doesn't move, the way the small smile is plastered on her lips, the way she keeps glancing at me as if to say 'is this over yet?' Unfortunately, it's only just started.

———

"What's the matter, Stella? Why won't you give your Uncle Tony a kiss?" CeCe's nasal voice carries across the living room, where we've gathered with our plates of cake now that our catered dinner is over, but it's her words rather than the annoying quality of her voice that has my head turning.

"No, thank you," Stella says as she turns her head away from where he stands above her, dips her fork into her cake, and takes a bite. The game of Sorry sits forgotten on the small table between her and her aunt.

"I don't bite, you know," Tony chuckles.

Even from across the room, I can see the way Stella's shoulders bunch up as she shrinks into herself. Next to me, Petra stiffens. "What the fuck?" she whispers under her breath.

Does Tony not see how uncomfortable he's making Stella? Or does he just not care?

"It's just a kiss, Stella-Bella," CeCe says.

"I just don't want to kiss anyone, Aunt CeCe," Stella says less audibly.

Petra looks at me pointedly, as if to say *Why aren't you doing anything about this?*

As much as I want to punch Tony in the face right now, I know I can't do anything to antagonize him or CeCe. Tom warned me about how tenuous my guardianship is. One wrong move could give them the ammunition they need to get custody, and I can't give them that. Instead, I grind my teeth together, thinking I should probably tell Stella it's time for bed. I suspect she'd go willingly, even though it's early.

The look in Petra's eyes lets me know my lack of instant action is not the response she was looking for.

She's on her feet and heading across the room when Tony starts making smoochy kissing sounds and leaning down toward Stella. Petra's hand is on his shoulder, pulling him back before I can say anything to stop this.

"The appropriate response when someone says they don't want to kiss you is to back off," Petra tells him, her voice steady and possibly louder than is absolutely necessary. "Not to use your superior size to force yourself on them."

Tony takes one look at her hand, then eyes her like she disgusts him. She looks back at him like the feeling is mutual. *Good, let her see how horrible they are.* I don't want my niece to suffer, but it's necessary that Petra see the shit that makes the idea of Stella living with them so repulsive.

"I just wanted a kiss from my niece," Tony says. "Don't try to make it sound like something it's not."

"I'm sorry," CeCe says to Petra from her seat at the table, "but why is this your concern?"

Petra's look conveys exactly how pathetic she thinks CeCe is for not only being married to this piece of shit, but for defending him as he makes her niece uncomfortable.

"Any time a child feels powerless to stop an adult from touching her in a way she doesn't want to be touched, it should be *everyone's* concern."

Her words trigger a memory in the back of my mind, but I can't grasp hold of it because I'm too distracted by CeCe's nasally voice as she says, "Oh Jesus, Petra, get over yourself," she rolls her eyes. "It's just a kiss."

Petra glances over her shoulder at me as I lean forward in

my seat and begin to stand. Her look tells me I'm reacting quite a bit too late.

She turns back toward Stella. "Ready for bed, sweetie?"

Petra reaches out her hand and Stella is out of her seat and has her arms around Petra so quickly it's like she has the ability to travel at warp speed. Petra wraps her arm around Stella's small shoulders as they turn back toward the wide doorway to the entryway.

"Thanks for coming over," I say to CeCe and Tony as Petra leads Stella out of the room. "It's been a pleasure, as always." I doubt they miss my sarcastic tone.

"You do always have the most interesting friends, Alex," CeCe replies. "Careful you don't let people like her have too much influence over our girl. I'd hate to have to bring the fact that you hang out with lingerie models to the court's attention."

Oh, the icy notes of jealousy.

There is so much I want to say and it's on the tip of my tongue, but I know she's baiting me and I won't fall into her trap. Petra has more integrity and drive than most people I know, and having walked down the catwalk at the world's most famous and controversial fashion show years ago doesn't change that. And in the few short days she's known my niece, she's shown her more love than Stella has ever seen from her aunt and uncle. But letting CeCe know any of that might do more harm than good. So instead, I walk them to the entryway and wait for the elevator to arrive. And when those doors finally close behind them, I breathe a deep sigh of relief.

I head down the hall toward Stella's bedroom. When I arrive, Stella is already kneeling in front of her nightstand like she does every night. Petra sits next to her on her bed, observing the ritual we created together to help her continue to honor her mother and father. I join Stella on the floor, trying not to think about what it means that I'm letting Petra into this extremely private part of our lives. That I'm literally on my knees in front of her.

We recite the Russian prayer for the dead as Stella takes each of the wooden nesting dolls and places them inside of each other until there's only one large doll on her nightstand. In the morning, she'll take them apart and set them up individually so that we can repeat this moment again tomorrow evening.

"Okay," I say, kissing the top of Stella's curls. "Time for bed."

"Is it okay if I want Petra to tuck me in?" she asks me.

"Of course it's okay," I say, glancing over my shoulder, "if Petra doesn't mind."

Petra swallows. "Of course I don't mind." Is it my imagination or is her voice even thicker than normal?

I head back to the living room to give them some privacy. I'm on the far side of the room looking out the window and across the terrace, wondering what will happen if Petra doesn't agree to help me get citizenship and wondering how long I should wait before I press her for a decision, when I hear the clicking of her wedges on the wooden floor. She moves across the rug silently, but I feel her approaching the same way you feel a storm coming on: the temperature drops a few degrees and the air feels calm and thick, but you can hear the thunder in the distance and feel the electricity in the air. I brace for impact, because if Petra is upset—really and truly upset—that's not good.

She stops with her shoulder next to mine, her arms crossed over her chest. She doesn't look at me, just gazes out the window as she says, "How could you put her in a position like that, Aleksandr?"

What is she accusing me of, exactly? "I don't have any control over how Tony acts."

She spins toward me and pushes her finger into my chest so fast I almost stumble backward. Almost.

"Bullshit," she spits the word at me like it's a bullet. "How can you love her like you clearly do and then stand by and watch her languish in a dangerous situation? Why didn't you stop him when you saw how uncomfortable he was making Stella?"

"She wasn't in any danger," I remind Petra. "I was right there." I want to give her my real reason, but she doesn't give me a chance.

"What you just witnessed was your niece being *conditioned* to accept unwanted attention from men. She very clearly said she didn't want to kiss him, but he didn't let up and the other adults who should have protected her made it seem like *she* was being the unreasonable one." Her voice is frantic and high-pitched and I don't know what to make of it. "How many times do you think that needs to happen before she finally stops pushing back? And once she does, what else will he—or someone else—try?"

I take in her wild eyes, the absolutely livid expression on her face, the fact that her finger has pounded into my sternum so many times it's going to leave a mark. This is about Stella, sure. But it also feels personal. "What happened to you?" I ask, keeping my voice calm and steady.

"None of your fucking business. You need to focus on

Stella. Protect her, Sasha. Teach her to be strong and to demand that other people respect her boundaries. Don't set her up to get taken advantage of over and over again." Her voice breaks and she turns away, then starts walking across the room toward the entryway.

"Wait!" What the hell is she talking about? "Where are you going?"

"I have plans tonight. I told Stella I'd stop by tomorrow afternoon to say goodbye."

"You're leaving?"

"I told you I wasn't staying in New York. I told you I have a life. I told you it wasn't fair of you to ask me to stay," she says, but I'm not sure what that means. Is she not willing to help me get citizenship? Or she will, but not by living in New York? "I hope you do right by Stella, Aleksandr. She's perfect —feisty and innocent and beautiful. Let her stay that way."

"I'm not sure I know how to do that," I tell her. I hate the raw consistency of my words, and how they fall away, peeling back pieces of my armor and revealing just how helpless I feel.

She turns back toward me but keeps walking backward toward the elevator. "You do. You'll figure out what she needs."

"You've known her for three days and you understand her better than I do."

"That's because once upon a time, *I was her*. But I'm not her parent, you are."

"Your instincts are great," I tell her. "You're going to make an unbelievable mom someday." I shouldn't feel a pang of loss at the statement. But suddenly my head is filled with images of her and Stella, together. And knowing those are dreams and not reality hurts more than it should.

This is what my father warned me about, the infatuation that only ends in self-destruction. *Let her walk away so you can save yourself.*

"I won't be an unbelievable mother," she says. "I decided a long time ago that I'm not having kids."

"I don't see how someone who's such a natural with kids could not end up with kids of their own." My thoughts spill out before I can think about holding them in.

"Luckily, I make my own decisions about my body," she says, and spins on her heel to push the elevator button.

I stand there like an ass, unable to form any words at all, let alone the ones that will keep her here. Because I remember a time when I used her body as an excuse to push her away. And I wish that were the *only* betrayal that happened the night we said goodbye for the last time.

Chapter Nine

ALEKSANDR

Fourteen Years Ago
Innsbruck, Austria

"A leksandr," my father calls as I pass the library doors. My back stiffens. I don't like to be summoned, but he literally does not know another way to interact with people.

I step between the half-open pocket doors of the extra wide doorway and wonder if he's been sitting at this desk in the hour since we signed those papers. He doesn't even look up when he feels my looming presence. "I need you to sign one more thing before you go."

"What else is there?" I ask, annoyed at this distraction while I'm on my way to see Petra. "I thought we signed everything earlier."

"You need to sign the bank draft too."

I'm having a hard time listening to what he's telling me because I'm too keyed up at the thought of being alone with Petra, in the dark, and so consumed by the memory of the way we locked eyes in the library.

I step up to his desk, and my father slides a piece of paper toward me. The name of the bank is displayed prominently at the top. FIFTY THOUSAND DOLLARS is written in capital letters on one line, and below it is the name of my trust and Petra's father's name. I sign along the line on the bottom of the page and wonder why I don't remember seeing a dollar amount in the agreement we signed earlier.

That paperwork is sitting on my father's desk, so I pick it up as I set my pen down. It's written in Russian, and until this past year I could barely read more than the simplest two- and three-letter words. But living in Russia this last year has meant I had to learn to read the language I've been speaking at home my whole life. I'd been too focused on Petra to spare a glance at the paperwork I signed earlier, but now I stare at the words across the top of the page.

MARRIAGE LICENSE

I can feel my father's eyes on me as I scan the page. It takes me three times as long to read it as it would if it were written in German or English, but I make it through the document eventually.

Then I turn to the second piece of paperwork we signed. MARRIAGE CONTRACT.

My eyes meet my father's.

"Explain this." It's not a request.

"I bought her for you. Or rather, you bought her, since the money is coming from your trust."

My eyes narrow. "What do you mean you *bought* her for me?"

"I see the way you look at her. I see the way you feel about her even while you try to act like she's only a friend."

As he speaks, fire runs through my veins—embarrassment and anger and shame combined into one rush of heat. I thought I'd kept my inappropriate feelings locked away, hidden so well that no one suspected a thing. I should have known my father's shrewd eyes would pick up on any clues.

"When I said I wanted to pay for her education with no strings attached, I didn't mean bind us together permanently for the rest of our lives." I knew there was no way Petra would ever accept the money from me, which is why I had my father arrange this whole deal. But where the hell had this marriage idea come from? Why would he think that, at nineteen and at the beginning of my professional hockey career, I'd want to be married?

"Sasha," he says, and I bristle at the nickname. He only ever calls me Aleksandr and my older brother Nikolai, as if using the diminutives that all our friends call us would somehow make him less of an authority figure. "I will not watch that girl wreck you the way her mother wrecked me."

Oh, so we're finally talking about this.

"*She* wrecked *you*?" I say, my voice harsh. "You threatened to tell her husband that something was happening between the two of you, and she died because of your lie."

The look on my father's face is one of absolute shock. He really didn't know that I knew.

"How do you know about that conversation?" His voice and his eyes are serpentine, and I wonder if he's getting ready to strike with some low blow—something he planned and I'm not expecting. That's how he operates.

"Because I overheard your conversation," I say, thinking back to their quiet, angry whispers before the car accident three years before.

Petra's father was in our home when the police arrived to tell him his wife's car took an icy turn too fast, and they asked what she could have been speeding home for. Of course her father didn't know, but *mine* knew.

"You knew she was rushing home after picking Viktor up from hockey practice, hoping to prevent you from saying something untrue to her husband. Petra lost her mother and brother, and I lost my best friend. All because you threatened her mother."

I don't mention how I've struggled with my own guilt over this event. Since we lived on the same property, I normally gave Viktor rides home from our hockey practices. But I stayed home sick that day because I had a minor cold and didn't feel like going to school. Mrs. Volkova wouldn't have been going to pick him up if I had been there like I was supposed to be. So maybe it's more my fault than my father's, even.

My father, sick bastard that he is, actually laughs. "You *think* you know what happened, but you have no idea. It wasn't an empty threat. She had been leading me on for *years*. You can think she was innocent if you want, but she wasn't. She knew how I felt about her and she used every available opportunity to manipulate me, sharing little pieces of herself here and there when it was convenient for her, then denying there was anything between us and telling me I was a jealous fool. And I've watched Petra do the same to you over the last two years."

"Like hell you have." Petra has made it very clear that she thinks of me like a brother. There's been no leading me on, no stolen kisses. Nothing but friendship.

Until this summer.

"You watch her like a hawk watches a mouse. You might think no one notices. You might even think she doesn't know. But how could she not? And now you've decided to pay for her boarding school out of your trust fund, because you want to see her dreams come true. And you're so naive you think you came up with that idea on your own, rather than her planting the seed and nurturing it."

That money is a tiny sliver of what's sitting in that trust fund. I won't miss it, and she'll get a shot at her dream—Olympic-level skiing. I'd be a selfish bastard not to help her when it costs me so little. Though, I'd help her even if it cost me everything.

"Unless you told her, she has no idea that money is coming from me." Petra is a lot of things, but manipulative is not one of them.

"You sure about that?" he asks, steepling his fingertips together while his elbows rest on his desk.

"I'm positive." She wouldn't do that.

"Well, one way or the other, she's yours now."

"That's where you're wrong. You don't *buy* a girl like Petra, you *earn* her. Her mother was the same way, and that was always your mistake. You assumed you could buy her like you do everyone and everything else." I pause and he doesn't respond. "Petra doesn't want to be bought. She wants to be loved."

"Well, as her husband, you'll be in a position to do that too"—his voice carries notes of boredom, as though he's already tired of this conversation—"if that's what you want."

How could I ever earn Petra's trust—or more importantly, deserve it—after the role both my father and I played in her mother and brother's deaths? And if I told her the truth, there's no way she would ever want to get involved with the son of the man her mother was allegedly having an affair with.

"I'm not marrying Petra under these circumstances," I say, slamming the papers down on the desk. "How do we undo this?"

"We don't. Everyone has already signed."

"This can't be legal."

"It will be once the paperwork is filed."

"What would make Petra's father agree to this?" I ask. He only knows Russian, which is why this once-brilliant engineer couldn't get a job in Austria and has worked as our property's caretaker since fleeing political persecution in the motherland before Petra was born. He obviously knows what that paperwork said. What would make him sell his daughter off like this?

My father just shrugs. "I'm sure he had his reasons."

My hand curls into a fist where it rests on top of the paperwork on the desk, and my father eyes it like he's daring me to punch him. As many times as I've had that desire in my lifetime, it's never been quite this strong.

"The marriage license will be filed tomorrow, and the contract in three days' time. Unless . . ." He lets the word hang there between us, and it's obvious he's not going to tell me what I have to do to prevent it unless I ask.

"Unless what?"

"I won't file them if you swear to never see Petra again. Let her go. Let your obsession with her go"—his voice is as hard and cold as ice—"or it will ruin you like my feelings for her mother ruined me."

I take in the lines around my father's eyes, the deep

grooves across his forehead from the perpetual frowning. He looks like a man who, despite having everything money can buy, is exhausted from life. He looks like a man who's never known happiness.

Is that the path I'm on?

"What makes you think I'd follow the same road you have?" I ask. I want to believe I'm emotionally tougher than he is, but my pull toward Petra is unequivocally strong no matter how much I try to repress my feelings.

"Because you are more like me than you want to admit. Once you commit to something, you're all in. I don't want to see you commit to a lost cause that will destroy your happiness."

Even though everything he's saying goes against everything I want, I see the truth in his words. I think about Petra all the time—what it could be like between us if she wasn't so much younger and if she felt the same way. I'd hoped that maybe now that she's sixteen things might change between us, but with me headed back to Russia and her headed to Switzerland . . . how much longer can I torment myself? Maybe cutting things off between us entirely is the safest course of action. She gets to go to chase her Olympic skiing dreams, and I can focus entirely on my hockey career instead of dividing my attention.

You'll both be better off that way, I tell myself.

"I'll say goodbye to her tonight."

"A permanent goodbye," my father says. "You need to break things off in a way that she won't keep trying to revive the friendship."

The knife in my stomach twists. The pain is unbearable and I haven't even ended things yet. I'm not sure I'm strong enough to do this, but I have to do it anyway. I can't marry her under these circumstances. She deserves better than this. "I understand."

"Good," my father says, "because if you try to see her again after this, I'll have to tell her where the money for her schooling came from. And why."

My eyes bulge at his words. Petra would leave school if she knew I was paying for it. She'd never accept a gift like that from me—I still can't believe she accepted help from my father. "You wouldn't."

His eyes are ice. "Oh, son. I would."

I thought it would be impossible to hate him more than I do, but I was wrong.

I turn and leave the room, trying to imagine what life without Petra will even feel like.

This boarding school and ski training is the only way for her to achieve her dreams, I remind myself. *If you really do care about her, let her go.*

———

I come around the bend in the garden, resolved that I won't tell Petra about the marriage. I'd have to reveal too much about the way our family's history is intertwined, too much about my own feelings for her. I'd have to tell her that her father apparently loves her so much he's willing to do whatever it takes to help her achieve her dreams, but respects her so little he essentially sold her off to do so.

When I reach the top of the ladder, Petra is on her hands and knees, lighting a candle. "What's this?" I glance around the treehouse and notice other candles and a blanket she's kneeling on. The whole scene is very romantic, and I keep my face expressionless so she won't see how this scene is everything I want, right when I know for sure I can't have it.

Her skirt is bunched up around her thighs and I know my eyes pause there for a second, just like they lingered on her body earlier in the library. I slide my gaze up to her belly, focusing on that sliver of skin between the waistband of her denim skirt and the tight button-down sweater she's wearing. *How am I going to say no to this?*

"I wanted to be able to see you in this dark, old place," she says.

In my momentary internal war with myself, I forgot I'd even asked her a question. I give her a small smile because if I wasn't here to end things, this would be a perfect scenario. God, how I wish I could at least kiss her before having to back away, but that would make what I'm about to do even worse.

"Well, are you coming in or just going to hang out on the ladder all night?"

I plant my hands on the floor and pull myself up into our secret hideaway. It's cramped up here now that we're fully grown, so I sit cross-legged on the blanket facing her. I need to keep some distance so I can keep my head.

For a minute we just stare at each other. I've tried to hide my true feelings this summer, but they seem to have saturated the space anyway. She looks at me like she can read my mind.

I reach behind me and grasp the book I've brought her. "Here," I say, shoving the book toward her. "I found it for you."

"Oh my gosh, Sasha!" Her voice carries the notes of delight I'd hoped it would. I spent too fucking long finding that book for her—months of searching through used book shops in half the cities in Russia. I've had it since I came home a month ago, but wanted to give it to her as a going away present—something to remember me by. She gazes at the cover like she's soaking it in. "I can't believe it."

"Why would you even want a first edition of *War and Peace* in Russian? You don't know how to read it." This fact has made her a pawn in my father's games.

"I told you," she says, like I don't listen to a word she says, "it was my mother's favorite book." She glances at the cover again, then continues like she often does—giving me small snippets of information, doling them out like treats. And like a fool, I collect them, hoping that one day I'll have a complete picture of who she is and what makes her tick. "Mama had one just like this and she lost count of how many times she'd read it. It was practically falling apart. But I don't know what happened to it after she died. It's like it disappeared off our bookshelf."

A shiver runs up my spine as the darkness surrounding us seeps into me. I know exactly where that tattered book is. I've seen one matching its description on a shelf in my father's private study many times and thought nothing of it. Another piece of her family he's taken from her and she doesn't even know it.

"Well, now you have your own copy." My words are gruff, full of finality. I shouldn't be running all over Russia doing her bidding when I'm supposed to be focusing on my hockey career. Half the reason I joined up in the KHL was to get the hell away so I could stop obsessing over her. It clearly didn't work.

I've never stopped thinking about those dark curls I want to dig my hands into, those lips I need to taste, that sharp tongue I want to feel on my skin. From her ridiculous body to her inquisitive mind to her guarded heart, there is no part of her that does not fascinate me. And if I don't get away from her, I'm going to do something about it, thus ruining her future.

"Thank you," she says as she hugs the book to her chest before stretching to set it down at the edge of the blanket. When she turns back toward me, she catches me staring at her again.

I open my mouth to tell her this is over, but no words come out. The way she watches my face, I can sense that she knows how much I'm hurting.

"What's wrong?"

I swallow. "Nothing." I feel jittery, like my muscles are spasming and I have as little control over them as I have over my emotions. I fucking hate this feeling. Is this what it feels like to love someone? Reckless and powerless and foolish?

She scoots toward me until we're only a foot apart. "Sasha, you're my best friend and I need you to stop lying to me."

What can I say? That wanting her is a sickness my body can't fight off? That as inappropriate as it is for me to lust after the younger sister of my dead best friend, I can't seem to stop myself? That until this summer I never dreamed she'd feel the same way, but that I know things are shifting and that even though this *could* be our chance, it can't be?

"What's wrong?" she asks again, leaning in close enough that my body can feel her even though we're not touching.

I breathe deeply through my nose, demanding control of myself. I will not think with my dick, there is too much on the line here. For her future, and for mine.

"Petra," I choke out, wondering if this is the last time I'll be able to call her by her name, "nothing can happen between us."

She blinks in surprise and her lips part slightly. I can't take my eyes off them. I could just lean forward the tiniest bit and finally know what it's like to taste her. *But I can't.*

"Why are you doing this, Sasha?" she asks. I wonder if the way her voice cracks is her holding herself together.

"You're a child, Petra." The condescending tone surprises me, even though the words are coming out of my own mouth. "I don't see you like that." Every fiber of my being stretches toward her even as my words push her away. But I think that sounded believable enough?

"Bullshit," she spits out the word as she studies my face.

I could love this girl. Maybe I already do. A part of me wants to tell her the truth and see if we can find a way to work this out. But I think the truth would break her. I'd rather her think I'm the one who's broken her than to know her father betrayed her this way, to know that my father is responsible for her mother's death. So I'll do the last thing in the world I want to do.

I do everything in my power to get the next words out without breaking down. "I don't feel that way about you, and if you don't realize that, you're a fool."

"Why are you saying these things?" she whispers, trying to hold back the tears that are gathering in her eyes.

What would my father say in this situation? Somehow, I know that channeling him will allow me to be as cold and indifferent as I need to be right now.

"Because you need to hear them. You're playing a dangerous game, flirting with every man around you." I think about how she shamelessly flirted with the gardener, Felix, when I first arrived home. Was she trying to make me jealous? "You're sixteen, but you look a lot older, and you're going to get yourself into trouble one of these days."

"You sound like all the jealous, catty girls at school. Is that what you are, Aleksandr? Jealous and catty?" When I don't respond, she says, "I can't help what I look like."

"You need to be careful," I tell her, because it's true. I've seen what men do to women who are too beautiful and too trusting.

"Oh." Her single word is an icicle dangling between us. "You're one of *those*."

"One of what?"

"One of those people who thinks that instead of teaching boys to respect girls, we need to teach girls to be careful not to attract too much attention from boys."

Time to end this. "No, I'm just someone who used to be your friend, but I don't think we should be friends anymore."

She bends forward at the waist, one hand on her heart. "What?" The word escapes through clenched teeth.

"You heard me." My face is expressionless. "This is goodbye."

"Sasha. No. I can't lose you too." The words are a whispered plea floating off her lips. I already know this conversation will haunt me for years, maybe forever. But for her sake, her plea must fall on deaf ears.

"You have no choice," I say, keeping any evidence of emotion out of my voice.

I turn and descend the ladder as quickly as I can. I need to be away from her or I'm likely to pull her into my arms, tell her I love her, and suggest we run away together. The trust fund from my mother would allow us to live a comfortable life, but I know that idea is madness. We are too young. And more importantly, she has dreams she wants to pursue, and so do I. Goodbye is the only way we can both get what we want.

Chapter Ten

PETRA

By the time I hit the lobby, I'm so angry I want to punch something. Damn Aleksandr. I'd hoped that in the last fourteen years he'd have learned how to grow a fucking spine.

Normally, I'd either head to the boxing gym that's around the corner from my apartment, or I'd head out to meet a guy. Fight or fuck—I don't get angry often, but those are the only two ways I know how to deal with my anger when things get to that point.

Martin holds the door open for me and warm spring air blows into the lobby. "It's a beautiful night, Ms. Volkova. I hope you enjoy it."

"Oh, I plan to," I give him a wink as I sail through the doors and into a beautiful Thursday evening. It's dark already, but the air smells like spring . . . a combination of the rain earlier this afternoon and the sweet fragrance of the blossoms on the trees overhead. I head south on Fifth Avenue and fish my phone out of my bag. I bring up my contacts and search for the newest entry—Sam Renaud. The man is perfect for me: stupidly attractive, and available for a night. No risk of commitment. Just how I like them.

And then the realization hits me so hard and fast that I stop in the middle of the sidewalk.

Shit. I'm married.

I stand there, frozen. I look up at the sky, but instead of the wide swath of brightly burning stars scattered across the Milky Way that I'm used to seeing in Park City, all I can see is the light pollution from the city that never sleeps reflected back toward me.

Call him anyway, I tell myself as I stare up at the sky, searching for even a single star visible through the haze. *Sam will be fun, just the release you need. Aleksandr doesn't deserve your chastity. Besides, he'll never know.*

But the reality is, until I've decided whether I'm going to help him get citizenship, I probably shouldn't risk something like this. How could our marriage story ever be believable if it came to light that I slept with someone in New York while I was here this week? Hopefully I didn't give my name to the guy I slept with my first night here. Then I think of the countless other men I've had sex with over the past fourteen years. I haven't even attempted to keep track or keep count. Sex is a biological need, nothing more. No reason to catch feelings or make it into more than it is.

My feet pound the pavement and I'm five blocks further south toward my hotel before I've definitely convinced myself that I shouldn't call Sam. Instead, I call the one person in my world who I trust for advice.

"Hey," Jackson says when she answers her phone. "Please tell me you are coming home early so I can see you even sooner?"

"I wish," I say. *Do I tell her about Aleksandr and Stella?* No, not yet. "I just have to finish up the planning I'm doing in New York and I'll fly home Saturday morning. Maybe we can grab dinner that night and catch up?"

"We're just settling in tonight, and we're meeting up with Lauren and Josh tomorrow night, so dinner Saturday would be great. And I can't wait to ski with you on Sunday!" It's not a squeal because that's not Jackson's style—she's one of the most composed, competitive, and caring people I know—but there's true excitement in her voice.

"Same. Seriously, I have no one to ski with in Park City since you moved away." With Jackson and I having both been professional skiers, it's hard to find anyone else who skis at our level. And even though she traveled for most of the winter when she was working for the National Ski Team, we got to ski together any time she was home.

"You need to find new friends who are as passionate about skiing as you are."

"Easier said than done." Most of the time when I meet people on the mountain who are truly exceptional skiers, they are pros who are just passing through as they travel to different mountains every week or so. I've met a lot of great people that way, but there's no one I can call up to ski with except for Lauren's husband Josh, who was also on the National Ski Team at one point.

"Hey," she says, clearly shifting the conversation. "What's this big news you said you had?"

For a split second I panic, thinking she's talking about Aleksandr. Then I remember that I was going to tell her about the show.

"This is still top secret," I tell her as I amble down the sidewalk, in no hurry to get back to my hotel room alone.

"Oh, my favorite kind of secret." She laughs.

"No, seriously. I signed all kinds of paperwork and I'm only allowed to tell immediate family. Which basically means you're the only one who can know." Jackson is pretty much a sister to me and she's also a vault. On the rare occasion I've ever said anything about my past, she's held those secrets close, not even sharing them with our other best friends, Sierra and Lauren. Or, as far as I know, with her husband Nate.

"I'm honored," she says, a tiny hint of teasing in her voice.

"About a year ago, I planned a wedding for the daughter of this really famous television producer. Seriously, this woman is a total badass." I tell her a bit about the shows she's produced and even Jackson, who isn't easily impressed, is impressed. "I worked pretty closely with her through the planning process, and right before the wedding, she said she was going to keep me in mind for the right TV opportunity. I assured her I had no interest in television work."

"Too much objectification?" Jackson asks.

"Yeah, pretty much anywhere a camera is involved." I roll my eyes even though she can't see me. She knows exactly how I feel about the way the media treats women. "Anyway, she was persistent. She's contacted me with opportunities a couple times and each time I've emphatically said 'no.' And then a couple months ago she called me with something totally different. A talk show about the female experience in America. The chance to interview women with extraordinary stories from all walks of life. And something about that really spoke to me."

"I'll bet. That's right up your alley," Jackson agrees. "So did you audition?"

"Yes, I flew to LA a couple months ago for the audition, and then I didn't hear anything for a while, so mentally I moved on. Then a couple weeks ago she called and offered me the job. I really had to think about it. When I left New York, I swore I was never stepping in front of a camera again. But this . . . this feels worth it."

"Wow. So what's this entail? Do you have to move to LA?"

"Yes, for the next few months. We'll film the entire first season in about six weeks, and then I need to stay in LA for the publicity and promotion. I've been assured that after that, I should be able to just fly back and forth for filming. I'm going to tell my events team about it next week, and we'll figure out a plan for running my business while I'm in LA."

"This is a lot to process," Jackson says. "You've been so private since you stopped modeling. But good, you're finally back to being yourself. This is such a great opportunity, I'm really happy for you."

"I went back and forth about it for a while, but can you imagine? I get to talk to all kinds of women about the exceptional lives they've lived, the things they've overcome to get where they are. And I get to promote them and their successes. That's the dream, right there. I'm not relishing the idea of being in the spotlight again, but if it helps me empower and maybe inspire other women, I'll do it. In fact, the more I think about it, the more excited I am!"

"I can't wait to hear more about this when I see you on Saturday," Jackson says. She sounds distracted, and as I hear Nate's voice in the background, I know why. Even though they've been back together for over a year and married for a few months, it still feels like they're playing catch-up for all the years they lost between their epic breakup and their reunion.

"Okay, I'll let you go," I say. "Looking forward to seeing you soon."

"Me too. Love you," she says.

"You too," I say. I hang up as I'm approaching the doors of my hotel. But instead of turning and going in, I keep walking toward Midtown. I'm too keyed up to go up to my room and relax, so I figure I'll just walk until some of this anxious energy dissipates. And maybe the fresh air and the time to think will help me figure out what to do about Aleksandr and Stella.

———

Riding the elevator the sixteen floors to Aleksandr's apartment is starting to feel normal, which is surreal considering that five days ago I didn't know he was in New York or that he had a six-year-old niece who I'm actually going to miss. But I have to get back to my life, I can't stay here forever.

When the doors open, he's waiting for me in the living room, sitting there casually on one of the couches with one foot resting on the opposite knee and a *Sports Illustrated* in his hands. His eyes lock on mine and he studies my face like he's trying to figure out how I'm feeling about things after last night's conversation. Or was it a fight? His face is as impassive as mine, each of us refusing to let the other know how we're feeling right now.

"Thanks for stopping by," he says. There's no tone to decipher in his voice. It's neither a heartfelt statement nor a sarcastic one, but rather the type of bland comment I'd make at the beginning of a meeting with a new client.

"I wanted to say goodbye to Stella," I reply. Even though he already knows this from my texts earlier today, I feel the need to remind him that I'm here for her, not for him. "And I brought some pictures of the possible party locations I visited today."

I don't like fighting with Aleksandr. I never have. When I was a teenager, I relished arguing with him because it was the only way I could see the cracks in his calm exterior, but it was always lighthearted teasing, seeing if I could get him worked up. That's not what this is—on my part, this is actual anger about how he didn't step in and protect Stella from her uncle.

"She's in her—" He starts, but then there's a flash of purple barreling toward me.

Stella's whole body hits my legs as she wraps her arms around me, and I have to reach out and steady myself on the wall so I don't fall over from the impact. "Hey," I say, smoothing my hand over her curls. "Did you have a good day at school today?"

She nods, her cheek sliding against my pants. "Guess what?" she says, looking up at me. "When Jason was being mean to me today, I told him what you said to say. He didn't even know what to say back. He went and sat with other people, so at least I wasn't by him for circle time."

I have no idea what circle time is. "I'm glad it worked."

"I think he's lonely. He's mean to everyone, so no one wants to be friends with him."

"It's always good to be kind to people, especially if they

don't have a lot of friends," I tell her. "But at the same time, you shouldn't put up with him treating you like that. He has to learn that people will be more likely to want to be friends with him if he's a good friend too."

I glance over at Aleksandr, who is watching us closely. His face is still a mask, and as always, I wish I knew what he was thinking. He's only let down his guard around me twice this week, that first night I came over when he told me about wanting to adopt Stella, and last night in his kitchen. My stomach flips over at the memory of his body that close to mine and the way his eyes swam with desire right in front of my face. That moment was the basis for all my fantasies last night, and I hate myself a bit for getting off to visions of him fucking me in his kitchen. I shouldn't be thinking about him like that, both because I'm still mad at him and because he's Sasha. It's a hard and fast rule that I don't sleep with friends or clients, and right now, he's both. Or at least, maybe we're working back toward friendship.

"What's that?" he asks, nodding to the cellophane wrapped plant that I'm holding above Stella's head.

"This," I say, "is a little goodbye gift for Stella." Stella springs back enough to look up, and I hold the plant down at her level. "It's an orchid, like the ones we saw at the Botanical Gardens," I tell her.

Her eyes light up and her smile practically splits her face in half. "I'm going to take such good care of it," she tells me.

"Should we go put it on the windowsill in your bedroom?" I ask her and then look to Aleksandr for confirmation. He nods, and she starts pulling me toward her bedroom.

We've unwrapped the plant and set it on the windowsill

125

and I've explained to her how to care for an orchid when we hear a conversation in Russian coming from the entryway.

"Who's that?" I ask her. I can't make out the words at this distance, but the dialect is clear, as is the firm voice of the female Aleksandr is speaking to.

"Probably my new nanny. She's stopping by tonight so I can get to know her."

"You must be excited," I say with a smile.

"Not really. She's old, and I don't think she'll be as nice as Natasha."

"Natasha was your last nanny?"

"Yeah. She was the best. She always made sure everything we did was fun."

I wonder if she was like a big sister to Stella? I always wanted a big sister growing up, but instead I had Viktor, who ignored me in favor of playing with Aleksandr and Nikolai.

"It must have been hard when she left." There's a question wrapped up in that statement.

"I miss her so much," Stella says, "but now you're here, which is even better."

Did Aleksandr not tell her I'm leaving?

"Stella, you know that I'm leaving tomorrow morning, right? I have to go home."

"But you'll be back, won't you?" she asks. "To help *Dyadya* adopt me?"

I freeze, not sure what to say. "I'll definitely be back in a few weeks, but I don't know how long I'll be staying. I have to be in California in a month for something really important for work."

Stella's eyes fill with tears. "So you're not coming back for good?"

"Honey," I say as I kneel down in front of her. "I'm going to find a way to help you both, but I don't think that will involve me staying here in New York."

"But you have to!" she says, and those tears spill down her cheeks. "You have to. Everyone I love leaves me."

My heart breaks for her. I know how alone she feels, even though I was older than she is when my mom and brother died. But at the same time, she can't *love* me. She hasn't even known me for a week.

"I promise I'll visit, okay?" I say, but even as the words leave my mouth, I wonder how I'll find time for that in my schedule. Though a lot of my events are in the Park City area, my reputation as an event planner means people hire me for events in other locations too. I travel a fair amount for work, mostly on the West Coast. And besides, I'll be kind of tied to LA for at least the next six months.

She sobs in my arms as I struggle to figure out how we've come to mean so much to each other in such a short period. I really am going to miss her.

"And what do we have here?" The question, in Russian, comes from behind me.

"This is Petra," Aleksandr says. "She's a friend of the family."

"And why does she have your niece in such a state?" the woman asks, criticism dripping from every word. I hate her already, and I haven't even turned around to see her.

"Stella's just having a hard time saying goodbye," I tell her, in English, so Stella can understand what we're talking about. It seems rude to talk about her in another language in front of her.

"I don't want you to leave," Stella wails, doing nothing to try to calm herself down.

"This is ridiculous," the woman says, and I cast a glance over my shoulder at her. Stella's wrong about her being old. She's probably in her early forties, but she's got a severe look about her. I can tell she's a strict, no-nonsense kind of person, which is fine as long as she's caring too. "I have been a nanny for twenty years and have never seen a child so coddled."

"She's lost both her parents and a nanny she loved in the past few months," I say in Russian, because Stella doesn't need the reminder. "Have some compassion."

"I do not indulge whiny children," she says back to me, and now I'm glad Stella can't understand what we're saying. Her tears have slowed down as she watches this conversation volley back and forth, undoubtedly trying to figure out what's happening.

My back straightens, but I don't let go of Stella.

"She is not a whiny child," Aleksandr says, in Russian. "She's grieving. There's a difference."

"She needs to learn to deal with her emotions without tears. A child such as this . . . " She sweeps her hand toward Stella as she turns toward Aleksandr. "I cannot work with her if you are going to spoil her so."

I rise from the floor with Stella still wrapped around me like a koala on her mother. I stand there facing them, wondering where Aleksandr's backbone is. Before I leave, I'll make sure this woman treats Stella right.

"There is a difference between loving and spoiling. Loving means giving someone what they need in order to feel safe and cared for. Spoiling is giving someone what they don't need, just because they want it. You should learn the difference if you are going to work with children."

Her beady eyes go wide as the heat creeps into her cheeks. "I am the most sought after nanny on the Upper East Side for a reason," she tells me. "My charges become strong, independent people. And I will *not* be talked to like this." She looks over at Aleksandr as if she's waiting for him to say something.

"Maybe we should give Stella some time to get to know her new nanny, Petra," he says in English.

The nanny's eyes meet mine and her look is triumphant, which is fine because this gives me a few minutes to talk to Aleksandr about all the reasons why he can't leave Stella in this woman's care. There must be a hundred other people who'd do the job better than her.

"I'm going to go chat with your uncle," I tell Stella. "But I'll come say goodbye before I go."

She squeezes her arms so tightly around my shoulders I'm worried she won't let go. But she does, and as I set her back on the floor, I realize that at six she's braver than I was at thirteen. No one this young should have to shoulder so much loss.

We leave them in Stella's room, but instead of heading to the living room, Aleksandr walks through the dining room, through the butler's pantry, and into the kitchen. Which puts two doors between us and the rest of the apartment—like he knows he's about to get an earful from me, and he doesn't want Stella to hear.

He walks to the far end of the kitchen, to the small table that sits beneath two large windows, each with a million dollar view. I wonder if I counted all the windows in the apartment, would the total number equal how many millions of dollars he paid for this place? Probably.

I stop at the end of the cabinets and lean my hip against the countertop, keeping the kitchen table between us.

"You can't come in here and make things more difficult for Stella," he says. Gone is the easy camaraderie we had in here yesterday evening before Stella saw the spider. Gone is the palpable sense of attraction too.

"*I* made things more difficult for Stella?"

"Yes. Don't aggravate her nanny, Petra. You have no idea what it took to get that woman to come work for me. She wasn't exaggerating when she said she's the most sought after nanny on the Upper East Side."

"Stella doesn't need someone harsh right now, Aleksandr." His name is a bullet fired from my lips. "Do you not understand what she's gone through? How much she's lost in the last several months? How do you think giving her a militant nanny is going to be what's best for her?"

"I'm doing the best I can," he says, and runs both of his hands through his hair, pushing it off his face.

"Well, you have to do better," I tell him. There's no nice way to say that, it just has to be said.

"That's easy for you to say, isn't it? Just waltz in here and make her care about you, then waltz right back to your life in Park City. You don't have to make the hard decisions. No, when things get hard, you just leave. You're not the one here day in and day out with her. I am. I've hired Irina based on her references. She's a well-respected nanny, and she'll be good for Stella."

"How can you possibly say she'll be good for Stella?" I ask, my voice rising.

I don't get upset like this. I don't know what's wrong with me. I just want to protect Stella, and I can't figure out why he's not on the same page.

"Stella needs someone who's constant. Someone who will be here every single day, taking her to school, picking her up, taking her to her after-school activities. I travel a lot for hockey. I can't be here all the time. Stella needs someone who can."

"You've literally described the role of *any* nanny. Are you telling me that out of the probably tens of thousands of nannies who work in this city, you couldn't find *anyone* more caring and compassionate than that dictator?"

"It's going to be fine," he says, and his dismissiveness only riles me up more.

"You cannot possibly know that. Put yourself in Stella's shoes. She just told me that everyone she loves leaves her." I watch that sink in, and Aleksandr's long blink is the only indication that it's affected him. "Now you're going to go play your games and leave her with someone who not only doesn't care about her, but doesn't even seem capable of caring for anyone?"

"You're overreacting," he says, and he knows how to push all my buttons in the same way I know how to push his.

I drop my voice low. "Do not tell me I'm overreacting. These aren't the hysterics of someone making something out of nothing. I've been in Stella's shoes. After my mom and Viktor died, my dad was distant and consumed by his own grief. If it hadn't been for you, I would have been all alone. Please, Sasha. Don't be my dad in this situation. *Be your teenage self.* Be there for her, or make sure that when you can't, you have someone here who's going to care about her emotional well-being like she deserves."

"I leave for my first playoff game on Tuesday. There isn't time to find someone else," he tells me.

"So this is about you, then. Not Stella."

He puts both his hands on the back of the chair in front of him, and the only sign that he's as pissed at me as I am at him is the fact that he's squeezing the wood so hard his knuckles are white. "No, this is about needing to have someone living here with her when I can't be here. Natasha didn't give me much notice, and I got lucky finding someone so qualified in such a short time frame. She may not be all touchy-feely," he says, "but she's who we've got for the next year."

"I'm beyond disappointed in you," I say as I cross my arms under my chest. "This is not how you treat people you love."

"How would you even know?" A dark laugh tumbles through his lips.

I narrow my eyes at him. "What?"

"You never let people get close enough to love you," he says, but he's wrong. I don't let people get close enough to hurt me. There's a difference. "In your entire adult life, who have you ever loved?"

I loved you, I almost say, but I hold my tongue because in the end he walked away too.

"Exactly," he says when I don't respond. "I'm doing the work of loving Stella and raising her, even though I don't claim to be qualified for either. So save your criticism for someone who wants to hear it." His words are a dismissal and I know when to cut my losses.

"I'm going to go say goodbye to Stella," I say as I turn and rush out of the kitchen before he can level any more parting blows at me.

I walk through the entryway and down the hall quietly, feeling like an intruder. I thought I had Stella's best interests at heart, and I thought I could convince him to find someone else. Maybe I was wrong on both counts, which is just another reason why I don't belong here. It's good that I'm heading home, where I can think about this situation and try to find a way to help him adopt Stella without having to be around him.

I approach the door to Stella's room, and pause, listening to the nanny's words. "No, you can't go see your uncle. He doesn't want to be around you when you're crying like a baby. Get yourself together, and then you can see him."

"He does want to see me," Stella says, her voice heaving through sobs. I can't tell if she's trying to convince the nanny or herself.

"No one wants to be around a crying child," Irina says. "You will learn to control your emotions or you will spend every moment in your bedroom alone."

"No," Stella wails. She sounds so scared that my heart literally hurts.

"How dare you," I say as I step through the door to find Stella curled up into a ball on her bed, Irina standing above her. Everything about Irina's body language is threatening. "You've been here for ten minutes and you're already intimidating and threatening her? *This* is how you care for the children in your charge?"

She looks at me like I'm an annoying child. "I will not

have my methods questioned," she says. "Especially not by some outsider."

I feel rather than hear or see Aleksandr behind me.

"She's six years old," Aleksandr reminds Irina.

"I know exactly how old she is. Too old to be treated like a baby." Irina stands there ramrod straight, as if daring either of us to argue with her.

"You are threatening her with solitary confinement," Aleksandr says. "That will never be okay with me."

Finally, the man I know he can be shows up.

"I've had forty-eight different families reach out about becoming their nanny in the two weeks since I signed a contract with you," Irina says to Aleksandr.

"Maybe you can call one of them back," he says, his voice lower and colder than before, "since this is clearly not going to work."

She walks past me and practically elbows her way past Aleksandr where he stands in the doorway. He turns to follow her into the hall and I hear his low words, in Russian, as he tells her he's calling the placement agency to tell them about her threats.

I rush across the room to Stella, where I scoop her up into my arms. "Okay, *Zaichik*," I say, the nickname from my childhood slipping out from nowhere. "Let's get you cleaned up."

We head toward the bathroom and get her face washed off. Her eyes are so red and swollen she can hardly open them, but she looks at me so earnestly after drying her face and says, "Thank you, Petra. I was so scared I'd be trapped with her."

"No way," I tell her. "Your *Dyadya* loves you too much to ever let someone like her crush your spirit."

I don't know the first thing about raising a kid, but I know I could do a better job than that dictator Aleksandr tried to hire. All Stella needs is a little love, someone in her corner who's got her back no matter what. That doesn't seem like so much to ask.

I turn to head back into Stella's bedroom and almost jump out of my skin when I see Aleksandr standing there.

"I'm leaving for my first playoff game on Tuesday, and I have no one to stay with Stella." I can tell by his voice that he thinks this is my fault, even though he's the one who fired her. "Now what?"

"I don't know," I tell him, and I can feel myself frowning. He is stuck between a rock and a hard place, and even though I would do it all again, it does feel like I'm the one who put him in this position.

He lowers his voice and switches to Russian. "The guardianship agreement is clear that I'll have one person to stay with Stella when I have to travel for work. The consistency is key for a child in her situation. I can't just not show up to work. I have a contract. And I'm at the end of it, so if I don't play in the playoffs, I can kiss my career goodbye."

"I . . ." I stutter. I guess I didn't really think about the position I was putting him in, I only thought about what was best for Stella and I knew that witch Irina was not it. Even I would have been better than Irina. But I have a job, and a life, that I need to get back to.

Two thoughts war with each other in my head: *Someone needs to be here to protect Stella, to help her become strong and resilient.* And *I don't even like children.*

I do the mental math—what I gain and what I have to give up. The give up column is far longer, including seeing my best friend who I haven't seen in a couple months, the last day of ski season, catching up with my team at work, and being there in person for two upcoming events. What do I gain? Personally, nothing. But Stella will be safe and well cared for, and somehow that matters more than everything I lose out on.

"I could probably help you out for a week or two, just until you figure out a new childcare arrangement."

Chapter Eleven

ALEKSANDR

"You were looking a little slow out there today, old man," Owen Ramirez says as he jumps up from the locker room bench like the nimble little fucker he is.

"Go to hell, Ramirez."

"Dude, you're the captain. You gotta build me up, not tear me down."

"Your ego needs a readjustment," I say as I turn to walk out of the locker room. He follows me into the hallway. "You're never going to get more playing time if you're not more serious."

"I was a second-round draft pick," he says, his chest puffing out like a rooster who's damned pleased with himself.

"And how much have you played this year?"

He falls into step next to me as he considers the question we both know the answer to. His voice is substantially lower when he says, "Coach doesn't like me."

"No one likes a player with an ego they can't back up. You want to play, you'd better bring it. Stop relying on your college career as evidence of your ability. That got you here, but it sure as shit won't keep you in the NHL."

"So what do I do?"

Ah, the real reason we're having this conversation. In my "old age" I've become the team psychologist, the one the younger guys come to with all their problems. Either that, or it's because of the big "C" I wear on my jersey.

"Same thing I told you on day one. Start by taking a lesson in humility." We walk a few more steps and he doesn't say anything, so I remind him, "Who you were before you got here, what you did, it doesn't matter. It only matters how hard you work now. So work harder."

"Not everyone can be as focused as you are one hundred percent of the time," Ramirez says as we push open the doors to the parking lot.

"Yes, they can. It's a choice. Notice how I go home after games, not out chasing skirts?"

"But, dude, the girls," he says the word on a long exhale. "When else in my life am I going to have chicks all over me, chasing me down like this? I gotta take advantage of that while I can!"

"Do you, though?" I ask. "Is that where you want to focus your energy right now? Or do you want to improve your game?"

"Oh, I'm improving my game," he says with a low laugh.

"Wrong game," I tell him. He doesn't get it, and that's fine. I've seen a dozen guys like him come and go in my near-decade in the NHL. Everyone here is used to being the best —until they go pro. It's a fight to stay, to improve, and to play. Not everyone is willing to make the requisite sacrifices.

"You sayin' you're celibate, man?"

"No. I'm just saying that sometimes it's good to save up some of that energy you spend on women and redirect it into your game. Think how much pissed-off frustration you'd be able to channel into your defense if you hadn't been laid in a few days."

"Hmm," he says, like he'd never considered the idea before. Has he seriously never had a coach or mentor tell him this before? Could he not have figured this out on his own?

Daniel is parked in my space. "Just think about it," I tell Ramirez as I head toward my car, "because I think you're better than what you've shown us this year."

He nods, but looks too lost in his thoughts to reply. I throw my gym bag into the trunk and slide into the back seat. "Did you get Petra's stuff to my apartment earlier?" I ask as Daniel backs out of the spot.

"Sure did. Just a couple small suitcases."

"Okay." I glance out the window, wondering what it will be like to come home today and in the future and have Petra in my space. Will she be a distraction? Probably. But having her there may also fuel the kind of frustration I was telling Ramirez he needed. In fact, half the reason I had such stellar seasons in my junior and senior years of high school was because I was pissed off the entire time, missing my best friend and wanting his little sister, but knowing I could never have her.

As usual, Daniel and I don't speak much on the way home. One of the things I like best about him as a driver is that he isn't chatty. When I lived closer to the rink, I used to drive myself. I had a sweet sports car that I probably took too many risks in. But once an apartment became available in the building Niko and Colette lived in, I moved to the Upper

East Side to be closer to my family. The drive to practice was horrendous, though, which is when Niko suggested getting a driver so I could just relax on my commute. I traded my sports car in for a more comfortable model and used the commutes to take calls from my agent or the brands I had endorsement deals with, or listen to podcasts and audiobooks. It ended up being a good move since only a few months later I was suddenly the guardian for my six-year-old niece.

"Just a reminder," Daniel says as we turn onto Fifth Avenue, "that I won't be available tonight. It's my daughter's birthday."

"No problem. Enjoy the party," I tell him.

"Thank you, sir." I'm not sure that I'll ever get used to how formal Daniel is with me. I hate him calling me 'sir' or 'Mr. Ivanov,' but he continues to do it no matter how many times I tell him he can just call me 'Alex' like everyone else does.

He drops me at the front of the building and I'm out the door before the doorman can come open it for me. I grab my gym bag from the trunk as Martin holds the door to the building open for me. "Mr. Ivanov," he says as I enter. "Ms. Volkova is all settled in your apartment. Is there anything else you need?"

My stomach flips over. It's a feeling I'm unaccustomed to. "No, thank you," I tell him as I head toward the elevator. *What do I say to someone I spent my teenage years obsessing over now that she's living in my home?* Even after I left her the way I did, I continued to follow her every move. I watched every televised ski race she competed in; I may or may not have salivated over every photo and video of her during her modeling days; I fantasized about running into her when she lived in New York, even while I took every precaution to make sure it didn't happen. Once she moved to Park City and wasn't in the spotlight so much, it became easier to let her go. But she's always been there, taking up residence in my brain.

She's the one that got away, except I was the one who pushed her away the minute she tried to get close. I didn't have a choice, or at least, I didn't think I did. The irony—that I pushed her away to prevent a marriage she didn't want, but we ended up married anyway—isn't lost on me. My fucking father left the marriage certificate on the very top of the box labeled "Important Papers," like he was getting in one last jab at me even from the grave.

The elevator doors open to a silent apartment. I don't know what I expected, but there's nothing to indicate that another human being is here. No music, no signs of movement. It's disconcerting. I am setting my wallet and keys in the marble dish on the entryway table when the door between the dining room and butler's pantry swings open. Petra glides through it with a plate in her hand, then gasps and almost drops it. "Holy shit," she pants, "you scared the crap out of me."

"Sorry. Should I announce myself when I come home or something?" I'm only half kidding.

She rolls her eyes. "I just didn't realize you'd be home this early."

"Practice normally ends a bit later, but we're leaving in the morning, so we got out earlier today."

"Can we go over this week's schedule one more time before you leave?" she asks. I'd taken her with me to drop Stella off at school this morning so she'd know what to do for the rest of the week, and I'd made sure we updated the emergency contact paperwork while we were there. I'll bring her with me to ballet this afternoon too, so she knows what to do later in the week.

"Sure. How about while Stella's at ballet? The class is too short to make sense to come home during it, we can grab coffee or something nearby."

"Okay." She looks confident, but sounds nervous.

"It's going to be fine," I tell her.

"That's easy for you to say. You're the one leaving. I have zero experience with kids. What if I fuck it up?"

"You're not going to fuck it up. You're a natural with her, which is the only reason I feel comfortable leaving." I don't admit to her how much I prefer this situation over the nanny I'd hired. She'd looked so good on paper and her references had been fantastic. Now I'm back to square one, waiting to hear back from the placement agency. And in the meantime, I've got Petra.

She pauses. "I need to get back to work, but let me know when it's time to leave for ballet. Oh," she says as if she's just thought of something else, "and after dinner tonight I need to run out to the shops for some pajamas."

Confused, I ask, "You can't just wear whatever pajamas you brought?"

"Uhh." She pauses, then stands a little straighter. "Normally I sleep naked."

And now I'm busy telling my dick to calm the hell down and stop picturing her in my guest room, just on the other side of my bedroom wall, naked. I should have put her in the nanny's bedroom on the opposite side of the apartment, the part I never really go into. But I wanted her to feel welcome, and to have access to the solarium that she was so obviously impressed by the other night. The fact that both of our bedrooms have exterior walls of glass and doors that lead right into it is something I have to remind myself not to think about. It would be too easy to step out of my bedroom and right into hers.

"You're welcome to some of my T-shirts and boxers if you want."

She smiles. "Already trying to get me into your underwear, eh?"

"Jesus, Petra," I say because now I'm definitely getting hard. "You can't say shit like that. We're not teenagers anymore."

"Right," she says, and the word is clipped. "You made that clear back then. Don't worry, I haven't forgotten."

I was wondering how long it would take her to bring that up. Every word was a fucking lie, but I can't tell her that.

"I'll let you know when it's time to leave," I say, turning and walking down the hall toward my bedroom before she can see the bulge growing in the front of my jeans.

I shut my bedroom door behind me and lean back against it. *Fuck.* Having her here is already more difficult than I imagined. It's easy between us when Stella is around, but it seems like every time I'm alone with her, there's an undercurrent of sexual tension. I didn't really think through the fact that she'd be here during the day while Stella was in school. And shit, that long maxi dress she was wearing was super low-cut. Why does she have to have such fantastic tits?

I unbutton and unzip my jeans, because it's getting uncomfortable in there, then I let them drop to the ground. I'm halfway across the room, heading toward the bathroom in nothing but my underwear and T-shirt, when I glance through the glass on the opposite side of my bedroom and notice Petra sitting at the table in the solarium with her laptop in front of her and a plate of sliced apples next to her. Her back is to me, thankfully, but as I slip into the bathroom unnoticed, I realize that this whole situation has just gotten real.

I thought I let go of these feelings I had for her years ago, and it's taken less than a week of seeing her intermittently to have them all come rushing back. I'm a grown man now and I could have any woman I want, so why am I fantasizing about the only woman I can't have?

Water droplets from the shower are still clinging to my hair and my chest, and I have a towel wrapped around my waist as I walk back into my bedroom. Petra's standing at the wrought iron table in the solarium, putting her laptop, a notebook, and her phone into a pile and then sliding them into her bag. I manage to get over to the floor-to-ceiling glass doors unnoticed, but the minute I start pulling the curtains closed, her head snaps up and her eyes focus on that towel, then slide slowly up my body. She's checking me out and there's absolutely no shame on her face when she locks eyes with me and raises an eyebrow.

I'm so tempted to accept her challenge, to march out there and show her exactly how it could be between us. I'm about to reach for the door handle when I remember that this isn't about me and Petra. It's about Stella. And sleeping with Petra would only complicate matters. Instead, I slide one of the heavy linen curtains in front of me and reach over to pull the other one closed too.

W e lost our first game, two nights ago, and tonight we're tied 2-2 in the third period. I glance at the clock and see that we have slightly more than five minutes left to win it, or they do.

The next few minutes are intense. No one scores, and there are no penalties. It's like everyone is behaving themselves—especially me—because neither team wants to see the other have a power play.

As I pass the puck to Robinson and skate around one of their forwards, Coach pulls our goalie and sends in another attacker. I don't think Coach would take this risk in the regular season, but in the playoffs he doesn't want to risk a long, sudden-death overtime period. In these last few minutes, our shot of scoring is better with six players and no goaltender. Unfortunately, Philly's chance of scoring is also better with us not having a goaltender.

Robinson passes it back to me, but I don't have a shot on goal and it's a relief to be able to pass it to our extra player, Ulcheck, who's right where I need him to be. He takes the shot but the goaltender blocks it and the puck ends up back with Robinson, who passes it to Ulcheck again. One of Philly's defensemen slaps the puck away and I skate with everything I have to get back toward the goal and help our defensemen block their attackers. With no goalie in the net, we can't afford them to get too close to our goal. Unfortunately, Philly's three forwards are in control of the puck and all advancing on our two defenders. Robinson and Ulcheck are already getting in the mix, so I skate around behind our defenders. I hear the shot even though I don't see it happen, and I dive across the goal as I turn to see if I can figure out where the puck is. It's hard to miss, coming straight at me a little higher than where my body is. I raise my arm, hoping I can block it. The puck connects solidly with my right shoulder, wedging itself between my shoulder and chest pads, then bouncing off. I go skidding across the ice on my left side, but I see Robinson has control of the puck. Coach has already sent in another center and is pulling me, so I skate to our bench.

I'm greeted with cheers and slaps on the back and all manner of celebration, but my eyes are already back on the ice, watching for our opportunity to score. It comes when Philly's players are moving like a machine toward our goal and our left wing grabs the puck and breaks away toward their goal. His shot is sloppy but still, miraculously, gets past their goalie.

Coach puts in a whole new team, including a goalie, and we manage to hang on for the last thirty seconds to win Game 2. It's a win, though I much prefer a wider margin on the scoreboard. This was too close, on the heels of a loss. We have to be better than this if we hope to advance.

I walk into the press conference ten minutes later, my NY hat pulled low over my forehead and a scowl on my face. I hate these pointless media appearances. The press wants face time with us, but there's very little we can say about the game that won't risk giving away some strategy that might help us in future games.

I take my seat in front of my nameplate, hoping they ask Robinson most of the questions. Of course, they don't. The first question is about why I'm scowling after a win.

"I prefer winning by a wider margin."

"You spent a lot of time in the penalty box earlier

tonight," a young reporter says. I've seen him a lot this season, but he's still pretty green. "You were playing like you were mad."

I stare back at him, my face expressionless. "That wasn't a question."

"*Are* you mad about something?" His question suggests that there might be something going on with the team that has me pissed off, as if I'd tell him if there were.

I'm mad that the woman I've spent my entire life obsessing over is living in the bedroom next door to mine and I can't touch her. I'm mad that her comment about trying to get her in my underwear keeps rattling around my head, haunting me while I'm trying not to think about her. I'm mad that Stella likes her so much, even while I'm grateful for their developing relationship, because it doesn't seem like Petra will stick.

"Don't confuse aggression with anger," I tell the reporter. "I'm just out there playing the game the best I know how."

"You're rarely in the penalty box," the reporter chirps, "which is why tonight seemed notable."

I shrug. He's right, I'm known for my self-control and tonight I had a hard time keeping myself in check. "Anyone have an actual question?" I crack a smile so the media will think I'm joking with them. I'm not.

They ask more questions about the game, about what our approach will be as we move into Game 3 in a couple days. Our responses are tight-lipped—"score more goals" and "play better"—and then we're being ushered out so the next players can come in.

Relieved, I head back to the locker room, past the couple of reporters who are milling around in there, and take a shower. When we board the bus back to the hotel, a bunch of the younger guys are making plans to go out and celebrate.

"You coming, old man?" Ramirez asks me.

"Clearly, you took nothing from our conversation," I remark, then look back down at my phone. I just want to get back to the hotel and call home. I want to hear Petra's voice, see how she and Stella are doing. I never called Natasha when I was on the road. I texted with her occasionally to see how things were going, and I generally sent Stella a video each day to tell her I hoped she had a good day and I couldn't wait to see her when I got home. But looking forward to talking to Petra feels different and a little dangerous.

"Ivanov never comes out," our goalie tells him. "Just stop asking already."

"You always been this serious?" Ramirez asks. "Or is this like a thing that happens once you pass thirty?"

"You getting bored warming that bench yet, rookie?" The look I give him has the rest of our teammates cracking up.

"Fair." Ramirez frowns. He played tonight, but not nearly as much as some of us.

"Then focus on the right game," I remind him.

"Tomorrow," he says. "Tomorrow I'll focus on hockey. Tonight, it's all about the ladies. Join us, it'll be fun. You could use a release, you know?"

You have no fucking idea, I think to myself. But the only release I want is from this obsession with Petra that I can't seem to let go of, no matter how hard I try. It makes me feel weak and out of control, two feelings I absolutely loathe.

Chapter Twelve

PETRA

"I'm so sorry," I say to my team on our video call before glancing back down at my phone where it flashes the name and number of Stella's school across the screen, "I have to take this call."

I mute my microphone and my speakers on the laptop before answering. I haven't told them anything, just that I'm staying in New York "with a friend."

"Is this Petra Volkova?" a woman's voice asks when I answer my phone.

Momentary panic grips my digestive system and I feel like I'm going to throw up. "Yes. Is everything okay with Stella?"

"Stella is fine. But the boy she knocked down on purpose is not. We need you to come in and meet with the principal. She's being sent home for the day."

Oh shit. Just the other night, Stella had complained about Jason being mean to her again. He'd started pulling her hair when he was behind her, and flipping her skirt any time she walked by him. I'd told her she needed to defend herself if he put his hands on her, which means this is probably my fault.

"Okay," I say. "I'll be there as soon as I can."

I explain to my team that an emergency has come up and I have to go. I haven't told them about Aleksandr and Stella or why I'm still in New York. The less they know, the better —for now.

But as much as my life has changed over the past few days of Aleksandr being gone, my work days have been fairly normal because Stella has been in school. I didn't anticipate that there might be interruptions like this.

The school is only a few blocks from the apartment, so I'm walking through the doors less than ten minutes later. The secretary ushers me toward the door marked "Principal" and I feel like I'm about to get in trouble.

The man sitting behind the desk has on a pink collared shirt and a patterned bow tie. He's on the phone, but gestures for me to come sit in the chair next to Stella facing his desk. She grabs my hand the minute I sit down, and I give it three little squeezes which has her face lighting up. She gives me three little squeezes back. *I. Love. You.* She just taught me that last night—it was something she used to do with her mother, and I'm hoping that I can handle this situation in a way that would make Colette and Nikolai proud if they were still here.

While the principal finishes his conversation, I mouth *Jason?* at Stella and she nods, then looks down at the ground. "Hey," I whisper, "chin up." In my eyes, she's done nothing wrong here.

But as the seconds tick by, I realize I'm so wildly out of my element, and my panic grows like it's a seed in my stomach sending roots throughout my body. My intestines make such a loud rumbling sound that Stella laughs quietly. The principal hangs up a moment later and turns toward us.

"Ms. Volkova," he starts. "We have a zero tolerance policy for violence at our school. We teach the children to work out their differences with their words, rather than their actions."

Stella's grip on my hand tightens. "And what do you do when words don't stop certain behaviors?" I interrupt.

"When children can't work out their differences on their own, our faculty members are trained to help them," he tells me. He strokes his goatee and then tilts his chin, and I'm afraid he's about to start a long diatribe on the benefits of mediation.

"Did you ever ask for help?" I ask Stella.

"I told my teacher the things Jason was doing, lots of times, but he never does them when she's looking, so he never gets in trouble."

"What happened this time?" I ask. The question isn't addressed to anyone in particular, and Stella jumps in to answer first.

"He tripped me at recess and I fell down and skinned my knee." She points to the bloody scrape above her knee socks. "So when I got up, I pushed him and he fell down."

I look up at the principal. "So she's told her teacher multiple times that this kid is being mean to her, and each time nothing happens because the teacher didn't see him do anything. And then he trips her, and she gets hurt, and *she's* in trouble for defending herself?"

"She's in trouble because we have a zero tolerance policy for physical violence."

"But you don't," I say.

"Yes," he replies, heat creeping into his face behind that ginger goatee, "we do."

"If that were true, then there would have been consequences each time he'd hurt Stella. But there haven't been."

"I can't comment on previous instances that I'm not aware of."

"There have been plenty of other instances of him pulling her hair, poking her between the ribs, flipping up her skirt," I recite the instances Stella has told me about and he looks surprised that I know the specifics. "And when she's told her teacher about it, nothing has happened. Whatever training your teachers have had on how to help your students work out their differences, it's failed in this case. She's asked adults for help in navigating the situation and they haven't helped her. So tell me," I say as I lean back in the chair and fold my hands demurely in my lap. "What was she supposed to do? Continue to take his abuse while her requests for help go unanswered?"

"Are you suggesting that she should be allowed to hurt people?"

"Not at all. In fact, we've talked about many different ways she can handle the situation. She's tried avoidance and redirection, and clearly those have not worked. Neither has asking her teacher to step in. So what other options did this first grader have when he tripped her and hurt her?"

His jaw hangs open for a minute. "I'm sorry, it sounds like you've been working with Stella on this issue for a while. Didn't you just start as her nanny this week?"

Stella and I look at each other and burst out laughing, which clearly makes him uncomfortable.

"She's not my nanny, Dr. Leonard," Stella says as she

bites back a smile, and my shoulders tremble with a cold shiver as I consider how different this meeting and its aftermath would be if that horrible witch Irina were here instead of me. "She's my uncle's best friend."

"Best friend from childhood. Just in town for a couple weeks," I say, as much to set Stella's expectations as to explain this to her principal. "I'm helping out because Miss Stella here is in between nannies and Aleksandr is in Philadelphia for the first two playoff games."

"When he came in the other morning with you and added you to the emergency contact form, replacing Stella's previous nanny, we naturally assumed you were her new nanny."

"Naturally. Now, about that question I asked," I say, keeping my voice friendly while hopefully letting him know he's not getting off the hook that easily. "I really would like to know how *the school* would like Stella to handle these physical attacks in the future. Because obviously allowing her to be abused at school like this isn't an acceptable option for *us*."

He tugs at his bow tie. "I will make sure Stella's teacher is aware of what's going on so she can take swift action if there's another incident."

"Which I'm sure there won't be once you get done talking to the boy in question, right? With his parent too?"

The tiniest bit of spit flies off his tongue when he says, "We will handle it."

"Excellent." I stand and take Stella's hand.

"Where are you going?" he asks.

"I was told Stella is being sent home for the day. I'm taking her out to celebrate being a strong young woman who does *not* let boys push her around."

153

"But . . ." His mouth hangs open just enough that I'm tempted to reach across the desk and push it closed it for him.

"Oh, I'm sorry, did you want the honor of asking us to leave?" My voice is all sweetness but we both know it's an act. "By all means, go ahead if it will make you feel better."

He just shakes his head and flicks his hand to shoo us out of his office.

"When I get older, I want to be brave just like you," Stella tells me as we walk down the hall hand in hand.

"You already are the bravest six-year-old I know," I tell her. It doesn't matter that she's the *only* six-year-old I know. I could know a hundred other kids her age and I think she'd still be the bravest because of everything she's been through. Most people have no idea how much courage it takes just to keep living after losing a parent and she's lost two.

She squeezes my hand three times, and I squeeze back.

"Stella?" We both turn toward the voice behind us, and a woman I've never seen in my life stands in the hall. "What's going on?" she asks.

"Hi, Auntie Sofia," Stella says.

Ah, Colette's best friend. "Oh, hi, I'm Petra," I say as I stick out my hand to shake hers.

She takes my hand in hers and smiles. "Yeah, I figured. I'm so glad Alex connected us via text the other night, or I would have been so freaked out to see Stella walking out of school with a stranger."

"Petra's not a stranger," Stella says in her innocent little voice. "She's *Dyadya's* best friend."

"I think it's more accurate to say we were best friends when we were younger," I tell Sofia.

"Aren't you still best friends?" Stella asks.

"Well, you know how we didn't see each other for years and years? It's hard to stay best friends with someone you never see. But we're old friends, anyway." I shrug. I doubt the distinction matters to Stella, but it will to Sofia, I'm sure.

"Why's Stella leaving early today?" Sofia asks me.

"We just had a little meeting with the principal about an incident that happened at recess . . ."

"I'm being sent home for the day," Stella interrupts. She sounds proud of herself and while I don't condone violence, especially among little kids, I'm really fucking proud of her too. It is hard to learn to stand up for yourself, especially around someone who is bigger and stronger. "Because I pushed Jason down after he tripped me, and he cried like a baby, so I got in trouble."

I glance around the wide, bright hallway. There's no one around except the three of us, but all the classroom doors are wide open.

"That's enough, Stella," I say quietly.

"I'm about to go volunteer in the library. Maybe you could tell me and Harper the story later?" Sofia smiles at Stella. "Could we go for ice cream after ballet this afternoon?" she asks me.

I had been planning to march Stella out of here and straight to grab some ice cream in celebration of her standing up for herself. But when I see the way Stella's face lights up at the suggestion of including her best friend, I suppose we can wait until after ballet. "Sure, that would be great."

"I love watching the two of them together," Sofia says as we wait for ballet to end. I've been here the whole time, but she just got here.

"They are adorable," I agree, as I watch them practice their pliés while holding hands.

"They remind me so much of myself and Colette when we were their age."

"You and Colette knew each other when you were that young?" I knew they were best friends, but had no idea it had been a lifelong thing for them.

"Yeah, we met in kindergarten," she smiles a sad smile.

"I'm glad you had such a great friendship, and I'm really sorry for your loss."

"Thanks. At least we still have Stella, though. She's got Colette's face and reminds me so much of her mom when she younger—strongly opinionated, but scared to voice her thoughts."

I chuckle. "I guess I've seen a different side of her."

"I think maybe you bring out a different side of her," Sofia says affectionately. "Alex says she's really taken by you. He seems to think you're a good role model for her."

They've talked about me? "I hope so. I want her to grow up to be strong and independent, but I also don't have any idea how to teach a kid those lessons." I had to learn them all the hard way.

"Well, Alex seems to think you're doing a great job," she tells me. "When is he coming back?"

"Tomorrow afternoon."

"Ah, okay. I'm trying to convince him to let Stella come over for a sleepover, and I'm hoping for this weekend."

"He won't let her come for a sleepover?"

"He hasn't ever said 'no,' he just tells me that he'll think about it and never says yes."

"Has she never had a sleepover before?" Maybe he's hesitant because it's new. But that seems odd to me since Stella and Harper have been friends since birth. How could they have never had a sleepover?

"The girls used to do them all the time. But after Colette and Niko died, Alex has been really hesitant to let her out of his sight. Which I understand, but at the same time, I think the girls need each other now more than ever before."

"I'm inclined to agree with you. Why don't we plan something for Saturday? I'll make sure it happens."

"Really?" she sounds skeptical. "I don't want to cause any problems between you and Alex. And I don't want him to think that I went behind his back to plan this with you."

"I never had a friendship like Stella and Harper's when I was a kid," I tell her. "What they have is special and we need to nurture it. I'm happy to go to bat with Aleksandr about it." Honestly, I'm even looking forward to it. Maybe it's a holdover from our childhood, but if there's anything I like more than seeing the cracks in that mask of his when we argue, I don't know what it is.

"Are you sure? If he's not ready to let her come over, I don't want to push it," Sofia says.

"What do you think is best for Stella?"

"I think getting back to normal as much as possible."

"And were sleepovers a normal thing before her parents died?" I ask.

"Yeah, honestly, they were. Either Harper would stay at Niko and Colette's, or Stella would stay with us. All the time." She tells me a little more about the routine frequency of their sleepovers.

"Then getting back to that will be a good thing, and Aleksandr will just need to get over himself."

Sofia laughs. "I've honestly never heard anyone talk about him that way. Everyone's so intimidated by him."

I roll my eyes. "I've known him my whole life. He doesn't scare me." At least, not in the way other people might be scared of him. What scares me, instead, is how my body betrays me when he's around. Last week in the kitchen before CeCe and Tony came over, the way he looked at me and the raw desire I saw on his face, is everything my sixteen-year-old self wanted to see from him. And even as badly as he hurt me back then, some part of me still wants to see it. I just can't act on it. Good. Let him desire me and not be able to have me. It'll serve him right to feel how I felt back then.

"He doesn't scare me," Sofia clarifies, "but he still intimidates the hell out of me. I can never tell what he's thinking, and with how little he actually speaks—it's unnerving. But I've also seen him at his absolute lowest, right after his brother died, and I've helped him learn to parent Stella. So I also feel like we have this understanding."

"I'm glad that he and Stella have you," I tell her as class wraps up, "They'll continue to need you . . ."

"After you leave?" she asks. I can't tell by her tone how she intends that statement. Concern? Judgment?

"Yeah," I say as I swallow down the thought of leaving Stella. How has this little girl wound herself around my heart so quickly? I thought I'd hardened myself off against these types of feelings, but I'd always focused on not feeling them toward men.

I know they say that the love you feel toward your child is instant and unconditional. But it never occurred to me that I could care about a child who wasn't even mine so swiftly and so completely. *The important thing is to not let her get attached to you,* I remind myself. *Then you won't hurt her when you leave.*

The girls come running out of class in their black leotards with their pink tights and ballet slippers still on their feet. I help Stella into her post-ballet shoes and get her into her fleece, and then we're fighting the cold gray mist that's settled over the city this afternoon. We slip into the back of the car and I tell Sasha's driver where we're meeting Sofia and Harper for our ice cream dinner.

———

"You did *what?*" Sasha says on the other end of the phone. I can't tell if he's upset or just surprised.

"I took her out to ice cream for dinner to celebrate." I bring my feet up onto the bed and pull the throw blanket at the end over my legs.

"To celebrate the fact that she got sent home from school?"

I get distracted by the view out the glass wall on the opposite side of my room and into the solarium. The moon has finally peeked through the clouds and it's lighting up the plants inside. I could get used to this. *No, you can't,* I remind myself. *You're leaving in a week and a half.*

"Petra, that's not something to celebrate," he admonishes when I don't respond.

"We weren't celebrating the fact that she hurt someone or

that she got sent home from school. We were celebrating her standing up for herself."

"And you think she knows the difference? What makes you think she's not going to feel empowered to deal with every situation with physical violence now?"

"How would you have suggested she deal with this type of bullying if she were a boy?" I ask.

His pause is his answer.

"Well, she's not a boy, is she?" His dry sarcasm is the wrong approach.

"Certainly you're not suggesting you're going to raise her to be a submissive weakling just 'cause she's a girl? Because I can give you a hundred examples of what happens to women who aren't empowered to stand up for themselves and to take control of their own emotions and bodies. And that's not what you want for Stella." It's the only reasonable way to raise a girl in this world.

"No, I don't want her to be a submissive weakling." He sighs and I wonder if, like me, he's curled up in his hotel room. Or maybe he's getting ready to go out with his team. They had a narrow win tonight, maybe he wants to celebrate. "But maybe the kid had it coming." I hear running water, like he's turned on a faucet, and I'm trying to picture what he's doing. Brushing his teeth before going out?

"I hope he keeps his hands off her from now on. If not, he can deal with me."

"Whoa," he says with a sigh, "I draw the line at *you* beating up a kid. No matter what a little shit he is."

"All right," I admit, "me beating up a little kid is *probably* not okay. But it makes my blood boil to think of her having to put up with him, or him laying a hand on her. She doesn't deserve that."

His pause is longer this time. Finally he says, "I'm glad you're there with her. I'm glad she's learning these lessons from you. Sometimes I think maybe I'm shit when it comes to this whole parenting thing, and yet you're such a natural at it."

"I'm sure there's a learning curve, give yourself some credit. You went from being a single guy to having a six-year-old, and she's still pretty great, so you can't be messing it up too much. And I know *nothing* about parenting, so if it seems like I do, then I'm just getting really lucky that what Stella needs right now is within my skillset to deliver."

"I think maybe *you* need to give yourself some credit." The running water turns off.

I burrow deeper into the pillows as I watch the mist that's turned into a steady drizzle slide down the roof and walls of the solarium on the other side of my room. The moon is already obscured again by the clouds.

"What are your plans tonight?" I ask him as I glance at the clock on my bedside table. It's 11:00 p.m. and I'm exhausted from my big afternoon of telling off Stella's principal, taking her to ballet, befriending Sofia, going out for an ice cream dinner, then getting Stella home tonight, fed real food, showered, watching some of the game with her, getting her in bed, and then watching the end of the game. And I still have a good hour or two of work I need to catch up on since I wrapped up early today. No wonder parents are always so tired!

"Sleeping. But first, a *really hot* bath."

"Is a *really hot* bath where multiple puck bunnies show up in your hotel room for a bath with you?" I tease.'

His laugh is more of a snort by the sounds of it. "A really hot bath is one where the water is so scalding I'm having a hard time forcing myself to get in the tub."

Oh shit. So what he's telling me right now is that he's standing there naked while talking to me. And now it's impossible not to picture the scene in my mind. His hard body . . . *no, not going there.*

Seeing him in his towel after his shower on Monday was enough to keep me up half the night fantasizing about that body. I knew he was muscular, but he's even bigger than I thought. His wide shoulders and broad chest are nothing but well-defined muscle, and don't even get me started on that eight-pack he's sporting. I can't stop thinking about how things might have gone if I'd had the nerve to walk over to that glass door and open it. He can act like he doesn't want me, but in the moments when he forgets to put that mask of indifference on, I see the desire pooling in his eyes. But he's still lying to himself, and I'm still not sure why.

Or maybe it's just been too long since I've had sex and that's why I can't stop picturing him without clothes on?

"Why did you make the water so hot?" Why does my voice sound so breathy? I clear my throat to stop that nonsense.

"Our trainer insisted I needed to soak in the hottest water I could stand."

"Why? What's wrong?" Suddenly I'm sitting up straight. It was a tough game tonight, but he didn't appear to get hurt. Spent a shit ton of time in the penalty box, though.

"I'm getting old."

"You're thirty-three." Can he hear my eye roll through the phone? I hope so.

"Which means I've been doing this to my body for twenty-five years. My hip's just been a bit stiff lately. Nothing too bad, but I'm doing some PT to help."

On the other end of the phone, there's a noise that's somewhere between a groan and a sigh, which I imagine means he's lowered himself into the water. *Do not think about his naked body,* I remind myself.

"Did everything else go okay today?" he asks, and it sounds like he's talking through clenched teeth.

"Everything's fine." I don't tell him about the sleepover Sofia and I promised Stella and Harper. We can cover that tomorrow when he's back.

"All right. Thanks again for everything, and for checking in with me while I'm gone. Tell Stella I can't wait to see her when she gets home from school tomorrow."

"I will," I tell him. "Goodnight."

"Night," he says, and the line goes dead.

Chapter Thirteen

ALEKSANDR

I t's early afternoon when the doors to the elevator open into my apartment. I step into the entryway and am met with . . . nothing.

What did you expect, a fucking welcoming party?

When I first bought this place, it was my refuge. My calm oasis in the busy city. I could open the door and walk into silence, leaving the stress of practice, the chaos of the streets below, and the pressure of the game all behind me. When I didn't want to see or talk to anyone, which was most of the time honestly, I could hide out here. But over the past few months, I guess I've gotten used to Stella being here, usually with a nanny, sometimes also with a housecleaner or a private chef.

So today's silence is leaves me feeling, I don't know . . . alone? But not in the good way.

I've finished getting my bags out of the elevator when Petra's text comes in.

PETRA

> Just picked up Stella at school, and we are going to run some errands. We'll be home in a couple hours. What do you want to do for dinner tonight?

For some reason, a couple hours feels like an eternity. I've been away from them for nearly four days. I miss Stella like crazy, and Petra, well, I always want more time with her.

ALEKSANDR

> How about I order something. What sounds good?

PETRA

> I have a voracious appetite, everything sounds good. Let me see what Stella wants.

Why does her comment have me wondering if she has a voracious sexual appetite as well? I bet she does. She strikes me as someone entirely comfortable with her own body, who wouldn't let feelings or relationship status get in the way of satisfying her needs. Which makes her all that much more dangerous to be around. Because it doesn't matter that I've wanted her since I was seventeen. I can never have her, even if it's what she wants. I don't know why she would want that, given that I made it abundantly clear when we were teenagers that I did not see her like that.

And since she's been back, I've continued with that charade, plus I've lied to her, basing our whole arrangement on partial truths. She can't, and shouldn't, trust me. Not to mention she's working for me planning our end of season celebration in addition to being responsible for Stella. Having sex with her would be wrong on *every* level.

I shake my head. How did I even go down that path? There is no indication Petra is even interested in a sexual relationship. Except, the way she was looking at me that day in the kitchen when I took my shirt off, and that moment we shared right before that frigid witch Irina showed up. The way she looked at me when I got out of the shower the other day, and her voice grew even more husky on the phone last night when I told her I was getting into the bath. I'd be lying to myself if I couldn't admit that there was some heat in those moments. But most of the "heat" has come in the moments she's mad at me, which seem to outnumber the moments she looks like she's undressing me with her eyes.

> **PETRA**
>
> Stella says pasta.

> **ALEKSANDR**
>
> Okay, I know an Italian restaurant she likes. Want me to order a few different things and we can just share?

> **PETRA**
>
> Sounds great.

> **ALEKSANDR**
>
> Anything you don't eat?

> **PETRA**
>
> Nope. I'm an equal opportunity consumer of all food. Get dessert too!

A couple hours later, they still aren't home, and I'm heading downstairs to grab the food delivery when Tom calls. It's as if he could sense that I just spent a couple hours trying *not* to think about whether Petra spending more time with Stella is making her any more likely to help me get citizenship so I can adopt my niece.

"Any progress?" he asks.

"Nope."

"You said I needed to let you do this your way," he says, "but the needle has not moved forward enough since you two were in my office."

"You don't push a woman like Petra," I tell him. "She'll decide in her own time."

"Well, let's just hope nothing happens while we're waiting for her to make up her fucking mind." Tom sounds pissed off.

"What's up?" I ask. "You aren't this mad about my situation. What's got you so spun up?"

Tom sighs. "Avery's going away with her girlfriends this weekend."

I try not to let my laughter escape as the elevator doors open. I take the bag from the delivery man who's standing there, nod my thanks as I hand him a cash tip, and step back into the elevator before it closes. "You sound so pathetic right now."

"I know. Trust me, I know."

Tom's been dating his assistant for a few months now, and after a very tumultuous beginning, they're practically inseparable.

"Is this the first time you'll spend a night apart since she moved in?"

"Yep. What are you doing tonight? I probably need to get out of my apartment, want to go grab a drink or something?"

"Can't. I just got home, haven't seen Stella in a few days.

Besides, Petra probably has plans tonight since she's kind of been stuck home while I'm gone."

Tom starts to say something, then pauses. Finally, he says, "Avery wants to see Petra again."

"Why? Do they know each other?" Didn't they only meet for like two seconds when Petra came to Tom's office last week?

"Petra sent her flowers on Friday as a thank you for arranging her hotel, and they've been texting since then. You guys want to come over for dinner one night or something?"

"When's Avery back? Sunday?"

"Yeah."

"I have a game Sunday night, but maybe Monday?" I ask as I walk back into my apartment and bring the food into the kitchen.

"Sure," he says.

"I don't really have a sitter for Stella, so how about you guys come here instead?" I take the containers out of the bag and set them on the counter.

"Fine." The word is clipped, his voice annoyed.

"Man, you sound like a real asshole right now. Go out and have some fun while Avery's away. You used to know how to do that before her, remember?"

"Before her, I used to know how to go out to pick up girls. Can't really do that now," he says. "Or, I don't want to anyway."

I hear the elevator doors open. "Okay, Stella and Petra are home, I gotta go. Go get drunk tonight or something," I suggest. "Don't just sit home pining for Avery."

"Asshole," Tom mumbles as he hangs up the phone.

I hang up the phone and walk into the entryway, and

Stella runs to meet me in the dining room, then wraps her arms around my legs so I'm immobile. I run my huge hand over her hair. "I missed you," I tell her.

"Missed you more," she says.

"Who were you talking to?" Petra asks as she follows Stella into the room.

"Tom."

"Your lawyer?"

I nod and bend down to pick up Stella for a proper hug.

"Why is he pining for Avery? Isn't she his executive assistant?"

Oh, she doesn't know. Of course she doesn't. "They've been living together for a few months."

Her mouth forms a perfect little O. "I had no idea. Maybe *that's* why she loves her job so much?" Petra laughs, and the sound rumbles around in my belly the same way it rumbles around in her throat.

She glances at Stella where she rests her head on my shoulder, the back of her head toward Petra. "Think they have sex at work?" Petra mouths silently.

I raise my eyebrows and nod my head knowingly, and Petra laughs.

"Can we eat dinner?" Stella asks. "Then I need to go pack my bag."

"Pack what bag?" I ask.

"For my sleepover with Harper tomorrow." Stella gives me such a huge grin that I don't know what to say in response. "Thank you for saying yes!" She gives my neck another big squeeze before wiggling out of my arms and moving toward the kitchen.

Petra opens her mouth to say something, but I silence her with, "We'll talk about this later."

She raises an eyebrow like she's looking forward to going toe-to-toe with me over this. I don't know if I love it or hate it that she never backs down from a fight.

Over dinner Stella catches me up on the last few days, including updating me on the situation with Jason, who hasn't so much as said a word to her since she pushed him down at recess. Petra looks absolutely imperious about this, but it's only been a day. We'll see if the truce lasts.

"When do I get to come to one of your games?" Stella asks, out of the blue.

"You want to come to a game?"

"I bet it would be more fun to watch in person than on TV!"

"You watched my games?"

"She watched the first period of each game this week," Petra clarifies. "The second and third periods were too late for her to stay up for."

What is this tightness in my chest?

"You watched the games too?" I ask.

"Of course." I can't decipher the look she gives me. She seems confused at my surprise, but I know for a fact she hadn't watched any of my games before this week.

"I used to watch them all the time with Papa," Stella says, and I marvel at how well-adjusted she sounds when she talks about her parents. Meanwhile, I can hardly think of Niko without evoking all kinds of rough emotions.

"I could probably get tickets to Sunday's game," I say, "if you both want to come." I don't want to assume that just because Stella wants to be there in person, Petra does too.

Stella and Petra look at each other and grin. "Perfect," Petra says. "But see if you can get tickets close to the ice. I don't want to be stuck up in a box away from the action."

That makes me chuckle, because of course she wants to be where the action is. And in a way that's easier for me too, because if she showed up in one of the luxury boxes where most of the other wives and girlfriends will be watching the game, my teammates would be all over me in two seconds. As far as they know, Alex Ivanov lives, breathes, eats, and sleeps hockey—there is no time for anything else.

They don't even know about Stella, so how in the world would I explain Petra?

———

"Explain to me why I just helped my niece pack for a sleepover I already said no to," I say as I walk into the den after putting Stella to bed.

Petra's curled up on one end of the couch with her laptop on her knees, so I take the chair closest to her. I try to ignore the long expanse of smooth skin on her legs. Those sleep shorts she's got on are incredibly short and leave nothing to the imagination.

She turns to face me. "Did you say 'no'? Or did you continuously brush Sofia off when she asked?"

"Either way, I didn't say 'yes.'"

"You do know that Stella and Harper used to have sleep-overs regularly, right?"

"Define regularly."

"Like usually once a month they'd stay with Sofia and her husband, giving Niko and Colette a night off, and once a

171

month they'd stay with your brother, giving Sofia and her husband some alone time. It was a normal part of Stella's life, and it sure seems like you've—" She pauses like she's considering her words. "—unintentionally taken that away from Stella."

It pisses me off that she's right, but also she doesn't know how much I hate letting Stella out of my sight. She's the only family I have left. "You don't know the whole story," I say.

One of her eyebrows rises higher than the other. "You're going to have to give me more than that if you want me to understand your reasoning."

"You don't have to understand," I say, the frustration evident in my voice. "I just need you to do what I say when it comes to Stella."

She sets her laptop on the couch and stands, which has me standing too. It's a face-off without the puck. Arguing with Petra has always been a favorite pastime.

"I'm not here to do your bidding. I'm not your fucking employee," she says, her words slow and deliberate, and so low they sound like sexual seduction instead of the frustration they actually are. "I'm here to do what's best for Stella."

"What I decide is best for Stella, is best for her. I need you to trust me on that."

She inches forward so we're nearly toe-to-toe. "How can I possibly trust you when you're not being honest with me?"

"Because it's *me*," I say, and I know my words sound desperate. I need her to go back to trusting me and all I can do is appeal to the reminder of the friendship we once had. "Because we were best friends once, and because even though you're obviously still mad at me, I think deep down you know that I have your best interests at heart too. Always have."

She barks out a scornful laugh. "Right."

"What the hell does that mean?"

"Exactly what it sounds like. You want me to trust you, because you're *you*? You are the one person in this world who has disappointed me beyond everyone else. My life has been a series of men disappointing me, so for you to have first place in that category speaks volumes." There's color creeping into her cheeks. Petra doesn't blush. I know because I spent my entire childhood trying to get a rise out of her that way before realizing it was impossible. So this blush can only be her anger creeping into her skin.

I know she intended for those words to slice into me, and they do. I don't know what's stopping me from telling her why I left her like I did. I could tell her I did it for *her*, to protect her from an unwanted marriage. I suppose I hold back because in telling her the truth, I might have to admit the depth of my feelings, or the fact that it was me—not my father—who paid for her boarding school. But mostly, I think, because I'd have to explain why my father's ultimatum was to either marry her or never see her again, which means I'd also have to tell her the truth about him and her mother. And I don't think I can do that without permanently ruining things between us.

Now that she's back in my life, I'd rather have this fractured relationship with her than have her never speak to me again. But even more importantly, and the only thing that *should* matter to me right now—I need her to agree to help me adopt Stella. And if she knew the truth, she might not.

"You've got nothing to say about that?" she asks when I've been lost in my own thoughts for too long.

"I know I hurt you, Petra, and I'm sorry," I tell her as I put my hands on her shoulders. "But I need you to know that I've only ever acted to protect you, just like I'm doing now for Stella."

"To protect me? By *leaving* me? What am I missing?" Her eyebrows dip and I want to cup her face in my hands, smooth out her furrowed brows with my thumbs.

I can't say what I really need to say, so instead I tell her, "You were so young. I wasn't what you really wanted."

"What you know about me, and what I wanted back then, could fill a thimble. You don't get to make decisions *for* me, Aleksandr. Not then, not now. But you do get to make decisions for Stella, and I fail to see how keeping her from returning to normal things, like sleepovers at her best friend's place, is what's in her best interest."

She's on her toes, leaning up toward me as she drills her finger into my chest. She's so fucking close it's hard to breathe.

"I just want to keep her as safe as possible. I know she's safe here."

Petra's voice softens when she says, "Part of why you want to adopt Stella is to make sure that Sofia becomes her guardian if anything were to happen to you, right? So there's no one she could possibly be safer with."

She does have a point and if I have to bend somewhere, this is probably the right place.

"Besides"—she shrugs, which has my hands falling from her shoulders—"you trusted her with me after I'd known her for a week. Sofia and Harper are practically family to her."

"Of course I trust you, I've known you my whole life." I soften my stance, no longer feeling like we're ready to go to battle.

"You have a funny way of remembering things." Her lip curves up and her laugh is sardonic. "Until I was thirteen, you wouldn't give me the time of day. When I was sixteen, you disappeared from my life. Don't give me this 'I've known you my whole life' shit when we really only knew each other for three years."

I can feel the muscles in my back tense up. It makes sense that this is how she remembers things.

"You think I didn't know you before then, and haven't followed what you've been up to since?" I'm dangerously close to saying too much, and willing myself to shut the hell up.

She folds her arms across her chest. I wish she wouldn't do that. All it does is push up her cleavage into the scooped neck of her T-shirt so I have a hard time focusing on anything but her chest. I drag my eyes away, looking up at her face, but it's impossible not to focus in on those lips. Wide and full, they mock me because all I want to do is taste them. Fuck, I didn't think through this whole having her move in plan before jumping into it.

Finally she says, "Careful, you're sounding a lot like a stalker." Her voice is teasing, and she steps away from me, the moment of tension broken.

When she sinks back into her seat, I do the same, crossing my ankle over my knee. I'm half relieved that she deescalated this before it turned into something more, and half disappointed to not find out what that "something more" would have been. Fighting with her has always felt like foreplay.

"I have to be honest, I didn't even once envision a scenario where my wife called me a stalker."

"That is so weird," she says, shaking her head.

I know very well what she means, but I can't help teasing her more. "You think I *should* have envisioned a wife who thought I was a stalker?"

She laughs when I wink at her, then shakes her head again. "Can you not call me your wife? It's just . . ."

"I know," I say with exaggerated sympathy, "it takes a while to get over the horror of marrying me, doesn't it?"

"Don't be a dick." She rolls her eyes. "One day you're telling me you never want to see me again, fourteen years pass, and the next time I see you, you're telling me we're married. Sorry if I'm not exactly doing cartwheels at this progression of events."

I skip right over justifying how I left things with us way back when. The longer I can go without having to explain that night, the better. "Have you at least given our situation some thought?" I have to ask—not because Tom called earlier, but because it's been eating away at me. It's the giant anvil hanging over my head at all times, and it's hard to keep pretending that I'm not constantly thinking about it.

"I have," she says, and rests her head on the back cushions of the chair. She's looking up at the ceiling, not at me, which makes it hard to read her. "And I'm trying to figure out a way to help you that doesn't involve us lying about being married, having lived together, all that. There has to be another way for you to adopt Stella."

"Tom's read through the laws pretty closely. New York only allows US citizens to adopt children who are US citizens."

"I know the US naturalization process is really complicated. I'm sure Tom's great, but maybe we should talk to an immigration lawyer instead?"

Even though it's not actually possible and totally cliché, it feels like my heart skips a beat. "We?"

"Well," she hedges, "yeah. We."

I nod and hold in the smile that's trying desperately to claw its way out of me.

"Okay. I'll ask Tom for a recommendation."

"Speaking of recommendations," she says, "any progress on a new nanny?"

"Yeah, the agency sent over some bios earlier today. Want to see them?"

"Obviously."

"You don't trust me after Irina, huh?"

"Should I?"

"I want to do right by Stella," I assure her.

"Then you need to find someone who's going to love and support her, not some tyrant on a power trip."

I both hate that she's right and love that she understands what Stella needs and is willing to let me know when I've fallen short. I pull up the bios on my phone and move onto the couch cushion next to her, keeping enough distance that we're not touching but that she can see my phone.

I reach across my body with the device so she can take it and look through the options, but instead she leans over, resting her head on my shoulder and looking down at the phone. I hold my breath, trying not to breathe in her scent, not to notice how warm her body is where it's pushed up against mine, and definitely trying to forget about the fact that from this angle I can see right down her shirt and she doesn't seem to be wearing a bra. I shift to rest my free hand under the arm that's holding out the phone. Hopefully, she thinks I'm supporting my arm instead of trying to hide the bulge that's growing in my pants as I soak in her proximity, her smell, and her amazing body.

She swipes through the bios, reading each resumé carefully and analyzing each person's photo, then returns to a few for a second look. I try not to be the creep checking her out while she's focused on important details regarding my kid, but I can't help it. I've never been able to stop my reaction to Petra.

She tells me the three that would be her top choices, justifying each with statements like "she's nannied for an only child before," or "she really seems to love kids," or "I like her approach to teaching self-discipline."

"I'll follow up with the agency and see if we can get interviews with them . . . assuming you want to be part of that?"

"Of course I do," she says.

"Thanks," I say, resting my cheek on her head for a brief moment.

She burrows her head deeper into my shoulder, a shared armless hug that makes it feel like we're progressing into trusting each other again. Then she stands abruptly. "I'm headed to bed."

The disappointment flows through me like a heavy metal, making me feel lethargic and half dead. Then in response, my adrenaline surges. I want to fight to keep her here in this room with me. *Let her go. You're playing a dangerous game.*

I know that in the end, Petra will leave. I know she has a life she loves and wants to get back to. I know that keeping her here with me and Stella, even in the short-term, isn't fair to her. It's like caging an eagle. She's meant to be soaring somewhere else, not tied down here. And hoping for anything else is just setting myself up for disappointment. More importantly, the longer Petra stays, the more likely it is that Stella will be heartbroken when she leaves. That'll make two of us. So I vow to keep Petra at a distance to protect both Stella and myself from the inevitable grief of losing her again.

"Goodnight," I say, picking up my book off the coffee table. I refuse to look at her as she leaves, afraid that she'll see what I'm feeling written plainly across my face.

Chapter Fourteen

PETRA

I wake up pissed off. Last night I claimed I was headed to bed, because I had to get out of that sitting room. Being around Sasha, just the two of us, was bringing back way too many feelings. The attraction and heat, which are so much more intense than when I was a teenager. The loss and devastation, which haven't faded enough to fully heal. I was feeling them in a repeating cycle, like watching our history play out over and over again. It left me feeling vulnerable, and I don't do vulnerable.

But when I climbed into bed after finishing up some work, all I could think about was that if I walked out the glass door and into the solarium, I could walk right into his room. I wanted that so badly my body hummed with the need to feel his hands on me, to taste his tongue against mine, to feel him stretch me wide open as he entered me slowly. And then I remembered all the reasons that was a terrible idea.

As much as I am still attracted to him, and even though I think he feels the same, our history and our present are both too complicated to further confuse things by having sex. So I settled for getting myself off to visions of him, which honestly has been the standard for a decade and a half—envisioning myself with the one who got away.

Except now that he's back in my life—so much hotter than he was as a teenager and even better than I've been picturing as an adult in my fantasies—thinking about him while pleasuring myself no longer leaves me feeling satisfied. It leaves me feeling disappointed because I want the real thing instead. The man who now sleeps in a bed on the other side of my wall.

Fuck. In the early light of the morning, I'm feeling just as dissatisfied and sexually frustrated as I felt last night.

I get up and shower, piling my curls up on top of my head because I do not have the energy to deal with washing my mountain of hair today. I scrub every inch of my body, then shave until my legs and lady parts are silky smooth. By the time I'm out of the shower, I feel more human, less frustrated, and ready to have a relaxing Saturday. And I have the perfect plan: I'll see if Emily is free for lunch, then get a little shopping in and see if I can get an appointment for a blowout. Spending a day away from Sasha and Stella is probably the best thing for me right now.

But when I go to make my blowout appointment online, I notice that they do blowouts for kids too. My first thought is how fun that would be for Stella to get to go do such a grown-up thing. I would have loved to do something like that with my mom when I was a kid.

You're not her mom.

The thought flashes through my mind, and it's the reminder I need. Except, I would have loved to do something grown-up like that with an aunt or one of my mom's friends too. Not that blowout bars existed when I was a kid, nor did we have the money for frivolity like that, even if they had. But I still distinctly remember how much I loved to get dressed up for a special dinner out or for an important family event, that feeling of getting to do something out of the ordinary.

I pop off my bed, determined to go ask Sasha if that's something Stella would enjoy and want to do if they don't already have other plans. I'm hoping I can ask him before she wakes up. Given how I've had to drag her out of bed every school morning this week, I'm guessing she likes to sleep in.

But the minute I step into the hallway and head toward the living area, I can hear her laughter. I find them in the kitchen. Sasha's standing over a griddle pan on the stovetop with his back to me, his T-shirt pulled tight across his muscular back and arms. Stella's sitting on the counter in her pajamas, close enough to see what he's doing but not so close she could get burned. Her hair's a mess of curls and her angelic face is looking up at him like he hung the moon.

"Make a dog," she insists, her voice delighted.

"I suspect it's going to come out like the cat," he says. His voice is a low, sexy rumble that has my thighs clenching together. He sounds like he just woke up, his voice is rough and his tone is tender. He sounds like himself in my fantasies.

"You mean the blob?" she giggles, closing her eyes and scrunching up her face in a way that can only be adorable on a little kid.

When she opens her eyes again she spots me, standing in the open doorway between the kitchen and butler's pantry, and squeals my name. Aleksandr's spine stiffens in response, his upper body going rigid. *Oh.* Is he not happy I'm intruding on their breakfast?

"Good morning, kiddo," I say as I walk in. Stella holds her arms out to me, so I go and pick her up off the counter. She wraps her legs around my waist and gives me a giant hug.

"I wasn't allowed to wake you up," she says into my neck as she snuggles her head against my shoulder. "But I really wanted you to have breakfast with us."

"I'd love to have breakfast with you. What are you making?"

"*Dyadya* is making pancakes. He said he'd try to make them into something besides circles, but everything just looks like a blob."

"Hmm," I say, peeking over his shoulder. "I see what you mean."

"It's harder than it looks," he mumbles.

So many sexual innuendos threaten to spill out of my mouth, but I hold them back because I don't want to traumatize the kid in my arms.

"Is that so?" I ask, my voice just as suggestive as I intend it to be. The way his head snaps toward me, his eyes going wide like he's reminding me to behave in front of the child, is enough to make me laugh out loud.

"Can you make them?" Stella asks me. "I bet you can do it better."

"Oh, honey, one thing you should know about girls . . . we do just about everything better."

The laugh that rumbles around in the back of Sasha's throat has my thighs clenching together again. Why is this man so damn sexy?

"Prove it," he says, stepping aside and gesturing for me to step up to the stove. The fact that he doesn't argue that point, and instead gives me the opportunity to prove myself, makes him even sexier in my book.

I step up to the counter and plop Stella back onto it, then step over to the stovetop, where his pancakes are about to burn on the griddle because they need to be flipped. "These ones don't count," I say, intentionally smirking at him in between flipping the pancakes already on the skillet. "I'm just cleaning up your mess."

"You know they taste the same no matter the shape, right?" His sarcasm is perfectly placed.

"Do they, though?" I raise an eyebrow. "Because these were about to burn. You weren't even paying attention. And burned pancakes don't taste good, no matter the shape."

"Touché," he says, as Stella watches our conversation closely without saying anything.

I'm not a person who likes sweet things for breakfast, so I've only made pancakes once or twice. The last time was a girls' ski trip I took with my friends, where Sierra was hung over and begged me to make her pancakes. I remember that when I looked up the instructions, there were a few keys to successfully cooking them and I rack my brain for those details now.

I turn the heat down on the skillet. "What do you think, kiddo?" I ask her. "What could make these pancakes come out better?"

She purses her lips as she thinks. "I think maybe you should pour the batter with something smaller. It's coming out of the bowl too fast and you can't really make a good design that way."

"Maybe we use a spoon for the whole thing, so we have more control?"

Stella nods her head vigorously, her curls bouncing up and down. "Let's try that," she says.

Beside me, I can feel Sasha move away like he's giving me this moment with Stella. But I don't want him any further from me, even though that's exactly where I should be keeping him. "Hey, Top Chef"—I wink at him—"watch and learn."

Ten minutes later, I've successfully made four cats and four bunnies, several sizes and shapes of hearts, and have pancakes that can (barely) pass for a horse, a dog with droopy ears, and a pig.

"Not bad," Sasha says as we sit down to eat. "But you probably do this all the time."

"Yep, I definitely don't go out to brunch with friends on weekend mornings. I just stand in front of my stove mastering animal-shaped pancakes on the off chance that a kid is going to ask me to make them."

His gray eyes are focused on me and his lips move into a smile, even though he looks like he's trying to stop that from happening. Then he turns toward Stella. "Want me to cut those up for you?"

"I want to try myself," she says.

We eat in silence for a minute while Stella works on cutting her pancakes.

"So, what do you have planned today?" Sasha asks me.

"I might go to lunch with a friend, then I think I'm going to go to the salon and get a blowout."

His lip quirks. "A what?"

"A blowout. You know, where they wash your hair and blow-dry it?"

"Can't you just do that yourself?"

"Yeah, but it's more relaxing and fun to go to the salon and do it there. Besides, you can't even imagine how hard it is to blow-dry all this," I say, pointing at my curls, "straight."

"I wish I had straight hair," Stella sighs.

That has alarm bells going off in my head. "Why's that?" I ask.

"Everyone else has straight hair. I want to be able to brush mine when it's dry and have it be all shiny and pretty like Harper's."

"First of all, your hair *is* shiny and pretty. And second, do you realize how lucky we are to have beautiful curly hair? Lots of girls would trade you their straight, boring hair for your beautiful curls."

She appears to think about this for a moment. "I still wish I could have straight hair for a day. *You're* going to have straight hair . . ."

I glance at Sasha, wondering if it's okay to ask to take her with me in front of her. If they have other plans, I don't want to interfere.

"Hey, Stella," I say. "Could you do me a big favor?"

She nods.

"I left my phone in my bedroom and I'm waiting to hear back from someone. Could you run and get it for me? It's on my nightstand."

She jumps up like she's delighted to help, and the second she's out of the room, I whisper to Sasha, "I was coming out here earlier to ask you if I could take her with me."

His blank look makes me think he doesn't understand.

"You know, so we could get our hair done together?"

"This is the one day I'm home all day. You could have the

whole day off," he says, "to do adult things. And you want to take Stella to get her hair done because . . .?"

His eyes are turning a darker shade of gray again, but I'm not sure why.

"Because it'll be fun for her. Something special that she hasn't done before." I wait and he doesn't say anything. "What's wrong?"

"I'm . . . kind of speechless."

"Because . . .?"

"I just figured you'd be dying to get out of here, to hang out with other adults. You know, have some distance."

"Stella's great, why would I want distance?" I say. He gives me a half smile; we're in agreement that his niece is wonderful. "And I only have another week with her. Plenty of time for adult stuff once I'm back home."

Just then, Stella comes bounding into the kitchen. "Here you go," she says, handing me my phone. Then she lets out a big sigh and collapses into her chair like she's just run a marathon.

"Thanks, sweetie." I look at Sasha for confirmation that he's okay with me asking her and he gives me a curt nod, then takes his napkin off his lap, crushes it in his fist, and drops it on his plate. *Wait, is he upset about me taking Stella out? Maybe he wanted to spend this time with her?*

As Stella picks up her fork and stabs a piece of her pancake, I pretend like I'm scratching the side of my face, so my hand blocks my mouth from her view. *What's wrong?* I mouth.

His voice booms in the silent kitchen when he replies, "Don't you have a question you want to ask Stella?" I guess he's ignoring my question and the secrecy with which I asked it.

Her head snaps toward me, her eyes huge like she just knows something really important is going to happen. I hope she's not expecting something more exciting.

"I was thinking that maybe you'd like to come with me this afternoon and get your hair done too?"

"Yes," she squeals as she jumps out of her chair and climbs into my lap, wrapping her arms around me once again. And I can't help but wonder why those small arms squeezing my neck don't feel as claustrophobic as I always imagined they would.

———

"You've got to be fucking kidding me," Emily hisses, and I follow her gaze out the glass door. "How in the world are you living with that man and not sleeping with him?"

Outside the restaurant, Sasha stands with his hips resting against a concrete planter so large it holds a full-size tree. He's got one foot crossed over the other in a deceptively casual stance, his chin tilted down toward Stella as he listens to something she's saying. His aviators and baseball cap hide most of his face, and his hoodie hides the bulky muscles of his upper body and neck, but I can tell by the rigid lines of his shoulders that he's not relaxed. He's large and imposing, and pretty recognizable even though he's trying not to be. He seems on edge about it.

I glance around the entryway of the restaurant to make sure no one else is close enough to hear our conversation.

"Emily, he's my oldest friend. It would be like sleeping with my brother." I wish I believed that.

She gives me the side-eye. "You're trying to tell me you're not attracted to him?" she asks as she slips her arms into her lightweight jacket and grabs her sunglasses from her bag. I glance out the window again, taking in the pale blue sky strewn with clouds. It's warm again today, the typical fluctuations of an East Coast spring.

I want to talk to her about our history, about how I'm feeling about him, about the sexual tension that's so thick you could carve it with a knife and serve it up on a plate. I want to tell her we're actually married, on paper only, and about adopting Stella and how conflicted I am. But I haven't told her anything more than I'm living with them for a couple weeks and helping out with Stella—and even that I swore her to secrecy about—because talking about the rest of it would make it all too real.

"I'm saying that we're friends, and that's all," I tell her.

Just then, he glances up at the restaurant doors. I can tell he sees us standing on the other side of the glass by the way he freezes, his mouth slightly open but unmoving. "Uh huh," Emily laughs. "Sure."

To escape this line of conversation, I push the door open and take a step out, holding it for her as she follows behind me. Behind his sunglasses I can tell Sasha still hasn't taken his eyes off me when we arrive in front of him and Stella, and the intensity of his focus is doing funny things to me. My legs feel shaky even as my thighs clench with longing, my stomach feels like it's dissolved into a million pieces that are floating off into space, and my heart is beating erratically. *After all this time and everything that's happened, how does he still have this effect on me?*

"Good lunch?" he asks when I fail to greet him.

I blink, pulling myself out of my stupor. "Great lunch. Emily, this is Aleksandr. Aleksandr, my friend Emily." There's no question they each know who the other is.

"Nice to finally meet you," Emily says as she extends her hand to shake his. "I feel like I've heard a lot about you."

With his free hand, he takes his sunglasses off and casually tucks them into the neck of his hoodie. "All good things, I hope."

"Depends on who's talking about you," Emily teases with a knowing smile. "But yes, only good things from Petra."

"That's all that matters, then," he says. His gaze flicks to mine, and I swear my insides melt. They're a big pile of goo trying to find their way out of my body. *This man.* Half the time I'm not sure if I love him or hate him, but there's no question he still does things to me that no one else can.

"And who is this cutie?" Emily asks as she glances down at Stella.

"I'm Stella," she says at the same time I say, "This is Aleksandr's niece."

"Well, it is very nice to meet you, Stella," Emily says. "Are you going to get your hair done too?" She asks like she doesn't already know they're here because I'm taking Stella with me.

"Yes! I'm going to get straight hair today!" Her excitement is rolling off her in waves.

"You know," she says, "my hair is curly too. But more wavy than curly, and I'd love to have your beautiful, perfect curls."

Stella eyes Emily's straight hair. "Your hair isn't always straight?"

Emily pulls her phone out. "Nope. Here, let me show you a picture." She opens her social media and scrolls back to a picture I remember her posting this past winter when she was on a yacht in the Caribbean with some friends. I remember her makeup-free, curly haired look and how carefree and happy she seemed in the pictures. Emily squats down next to Stella to show her the pictures. "See, this is what my hair looks like when I don't do anything to it."

"It's beautiful," Stella says.

"Yep, because curly hair is awesome. And if I had your perfect curls, I don't think I'd straighten my hair very often. Don't forget that!" she says as she stands back up.

"Thank you," I whisper as I hug her goodbye. I love how she instinctively knows we need to empower the next generation to love themselves, to not listen to all the bullshit about how you need to look a certain way in order to be loved, accepted, or desired. And I love that her modeling priorities these days reflect that, how she's working to change that industry from the inside out.

We walk half a block to the car, and Sasha holds the door open for Stella to climb in first. When I move to step in behind her, he stretches his arm out and rests his hand on the roof of the car, blocking the door. "Is everything okay?"

I look up at him, the confusion likely evident on my face. "Yeah, why?"

He dips his head toward mine and my heart speeds up. "You just called me Aleksandr several times."

"That's your name."

"You only use that name when you're mad at me."

I pause, then let out a small and silent laugh. "Maybe you're right. But apparently I'm the only one who calls you Sasha. To everyone else, you're Alex. That just sounds wrong to me, so I will probably always call you Aleksandr in front of other people."

"Okay." His nod is curt.

"Do I really call you Aleksandr when I'm mad?"

"So far as I've noticed." He moves his arm out of the way and gestures me into the car, then closes the door and goes around to the other side to sit behind the driver.

When he gets in the car, I glance at him over Stella's head, and the desire that runs through my veins is reminiscent of being sixteen again.

"How soon after our hair appointment am I going to Harper's?" Stella asks as the driver pulls away from the curb. "I can't wait for her to see me with straight hair!"

Sasha and I share a look. I think we've both just realized that we'll be alone together tonight. My body visibly shudders as a wave of longing moves through me. This is so very dangerous.

———

"What are you crazy kids going to do with your night off?" Sofia jokes as Stella and Harper take off at a run into the depths of the apartment.

"Probably sleep," Sasha responds with a shrug, his voice sounding like he's bored just thinking about not having Stella around for the night.

I shrug too. "I probably should have made plans or something, but this has been a busy week," I say. "Just having time to relax sounds great."

"Well, enjoy the quiet," she says as the sound of the girls' laughter in the background rises to a shockingly high decibel level. We lock eyes, and I can tell we're both thrilled we could make this sleepover happen.

I glance over at Sasha, whose face remains stoically placid. I can't tell what he's thinking, and I hate that. I hope he sees how happy Stella is and is himself happy that he allowed this. Or got roped into it. Whichever.

Sasha doesn't respond to Sofia's comment. "I will," I tell Sofia, not wanting to speak for Mr. Silent standing next to me.

He's quiet in the elevator ride down to the car, and silent as we climb into the backseat of the car next to each other. He doesn't speak as the driver—who I now know is called Daniel, but who has never said more than a handful of words to me despite the number of times I've been in this car over the last week—pulls into traffic and heads back to Sasha's apartment.

I cast a glance at him out of the corner of my eye, but he's facing the front, focused on the back of Daniel's headrest or looking out the front window. I can't tell what he's thinking any more than I can tell what he's looking at. I glance down at my phone in my lap, wondering if maybe I should plan on going out tonight. He looks . . . angry? Tired? Like he wants solitude? But also, it feels like there's a nervous energy just below the surface, pulsing between us. He shifts slightly away from me, toward the door on his side of the car.

He's always been a hard one to read. Gentle and quiet, even though you'd think the opposite to look at him. His tight mastery over his emotions and his actions is one of the things that drew me to him. As someone seemingly without a filter, prone to spitting out the first thing that came to my mind, I always marveled at his ability to control everything about himself. Maybe it's my age or that I don't like to play games, but I find that now I'm tired of having to work so hard to understand him, to know what he's feeling.

My phone buzzes in my lap and I glance down to find a message on the group chat I have with my best friends.

LAUREN

OMG! They. Are. Mobile. God help me!

I make sure my sound is silenced, and tap play on the video she's sent. Both twins are on their hands and knees, and in a few shaky movements, one of them crawls toward the other.

My inhale sounds like a gasp in the silence of the car, and I can feel Sasha's eyes on me. I hit play again, and can't help it when I choke up a bit. Less than a year ago, I was holding these babies in the NICU. Sierra and I would take turns showing up every other day to help Lauren and Josh however we could. Now these baby girls are freaking starting to crawl, and it feels like it's all happening so quickly.

"Are you okay?" It's a tender question asked in an unusually quiet voice. He's not whispering exactly, it's more like a verbal caress and it has heat pooling in my stomach and spreading through my chest.

I hold my phone so he can see it and hit play again. "These are my friend Lauren's twins. They are ten months old, and I feel like they're growing up way too fast."

He's silent for a beat, then says, "Kids have a way of doing that. I feel like Colette was just showing me how to change

Stella's diaper, and here she is in first grade." I shift my eyes toward him in time to catch his Adam's apple bobbing as he swallows down whatever thoughts or emotions he's holding back.

"I don't know how people do it." The words are out of my mouth before I can think better of it, and even though that's par for the course with me, I wish I somehow could take them back. I already know he'll press me on my meaning, and it feels like too vulnerable an admission to someone I used to know, in a car with a driver who's essentially a stranger to me.

"Have kids?" he clarifies.

"Yeah." I shrug, hoping he'll drop it.

"Why not?"

"It just seems so . . ."

"Hard?" he prompts.

"No." I'm no stranger to hard work. "Painful, I guess. Watching them grow up so quickly, knowing they'll experience pain you can't fix, knowing that there'll be heartbreak and obstacles you can't prevent."

"But that's life." His voice isn't dismissive or judgmental. Any time I've voiced something like this around my friends, they've basically dismissed it—not because they're jerks, but because none of them grew up with the kind of loss I experienced, nor had every single person they loved disappoint them over and over again. "And it's filled with joy and successes too," Sasha continues. "And as a parent, you get to . . . I don't know . . . help them learn to live through both, I guess."

I love the way he sounds like he's still figuring all this out, too. Like he doesn't know exactly what he's doing, but he's willing to make it work. So often I feel like everyone around me has their shit together, has built the life they want, and I'm over here still trying to figure out what that life even looks like for me.

I very intentionally make it look like I love this life I've created for myself, but the truth is that even at thirty, I don't know where I'm going or what I really want. I work hard and I've gotten lucky too. I've been able to essentially reinvent myself and my life and my career over and over. But the result is that instead of feeling successful, I feel like everything is temporary. That's a scary feeling, one that I tamp down deep so I don't spend too much time thinking about it.

"You're doing a good job." I reach over to pat his forearm in what's meant to be a supportive gesture, but instead I'm blindsided by the rush of heat I feel when my hand connects with the strong muscles beneath his hoodie. Hoping to turn the conversation away from my admission and from the sudden feelings of longing, I add, "Irina aside."

That earns me a small smile. "I feel like I don't know what I'm doing half the time."

"I'm sure every parent feels that way with their first kid. And you didn't have the luxury of growing in your parenting skills as Stella grew up, since she's only been yours for a few months. But you two are figuring it out together and it'll all work out. You're great with her, and she clearly loves you."

His lips part like he's going to say something, and I realize how close we are now that we were leaning toward each other to watch that video of Lauren's kids together. He doesn't say anything, though, just stares at me like he's trying to memorize my face.

I can't help the way that heat from my chest spreads. It's like tiny pins and needles dancing over my skin. He licks his lips and my core muscles clench involuntarily, which has me pressing my thighs together to ease the pressure I feel between my legs. His eyes travel down my body, and mine follow his path. My taut nipples are visible through both my bra and the white satin camisole I'm wearing, and the fabric of my black pants is bunched together at my crotch where I'm squeezing my thighs together so tightly they could bend steel.

I'm not sure how he has this effect on me, but I am aware that I need to tamp it down like I do with everything else that doesn't help me accomplish my goals. Because getting involved with Sasha is a detour I can't afford.

His eyes travel back up my body until they meet mine. He opens his mouth again, and again no words come out. It's like we both have forgotten what we were talking about, and instead can only focus on these glances, the small touches—the sexual tension that's filling the car.

Our eyes spring away from each other when Daniel clears his throat. "We're here," he says.

I glance out the window to find that we're at a standstill in front of Sasha's building, which we didn't even notice because we couldn't take our eyes off each other. Well, that's embarrassing.

Sasha reaches for his door handle and scoots out, holding the door open for me to follow. He gives me his hand as I step out, and even though I certainly don't need his help, I take it because it would be rude not to. I'm so unprepared for the feel of his fingers as they run along my palm and then grip my hand. He supports a little of my weight until I'm standing, then pulls his hand away like he's touched something poisonous. I'm simultaneously relieved that he's no longer touching me and looking for a reason for him to touch me again.

We walk through the lobby without speaking, and then the mechanical sound of the elevator moving swiftly upward drowns out the pregnant silence as we take turns casting glances at the other and looking away a second before being caught. When the elevator dings to announce our arrival at our floor, I almost jump out of my skin. I know this restless feeling of desire, and the only way to rid myself of it is to have sex. I could head to my room and try to take care of this problem myself, or I could go out and find someone to take care of this problem for me. The thought of my body sliding along someone else's, those touches, that heat, the feeling of someone moving inside me has my underwear drenched and my nipples aching to be touched—probably because I'm picturing myself with Sasha.

When the doors open, I fly out of the elevator and down the hall to my bedroom, shutting the door behind me and resting my back against it. My hands want to roam over my body, do something to alleviate this need that's grown so hot I'm burning up with it. But I know that won't satiate me enough tonight. Tonight, I need real human contact.

I head into the closet where I strip off my clothes and pull on clean underwear and a white dress. The smocked top holds my breasts in so I don't need a bra, but the way the fabric scrapes along my still-hard nipples with every move-ment has me so revved up I'm about to explode. I slip my feet into some wedges that lie on the floor, then head to the bath-room to freshen up. Five minutes later, I'm heading down the hall to let Sasha know I'm going out for the night.

I find him in the kitchen, guzzling a bottle of water like a man parched from days in the desert. *Good, maybe he's as hot and bothered as I am.* I watch for a moment as his throat bobs with each swallow, his neatly trimmed bearded jaw moving rhythmically as he gulps the water.

I open my mouth, intending to tell him I'm headed out, but instead the real question I've been wanting to ask slips out.

Chapter Fifteen

ALEKSANDR

I take a long drink of my water, letting it cool my nerves about Stella's absence and the blatant attraction I'm feeling toward Petra. When I tip the bottle back down, she's standing in the doorway between the kitchen and the butler's pantry, wearing a white dress with wide straps and a full, but short, skirt. She's got on platform wedges with tan leather straps that barely stand out against her olive skin and make her legs look a mile long.

"If we're married, why aren't we having sex?"

Her question is so unexpected that the water slips down the wrong pipe and my throat spasms. I can feel the liquid tickling my lungs and I need to cough, but it's like my entire esophagus is paralyzed. I can feel my eyes widen as my lungs contract, but the cough is frozen inside them. Finally, everything releases and I'm left sputtering.

I bend at the waist, coughing violently into my elbow. When the liquid is out of my lungs, I look at her and say, "This isn't that kind of marriage."

"I fail to see what I'm getting out of it, then."

It's a fair point. "Petra, we're doing this for Stella."

"A woman still has needs," she says, then she spins on her heel and stalks through the pantry.

"Where are you going?" I ask, too stunned to follow her at first.

"Out," she calls over her shoulder as I follow her through the dining room. In the entryway, she grabs the jean jacket and straw purse sitting on the cushioned bench. "If you're not going to meet my needs, then I'll find someone who will. I'll be back in the morning."

I'm practically on top of her before she can even get her first arm into her jacket, backing her into the wall. I plant my hands on either side of her head. "Like hell you will. You're a married woman."

She snorts, a derisive sound that emanates from the back of her throat. "Are marriages even real if they're not consummated?"

She's been married for fourteen years and I'm confident she's slept with her fair share of men in that time. But she *knows* she's married now, and that should make a difference to her like it's made a difference to me.

"You have no idea what you're asking," I growl, my face inches from hers.

She lowers her eyes to my lips. "I don't ask," she says quietly.

Yes, this is a woman who is used to calling the shots.

"You're going to beg," I say, my voice low, steady. I can't control this desire any longer, not when she's standing in front of me challenging me to do the thing my body most wants to do. "And you're going to like it."

I swallow her scoff with my lips, and her mouth parts for

me like she's been waiting for this since she first walked into my apartment over a week ago. I have sixteen years of pent up sexual frustration when it comes to Petra Volkova, and it's going to be damn near impossible to take this slow, with the attention and reverence she deserves.

With one of my hands, I cup the back of her head, digging my fingers into her thick hair until my fingertips rest against her skull. Her tongue laps at mine, presses into it, circles, retreats. I chase after her, pressing her further back against the wall as my whole body advances toward her. The need to touch her, to feel her against me, supersedes everything else. I am out of control, and I don't lose control. This woman makes me crazy.

She pushes her hips forward, tilts them up so she presses along the hard length of me, then she sighs into my mouth and leans her head back against my hand to break the contact as she breathes deeply. Her neck is elongated and exposed, so I trail kisses along her jaw and down the column of her neck. I nip at her collarbone and slide the strap of her dress off her shoulder so I can taste her smooth skin. Then I trail kisses across her cleavage, but the minute I move up the other side of her neck, she's pushing her chest into me. I don't have the superhuman strength it would take to resist her.

When my lips meet hers again, she wraps her hands around my lower back, anchoring our bodies together. She runs her fingers under the hem of my shirt and the sensation of her fingertips riding the ridges of my muscles has me groaning into her mouth. The need is consuming, like a fire just waiting for a lick of oxygen before it explodes.

The small dose of oxygen comes when she unbuttons the waistband of my jeans, then slides them down over my hips and pushes them past my thighs and lets them fall to the floor. Suddenly, the only things standing between us are the thin cotton of my boxer briefs and the gauzy material of her dress. The fire explodes into an inferno.

I pull away from her, just enough to see her face as I bring my hands to the straps of her dress. I watch her eyes as I slide the other strap off her shoulder, and she raises one eyebrow like she's challenging me to actually slide that dress down her body. With careful hands, I pull the straps along her arms, and that smocked top follows as it drags along her sides.

Her breasts spring free and my cock swells even bigger and harder than I thought possible. I want my mouth all over those tits. I want to fuck them, I want to feel them dragging along my abdomen as she lowers herself to her knees in front of me, I want to see them spread before me as I hold myself over her and plunge into her, I want to see them bouncing as she rides me, I want my hands on them as I bend over her back with my hips pressing into her from behind. There's no shortage of ways I want to be with her. And I already know, with absolute certainty, that once will not be enough. Tonight will not be enough.

I'm not sure there is an "enough."

I continue pulling the straps down until the fabric slides over her hips and pools at her feet, where I drop on one knee to pull the dress aside as she steps out of it. I gaze up at her from the floor. The sunset has golden light streaming in from the glass ceiling above us, so she's literally glowing. It's like looking at a painting of the goddess Venus, but Petra is far hotter than any Venus I've ever seen captured on a canvas.

From here, my head is at her waist, so I drag my tongue

along the top seam of her skimpy underwear, then up to her belly button. I continue my path up the center of her abdomen as I slowly stand until my tongue is between her breasts. I cup one in each hand, wanting to both devour them and worship them at the same time. When she moves her hand between us and wraps it around me through my boxer briefs, I dip my head so my mouth meets one of her nipples. My tongue laps at it, and she leans into me, pushing her breast further into my mouth. My lips latch over her skin as I suck, gently pulling her nipple deeper as I slide my tongue over it. Her response is exquisite: the way her hand tightens on my cock, the groan that escapes her throat, the way she whispers, "Yes, Sasha."

I let one of my hands travel down to her bare ass, where I give her a playful squeeze that has her hips pushing forward, seeking me out, so I trail my fingers around her hip and dip my fingers into her underwear. I slide them down, brushing over her clit, then trailing along her slick seam until they arrive at her entrance. She's so wet for me—this would be a turn-on no matter what, but it's all the sweeter because I have wanted her forever.

I dip one finger into her and pull out slowly, then enter with two fingers. "Yes," she hisses, and her hips move like they have a mind of their own so that her warm, tight pussy slides back and forth over my fingers. "Holy shit," she sighs, and I glance up at her from where my tongue still plays with her nipple. Her lips are forming a small O, and her eyes are heavily lidded, almost half-closed in pleasure. She's close, and there's no way the first time I make her come is going to be against a wall in my entryway. It's bad enough that I'll never be able to walk into my apartment again without hearing and seeing her exactly like this, I don't need to remember the sound of her coming every time I walk in here too.

I pull my fingers out of her as I fully stand, and she whimpers. It's an intoxicating sound that makes me feel powerful, like I have some modicum of control over this uncontrollable creature. With both arms, I reach around her, my hands coming between her thighs from behind and lifting her so she's wrapped around my waist. Her legs grip my hips as I turn and walk her down the hall, and she bends her head to trail her tongue along my earlobe before capturing it between her teeth. "Walk faster," her husky voice demands.

When we reach my bedroom, I set her at the foot of the bed, then I slide her underwear down her legs and pull her wedges off her feet one at a time. When I stand, she's got her hands in my boxers and is pulling them down my legs. They don't come off easily, it's always hard getting them past my muscular thighs. She's squatting, sitting on her heels at my feet and her eyes are firmly locked on my cock where it juts out from my body at a hard angle. She reaches up and wraps her hand around my shaft as she takes the head into her mouth, swirling her tongue around the tip before closing her lips around me and sliding me all the way to the back of her throat.

"Shit." It's the only coherent thought I have as I reach behind her and grip one corner post of my bed. She slides me out of her mouth, then takes me in as far as her throat will allow a few more times, and I'm feeling way too close. This isn't ending with a blow job.

I take her chin in my hands and tilt her face up until I slide all the way out of her mouth, but she's still got the base of me firmly in her hand. Her lips are wet and her eyes are wild as she looks up at me. "The first time we do this, I'm coming inside you."

"That's fair," she says as her lips curve into a smirk. She stands. "The inside of me feels amazing, if I do say so myself."

Holy shit.

I push her backward onto my mattress, pull my shirt over my head, and pull her knees up over my shoulders as I kneel at the end of the bed. She's laid bare before my face, her slick folds are mesmerizing in their silkiness. I run my tongue over her clit and watch as her entire body convulses in response. It only takes a few more passes of my tongue over that sensitive area before she's saying my name with reverence and longing. I enter her again with two fingers while my tongue works her clit, and she lets out a guttural moan. I know she's extraordinarily close, so I slow down.

"Don't stop," she says with that throaty voice that's sexy as hell. "Please, Sasha, I'm so close."

I keep up the slow pace even as she wants more.

"Please, Sasha, make me come."

I'm so hard I'm going to explode if I don't get inside her soon, so I continue as she asked. She's chasing her first orgasm and in my mind I'm already planning out her second.

"Yes," she chants, as I feel her muscles contract around my fingers. "Yes, yes, yes."

I slow my assault, giving her a moment to ride the wave of her orgasm, then I stand and reach my arm under her back as I drag her up the bed with me. "I told you you'd beg," I say, brushing my lips across her eyebrow.

She reaches behind me and smacks my ass in response. "I *let* you make me beg."

"Whatever you say." She rolls her eyes at me as I reach

over to the nightstand where I keep my condoms, even though I've never once brought a girl back to my place. The thought of sharing my own bed with someone has never crossed my mind. Until tonight.

She sits up, taking the condom from me where I stand on both knees in front of her, then tears it open and rolls it on. The feel of her fingers skimming over my erection has my eyes rolling back in my head.

"Not too quickly," she says as she looks up at me through her eyelashes. "You owe me at least one more orgasm."

I push her shoulder so she falls backward onto the pillow, then drop my hand on one side of her head so I'm propped up over her. "Are you always this demanding?"

"There's nothing wrong with a girl who knows what she wants and goes after it." Her eyes challenge me to disagree.

"There certainly isn't." In fact, there is nothing sexier than a confident woman who knows what she wants in the bedroom.

Sliding into her feels like coming home, like making a full circle. I've wanted her and us and this for what feels like my entire life, and so I refuse to think about all the reasons that I insisted it was impossible. Instead, I focus on her face—the bright blue eyes that are locked on mine, the straight ridge of her small nose, the perfect Cupid's bow at the top of her full lips—as I pause, giving her time to adjust to me.

She reaches up, cupping the side of my face in her hand. "What are you waiting for?"

I pull out about halfway and slide back in slowly, and the small moan that escapes her mouth has me gritting my teeth. Her dark hair is splayed around her, the silky strands so different but no less sexy than her normal curls. Her lips are swollen and her breath is coming in shorter pants, her ribcage expands and contracts with each inhale and exhale and the way her breasts roll with the movement has me wanting my mouth on them again. I pull out again and slide back into her, trying to memorize the feel of her skin sliding along mine and the way her muscles grip me as I enter her.

She slides her hands from my face down to my neck. "Yes." Has one word ever sounded so right before? My hips start moving to their own rhythm and she matches each thrust with the upward motion of her own hips. I'm trying to focus on her face, on the way her half-closed eyes are focused on my lips, the way her mouth is parted and letting out small gasps of pleasure. But I'm again distracted by the way those perfect breasts are bouncing with each thrust of my hips and I just want my mouth on them, which is impossible from this angle. So I sweep my arm under her back, and lift her with me as I sit back on my heels.

With her thighs spread on either side of my hips and her legs wrapped around my lower back, I can't imagine that I could penetrate her any deeper than I already am. She rocks her hips away and toward me and moans another "Yes!" as I hit the deepest recesses of her. Then she leans back a little, resting one of her hands on the bed behind her while the other grips my neck, and with her back arched like this, those sexy-as-fuck pale pink nipples are pointed up like she's waiting for me to devour them.

I bend my head down, sucking first one, then the other, into my mouth. Petra's arched body slides along my abdomen as we move in tandem, joining and parting, skin slapping each time she sinks down onto me. I lift my mouth from her and try to memorize each movement, each moment, each look she gives me, but there's not enough time. We're both panting and I'm already feeling that tightening at the base of my spine. I grit my teeth and increase the pace, biding my time and watching as she half closes her eyelids while her lips part. I swear the sound of our bodies meeting is the most erotic thing I've ever heard, until she whispers, "Fuck, yesss."

Her muscles are clenching and releasing rhythmically, and she's bucking her hips wildly against mine. I hold back as long as I can, wanting her to ride out every second of this orgasm, and then I move my hands to both her hips, pulling her down to me over and over as I spill everything I have into her.

We collapse back onto the bed, me on top of her. I want to prop myself up on my elbows but I can't muster the energy, so I roll to my side instead, bringing her with me so we're facing each other.

"Why haven't we done this before?" she asks.

I just stare at her, unsure how to respond.

"Did you not want me like this, back when we were teenagers? Did you just think of me like a little sister?"

Her question stuns me. "I've *never* thought of you like a little sister, which is half the problem."

"I don't see why that's a problem. But what's the other half of the problem?"

I can't tell her the truth about my dad and her mom, can't tell her that her mom and brother's blood is on his hands—or that I've known about it the whole time. I can't tell her that I kept her in the friend zone out of guilt and a respect for my dead best friend, and so I wouldn't have to tell her the truth about her father's role in this arranged marriage. So instead, I say, "It's just an expression."

I reach my fingers up and trail them along her face, noticing how her features soften. It's like watching someone let down their metaphorical guard.

"You really hurt me," she says. "Back when you left."

"I know." I see the question in her eyes, but I can't answer it. I want to tell her that I had to, but I won't have an explanation if she asks "why." So instead, I opt for another truth. "And I've never not been sorry about it."

She stretches herself over to me and takes my lips in hers, kissing me slowly, lazily, like we have all the time in the world. But we don't. Stella will be back midmorning tomorrow, and we have a lot of catching up to do before then. I deepen the kiss and run my hand up the side of her thigh, along her obliques, over her breast, and then down her abdomen to her center.

She pulls back and looks at me. "Already?"

"Don't plan on sleeping tonight," I tell her, then pull her against me to begin round two.

———

I know she's in the stands, but I've managed not to look for her this entire game. I've never let my eyes track up to the eighth row where I know she's sitting. I can't let her presence here distract from my game. In the regular season, that wouldn't be okay. In the playoffs, it would be unforgivable.

Head down, I take the puck up the outside, passing it to Thompson just before their left defenseman reaches me. Thompson stops the puck, spins, fakes a pass to me and instead slaps it to Ottowan, who acts like he's taking a shot on goal but instead passes it across the ice right to where I'm waiting. I slap it into the top right corner of the net.

The horn signaling the goal echoes in my ears. I skid across the ice on my knees, then hop up to my feet, holding my stick in the air.

My eyes involuntarily turn up, searching for Petra exactly where I know she'll be. She's holding Stella up so she can see, while jumping up and down cheering. Her cheeks are pink, her smile is huge, and her straight hair is tucked behind one ear.

It feels like the muscles in my chest have tightened, so much so that it's hard to breathe. That C on the jersey she's wearing—without even seeing the sleeve, I know she's wearing my number. I know my name is printed across her back, like I can see it printed across Stella's, and the clarity of what I want is astounding: she should be, and in many ways already is, mine. As much as I've fought against that desire my whole life, I realize it's fruitless. I will never be happy until we're together. It's the inevitable ending of our story.

She glances down at me, her eyes locking with mine, and I can no longer hear the thousands of cheering fans, I can only hear the thumping of my heartbeat, which sounds like it's between my ears.

She holds my gaze, heat burning in that hungry look. I'm frozen in place until Stella points up and Petra looks at the jumbotron above the rink. I follow her gaze to see myself reflected there. Every person in the rink was just watching me watch her. *Shit.*

The impact to my body when Ottowan crashes into me in celebration would be enough to knock me on my ass while I'm this distracted, but Thompson is behind me, cheering and holding me up and mumbling "keep your head in the fucking game" as his eyes follow my gaze and land on Petra. "No chick is worth getting this distracted."

I shake my head to clear it. I need to be at the top of my game tonight, and he's right that I can't let her distract me. He's wrong about her not being worth it, though.

We hold our one-point lead for the remaining three minutes of the final period, and when the buzzer sounds to end the game, my teammates on the ice pile together with our sticks in the air and the rest of the team hops over the boards and surrounds us. It's a sweet victory because now we lead this series by one game, only two more to clinch this round and move on. I have to remember not to get ahead of myself.

The minute we're back in the locker room, I text Petra to ask her to wait for me after the game, letting her know how to get to the hallway that leads to the players' indoor parking area. I check my phone after my shower, and again after I'm done with the invasive interviews the press insists on conducting in the locker rooms, but there's no response. I try not to let that bother me. She was probably rushing to get Stella home and in bed because she has school tomorrow morning and it's already after 10:00 p.m. Or maybe she didn't want to be seen waiting for me, didn't want the attention that might bring. Or maybe she didn't even see the text. In my head, I run through a long list of reasons she might not have responded as I look at my text message and her lack of response while walking with a few teammates down to the parking garage. I'm so lost in my thoughts that I'm not sure why Thompson is elbowing me in the ribs until I hear Ramirez say "Damn, Ivanov" under his breath.

I glance up and Petra is leaning one shoulder against the

cinderblock wall. Stella is wrapped around Petra, her head resting on Petra's shoulder, her arms hanging limply by her sides, and her legs dangling from each of Petra's hips. I focus on how supporting Stella's dead weight like that must be killing her back, shoulders, and arms, rather than focusing on the way my heart seems to be twisting around itself at the sight of them together waiting for me after my game. It's everything I didn't know I wanted.

"Can I take her for you?" I ask as I approach them. Behind me, my teammates move on toward their cars.

"Please," she groans.

Stella wakes up when I shift her to my arms. She looks up at me adoringly and says, "Dada," before resting her head on my shoulder and closing her eyes. It's only the second time I've heard her call me Dada instead of *Dyadya*, and it does funny things to my insides just like it did the first time.

She's dead weight in my arms, and I can't even imagine how Petra held her like this for any length of time. Petra bends to take my bag that I'd set down on the ground. "I can get that," I tell her.

"Please, this is nothing compared to holding Stella for the last half hour."

"I'm sorry it took me so long," I say as we start walking. "I didn't know you'd be waiting."

"It's fine. I was going to text you once we got down here, but Stella fell asleep in my arms right after security let us through, and I couldn't get my phone out of my bag after that."

"Thank you for waiting for me," I say, glancing down at her as we move.

She tilts her head up toward mine, like she's going to say

something, but instead she just gives me a smile, then says, "Of course."

"Your body must be killing you." In my arms, Stella is like a fifty-pound sack of flour.

Petra just raises her eyebrows in response and gives me a tiny nod of her head. I don't know how she manages to make the movement so sexy. It's got to be the way her face changes when her features move. Those big blue eyes under perfectly arched brows, the angular line of her cheekbones under her smooth skin, those full lips that are as sexy right now covered in lip balm as they are when they're painted bright red. And I love her curls, but there's something incredibly sexy about her with straight hair. And just like that, I'm flooded with memories of last night and the way she looked with her hair spread out on my pillow. I want to know what that hair feels like wrapped around one of my hands, with the other on her hip as I enter her from behind, what it would feel like to own a piece of her, to know she was mine.

That got serious quickly. I don't know why my thoughts keep going to this "forever" state. That's not the path Petra and I are on. She might help me with Stella, but she's not staying in New York, she's made that very clear.

"Let me give you a massage when we get home," I say quietly as we step into the garage.

She rolls her shoulders, stretching them out a little. "You're the one who just played two hours of hockey. Shouldn't I be offering up the massage?"

The thought of her small hands being able to massage my body in a productive way is comical. "I'm all set. I want my hands all over you now."

"We'll see," she says with a small shrug.

I raise an eyebrow at her. Last night was not one and done, and we both know it. Not only because we had sex four times before we finally fell asleep, but also because I woke up this morning to her climbing between my legs and waking me up with a blow job. Then there was the sex we had in the kitchen after we ate breakfast, and the way I came up behind her while she was doing her makeup before we went to get Stella, my fingers dipping into her underwear and getting her off while we locked eyes in the mirror. I'm trying to forget the way she sank to her knees after that and gave me my second blow job of the day, because the way she looks with her lips around my dick is something I will *never* get over.

When we get to the car, Daniel opens the door for me. I buckle Stella into her booster, and though she wakes for a minute again, she slumps toward the door as soon as it's shut.

Daniel goes to the driver's side and gets in as Petra and I go to the back of the car to drop my bag off. When the trunk is popped and blocking Daniel's view of us, I slip the bag from her shoulder, letting my fingers graze a path down her arm and trail over her hand.

My mouth is mere inches from her face when I ask, "Is it wrong that all I can think of right now is getting you back into my bed, preferably in that jersey?" The thought of her in nothing but my sweater has my dick trying to escape through the waistband of my pants.

"It depends on what you plan to do to me while I'm there." She fucking winks at me, and it has a growl escaping the back of my throat. I'm so turned on right now that I'm contemplating dragging her to the other side of one of the enormous pillars, where we *might* be out of view, and getting naked with her. I've never had sex in public, but right now it

215

feels like the reward might outweigh the risk. She looks at me like she can read my mind, then says, "In the meantime, let's get Stella home and in bed."

In the back seat, she snuggles up next to me and I throw my arm around her shoulder, pulling her even closer. She trails her fingertips up my thigh and back down, and from her vantage point, I'm sure she can see how hard she's got me. But even though she drags those nails up and down my leg, getting closer and closer each time, she never actually touches me where I need her to.

I'm so keyed up when we get back to the apartment that I don't even care if anyone else notices I'm sporting a huge boner while carrying my kid through the lobby toward the elevator. Petra's eyes never leave mine the entire ride up to the apartment, and the tension that's building between us is exquisite. We go together to Stella's room to get her in bed. Petra insists we take the jersey off her because it's too loose to be safe to sleep in, but otherwise we leave her in her clothes as we tuck her into bed.

And the minute we are in the hall with Stella's door closed behind us, Petra says "Meet me in my room in five minutes" and walks away without looking back.

Chapter Sixteen

PETRA

My underwear is absolutely soaked when I strip them off in my closet. I don't know how I could get so turned on walking to a car next to him, but it happened. And then the car ride back, where he wrapped his arm around me and pulled me into his side, where I dragged my fingertips down his thigh and raked my nails back up. If Stella hadn't been in the back seat with us, there's no doubt in my mind I'd have given him a hand job right there, even with Daniel in the front seat.

Slipping the jersey back on, I loosen the laces that run from the neck down the shirt so that it gapes open between my breasts. I want him to think of me like this every time he slips his own jersey over his head.

After I quickly brush my teeth and wash my face in the bathroom, I hear the glass door at the other end of my room opening as I'm drying my face. I step out of the bathroom, my hair still up in a ponytail and my face still damp, as Sasha walks through the door from the solarium in nothing but a thin pair of jersey shorts. I pause in the doorway, noting that the steel pipe that was threatening to break out of his pants earlier is gone. It's a disappointment until I realize that I can easily make it reappear.

As I lean against the doorframe, I cross my arms over my chest and can feel my boobs squeezing together, hopefully giving him a nice view of my cleavage. He stalks across the room toward me, his eyes never leaving mine, but he stops about a foot in front of me. My body, expecting his touch, reacts by stepping forward toward him. I stop about an inch away, and he lets out a sound that's half sigh, half groan.

He takes my hand in his. "Come here," he says as he turns and starts walking back toward the solarium. Once inside, he walks across the space to the low brick wall with the glass rising from it. He steps behind me so I'm facing the lights surrounding Central Park and plants his hands on my shoulders, those thick fingers of his expertly running along the ridges of tight muscles there. Holding Stella for half an hour while we waited for him was a lot more painful than I let on. It would have been fine if she were awake, but as dead weight, it was a killer. Still, I'm not upset we waited.

I let my head drop back to rest along his collarbone as he massages my shoulders, then I tell him that my lower back is killing me too. He gently slides his hands under the jersey and uses his thumbs to work out some knots there also. The force of his hands on my back moves my upper body forward, and I plant my hands on the glass to hold myself upright. Behind me, he steps closer and fits the length of himself between my ass cheeks.

"You're not wearing anything under this," he growls.

Instinctively, I push my hips back to slide along him. A low sound rattles around his throat, but he doesn't stop massaging my back even as he pushes his hips forward to increase the pressure between us.

I watch the spectacular view of the city as his hands work their magic on my lower back for another minute until his hands move to my stomach and then up the front of my body to my breasts. He cups them in his hands, rolling my nipples between his thumb and forefinger and in response, I push my ass back against him even harder.

He dips his head so his mouth is next to my ear and in a low voice tells me, "I am absolutely obsessed with your body."

"Good." I turn my head enough for our lips to meet, and kiss him gently, our lips toying with each other for a minute until he deepens the kiss and lets one of his hands trail down the front of me until it meets my center. He drags two fingers from my clit, through my slick folds, back to my ass, then switches direction again. My hips move to meet his fingers, wanting them inside me to fill the aching emptiness that's suddenly desperate for him. But he tortures me by dragging his fingers back and forth along my seam until I'm saying his name, begging him, "Sasha, please."

"Still begging," he teases.

The sigh that escapes my lips when he enters me with his fingers is otherworldly, and I can't be responsible for the sounds that escape my lips as he begins stroking me deeply inside while his palm slides along my clit with each thrust of his hand. Between the feel of his enormous cock along my ass, the miracle his fingers are working inside me, and the way he's gently pinching my nipple with his other hand, he's got me ready to orgasm in record time.

"I'm so close," I whisper, then want to cry when his hand

leaves my breast. But he uses it to push his shorts down his legs, then he's back with his bare skin against my ass.

Then he's moving again, and I'm having trouble deciding which I appreciate more: the way his long fingers can reach the parts of me that need his touch, or the way his rock-hard muscles are cradling my body from head to toe, making me feel protected and cherished. I consider myself pretty well versed in sex, and this still feels different somehow. More intimate, more meaningful. Less about getting off and more about the connection. I mean, this is the first time in years that I've spent more than one night with a man.

I'm wondering if the same is true for him, or if he's had successful short- or long-term relationships, when the pulsing deep in my core begins. It spreads, making my legs shake beneath me and my arms feel tingly. My breath comes in short inhaled gasps and long exhaled moans, and I don't even know what I'm saying, but words are tumbling out of my mouth.

When my muscles stop pulsing around his fingers, he pulls out and I hear the rip of a condom wrapper, but I'm too exhausted to even move. "When I saw you at the game tonight in my jersey, all I could picture was bending you over," he says, one hand coming to my hip and the other guiding my back down so my hands are resting on the cast iron table next to us. The jersey moves up my back as his lips trail kisses along my spine. "Even mid-game I wanted to be inside you," he says, his mouth next to my ear as his body cups mine. Between my legs, he rubs the hard, long length of himself along my slickness.

My hands rest on the table, still warm from the sun even though the air is turning cold this late at night. A shiver of anticipation runs through my body. "I live to make dreams come true," I say as I push my hips back into him.

His responding growl sends another shiver through my body as the realization that I can have this effect on him floods me. He pulls back and then he's stretching me open as he slips into me. I'm still sensitive from my orgasm and the feel of him sliding along the nerve endings inside me, dragging that magnificent cock along the slick walls of my core, has me keyed up way too fast.

Then he wraps his hand around my ponytail and he must stand because his chest is no longer pressed against my back. A tiny tug has my neck arching backward.

"Look at me."

I glance over my shoulder and am surprised at the possessiveness I see in his eyes as they scan my face and then travel down my body before returning to meet my eyes.

"You have no fucking idea what you do to me, Petra. Watching myself enter you like this—You . . . this . . . is even better than I always imagined."

I'm sure my eyes go wide at the word "always." *He pictured us together like this?* Is *that* what he meant last night when he said not seeing me like a little sister was half the problem?

"Everything about you," he says as he drags himself slowly in and out of me, stoking a fire right between my legs, "is exquisite. Everything. Your smart mouth, your drive and ambition, the fierce way you care about people, your protectiveness. And this body . . ."

He picks up the pace, his thrusts coming faster and harder and leaving me breathless in the best possible way. "Talk to me," he says. "What are you feeling?"

I'm too focused on his words, the feeling of his fingertips as they press into my hip, the way he's hitting that spot deep inside me exactly as I need him to hit it, the way his hand is still wrapped around my hair holding my head in place. It takes me a moment to find the right words. "I feel . . . over-whelmed . . . possessed. I feel like I want to do this as often as possible. Like this is what was always meant to be between us."

The last sentence has him grunting in agreement as he pounds into me, his movements forceful and gentle at the same time. Then he stops suddenly, pulling out right as I was starting to feel the first traces of my next orgasm.

"I want to see you," he says as he flips me over, lifting me up and laying me back on the table. "And I want you to see me too." He pushes back inside me, then reaches his hands inside the open neck of the jersey and cups my breasts before bringing them up so that the neckline of the shirt holds them in place like a push-up bra.

"You like that I'm wearing your number?"

"I normally avoid jersey chasers like the plague," he says. "But you in my jersey . . . it's the biggest fucking turn-on."

He hooks his hands under my knees, bringing them up to the sides of his chest. At this angle, he's so deep, and I'm stretched so wide from the thickness of him. His eyes are still on my breasts, so I bring my own hands up and cup them, rubbing my thumbs over my nipples. I see the heat in his eyes, those molten gray irises swimming with lust, his pupils so large they almost take over the irises. "You like it when I touch myself?"

"Hell yes," he grunts, his dark hair falling forward into his eyes as he looks down at me.

I bring one finger up to my mouth, swirl the tip of it with my tongue in the most suggestive way I can manage, then bring that finger down to where our bodies join together. I'm well on my way to another orgasm, but might as well help him out if he enjoys watching. A couple of swirls and flicks of my clit with my finger and my hips are moving to meet his in time with each push and drag.

"Shit, Petra," he grunts out. "You are so fucking sexy."

In response, I pinch my nipple with my other hand, and my eyes half close with the pleasure coming from so many parts of my body. I can feel my muscles clenching around him as the orgasm starts deep inside, but it's chased by a second orgasm from the feel of my finger on my clit, and experiencing both at the same time has me gasping and panting out expletives over and over as the waves of heat and sensation roll through me.

Sasha's eyes close tightly as he pushes into me with one final thrust, and feeling him pulsing against my inner walls sends me completely over the edge. I come apart with a sound that's half scream, half sigh, but he reaches down and covers my mouth, bending forward whispering, "This ends very differently if we wake Stella up."

I glance around, for the first time considering that she might be able to see us or hear us from her bedroom. But then I remember that her bedroom looks out onto the terrace, and from that angle it'd be impossible to see us in here.

"How does it end if we don't wake her up?" I ask as he pulls back to look at me.

He looks over his shoulder toward my bedroom door. "Let's find out."

———

When I wake up in the morning, everything is sore. My body feels like I spent last night doing gymnastics, which in a way I guess isn't far off. Sasha was asleep with his arms around me when I dozed off, and even though I know he wouldn't have wanted Stella to find us here together, it's still disappointing to wake up alone.

I roll over to find a note on my nightstand.

I am taking Stella to school—didn't want to wake you. Then I'm off to practice and a media event and will be home midafternoon. Text me if you have a busy day and want me to pick Stella up from school. Also, don't forget Tom and Avery are coming over for dinner tonight.

I glance up at the clock. *Shit!*

I fly out of bed so fast I almost levitate. I forgot to set my alarm last night, and I have a meeting in Brooklyn in half an hour to go over decorating the rooftop I've rented for Aleksandr's end of season party with the rental company that will be supplying the decor. Even if I walked out the door right now, which I can't do because I'm naked, there's no way I could make it there in time. I shoot off a text to the building manager and my contact at the rental company letting them know I'm going to be late, and asking them to start measuring the space and getting any other details they need while they wait for me to get there. Then I order a ride and give myself the ten minutes until they arrive to get dressed and ready, all the while reminding myself that it's not Aleksandr's fault I overslept.

———

When I walk back into the apartment at 6:30 p.m., I'm in a mood. It's been a long day, the kind where everything that could possibly go wrong has gone wrong.

"There you are," Aleksandr says, walking into the entryway as I'm setting my bag down on the large bench that sits against the wall. He takes one look at me, all sweaty and disheveled because I didn't check the weather and dressed way too warmly for this spring day, and asks, "What's wrong?"

I remind myself again that it's not his fault I overslept. I'm a big girl and can be responsible for setting my own alarm. But if he'd just woken me up before he left, this day would have been very different. Or if I just hadn't slept with him last night, I'd have woken up well-rested and ready to take on the world. The worry that's been running through my mind most of the day returns—was getting involved with him in this way a mistake?

"It's been a day."

His face softens. "Is there anything I can do to make it better?"

"Doubtful." I'm not pouting exactly, but I'm also glancing into my bag like I'm looking for something, so I don't have to meet his eye. I'm afraid he'd see right through me—through the bravado and the success—and find someone who's actually just barely holding it all together.

"How about if I make you a drink while you hop in the shower? Tom and Avery will be here in an hour."

I try not to physically deflate at the mention of having company tonight. I completely forgot, and I don't feel up to that at all, even though of course I'd love to see Avery again. I feel like she's the kind of person I could be friends with—real, unassuming, fun—if I were staying in New York. *But you're not*, I remind myself.

It's a well-timed reminder because Aleksandr wraps his arms around me, giving me the supportive hug he somehow knows I need. I rest my head on his shoulder, thinking how easy and natural things feel with him when we're not fighting. Though even the fighting feels like foreplay. And yet, this is all temporary. It has to be. I have a life and career back in Park City and a talk show that's supposed to start in LA soon. I can't stay, even if I wanted to.

But I don't, right?

"What's wrong?" I hear Stella's voice and open my eyes to see her standing behind Sasha.

"Nothing," I tell her, thinking that she must have seen my emotions flashing across my face. If I don't intentionally guard myself, my face shows everything I'm feeling. "I just had a bad day and needed a hug." I step back and Sasha's arms fall to his side, then I take a few steps past him toward Stella. "It helped, but maybe I need one from you too?"

She wraps her arms around my waist and squeezes as hard as she can, and I glance over my shoulder at Sasha. He's standing there with his hand on the back of his neck, his button-down shirt rolled up at his elbows and pulling tightly across his chest and shoulders, and another unreadable expression on his face.

I glance back down at Stella. "I have to go hop in the shower and get ready for dinner."

"Why do you have to get ready for dinner?" she asks.

"Because I had a rough day and feel gross, and I want to shower and start all over."

Her eyes light up like the thought never occurred to her that a shower could have the power to wash away a bad day and let you start fresh. "That's a good idea," she says. "Maybe I should take a shower and wash away my day too."

"You had a bad day?" I ask.

She nods and I take her hand. "Come tell me about it while I pick out something to wear tonight, then we'll both take our showers and wash the ickiness away, okay?"

We head down the hall together, hand in hand, and I let her tell me about all the things that went wrong in her day: she didn't get to sit next to Harper during circle time, she struggled with subtraction at one of her math stations, Jason got her out during dodgeball in PE, and their music teacher was sick so they had to watch a boring video with a substitute instead. I'm reminded of what I've heard so many parents say: *little people, little problems.* But they are big problems to her, and I'm glad this is the stuff she's focused on instead of worrying about things like how her uncle will manage to adopt her.

I've just stepped out of the shower with a towel wrapped around me when my phone buzzes rapid-fire on the counter. I pick it up to see several messages from Sierra. I do the math and realize it must be close to midnight in Europe, which is where I think she is right now.

SIERRA

> Beau was just catching up on the playoff games from the last few days. He paused during the New York/Philadelphia game and was like "Is that Petra?"

227

SIERRA

Imagine my surprise to see you at a game in New York, wearing a player's jersey and giving him fuck-me eyes on national television?!?!

SIERRA

What the hell is going on, and whose kid were you holding?

Oh shit. Well, this is going to be hard to explain.

PETRA

It is a REALLY long story and I can't explain right now because I am about to host dinner for two people I hardly know. Can we catch up about this in a few days? I'm back in Park City this weekend. Let's chat then.

SIERRA

You're seriously going to make me wait almost a whole week for answers?

PETRA

Sorry babe, but yes. I am still in NY and can't really talk about this while I'm here.

SIERRA

Wait! Still WHERE in NY? Like, you're not dating this guy, are you?

PETRA

No, definitely not dating him. I'll catch you up on all of this soon. Promise!

There is no way I can update Sierra on this without telling Jackson and Lauren, too, and I can only imagine that Jackson is going to be hurt I didn't tell her when I talked to her last week. And now she'll know that it wasn't work that kept me from seeing her when she was in Park City, it was staying here with and for Aleksandr. Oh shit, how much can I even tell them?

There's a knock on my bathroom door and it's cracked open. I throw my phone down on the counter as if I have something to feel guilty about.

"Okay if I come in?" Sasha's voice floods the room, and I swear I can feel it glide over my skin like a caress. I feel that familiar pull between my legs and have to remind myself that I spent most of the day thinking that sleeping with him was a mistake. *It's only going to make an already complicated situation that much more difficult.*

"Sure," I say.

He pushes the door open and reaches over to set a copper cup on the counter. "I made you a Moscow Mule. I hope you like those?"

"I like any drink that's not too sweet," I tell him.

His gaze flows over me, taking in my hair piled in a messy bun on top of my head, my makeup-free face, my bare shoulders, and the towel that's wrapped around me and tucked in between my breasts. His eyes are hungry, and I glance down to where his pants now look like they're too tight in the crotch. I look back up at him, smirking intentionally.

"I really want to take that towel off you and see how much fun we could have before Stella gets out of the shower," he tells me.

"Too risky," I say.

"It took her forever to pick out pajamas for tonight. She just got in the shower. We've got at least ten minutes."

I feel my nipples hardening against my towel.

"We don't have time," I say. "Tom and Avery will be here soon."

His look is both tender and possessive, like he wants to own me, but gently. "I bet we can manage it."

I know we shouldn't. It'll make things feel rushed before our company comes and it'll make things between us even more complicated than they already are. But my vagina isn't having any of my logic, it's literally seeping with desire and sending waves of longing through me.

"How quick can you be?" I ask.

He steps in and closes the door behind him, pushing the button to lock it. "I guess we'll find out."

When his lips land on my neck and my towel drops to the floor, the only thought running through my head is: *this is how all bad days should end.*

Chapter Seventeen

ALEKSANDR

"You fucking slept with her." It's not a question.

I glance up at Tom as he takes a sip of his whiskey, then toward the door to the den. It's closed, as is Stella's window, giving us some privacy on this terrace.

"What are you talking about?" I respond, my voice low.

"I can see it in the way you look at her with those stupid, gooey eyes. I recognize that look because I think I wore the same one every time I was around Avery after we first got together." He tugs at his loosened tie, and I remember how he did the same thing sitting in a bar in Midtown when he first told me about him and Avery.

I just shrug, neither confirming nor denying his assessment.

"I should have realized this would happen," he says. "It's the inevitable wrinkle in the plan. How did I not see it coming?"

I hold back the jokes about coming that spring to my mind. "I'm not saying I slept with her," I say, keeping my voice low so they don't hear us from inside, "but would it be so wrong if I had?"

"Yes!" His outburst is unexpected and so is the way his palm lands on the table, making the remaining glasses rattle. "Yes, it fucking would. You're trying to enter into a legal agreement with her, and sex screws everything up. It puts emotions into the equation, and that will mess shit up quick."

I don't have a response to that. There's no question that emotions are involved, at least for me, but they always have been. I'm less certain how she's feeling. I wanted her to tell me more last night in the solarium. I opened up about my feelings, told her I'd always wanted this kind of sexual relationship with her, and told her the things I loved about her. In response, she told me how good the sex was. It's not like I didn't want to hear that, but I was hoping for a bit more.

Perhaps expecting to have a meaningful conversation when I was balls deep inside her wasn't realistic, but the words about feelings flow more naturally when we're intimate. For me, at least. For Petra, it feels like she has one foot out the door when I want her here permanently.

"So, what are you going to do about it?" Tom asks when I don't respond.

"Do about what?"

"Are you planning on making this an actual marriage, rather than a marriage on paper only?"

The question makes my heart speed up. *Is that what I want?* I loved my single life. It allowed me to focus on skating, to become one of the best hockey players in the league. I made more money than I knew what to do with, there were always women around, and I had Niko and his family nearby. It was perfect. But something changed when I got

Stella. She's a type of happiness I didn't know I wanted, and having Petra here with us has made me think, for the first time ever, about how I want a family of my own. I don't want to just be the guardian of my niece. I want to adopt her, to be her father, and to share that responsibility with someone else. To have more kids. To have something worth coming home to.

But Petra's already told me that's not what she wants in life. She said she didn't want kids, and after watching her with Stella for the last two weeks, I don't understand how that could be true. I don't *believe* it could be true.

"I don't think that's what Petra wants," I tell Tom.

"You don't *think*? You haven't even talked to her about it?"

"I told you, you don't pressure a woman like her. She'll come to a decision in her own time."

"I found you an immigration attorney," Tom says, as if this attorney can save me from myself. Before he's even done with his statement, the door to the terrace opens. Petra steps out with Avery on her heels, and they cross over to the table in just a few steps. Petra has a bakery box in her hand with the dessert Avery and Tom brought.

"Stella is the cutest," Avery sighs as she sits down, which I guess means bedtime went well. She looks over at me. "You're doing a great job with her, Alex."

"I'm trying. But for all my work over the past few months," I say and glance over at Petra, "she's only really seemed happy the past couple weeks, since Petra's been here."

Her eyes widen before her face relaxes into a serene mask. "Don't let him fool you," she tells Avery, "she's amazing in her own right, and he's doing a great job raising her. The issue of finding a nanny, aside."

"Feels like there's a story there," Tom says, then takes another sip of whiskey. Petra regales him with the story of Irina, the evil Russian nanny who sounds even more like a witch when Petra retells it.

Avery alternates between laughing and looking horrified. "So, did you find someone new yet?"

"I've got several meetings set up this week," I tell her. "We're interviewing the first two tomorrow morning."

Petra looks surprised by this information, even though I'd watched her put the meetings into the calendar on her phone when I told her all the dates and times. I realize how much she must rely on her assistant to keep her schedule straight, set up meetings for her, and so on. I wonder what it would be like to be juggling so many balls at once. Before Stella, I had two balls: hockey, and all the shit—media appearances, brand relationships, etc.—that comes with it.

Petra opens the bakery box and hands each of us a small dessert plate. We all choose something, and then Petra says to Tom, "Did I hear you say you'd found us an immigration attorney?"

Tom glances at Avery. I'm guessing he doesn't normally discuss confidential client information with her. "It's fine," I tell him.

"Actually," Avery says, "I'm going to go use the restroom." She excuses herself and disappears through the door back into the den. I appreciate her discretion, even though I don't mind her knowing the details of our situation. If Tom trusts her, I trust her.

"Yes," Tom says once the door closes behind Avery. "She

specializes in both immigration and adoption law. I talked to her yesterday, explained the situation to her, and she's happy to take on your case. She said there are a few different options." He picks up his phone and asks for Petra's number. When he sets his phone down, both our phones buzz with a text from him containing the contact info for the lawyer.

Petra looks like she has questions, but she's chewing on her lower lip instead of asking them. "What are you thinking?" I ask her.

She pauses a beat before responding. "I'm not willing to lie about our marriage," she says apologetically. She turns toward Tom. "I'm not sure if you expect us to walk in there and tell her that we've been living together off and on like you'd suggested in your office, but I don't want to lie. I need us to be honest with her and let her tell us the best way to proceed."

Tom opens his mouth. "Done," I say, the word so definitive there's no point in him arguing with me about it. "Lying about this isn't worth the risk. I don't want to jeopardize my guardianship of Stella or my potential path to citizenship. Let's trust the process."

Tom shakes his head. "You're in for a much longer road this way," he tells us.

"That's fine," I tell him. "At least it's not unethical."

I notice the way his shoulders tighten at the mention of ethics. "Hey, you told me to figure out the *fastest* way for you to adopt Stella, and that's what I did. You didn't tell me to find the most ethical way."

"I know." And if Petra had been willing, maybe we'd be on that path. But now that I'm spending more time with her, I can't believe I ever hoped that she'd go along with his plan.

She's a lot of things, but a liar isn't one of them. "And I'm sure that was the only option for adopting her quickly. Now I guess we take the long but legal route."

He smiles wryly at that. "If you wanted the long but legal route, you should have just said so." He takes another sip of whiskey.

Under the table, Petra grabs my hand and squeezes. "We're thankful for your help, Tom. We know you were just doing what was best for Aleksandr and Stella."

He's saved from responding by Avery's reappearance. She sends Petra a questioning look, and Petra nods her head toward the table.

"Did I tell you I went to my first professional hockey game last night?" Petra asks Avery when she sits.

"No, but I saw you on TV."

"Wait, what?"

"Uh . . ." Avery stumbles, like she wishes she hadn't said anything. I remember Tom saying one of the things he found sexy about her was how adorable she was when she was flustered, and I see what he means. She gets this pale pink flush on her cheeks that blends with her freckles and she closes her eyes for a minute, which makes me realize how long her lashes are. I'm not trying to check out my friend's girl, especially not with Petra sitting next to me and holding my hand, but I do recognize what he was telling me months ago. "When you guys were staring at each other after Alex's goal in the third period?"

"I didn't think about the TV coverage," Petra says quietly, and her hand slackens in mine. In response, I hold on tighter and at least she doesn't pull away.

"It's typical for them to focus on the player who scored

the goal and the fan's reactions," I say. "It's my fault, because I should have realized that the cameras would all be on me, and then would turn to whoever I was focused on."

"Whatever," she shrugs and gives us a megawatt smile, the kind that I'd expect if we walked out of a restaurant to find the paparazzi waiting for us. I recognize it for what it is— her desire to move on and act like this doesn't bother her. But we'll be returning to this conversation later, whether she wants to or not. I'm not going to let one TV camera ruin what's building between us here.

"So, was the game as exciting in person as it was on TV?" Avery asks.

"It was. I hadn't watched hockey in almost fifteen years," Petra says, and this info is new to me. But it makes sense, given that she didn't know I was playing in New York. She would have had to be actively avoiding hockey to not know this.

"Like, hadn't watched it even on TV?" Avery scrunches up her eyebrows, obviously wondering how Petra hadn't ever watched the sport I play professionally.

"Yeah, I . . ." She pauses. "I was kind of anti-hockey for a while."

"Oh," Avery says, and even though she clearly wants to ask more questions, she glances at me and then changes the subject. "So, my friend Taryn and I are going out for drinks on Thursday night. Would you want to join us?"

"Oh," Petra says, disappointment tinging her voice. "I'd love to, but I can't. Aleksandr's in Philly still, that'll be game 5. I'll be here watching it with Stella."

I weigh the fact that Petra sounds like she does want to see Avery again before I open my mouth. Hopefully that wasn't Petra trying to bow out of plans gracefully, because if so, this is going to piss her off. "You guys could always meet here. Plenty of drink options and you can watch the game together."

"I love that idea!" Petra says. "If you want to," she adds quickly, glancing at Avery.

"Of course I want to. That sounds perfect."

"Great, I might invite my friend Emily too," Petra adds.

On the promise of future plans, Tom says they need to get going. He mentions an early morning meeting, but I'm not fooled for a second because I recognize the way he's looking at Avery. It's exactly the way I'm looking at Petra—like I can't wait to get her naked and on her back.

———

"I do have my own place in the Village, so I wouldn't need to live here full time," the second nanny we're interviewing this morning says after we finish giving her the tour. So far, the interview's gone very well. I can tell by her body language that Petra thinks this girl is *the one*. With the first candidate, we didn't even bother showing her around because it was obvious we weren't going to hire her. "I'm happy to stay here overnight whenever necessary, but I do find that it's also good for everyone to have their own space."

I consider what she's saying. "That's great," I agree. Natasha was such a godsend those first few months Stella was with me, and I don't think I could have done the parenting thing without her. But Stella and I are settling into a routine now and it would probably be awkward to have a nanny here when I didn't need her. And even though what

I'll be paying her could warrant a 24/7 work schedule, I know that's not a healthy expectation either. "I'm just at the beginning of the playoffs now, and God willing, I'll be playing for another month or more. But then, summer should actually be much lighter in terms of how often I need you. Things will pick up dramatically when the season starts up again, but I generally have the schedule well in advance so we can see all the time I'll need you here late for home games, or for a few days and nights when we are traveling. Depending on the schedule, sometimes we're on the road for a week or more at a time. Will that work okay?"

She nods. "It will."

"Discretion is critical," Petra says. "That NDA you signed when you arrived is in place because Aleksandr is very private and Stella is still adjusting to this living situation, and it's essential that her new normal not be upset. Can you truly handle not telling anyone—your roommates, your family— who you are nannying for?"

"I don't have roommates or a family, and I can definitely avoid telling my friends."

I watch the way Petra's eyebrows knit together. "I'm not trying to pry," she says. "But if you're going to have such close access to this family, I do need to know what your situation is? How does a young woman like you live in the Village without roommates? And do you really not have any family?"

Raina, the potential nanny in question, steels her shoulders as she opens her mouth to respond. "My parents died in a plane crash in Alaska when I was a teenager, so I moved in with my aunt, who had a brownstone in the Village that she'd inherited when their parents passed. It had been in my dad's family for generations. My mom was an only child and her parents had already died by then, so it was literally just me and my aunt. She passed away from cancer a year ago. The reason I never finished at Columbia was because she got sick my junior year, and I had to take a leave of absence my senior year to take care of her."

Petra looks at me, her eyes wide, then looks back at the girl. "Will you excuse us for a minute?"

She nods, looking nervous, like she's said too much even though all she did was give us the honest answer to Petra's somewhat invasive question.

Petra stands and I follow her to the living room and then out to the entry.

"Hire her." The words are out of her mouth in a whispered, frantic plea the minute we're out of earshot.

"Without checking her references?" I ask. This seems very unlike Petra.

"Of course I want you to check her references." She uses her hand to sweep the air like she's shooing away that ridiculous notion. "But as long as they check out, this is our girl."

God, I love the way she's been using "we" during the interview and is saying "our" right now. But I need to not focus on that, because when we woke up this morning she had a text from her assistant about her flight home on Sunday. I need to accept that she's leaving. I need to prepare Stella. And then I need to figure out how to get her back here as soon, and for as long, as possible.

"What makes you so sure this is the one?"

"She's so chill. Like I could see her taking everything in stride—Stella's huge personality, your very public career, the erratic schedule. And most importantly, the fact that she lost her parents when she was younger means she will have

240

empathy for what Stella's gone through, unlike Irina." A shudder runs through Petra at the mention of the almost-nanny.

"I think she'll be fine," I say.

"That's it?" Her whisper makes it sound like she's hissing this question at me. Is my agreeing with her pissing her off?

"I agree with what you're saying about why she's a good fit." I shrug. "And I could see her here in our lives. I feel like she'd be very easy to get along with and not, I don't know, not take up too much space, you know?"

Her eyes narrow. "What do you mean by 'not take up too much space'?"

I'm not sure why this is the wrong thing to have said, but I can tell by her response that it is. "I . . ." I pause, considering my words. "I feel like Irina would have inserted herself into everything, insisting that her way was the only way. It would have been like living with a tyrant. Raina seems like the exact opposite. Like she'll be flexible and easy to be around, but firm enough with Stella when needed. I'm not worried that if I'm home while she's here with Stella, that she'll be trying to nanny me too."

Petra swallows. "Okay."

"Why, what did you think I was saying?"

"I don't know," she says, looking off down the hallway behind me. I hate it when she won't meet my eye. "I'm just sensitive to the idea that women 'shouldn't take up too much space.' That phrase is used often to try and keep women in small boxes so their successes don't threaten men."

I put my hands on her shoulders and wait until she looks up at me. "You do know that's not what I meant, right?"

"I do now," she says. "Let's not keep Raina waiting."

With that, she steps away and walks past me. Then she turns around quickly. "But when you offer her the job, can you make it contingent on her finishing up at Columbia? Stella is in school for six hours a day. She should at least be able to take some classes, even if not a full load. That degree is the key for her future, so she has options."

It occurs to me then that I don't think Petra ever went to college, and I wonder if she's somehow insecure about that fact. "Okay, but I didn't go to college," I remind her.

"You're a professional athlete." She rolls her eyes. "Your career wasn't dependent on it, and you're set for the future with what you've earned so far." She's not wrong.

"What about you?" I ask.

"I supported myself with skiing and the endorsements that came along with it, and then modeled when skiing was over. I saved enough money from modeling to start my own business. Most people don't have that luxury either."

I want to ask her so many questions about how she got where she is, about her father, and if he got to see her successes before he died, about where she's going from here. But she turns and walks back into the living room and I have no choice but to follow her.

"Thanks for your patience," Petra says to Raina when we each take our seats.

"Of course," she says.

Petra gives me a pointed look.

"We'd like to offer you the job," I start. "As long as your references check out. I can make the calls this morning."

"Thank you so much," she gushes, the excitement evident in her voice.

"There are a couple conditions though, so I want to make sure you're okay with them before I start making calls."

She gives a definitive nod and says "Okay," but her face drains of color. *What the hell does she think I'm going to suggest?*

"First, the NDA is essential. Stella's privacy is of the utmost importance. When you leave here, I'm sure you'll spend some time Googling me and seeing what you can find out." Her face flushes a bit when I say this, and I realize that she's probably already done this. "What you won't find," I continue, "is any mention of me being the guardian of my niece. For a variety of reasons, I want that kept as quiet as possible."

"Of course," she says.

"The other condition," I say, hoping she'll agree, "is that as long as you're working for me, you need to be working toward finishing that degree at Columbia."

She gets this hopeful, excited look before her face falls. "I don't think I can afford to do that," she says.

That hadn't occurred to me.

"Why not?"

"I got a scholarship to Columbia," she says, looking at the floor. "But when I looked into going back after my aunt passed away, they wouldn't finance any of my education because I now own this really valuable property in the Village. But it's been in my family for generations, I can't sell it. The financial aid officer at Columbia suggested I take out a reverse mortgage to pay for school, but how would I pay that back while also going to school? The property taxes alone take up a huge part of my salary."

"What about student loans?" I ask.

"That's really the only feasible option, since I wouldn't have to start paying them while I'm in school. But I did the math. Between the student loans and the property taxes, that would give me almost nothing to live on once I graduated. My major is child psychology. It's not exactly leading to a lucrative career path, at least not right away."

"You're making some really tough, but really smart, financial decisions right now," Petra says, and I realize that this is exactly the kind of math she's probably done her entire life. Especially when she was saving to pay my father back for that loan for school, not knowing that it was something that would never need to be repaid. I realize how much I have not once missed that money, how investing in someone else's future made me feel better than the money sitting in an investment account, growing me more money, ever could.

"I'll pay for the classes."

Petra's head snaps toward me and Raina sucks in a sharp breath. "Why would you do that?" Raina asks, the skepticism clear in her voice and the pinched look on her face.

"Because Petra pointed out that without your degree, your future options are limited. And because I can. Because I won't even miss that money. It'll do far more good this way."

Raina's mouth drops open. "How would I ever pay you back?"

"Just take good care of my kid," I tell her. "Be firm enough that she doesn't grow into a spoiled brat, and kind enough that she feels loved. Be there for her when I can't. And as long as you're working for me, I'll pay for you to take as many classes as you can reasonably manage each semester."

Raina's eyes are glassy with unshed tears.

"Say yes," Petra stage-whispers to her with a laugh.

"Okay," Raina says slowly. "Yes."

I stand and hold my hand out to her, and she stands to take it. We shake on it. "I'll call your references right away. I have to leave for Philadelphia in"—I glance at my watch—"a few hours. I'll have my lawyer email you a contract this afternoon."

"Thank you so much," she says. "I feel like you both have just changed my life."

"It's going to be so worth it," Petra says, "because I can already tell you are going to be good for Stella, and I'm glad you'll get more out of this than just a paycheck. I can't wait to see you graduate."

There's warmth spreading through my chest. It's a hot lump that grows in a way that's almost painful, but also amazing. Is it pride at being able to help Raina achieve her dreams, while she's here helping to raise Stella so I can achieve mine? Is it hope at the way Petra talks about seeing a graduation that's at least a couple years down the road? Is it admiration for the way Petra suggested something I never would have thought of and made such a huge difference in this girl's life?

I can't describe this feeling because I'm not sure I've ever felt it before. But it feels like my life is finally coming together like it was always supposed to.

———

Two hours later, I've finished up with my phone calls and Avery has assured me she'll have Tom's paralegal draft the contract and have Tom sign it today.

"It'll be in Raina's inbox before I leave the office tonight,"

Avery says. I can tell she senses I'm worried this won't happen quickly enough. "Okay?"

"Thanks, Avery."

"Anytime. Bye."

Knowing this is locked down, and being able to cancel the remaining interviews on Friday when I'm back, will give me such peace of mind. I want to know this search is over and that Stella will be well cared for once Petra leaves. That thought is a rock in the pit of my stomach. I know it's reality—she has a business to get back to. She has other events besides the one she's planning for me, and I'm sure planning them from afar like this is more difficult. I know she has friends and a life in Park City. But I want her life to be here, in New York, with us.

I stop my pacing when that reality hits me. I've known that I want Petra to stay since the minute I kissed her. Probably even before that. But that was selfish me, wanting to be close to her, wanting to be able to touch her and taste her any time I wanted. Wanting Stella to be able to keep looking at Petra with that adoration she so clearly has for my ex-best friend, now current lover.

But this reality is different. This feeling is different. I want her to stay for good. To see if we can make this marriage more than just a slip of paper. I can envision us here, together, with Stella and with more kids if Petra's willing, and with a happiness I never dared hope for. Until now.

I can hear the low rumble of her voice out in the solarium, which she's been using as her office during the day while Stella's in school. I head over to the glass doors that lead from my bedroom out there, and quietly pull one open so that I'll be able to hear when she's done with her call.

I glance at my watch. *Shit.* I have five minutes until I need to be downstairs where Daniel will be waiting to load my suitcases into the car and drive me to our training facility, then we'll head down to Philly on our team bus. I definitely don't want to interrupt Petra, but I want to talk to her before I go. I want to let her know that everything's a go with Raina, and also tell her how I'm feeling about our future. I want to plant the idea like a seed that can grow when it's ready.

"No"—Petra's voice is firm—"there's no way I can be in LA by the end of this week. Late next week, probably."

What the hell?

She laughs and that throaty, sensual sound rolls over me like it always does, springing to life a small flame of desire. "You don't *need* me, Charlie, you *want* me. There's a difference."

The hairs on the back of my neck stand up as a chill moves down my spine. *Who the fuck is Charlie?*

There's a pause as she listens to the response and then a low, disapproving "Hmm" rattles around in her mouth. "I've already given you my answer." Another pause and then, "No, I haven't found a place yet." *A place in LA?* "I saw a promising little house online, but I want to go see it when I get there." She laughs at whatever this asshole Charlie says. "Well, obviously, I want to be as close to you as humanly possible."

Another chill moves down my spine. Have I really been this blind, thinking that just because we have this history and we're having amazing sex and she's great with my kid, that it means she'd want to stay? Are my feelings really this entirely one-sided? And this whole time she's been seeing someone else? Is she moving to Los Angeles to be with him?

I don't know her at all.

She mumbles a low, "Of course." Like everything she says, it sounds sexy.

I shut the door as silently as I opened it, take a few quick steps across my bedroom, grab my suitcase, and head downstairs. I need to get out of here, to think about what I just overheard and to figure out what it means. And I need to be away from Petra to do that.

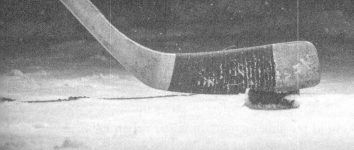

Chapter Eighteen

PETRA

The interview with Raina ran a little longer than planned thanks to my and Sasha's side conversation and the negotiation about Raina's college plans. I've literally never been more proud of anyone than I was of him for the way he handled that. So many people's opportunities are limited by the cost of the education they need in order to achieve financial independence. I hardly know Raina, but I already want to make sure that she has every opportunity in the world, especially if she's going to give the next year or more of her life to caring for Stella.

In any event, now I'm late for my meeting with my producer, Charley. She's not going to be happy about that, but at least I texted her assistant asking for her to call me ten minutes later than planned, and got a clipped *OK*. But I manage to make it to the solarium before my phone is ringing.

"Hello?"

"Petra, this is Annabeth. I'm putting Charley through."

"Okay, thanks."

Silence, then, "Thanks for making me wait, bitch."

Charley laughs. She's tough as nails, but I know I'm going to like working with her.

"Sorry, something really important came up."

"What could possibly be more important than talking to your first and favorite producer?"

"Ugh," I stall. "Something personal."

"If this show goes well, you're about to be a household name." That promise sends a shudder through me. I don't want the notoriety, I just want to be able to help women tell their stories, to inspire other women to persevere when they feel like giving up. I want to live my feminist beliefs in a way that helps other women take control of their own lives. It's a big dream, and this show is about to help me achieve it. "And if that happens, there won't be a separation between your personal and private life."

"Are you trying to talk me out of this, Charley?" I tease. "Because if so, it's working." She knows how on the fence I was about doing the show. She's the one who pulled me over to her side, fought with me tooth and nail until I agreed. She's been my biggest cheerleader and also a staunch realist about how my life is about to change.

I'd accepted these changes, and I was okay with them. And then Sasha had to walk back into my life, along with the sweetest little six-year-old, and now they've both wormed their way into my heart. I'd thought it was well-protected, that I'd hardened myself off to actually loving someone other than my best friends. And never in a million years did I think I'd be able to trust Sasha again after the way he left me when we were younger. It had taken years to recover from that, and then a series of other men tried to break me like he had, and it was enough for me to swear off ever caring for a man again.

Use them for what I needed, and get rid of them—that plan had worked so well for me until he showed up again.

"I'm just trying to prepare you for the reality of how things might change for you," she tells me. "I know you like your privacy, but that's going to be harder to maintain. It'll be more like when you were modeling, except we're not selling your body. We're selling your brain, your personality, your life experience. And people are going to pay attention, Petra. I can just feel it. This show is going to be great."

I take a deep breath, pushing back the trepidation that's rising to the surface. I've already agreed to this. Signed a contract. This is what I wanted. *Why does it feel so wrong now?*

I wonder for a moment if I should tell her about Sasha and Stella. Does she need to know that I'm legally married? If we're able to move ahead and find him a path to adopting Stella, and it somehow gets out in the news, she'll be furious that I didn't tell her.

Not yet, I decide. I'll wait until we meet with the immigration lawyer and I have more info.

"Why aren't you saying anything?" she asks.

"Sorry, just lost in my own thoughts," I say. "This is all a lot to process."

"Petra, you've had over a month to process this. Has something changed?"

Everything's changed. "No."

"Okay, good. Listen, I really need you here this week. The studio wants to film some promo stuff and there's an opening on Friday. So get your ass down here."

"No," I say, my voice firm. Obviously, there's no way I can leave New York this week. Sasha isn't even back from

Philadelphia until the end of the week, and I'm booked on a flight back to Park City Sunday afternoon. "There's no way I can be in LA by the end of this week. Late next week, probably."

"Petra, I *need* you here this week." She's not asking.

"You don't *need* me, Charley, you *want* me. There's a difference." I'm not under contract yet, so she can't force me to come to LA early.

"The sooner we get the promo material filmed, the sooner we can start advertising."

I'm sure that's an important aspect of the show's success, but there's no way I can be in LA this week and she's just going to have to accept that. I let a disapproving "Hmm" come out, then tell her, "I've already given you my answer."

"I'm starting to get worried about your level of commitment. Have you at least signed a lease down here?"

"No, I haven't found a place yet," I tell her. That's on the agenda for next weekend when I'm down there. "I saw a promising little house online, but I want to go see it when I get there."

"Just make sure it's close to the studio."

I laugh. "Well, obviously, I want to be as close to you as humanly possible."

"Just get your ass down here and nail down a lease, and I'll feel much better about all this. I'll be able to stop worrying that you're actually a flight risk. I hope you know how much I've stuck my neck out for you to make this happen. I *know* you're the right person for this show. Now we just need to show those stuffy execs that I'm not wrong about you."

Why does it feel so wrong to be doing something so right? This show is the right choice, I know it is. I'd hemmed and hawed about it when deciding, but once I commit to something, I'm all in. That's why I have been completely upfront with Sasha about not being able to stay in New York—I know it's impossible. But now I'm extremely torn. I'm starting to wish I hadn't committed to this show. Because if this commitment didn't exist, I might want to stay in New York a bit longer, to see if what's developing between Sasha and me now, as adults, is real and worth fighting for.

"You are still in, right?" Charley asks when my thoughts have kept me silent for too long.

"Of course," I say. The words come out with far more certainty than I feel.

"Good. Please don't prove me wrong here, Petra. You are going to be amazing. I'm not sure why you still seem so unsure."

"I have never liked being in the public eye," I admit.

"You were an Olympic skier and then a model. You literally lived in the public eye for like ten years."

She says this like I need the reminder. "I know, and it wasn't good for me."

"What do you mean?"

It already feels like I've said too much, and I don't even know where to start my explanation. "Nothing. I was younger then, and the attention was all too much."

"Well, you are older and wiser now. You'll be fabulous."

"I already am fabulous."

This gets me the laugh I was expecting, breaking the tension of the moment.

"That you are," she agrees.

I glance at the time on my clock, realizing Sasha needs to leave any minute and I don't want to miss saying goodbye. "I have to run. I'll see you in LA in a little over a week," I tell her. "Right on schedule."

I walk over to the wall of glass that leads from the solarium into Sasha's room, but he doesn't appear to be in there. I open the door and call his name to be sure, but there's no response. So I walk through his room and down the hallway to the entryway, expecting that maybe his suitcase will be there and he's puttering around somewhere waiting for me to get off the phone so he can say goodbye.

Nothing.

I wander into the living room and through to the sitting room, and still no sign of him. I head back through the living room to the dining room and into the kitchen. He's nowhere to be found. There's no indication that he's still here.

What the hell? He left without even saying goodbye? Without telling me whether we'll have the contract ready for Raina today? Without even leaving a note?

I go through to the solarium and find my phone where I left it on the table, and I don't have any missed calls or texts from him, and now I'm getting angry because it's a lot easier than admitting to myself how hurt I am. I shoot off a text to him.

PETRA

> You left without saying goodbye?

I respond to some emails and prep for a meeting with Morgan that's supposed to start in twenty minutes. And when I sit down for that meeting, I still have no response from Aleksandr. I know he's in the car on his way to the airport, so there's no reason he wouldn't see the text.

Maybe he's on a phone call and can't respond. Be patient.

Patience has never been a specialty of mine.

————

"**D**on't you like the burritos?" Stella asks.

I take a look at my half-eaten dinner and then give her a small smile. "I do, I'm just not very hungry." We'd made dinner together, and I can tell she's worried that I don't think she did a good job. "But I'm going to save the rest of my burrito for later, because I think this is one of the best I've ever had."

She beams. "I didn't know I liked guacamole, but you're right, it makes burritos even better." She looks at me like I'm some sort of all-knowing food goddess.

"My best friend, Jackson, is a taco guru," I tell her. "I've learned a lot about Mexican food from her."

"What's a guru?"

"It's someone who's an expert on something, someone you can learn from."

"Are you a guru too?"

I try not to laugh at the question, which is asked so innocently. "No, I don't think so."

"There's nothing you're an expert on?"

I'm certainly no relationship guru. I think about the fact that Aleksandr still hasn't replied to my text or returned my call after I left him a voice mail earlier this afternoon. I thought we had something, that we were building something. Here I was thinking how much I didn't want to go to LA because I just wanted to stay here with him and Stella, and obviously that was very one-sided.

"Well, I'm kind of an expert on event planning." My shoulder ticks up in a small shrug.

"What's that?" she asks through the huge bite she just took of her burrito, food threatening to fall out of her mouth.

"My job is to plan big events, like parties and weddings and retreats. People hire me to organize all the details and make sure that the event is a success."

"Is it fun?"

"Sometimes. But the point of work isn't that it's fun, it's that it's fulfilling."

"What's fuf-filling?"

"If something is fulfilling, it means that you're using your talents in a way that helps other people and also makes you happy. For me, getting to plan these kinds of events makes me feel that way."

"Are you a guru in anything else?"

I think about the show I'm about to start filming. "Well, I'm also really good at talking to people. At getting to under-stand their story, and when necessary, giving them advice to help them." My friends have always come to me for advice because I don't hold back or sugarcoat it. That may not be everyone's preferred method of "help," but they know that they are getting honest feedback.

"I think you're really good at helping people," Stella says.

For some reason, this makes me feel worse instead of better. Yes, I've helped her. I made sure she didn't get the evil Irina as a nanny, and I even gave up two weeks of my life to stay here with her (though that hasn't exactly felt like a sacri-fice). I made sure that little asshole Jason stopped tormenting her at school by teaching her how to stand up for herself, and

I helped find her a new nanny who I'm sure she's going to love. But . . .

But what? You've done more to help this little girl than anyone could reasonably expect.

But I haven't figured out a solution to help Aleksandr adopt her. I know we're supposed to meet with the lawyer Friday afternoon after he's back from Philadelphia, and I'm really hoping she has some ideas.

"And I think you've helped *Dyadya* more than anyone else," she continues.

This has my head snapping up to look at her across the table. "What do you mean?"

"He never smiled until you started staying with us," she shrugs. "I think you make him happy. He likes having you here and so do I," she beams at me.

I smile at her and mumble "Thanks," though my stomach is twisting itself into a knot around the small amount of dinner I've consumed. I want to believe I make him happy and if she'd said this yesterday or even this morning, I'd have agreed. But I don't know what to make of this nearly full-day of silence or the eerie feeling that I'm watching him cut me out of his life like he did so many years ago. It feels like history repeating itself, except now we have the kind of relationship I'd always dreamed we would—I was starting to see us as partners, which is what I thought he wanted, and the sex was amazing too.

"Are you finished eating?" I ask, nodding at the skeletal remains of a burrito on her plate.

"I'm too full to finish."

"Okay, why don't you go take your shower and get your PJ's on so we can watch the game. I'll clean up."

"Can we wear our jerseys like when we went to the game?"

"Sure, just wear it over your pajamas."

"And you'll wear yours too?"

"Uh huh." I can't say no to her request, even though right now putting his last name across my back feels a whole lot different than it did on Sunday night.

Half an hour later, we're watching the pregame show when Stella asks me to take a picture of us. We pose for a selfie together and when I look at the resulting photo, I'm shocked at how much we look alike. The same dark brown curly hair, the same ivory skin and high cheekbones, the same shaped eyes, though hers are brown where mine are blue.

"Will you send that to *Dyadya*?" she asks. "I want him to print it out so I can have it in my room."

"Sure," I say, noncommittally, because there's no way I'm texting him a photo of us right before the game starts, especially when he seems to have been avoiding me all day. How desperate would that seem?

"Let's send it now," she says.

"He won't have his phone on him," I tell her. "He's already warming up, see?" I point to the screen where, behind the commentators, you can see the hockey players going through their warm-up drills like miniature figures skating across the ice.

"But if we send it to him now, he'll see it right after the game," she says.

Yes, exactly what I don't want to happen.

"Here," she holds out her hand. "Will you show me how to send a photo?" Her big brown eyes are huge and pleading. "I know it will make him smile when he sees it."

I'm very afraid that she's wrong about that, but there's no way to tell her no without giving her a reason, and I don't have one I can share with her. She has Aleksandr's best interests at heart, and she just wants him to have a little piece of "home" while he's on the road.

As I hand her the phone and show her how to send the picture, it dawns on me that even though I'm the adult, I am absolutely not in control in this situation. Stella is one hundred percent running this show.

Chapter Nineteen

PETRA

ALEKSANDR

WTF is with that photo?

PETRA

What do you mean?

I wait for his response, but it doesn't come. The bubble appears to show that he's typing, then disappears again. Multiple times. I wait. And wait.

This whole day has felt juvenile beyond measure. Leaving without saying goodbye, then ignoring my texts? I knew he wouldn't call to say goodnight to Stella because of the game. But for both of his away games last week, he at least texted me midday with a video he'd filmed to say goodnight, so I was able to show it to her before bedtime. Today, nothing. And now he's upset that she wanted to send him a picture to make him happy? I'm pissed off on her behalf, in addition to being mad about how he's ignored me.

I hit the button on screen to call him, and I'm surprised when he picks up on the first ring.

"What?"

The one-word greeting further inflames my temper. "What the hell is going on, Aleksandr?"

"Why don't you tell me," he says. The cool, indifferent tone that carries across the phone surprises me.

"I don't even know what you're talking about, much less why you're upset."

"What makes you think I'm upset?" His voice couldn't be flatter, more devoid of emotion, if he were a robot.

"Besides the fact that you left without saying goodbye, ignored my messages today, and didn't even send Stella a goodnight message?" Not to mention his WTF response to the photo of Stella and me.

He pauses for a beat. "I forgot about the goodnight message for Stella. Today was really busy."

"Fair enough. But why are you ignoring me?" I hate that I have to ask this question. It feels childish, as though we're still teenagers who haven't figured out how to communicate with each other, instead of adults in a sexual relationship. Part of the reason I never sleep with anyone more than once is so I don't have to partake in these cat and mouse games.

"Why don't you ask Charlie?"

Now it's my turn to pause. "How do you know about Charley?"

"Accidentally overheard you on the phone with him before I left."

Several things click into place with the use of that pronoun. "Aleksandr, Charley is a woman."

I can hear his breath hitch and can envision his eyebrows dipping as he works through this new piece of information. "Wait, you're in another relationship with a *woman*?"

I can't help the laugh that escapes my lips. "A professional one, yes."

"Please explain." The words are flat, a demand instead of a request.

I consider that my contract prohibits me from sharing details of the show with anyone but immediate family. I shared that information with Jackson because she's essentially a sister to me, rationalizing that she'd be the only one that I'd tell. But Aleksandr is actually the only person my contract would technically permit me to tell about this, because we're legally married.

"I really wish we were having this conversation in person," I say, shifting to set my laptop on the bed next to me so I can lean further back into the pillows, letting them engulf me when I wish I was in his arms instead.

No response, just the sound of his breathing.

"I need to emphasize that everything I'm telling you right now is completely confidential. The only reason I'm able to even tell you is because we're married."

"Noted," he says.

"I need you to tell me that you will keep this information to yourself and not tell a single other person."

"What if it's something the lawyer we're meeting with this week needs to know?" he asks.

"She will need to know, and we'll tell her."

A small grunt escapes on the other end of the phone. "So this is relevant to me adopting Stella, then. When were you going to share this with me?"

I probably should have already told him, but I'd been so wrapped up in how things were changing between us, trying to figure out what our evolving relationship meant, that I didn't want to throw something else into the mix. He knew I was leaving, what difference did it make if it were for this show or for the business I'd been painstakingly growing for the past few years?

"I would have told you before we met with the lawyer," I assure him.

"Okay, so?" he prompts.

"I'm moving to LA. I'm going to be hosting a show, like a *60 Minutes*-type talk show that interviews women who have overcome great obstacles to redefine success in their field. It's called *And Yet We Rise* and we start filming in two weeks. This morning I was on the phone with my producer, Charley, finalizing some details about the start of the show."

There's a pause on his end as I imagine he needs a moment to absorb this information.

"Is this why you've been so insistent that you can't stay?"

"Yes."

"So, where does that leave us?" He sounds like he's just lost something he worked his whole life for. Totally defeated. Which is ridiculous, because we've been sleeping together for less than a week. And before that, we hadn't seen each other in fourteen years.

"I don't know. I've worked my whole life for an opportunity like this." Everything I do is about lifting up and empowering women—from the friends I keep, to the women I hire, to the types of events I plan. "This is my chance to really promote female voices, to help show young girls that women can overcome any obstacle, achieve anything they set their mind to. I want that kind of a show to exist in this world. I want something that women can watch with their daughters. Something that doesn't focus on all the misogyny, but instead focuses on the beauty of the female experience."

My phone buzzes in my hand as I speak, and Aleksandr's name flashes across the screen with a video call.

"I needed to see you," he says when I answer. He's sitting in a chair in a hotel room, beige curtains hanging behind him. His thick, dark hair is wet and a few pieces curl down into his face. "There was so much passion in your voice just now. I need to know what you look like when you're talking about something you're so committed to."

I glance at my video in the corner of the screen. I'm in a T-shirt, no makeup, and my hair is clipped back so it would stay out of my face when I was working. I watch a faint pink flush infiltrate my cheeks. I don't fucking blush. What the hell is this?

"Sometimes I get a bit carried away."

"Never apologize for your dreams, Petra," he says. "And definitely don't keep them a secret. Dreams are for sharing, for chasing, for achieving."

"I'm a little surprised you're being so supportive," I tell him.

"Why is that?" he asks, and even through the phone I can tell his eyes are searching my face, trying to understand me.

"Because it means I can't stay in New York and help you with Stella. This makes everything harder for you."

"What kind of a selfish bastard would I be if I tried to crush your dreams to achieve my own ends?"

I don't know what's happening to me. My whole body feels like it's melting from the inside out, like my heart has exploded and is oozing lava through my veins, disintegrating me from within. I expect that my skin will turn to ash at any minute, but it doesn't. It's just covered with a thin coat of sweat.

"You aren't saying anything," he murmurs.

I want to kiss his face, to hold it in my hands and run my lips over his forehead, his eyes, his nose, and his cheeks, ending with his mouth.

"I'm not sure . . ." I trail off, trying to find the right words, "that I've ever felt so *seen*."

"Are you crying?"

"No," I say, noting how watery my eyes are. I don't cry. Especially not over a man. But those words were the most honest, most touching thing anyone has ever said to me. "I just didn't expect you to be so supportive."

"I know what it's like to have dreams you've worked your whole life for."

"Did you ever believe you'd be this successful?" I ask.

"I always believed it, which is why it happened."

I love that he doesn't fake humility. He doesn't say "I got lucky" or some bullshit like that. He's worked hard for everything he's achieved, and I'm glad he's owning it.

"What about you?" he asks.

"I feel like my life has been me constantly reinventing myself, going from skiing, to modeling, to event planning, and now hosting this show. None of those things seem to have anything to do with the other, but I've let the things I'm passionate about dictate my path. I've worked hard for every one of those opportunities, networked my ass off to meet the right people and to be the right person in return. But the show did kind of fall into my lap." I explain how I met Charley and how she hounded me until I agreed to audition.

"Did it fall into your lap? Or did all that networking finally pay off?"

"A bit of both, I guess." I shrug.

"Don't do that," he says, his voice soft. "Don't act like you don't deserve this opportunity."

I'm not sure I do. "I'm having a bit of impostor syndrome is all. I feel like this is the kind of role that should go to someone more experienced, and I'm still not entirely sure why Charley wants *me.*" It feels good to voice what I've been keeping in my head all along. I'd never admit to anyone else that I'm scared.

"She obviously sees something in you and knows you're right for this role. Trust her experience. Trust the process and don't sell yourself short. Yeah, you've never done this before. But you'd never skied competitively, or modeled, or planned a huge event—until you did. Everyone starts somewhere, Petra."

I marvel at how his eyes have turned to a soft gray, how wrinkles appear at the corners when he looks at me like this. It's not the look of desire I've seen so often recently, or the look of fond affection he gives Stella. If I had to describe it, I'd say it was pride. And for some reason, it makes me deeply uncomfortable.

"Hold on," I say as I set the phone down and take my sweatshirt off. Heat is running through me again, this time from embarrassment.

When I pick up the phone again, his eyes slide up and down the phone screen. He takes in the spaghetti straps of my camisole. "Oh, are we at the taking-our-clothes-off part of the conversation?" His eyes crinkle in the corners as he holds in his smile.

"I mean, we *could* be," I tease, running a finger under one of the straps of my cami.

"I like that idea, a lot," he says, as he reaches behind his neck and pulls his shirt over his head. The phone is jostled as he switches it to his other hand to get the shirt off his other arm. "So, how does this work?"

"How does what work?"

"Phone sex. I've never done this before."

I love the combination of amusement and vulnerability in his voice.

"Me either." By the look on his face, my response surprises him. "I guess we'll figure it out together."

———

"H oly crap, Petra," Avery whispers when the kitchen door closes behind us. "A warning would have been nice. You know, something like 'By the way, my friend Emily is a *supermodel.*'"

I glance up at her and there's a bit of panic in her eyes.

"I'm sorry, it didn't even occur to me," I say as I hand her the tray with the glasses before grabbing the pitcher of margaritas off the counter.

"It's already awkward enough to be in Alex Ivanov's house watching him play hockey on TV. But hanging out with a supermodel too? That's next-level."

"First of all, Aleksandr's just a normal guy whose job it is to play hockey. You've known him long enough that you shouldn't feel awkward around him."

"Petra, in case you haven't noticed, I'm kind of an awkward person."

I take in her freckles and the big brown eyes behind her glasses, her light brown hair up in a bun, her black tank top front-tucked into ripped jeans with black leather slides, her wrist with gold bangles. She's casual and elegant and adorable. "Screw that. You are *not* awkward, and if you are, it obviously just adds to your charm. And also, Emily is a perfectly normal person too. She just happens to be more gorgeous than the rest of us."

"I love that hanging out with supermodels and living in a famous hockey player's apartment is all normal to you," Avery laughs as she turns with the tray to head back through the butler's pantry.

"My life is a lot less glamorous than it seems right now," I say as I follow behind her. Yes, I'm living in Sasha's multi-million-dollar co-op, but this isn't my life and I'm essentially his niece's nanny. But guilt niggles at the back of my mind, because as soon as my show airs, she's going to assume I was lying about the glamourless life. It's going to be hard work, and that's rarely glamorous no matter how it appears on TV.

"Uh huh," she says as she leads the way back through the dining room. Her disbelief makes me wonder if Tom knows Sasha and I are sleeping together and told her? He *is* one of Sasha's best friends, not to mention his lawyer, so it would make sense if he'd told him.

We head through the living room and into the sitting room. There on the couch is the least glamorous version of Emily I've ever seen. She has about ten small ponytails coming off her head in different directions and each has been braided. Some have colored barrettes at the end, and some have small Stella-sized scrunchies. She looks like one of those

Barbie hair salon dolls with the big head that a six-year-old got their hands on.

I laugh so hard I almost spill our drinks. How did Stella manage this in the few minutes we were in the kitchen? "I need a picture of you and Stella together," I tell her. "This needs to be documented."

Because she never takes herself too seriously, Emily happily poses for the photo. When I show it to Avery, I make sure to whisper, "See, totally normal."

We settle in on the couch and chairs right as the pregame show ends and the players return to the bench from their on-ice warm-up.

Sasha isn't on the ice for the face-off, but he's jumping over the boards and into the play only a minute into the game. I watch as Avery explains the logistics of hockey line switches to Emily, telling her why they're so frequent and how they know who is coming in and out of the game. She knows more than I do about the sport, and I grew up at the hockey rink watching my brother and Sasha play.

"How do you know so much about hockey?" I ask her.

"I used to play."

I'm sure my eyes are as wide as Emily's. "Really?"

"Yeah, I was on my high school team, and I played on our intramural team in college."

"I've never known a female hockey player," Emily says cautiously, "but I guess I envisioned them being bigger and tougher than you appear."

"Some are." She shrugs. "But like most women, hockey players come in all shapes and sizes. The important thing is how agile you are on skates, how much stamina you have, and that you're not afraid."

"Afraid of what?" I ask.

"Anything. The puck, the other players, getting knocked on your"—her eyes track to Stella—"butt."

I'd say Avery's body is average. She's probably five foot six and one hundred and thirty pounds, with smaller breasts and a slim waist. She does seem athletic, but the thought of her being checked up against the boards or knocked over on the ice is alarming.

"Do you still play?" I ask.

"No, but I teach a learn to skate hockey program specifically for girls on Sunday mornings."

"Really?" Stella says, taking her eyes off the game for the first time since it came on. "I want to take lessons with you!"

"Don't you already know how to skate?" I ask her. I've seen figure skates in her closet.

"Yeah, but only with those white skates for girls. I want to learn how to be fast on hockey skates. I want to skate like *Dyadya*."

Emily and Avery look at me, and I mouth *Uncle* so they know she's talking about Aleksandr.

"I want to surprise him," Stella adds. "Petra, will you help me surprise him?"

I want so badly to say *yes*. To tell her we'll set up times for her to have lessons with Avery while her uncle is out of town, so that when his season is over, she can surprise him with her new skating abilities. I want to take her to buy new skates, be there for her lessons, see the surprise on Sasha's face when he sees her in hockey skates. But I can't.

"I wish I could, honey. But you know I'm leaving in a couple days, right?"

The hopeful look on her face falls, and it's replaced by a

look that tells me I've just crushed her hopes and dreams. It about breaks my cold, dead heart because it's real and raw and I hate disappointing her like this.

"But," I continue, "how about I take you to buy a pair of skates after school tomorrow, and I'll set it up with Raina so she can take you to some lessons with Avery. Then maybe we can surprise your uncle when I come back in a few weeks?"

Stella nods her agreement but doesn't say anything. Then she gets up from her seat next to Emily on the couch and crosses to my chair, curling up in my lap with her arms wrapped around my neck and her head on my chest.

Over her head, I look at Avery. "Can we arrange that?"

"Of course," she says, but even she looks sad. Emily looks disappointed. I feel like shit. This is officially the worse playoff viewing party ever.

We watch the rest of the first period, and when it ends with New York in the lead by one goal, I take Stella to bed. She's tired and emotional and gives me a long hug. "I really wish you didn't have to go," she says.

I pause for a moment, resisting the urge to give her the reply that I'd normally make in circumstances like these. Instead of telling her I have obligations and explaining how work comes first, I tell her the truth. "I wish I could stay too. But I can't."

To her credit, she doesn't beg me to stay or even ask why. She accepts my leaving as inevitable, which only makes me feel that much worse. I promised myself I wasn't going to let her get too close because I didn't want to hurt her by leaving. I didn't want her to have to experience losing another person she cared about. And I've failed at that too.

When I return to the living room, Emily has taken her

hair out of the braids and she and Avery have their heads together looking at Avery's phone. I love seeing them getting to know each other because I love connecting people like this, building a web of friends. And that's what this would be, if I were staying in New York.

If someone had asked me a few months ago what "having it all" meant to me, I'd have described my life: a wonderful group of best friends, a successful business I'd built myself, and a contract to host a show that was about to begin filming. Now, standing in this sitting room, I feel like "having it all" could look very different: married to Sasha, adopting Stella, building a new group of friends here, moving my business back to New York.

No, this isn't the life you've chosen. You're already too far down the first path, backtracking would be ridiculous. You don't want to be married. You don't want kids. And you're about to become a household name when your show airs. You've built the life you wanted, now it's time to enjoy it.

"This is when he surprised me with a trip to St. Thomas at Christmas. It's when I knew for sure that he felt the same way I did." The look on her face is so tender, so full of love, that it makes my heart hurt. I remember what it was like to feel that way, but it only ever led to heartbreak and humiliation for me.

The life you've built is so much better than what any man could offer you, I remind myself.

Emily's smile is huge and genuine when she tells Avery, "You two are very cute together."

"I'm still kind of pinching myself that it's all real. I mean, initially I thought he was a total asshole."

Ah, the allure of the asshole. I know that well. Hopefully,

Tom turns out to truly be a good person, unlike my last boyfriend.

Avery looks at me as I sit near them. "Oh no, what's that look?" she asks.

I school my face into a neutral expression. "What look?"

"The look you got when I said I initially thought Tom was a total asshole?"

"Oh"—I shrug it off—"nothing. It just made me remember the last guy I dated, who turned out to be the worst when I thought he was one of the good guys."

"He really was the worst," Emily says with a wry little laugh.

"Oh no, what happened?" Avery asks, her concern evident in her voice. I can tell she has a big heart, and I hope for her sake that Tom guards it like it deserves to be protected.

"Well, he ended up in jail, so . . ." I never tell anyone this story. Emily knows, because she was involved, as were a few other women we used to model with. It's a well-known story in the industry, but outside of that, the only other person I've ever told is Jackson.

"He was our agent," Emily supplies when I stop talking. "And he was literally stealing from us—creating fake contracts that undersold what the companies we were modeling for were actually paying us so he could pocket the difference. He did this for years, to six of the models he represented. He and Petra happened to be in a relationship, so it was even worse that she was one of the women he was stealing from."

"Oh, wow," Avery breathes. "How did you find out?"

"I started to suspect something shady was going on, so I

hired a private investigator who wasn't afraid to get her hands dirty."

"What does that even mean?" Avery asks.

"I needed her to gather evidence, and I didn't care how she got it. Was there breaking and entering involved? Did she somehow pick her way into his safe? I don't know, and I don't care. She got me what I needed."

"Sounds like an utter badass to me," Avery smiles.

Alicia was a badass and a saint. Some people come into our lives just when we need them, and Alicia was that person for me. A chance meeting at a party and my fascination with her career choice led us to exchange numbers. I never thought I'd need to hire her, but I was so glad I had her in my contact list when I needed her.

"In a lot of ways," I tell Avery, "she saved me."

"You saved yourself, Petra," Emily insists. "You're the one who hired her, and when he was prosecuted, you testified against him."

"You had to testify against your boyfriend in court?" Avery gasps as she turns her head toward me.

"Hell no. He wasn't my boyfriend anymore at that point," I tell her. "I cut him loose the minute I had the evidence I needed to turn over to the DA. The worst part was realizing that I'd internalized a lot of things he'd said to me, like that I'd get paid more if I lost a few pounds. He was trying to make it look like I wasn't earning as much as I deserved by some deficit of my own doing, when really I was being paid fairly and he was just making excuses to cover that he was stealing from me."

"Wow, Petra. I'm so sorry that happened to you," Avery says. "And you, too, Emily."

"It wasn't as bad for me, for obvious reasons," Emily tells her. "But this is why Petra generally hates men."

What Emily doesn't know—actually, what no one knows—is that Ryan was the *last* in a string of men who did me wrong. She sees him as the thousand pound weight that broke the camel's back, when really he was just the final straw.

"That which doesn't kill you, makes you stronger," I quip. That little saying got me through a lot of heartache, and has helped me rebuild my life time and time again.

"I can't really imagine anyone being stronger than you," Emily says. "For real." Her words are supportive, but her smile is sad, so I direct our attention back to the game now that the commercial break is over.

Chapter Twenty

ALEKSANDR

"The good news is that you do have options."

The lawyer that Tom recommended sits behind her desk, across from Petra and me. She's a severe looking woman in her midthirties, with dark hair that's pulled tight into a low ponytail and dark magenta lips. "The bad news," she says, and Petra reaches across the small space between our chairs to grasp my hand, "is that none of them are as easy as what you're hoping for."

"What is our *best* option?" Petra asks.

"Your fastest option for adopting Stella is to stay married. Petra, you can legally adopt her because you're a citizen, and once you've adopted her, Aleksandr can also legally adopt her because you're married."

"But I'm moving to LA. We won't be living together. Stella will be here in New York with Aleksandr, and I'll be across the country."

"You could claim residency in New York, using Aleksandr's address as your permanent residence. Then wherever you live in LA could be a temporary residence you stay in while you're there filming. You'd have to come back to New York frequently though, at least every other weekend if you want it to be believable that you're married and want to adopt Stella together. And you'll need to move your event planning business to New York too, if you're going to continue with that."

"But all my employees are in Park City," Petra says, and I hear the worry in her voice.

"I'm not a small business attorney, but I don't think there would be any reason your employees couldn't continue to work from Park City. However, if you're going to be a resident of New York, your business should be here, too, or it will look suspicious."

Petra sighs, a long, low sound of frustration leaving her lips. I feel the magnitude of what's being asked of her.

"This feels like everything is coming down on Petra," I say to the lawyer. "Isn't there something *I* could do to make this happen that doesn't involve her sacrificing so much?"

She squeezes my hand in hers, a small offering of thanks or support or love—I'm not sure which.

"Unfortunately, whereas she's the US citizen, she's the one who is going to have to do the work here."

"That feels very unfair," I say.

"And yet it's what the law requires. You could always go the route of getting citizenship yourself, and then adopting Stella. But as you already know, that process might take a couple years. I suspect a judge would be sympathetic to you wanting to adopt your niece after her parents' death, and that the adoption process would be significantly quicker, but I also can't make any promises. And you'd have to get citizenship first. There could be any variety of delays, and even if we go for the faster option of Petra adopting Stella, the judge needs to believe that you two are married and living together and in this for the long run, or he might deny the adoption petition."

My frustration rattles around in the back of my throat, and Petra looks at me like she's shocked by the groan I've let loose in this office. "This feels like an impossible task."

"May I ask what the hurry is?" the lawyer asks. "Why not go through the process of becoming a citizen and adopting without involving Petra? You're already the legal guardian."

"If anything were to happen to me . . ." I trail off, but Petra picks up and explains about Nikolai and Colette's will, and how CeCe and Tony tried to get custody and how they are still sniffing around, trying to be part of Stella's life even though that's not what her parents wanted.

"You don't have any specific evidence that your brother and sister-in-law didn't want the aunt and uncle around?"

"No," I tell her. "Just that they had separate conversations with me and my sister-in-law's best friend, Sofia, where they explained their wishes to each of us." She's already seen the will, I don't need to explain that they clearly didn't include CeCe or Tony in any part of that.

"Keeping families together is almost always the goal," she tells us, and it's exactly what Tom had told me and exactly why I'm worried. "But if their wishes are clearly spelled out in their will, I don't think you need to worry."

"I wish that was the case, but when the judge decided in my favor, he also said he'd reconsider if I was ever unwilling or unable to serve as Stella's guardian."

"Whichever option you choose," the lawyer says, "I'd get started on it as quickly as possible. I do honestly think your *best* option is getting your citizenship and adopting Stella yourself. Given the . . . unique . . . nature of your marriage, having Petra adopt Stella may be the fastest option, but may not be the wisest."

"What do you mean?" Petra asks.

"Given the circumstances, if you don't plan to stay married, things might get messy when you separate. If you're the one who has adopted Stella," she tells Petra, "then that gives you a lot of leverage when it comes to the divorce. It's possible"—she looks over at me—"that you might not end up with Stella in the end."

Petra draws back, her eyes wide. "I would *never* do that. Stella isn't a bargaining chip, and I'm not looking to gain anything from this, except to help Aleksandr adopt his niece."

"That's true right now, but who's to say what might happen in a year? This whole process might take that long, and adoption is tough even for two people in a loving, committed relationship."

Her concern gives me a moment's pause. Petra has put her life on pause to stay in New York and help me over the last couple weeks. There hasn't been even the slightest indication she'd do anything that wouldn't be in my or Stella's best interest. *But.* The word rattles around in my head. *But could she?*

She's been extraordinarily honest about the fact that she doesn't want kids. I know the idea of getting a divorce also weighs heavily on her mind, as she doesn't want the attention that would bring. Could she—would she—ever use Stella as a bargaining chip to get what she wanted out of a divorce?

Petra wouldn't do that, I assure myself. But the question is there, digging into the soft spot in my heart that I didn't even know existed before I had Stella: *Are you sure?*

Do I know her well enough to know this for sure? How could I guarantee that she wouldn't cross me down the road to get something she wanted?

I glance over at Petra, who is gazing at me as if she can read my mind and looks disappointed in my thought process. "Thank you. We'll take your advice into consideration," I tell the lawyer as I reach for Petra's hand.

———

P etra is still working when I get home from picking Stella up at school, and she's quiet through dinner. It's a combination of watching her lost in thought and submersed in sadness—one minute she's staring off into space, the next she's choked up while answering a question from Stella. She's a hollow shell of herself. I've never seen her like this, and it's breaking my heart to watch.

After dinner, I suggest we walk over to the ice cream stand in the park, and while Stella practically hits the ceiling in her excitement, Petra just says, "You guys go, I should probably stay home and pack."

"Do you *really* have to leave? I want you to stay," Stella speaks the words I've been thinking for days.

"Unfortunately, I do," Petra says. "I have a lot of things going on for work right now, and I have to be there for them. But like I told you the other night, I'll be back in a few weeks." Her smile is small and pitiful.

"But at least come for ice cream, please," Stella draws out the last word for a few seconds, and I hate to see her like this, begging for Petra's attention. I equally hate watching Petra withhold it when she doesn't want to, like she thinks it'll be easier for Stella when she leaves if she starts pulling away now. I wish she understood that nothing will make her leaving easier.

If it's possible to regret letting someone into your life and also wanting to hold them tightly and never let go, that's how I'm feeling. And I'm pretty sure it's how Stella is feeling too.

"I wish I could, cutie," Petra says, then turns her head and gazes out the window.

"Why don't we take a walk and get some ice cream," I say to Stella, "and give Petra some time to pack. Then maybe when we get back, we can watch a show together before it's time for bed."

"Will you watch the show with us?" Stella asks Petra.

"Sure. I'll go start packing now."

The air is warm, and the sky is still quite blue as we head across Fifth Avenue and into Central Park. I'm confident Stella could find the ice cream cart with her eyes closed. As we take our treats and walk over to the playground where she sometimes likes to get her energy out at the end of the day, it occurs to me that soon I'll need to start teaching her how to navigate the city. Not that she'll be doing it on her own for about another decade, but just to make sure she always knows where she is and how to get where she wants to go. I never want her to feel lost or powerless.

I'll also need to teach her how to keep herself safe, which has me thinking of Petra and how she's the person I want to ask about this. I don't know how women keep themselves safe in a city or how they should react under different circumstances, but I'm confident Petra will be an expert in this area. It's interesting to me that the more deeply I think about it, the more I find that Petra fits well into *all* parts of our life. Not only because I want to be with her every minute of the day, but also because Stella looks up to her and Petra is exactly the kind of woman I want Stella to grow into—strong, independent, thoughtful.

"What do you think things will be like when Petra is gone?" Stella asks as she leans back on the lip of the fountain overlooking the playground.

My throat feels tight and my eyes burn at the thought of answering this question. "Probably a lot like before she arrived."

"I don't want to go back to our life without her in it." Stella's normally confident voice is small and pinched, and her eyes look a little lost as she gazes past me at the trees.

Neither do I. The words almost slip off my tongue, but I bite them back just in time. I need to appear unified with Petra on this front or it will be confusing and even more painful for Stella when Petra leaves. "We'll be okay," I tell her instead. "And you're going to love Raina. She's like Natasha, but even nicer."

"But do you think she'll love me like Petra does?"

The question slices through the last of my willpower. "I don't know." My voice cracks with emotion. "You and Petra have a special bond. But that doesn't mean you and Raina won't have a different, special bond too."

"But Raina will only be my nanny. I wanted Petra to stay and be my mom."

I look at her in alarm, but her face is hard and certain. My throat is so tight I feel like I can't speak, which is just as well because I don't want to give her false hope, and I also don't want to crush her dreams. Will Petra and I pursue the path of her being the one to adopt Stella? Will we stay married to make this all possible? Or will she leave for good, and I'll pursue citizenship instead so I can adopt Stella without her help? I don't know yet, and since Stella doesn't even know that Petra and I are married, I can't even begin to explain this possibility to her.

"I know," I tell her and reach my arm around her shoulders to hug her to my side.

"Do you think that will ever happen?"

"A lot would have to change for that to happen," I say tentatively. "I'd have to be your dad and—"

"But you already are my dad, aren't you? I mean, now that Mama and Papa are dead and I live with you?"

Goose bumps rise on the back of my neck. I'm not sure how I thought this conversation was going to go, but this isn't it. "I mean, yeah." I shrug because I don't want to make a big deal out of her questions and give her any reason to think maybe that isn't what I want. It's exactly what I'm trying to make happen.

"Can I call you Dada then, instead of *Dyadya*?"

"Sure." Why does my voice sound like it's being pushed out the spout of a steaming teakettle? "But even so, that doesn't mean Petra would be your mom." My chest feels so tight it's painful.

"But she would be if you marry her," Stella says, like it's the most obvious and simple thing in the world.

The urge to confide in my six-year-old niece is astounding. I want to tell her that I don't know how to be enough to make Petra want to stay, and the not knowing and the not being enough makes me feel so small and insignificant when Petra is such a huge part of my life already.

"That's not really how marriage works," I tell her. "You

have to love the person, be *in love* with them. And you both have to feel the same way about each other."

"But don't you guys love each other?" she asks before shoving an enormous spoonful of ice cream into her mouth.

"We've been friends for a long time, and we do love each other. But that's different than being in love."

"What's the difference?" she asks, her mouth full of ice cream.

"You can love someone like they're family, you know, like I love you. But being in love with someone is . . . more."

"How?"

I don't know how to explain this. I've loved Petra since she was thirteen and been in love with her since she was fourteen—and I'm not sure I even know what the difference is anymore? I only know that I've never felt this way about anyone else and that my feelings and attraction to her are even stronger now than when we were teenagers.

"I don't know how to explain it," I tell Stella, hoping that answer will suffice. How do I explain love and sexual attraction, and the difference between the two?

Stella looks up at me. "So, are you not *in love* with Petra, then?"

"I don't know, sweetheart. It's a really complicated situation."

"No, it's not," she insists. "We love Petra, and we want her to be part of our family."

"I wish it were that simple."

"It is, you just have to ask her to stay."

I love her confidence, her reckless belief that life is asking for what you want and then getting it.

"There are a lot of reasons she can't stay," I remind Stella.

We literally just had this conversation in the apartment, I'm not sure why she wants to rehash it out here.

"But have you *asked* her to stay?" she asks, her voice more insistent.

"No, because she can't, and I don't want her to feel bad about that."

"That's silly. Maybe she's just leaving because she doesn't know you want her to stay."

Could that be right? Could it really be that simple?

"I don't think so, honey." I pat her head affectionately.

"Well, you won't know unless you ask her," Stella says.

But I do know. I know what Petra's goals are, and I know she has to be in LA next week. There's no way she can stay, which we've explained to Stella over and over. But just like me, she's having a hard time wrapping her head around the reality of life without Petra in it.

I wrap my arm around her shoulders and give her a little squeeze. I hate knowing how much she's going to hurt when Petra goes, and I hate that in order to support her through it, I'm going to have to pretend that I'm not hurting just as much.

———

When we return from ice cream, Petra is waiting for us in the living room with a bright smile on her face. She's changed into the sleep shorts and tank top she's worn most nights, and she'd look so perfectly at home here in my living room if that smile on her face wasn't so fake.

Stella's so thrilled to see Petra waiting to watch a show with us that she doesn't even notice how all-wrong this is—

her lips stretched too tight across her teeth, the way her cheeks shake with the effort of holding the smile, her glassy eyes. How does Stella not see that Petra seems like a facsimile of herself?

In the middle of the couch, Stella curls up into Petra's side and I take a seat on the opposite end of the couch, so Stella's between us. Stella chooses a show and gets it started, and over her head I keep glancing at Petra. Memorizing the milky skin of her neck, the graceful slope of her shoulder, the way her dark hair curls into perfect ringlets that spring over her shoulder even as she tosses them behind her, the way her eyelashes swoop and curve, the small scar she has where her ear meets her jaw. Every time I look at her, I notice something I hadn't seen before. She's like a 1,000-piece puzzle where you spend ages looking for a tiny piece and immediately when you find it, you're already searching for the next one.

I stretch my arm out along the back of the couch and drag my fingers along Petra's bare shoulder. I feel her stiffen, and I'm about to pull my fingers away when she glances over at me—her eyes are filled with tears and her body relaxes. I stroke the soft skin along the column of her neck with the backs of my fingers, then cup her jaw in my palm. The pads of my fingertips play with the hair behind her ear, and she rests her head in my hand. With my thumb I trace the curve of her ear and the strong line of her cheekbone, trying to memorize it all—the way she looks, the way her skin feels under my fingers, the way she's welcomed Stella into her life, and how this domestic scene feels like everything I never thought I'd have.

When the show is over, Stella asks if Petra can put her to

bed tonight, and Petra agrees even though she wears all her reservations on her face. I want to gather her up in my arms and take away all her fears, and dammit, I don't want her to walk out that door tomorrow. Yet I want her to achieve all her dreams, and I hate that the two things are at odds.

When she comes out of Stella's room, I hear her quietly padding down the hallway toward the living room, and I'm up off the couch before she reaches the wide entrance to the space. I've been waiting to wrap her in my arms for hours. I want to kiss away those tears that have been threatening to fall since dinner. I want to spend our last night together wrapped in each other's arms, because even though I dread the dawn, I'm planning on making the most of this darkness.

"Well," she says when she comes into view. "I think I'll head to bed." She crosses her arms over her chest. "I've got an early morning."

"Come here, Petra." I keep my feet firmly planted on the floor, because even though I know I could go to her, I need to know she's willing to come to me.

"Aleksandr," she whispers.

"Don't do that," I say, keeping my voice low since we're still within earshot of Stella's bedroom door.

"Don't do what?"

"Push me away like that."

"How am I pushing you away?"

"You only call me Aleksandr when you're mad at me."

"I'm not mad . . ." She trails off, either unwilling or unable to finish that sentence. But she does take a few steps into the room so we're standing face-to-face.

"It doesn't make it easier on the person you're leaving if

287

you start pulling away before you're gone," I tell her as I put my hands on her hips.

She looks away, her gaze focusing on the windows on the far side of the room.

"I just don't want to make promises I can't keep. And being with you now feels like a promise for the future."

"I'm not expecting that." *Just hoping for it.*

"Yes, you are," she says, looking back at me. Her eyes are full of sadness, not the steely reserve I normally see there.

I'm not sure what to say to that. Do I admit that she's right? That I *do* want to know where this could go? That I do want her to stay so we can see what's possible between us? We barely talked about the lawyer's recommendation on our way back here after the appointment this morning because she said she needed time to think about it. There are so many strings left untied, and I want things wrapped up so badly, but at the same time, I know she needs time to process all this. *If she thinks about it in LA, far away from me and Stella, will that make her less likely to want to come back?*

I lock eyes with her, studying their bright blue depths. Her irises are like one of those prismatic pictures where all the colors are changed into geometric shapes that swirl into larger shapes. Hers are a mixture of the color of water in the Caribbean, the sky on a bright and cloudless day, and a dark storm over the North Sea.

"I promised myself a long time ago," she whispers, and her hot breath bounces off my lips, "that I'd never again do anything I didn't want to do, that I'd stay true to myself. And this—leaving—is me doing something I don't want to do."

Her admission is both hopeful and heartbreaking. "Then

don't go." I squeeze her shoulders tightly, hoping she can feel some of what I'm feeling right now.

"Don't you see, Sasha, I *have* to. I—"

"That doesn't mean this has to be over." I need her to give us a chance more than I've never needed anything in my life. I don't want to beg, but I can't let her leave without knowing how I feel. "You have to leave New York, but you don't have to leave this relationship."

"How could we keep this going across an entire continent?" Her words are weak and hopeless.

"Let's just see, okay? You need to go to LA. You have dreams and I want you to chase and attain them, to be everything you've always wanted to be. At the same time, I want to be with you and I can't follow you to LA because my team and Stella are here. But we can still try to make this work."

"You'd follow me to LA?" Her words are barely audible.

The thought hadn't seriously crossed my mind until it came off my lips. My thoughts of us together had always centered around her staying here, because logically, I knew that was my only possibility. "If I could, I would."

She leans forward, bowing her head and resting it on my chest. I wrap my arms around her back as her shoulders begin to shake.

"Why?" she asks. "Why does this have to happen right now? Why couldn't we have gotten together years ago or years from now? We had to pick the one point in time that is impossible."

She looks up at me and tears are streaming down her face. It's only the second time I've ever seen her cry.

"Nothing is impossible," I kiss her forehead and run my thumbs across her cheeks to smooth away the tears.

"It feels impossible," she mumbles, looking down at my chest.

"It's not. We just have to figure it out," I say, and I trail my lips down the bridge of her nose to her mouth.

Her lips meet mine in a hungry, greedy kiss. She's not giving right now, she's taking, and I'm here for it—for whatever she needs. I have a good idea what that'll be when she takes my hand and leads me down the hall, past Stella's door and past her own, to my bedroom. She closes the door quietly behind me, then reaches up and threads her fingers into my hair, pulling my head down to hers. Her lips are insistent as they part, her tongue demanding as it strokes mine. Her other hand tucks under my shirt and her fingers play with the skin at the edge of my waistband, teasing me as she slides her fingers across my abs and over my hipbone. In one step, I have her back against the door, and she trails a foot up my leg and snakes her knee around my hip, pulling me even closer to her.

With one hand on her thigh to anchor her leg in place, I push my aching dick against her center and am rewarded with her groan as it reverberates into my mouth. She leans her head back against the door, eyes closed, and says, "I want you so fucking bad."

I grip the hem of her tank top and pull it up over her head to reveal a bra I've never seen her wear. It's pale pink and sheer with lace trimming the cups and a lace band. "You are unbelievably sexy."

Her upper lip curves into a smile as she looks at me with those lust-filled eyes. The look says *I know*, but at the same time, it communicates so much more than that. I know Petra is well versed in the bedroom, but I also get the sense that there's an emotional component to our sexual relationship that doesn't exist for her otherwise. Or maybe I'm just projecting my own feelings?

I move my fingers to the waistband of her shorts and she drops her leg, letting me slide them down to her ankles. I kneel at her feet to pull them off, and the matching sheer pink thong does nothing to hide her body from me. I look up at her from the ground, then trail my fingers along the edge of that fabric until I'm at the seam between her legs. I sweep my fingertips under the fabric and marvel at how wet she already is. As I slide the thong to the side, I use my other hand to lift one leg over my shoulder. My lips trail up the inside of that thigh as I tease her by stroking back and forth along her folds with my fingers while never actually touching her clit or entering her. When my lips reach the top of her thigh, she uses her leg to pull my head closer and lets out a throaty growl. "Sasha . . . now."

In an instant I'm driving two fingers inside her while my tongue attacks her clit, and her whole body tenses with need. The view from here, looking up over her flat abdomen and across her lace-clad breasts, watching her mouth twisted in pleasure, her eyes shut tightly—this is the future I want. Petra, every single day. I want sex, yes. But I want *her*. I want her parenting Stella with me, I want her sitting at my dinner table, I want her wearing my jersey at my games, I want to watch TV on the couch with her at night, and wake up with her in my arms. I want her making decisions with me about our future together. I want us to be the family I never had, and the family Stella deserves. I want forever.

My tongue moves faster, my fingers stroke harder at that thought—forever. *She can't leave.* I pour all those feelings into the orgasm I give her, and the way she moans my name as her legs shake and her body convulses around my fingers gives me hope that she's feeling the same way.

The minute she's done, she reaches down, grabbing the neckline of my T-shirt and pulling me to my feet. Our lips meet in a possessive kiss, her tongue swirling around mine as she invades my mouth. Reaching behind her, she locks the door and then walks me backward, her lips never leaving mine, until the backs of my legs hit the bed.

Petra pulls back for a second, long enough for me to pull my shirt over my head and for her to unbutton my pants and slide them down my legs so I can step out of them. She looks at me then, her eyes sliding down my body to where my dick is straining so hard against the fabric of my underwear that it's actually pulling the elastic waistband away. She reaches out and snakes her hand between the fabric and my abdomen, then slides her fingers and palm down my shaft, gripping me as the muscles in my lower back contract into a shudder. *Holy shit, the things this woman does to me.*

While I strip off my boxers, her eyes never leave mine, not even when she slides her thong down her legs, leaving a trail of moisture along one thigh, or when she slides the straps of her bra off her shoulders and reaches behind her to unclasp it one-handed. She's the most amazing creature I've ever seen —naked or clothed, in a business meeting or being a surrogate mom to my kid.

It doesn't matter, I'll take her any way I can have her.

Chapter Twenty One

PETRA

I wake up cocooned by Aleksandr's warmth. His abdomen is pressed up against my back, one arm is slung over my ribcage and wrapped around my chest, and his knee is wedged between my thighs. Aside from how his heat smothers me like a hot, humid day, the other thing I notice immediately is the way he is already hugely hard and resting right against my ass.

I want to press myself back into him, wake him up with the motion of my body rubbing against him, and see if we can fit in a quickie before I have to get up and shower. I glance at the clock on his nightstand and see that it's only six in the morning. The alarm was set for seven. We have plenty of time.

I arch my lower back and run the crease of my ass cheeks along his impressive length. I feel the way he twitches against me, so I repeat the motion a few more times until his hips are moving forward, meeting me each time as he thrusts himself against my skin.

"I want to wake up like this every day," he says quietly, the words a whisper across my hair.

Me too. I don't say anything in response, just take his hand, kiss his knuckles, then move it to my breast. His fingers instinctively move across my nipple, gently at first.

I slide my own hand behind me, between us, and grip him tightly in my hand, sliding along his length in slick, smooth motions.

"Holy shit," he growls. "I want to be inside you."

"Then make it happen," I say.

He pulls away and I know he's reaching behind him toward his nightstand where his stash of condoms are, but I'm overwhelmed with the need to feel him bare inside me, to share that moment with him so that he can be the first man ever to have that honor.

I move my hand to his hip and pull him back toward me. "Now."

"Petra, I need—"

"Now, Aleksandr."

"Are you sure?"

"You're clean?" I confirm.

"Yes. And I've never not worn a condom. Ever."

It feels like my heart flutters in my chest, skipping a beat or two at his admission. So I'll be his first too.

"Same," I tell him. "I've never had sex unprotected."

"You're on the pill?"

"Yes."

He must lean up on his elbow because he's looking down at me, his face hovering above mine as I turn my head to look up at him.

"I want to know what you feel like inside me," I tell him, "with nothing between us."

He looks down at me, unmoving. Finally he says, "I don't know if I can do this, and then let you walk out of here in a couple hours." His voice is unsteady, choked with emotion.

I reach up and stroke his face with my palm. "It's only for a few weeks. I'll be back next month for the party."

"You know what I mean," he says, but his hips thrust against my ass again and I know how badly he wants me.

"We can use a condom if you want, Sasha." I make sure my words are soft and understanding, even though I want him inside me so badly I can feel the moisture dripping down the back of my thigh.

He quickly exhales through his nose—a short, quick grunt. And then he's lifting my top leg and sliding himself along the creases between my legs.

I sigh. "That feels unbelievable, and I *need* you inside me."

Aleksandr uses his knees to sweep my legs up so I'm curled into a C on my side, his body is wrapped around every part of mine. His groan as he slides into me is raw and loud enough that I'm actually worried Stella could hear it two rooms away.

I turn my head over my shoulder. "Shhh."

"Don't tell me what to do, woman," he says as he moves his hand to my hip, anchoring me in place.

Silent laughter rumbles around in my chest and my upper body shakes against him. And then he moves inside me with deep, deliberate strokes that take my breath away.

"Shit." The word rolls off his tongue in a grunt. "This. Is. Too. Good."

"And that's a problem because . . .?" I ask, driving my hips to meet his as best I can on my side.

"Because it's been ten seconds and I'm already close." He sounds frustrated.

I know exactly what will make me catch up to him. "Roll over and sit up," I say.

He pushes into me again. "I'm not saying I want to stop."

"And I'm not saying we're going to stop," I tell him, meeting his next thrust. "I'm just going to show you how to catch me up."

"Fine." The word is another growl, and he sighs as he pulls out of me slowly, like every inch of movement is against his will.

Once he's sitting, I roll over. I sit up and swing one leg over his hips so I'm straddling him. On my knees like this, my breasts are right in his face and as I sink down onto him, sheathing him inside me, he takes them both in his hands reverently. Until Sasha, I've never been with someone who makes me feel like he's worshipping my body and owning my soul.

As I move over him, his mouth and his hands are everywhere, licking and stroking every part of my body that he knows will bring me pleasure. As I tilt my hips and slide along him, I focus on making sure he hits that spot deep inside me that will bring me to orgasm. I look down at him as I sink onto him again, marveling at the way his eyebrows scrunch together at the effort of holding himself back until I find my release. There is raw desire in those eyes as he glances up at me. Eyes locked on my face, lips locked on my breast, his mouth is doing things that are driving me wild.

I pick up the pace and find the best angle so when he

rubs against that spot deep inside me, I about come undone. He sucks my breast further into his mouth, circling my nipple with his tongue as I slide him in and out of my body. When I groan with pleasure, he emits a sound from the back of his throat that is both desire and torture, and it reverberates along my skin. I speed up, my thighs and core working hard as I rise and sink over him, and the more I move, the closer I get to that orgasm I so desperately want.

Framed by dark lashes, his eyes are a swirling mass of gray liquid steel again. The way they focus on my face—assessing, studying, loving—makes me feel *seen*. He *knows* me like no one else. He *loves* me.

The realization hits at the same moment that my orgasm begins. My muscles clench in rippling waves that pulse around him as I buck my hips wildly against his. Without taking his eyes off me, he tilts his chin up, letting my breast fall from his mouth as he reaches one hand up to bring my head down to his. His lips are parted when our mouths meet and his tongue plunges into my mouth with the same relentless ferocity with which my muscles are clenching around his cock. I feel him pour himself into me as my orgasm brings about his, and both his hands cup my face as he kisses me like it's the last time.

It's too much, the way my body responds to his, the way he owns my heart. I don't know what to do with all these feelings. The physical ones I can deal with, even though I've never experienced anything of this magnitude, but the emotional ones are strangers. Is it just like this because we are saying goodbye? Or could I always have this if I stayed?

And more importantly, how does one walk away from this kind of earth-shattering experience?

———

The tears started falling when I walked onto the plane yesterday.

I held it together when Sasha and Stella dropped me off at the airport. I said my goodbyes and made it through security and to the gate without incident. But the moment my butt hit that first-class seat, the tears started falling. I slid my sunglasses onto my face and the flight attendant brought me napkins and a glass of champagne, but I cried silent tears until there were none left to shed. I managed to eat lunch without crying, though it was hard to get the food past the enormous lump in my throat. But the moment I handed the plate back to the flight attendant, the tears started falling again. If the businessman sitting next to me noticed me constantly dabbing my cheeks, sliding that napkin up under my sunglasses, he didn't say anything. I managed to collect my luggage and make it to the car Morgan sent for me without tears, but the minute I slid into the back seat, they started falling again. I cried even harder when I walked through the door of my apartment. Normally my refuge, now the sunny space felt like a jail cell.

It was like each time I transitioned into a new situation that would take me further from Aleksandr—the plane, the car, my apartment—I broke down. And I can't seem to stop breaking down over and over. Maybe these are the unshed tears from the first time he left me, back when we were teenagers. Maybe they are the unshed tears of all the men who have screwed me over time and time again. Maybe it's the acknowledgment that I've once again let a man into my life, not just into my bed, and this gives him the power to hurt me.

But I trust him. And maybe more importantly, I think I love him. And I think he feels the same way. Which is why it's so hard to have to walk away, even if it's not forever.

I take another tissue from the box I've left on the ottoman in the center of my closet, wipe my face and blow my nose, then toss it in the now almost-full trash can I've moved into my closet while I'm packing.

My phone buzzes with a text and I scoop it up, hoping to see Aleksandr's name. Instead, I have two texts from Sierra and one from Morgan. Nothing from Aleksandr. Which makes sense, since last night I'd told him I needed some time to adjust to being home. I told him I'd contact him when I felt ready to talk.

> SIERRA
>
> When are we going to talk? I know you're back in Park City, and you said we'd talk when you got home this weekend.

> SIERRA
>
> Petra, you can't hold this all in. Whatever is happening, you need to talk about it. If not to me, then call Jackson. I'm pretty sure you haven't talked to her either. We're here for you if you need us.

I fold a few more dresses and add them to my suitcase as I consider how to respond to her texts. In the past, I've been a confidant for both Jackson and Sierra. I've given them both advice they needed to hear, when they needed to hear it. At various points over the past couple years, they've each told me things they hadn't told each other, despite the fact that they've known each other since they were eight years old. It's always been easy for me to dish out impartial, practical advice because my heart's never been involved. And now that it is, I don't know what to do.

Call me when you have a minute.

My phone rings in my hand.

"Hey," I say.

"God, I've missed you and your sexy voice," she tells me. "How have you been?"

"There's, uh, been a lot going on lately." My voice is more raspy than usual because of all the crying.

"Spill."

As if it's that easy. "I don't know what to say."

"How is this hard?" she asks. But Sierra is an open book and the most empathetic person I've ever met. Loving is easy for her. Caring for other people is easy for her. The only thing she has trouble dealing with is the weight of her own expectations. But it's not like that for me. I don't know how to be that person, the one who gives up her dreams for someone else. My dreams and my success are too tied to who I am.

"You're not saying anything," Sierra says from the other end of the phone.

"I know. I'm thinking." I take a stack of neatly folded basic loungewear and add it to my suitcase. I never step foot outside without a banging outfit, carefully styled hair, and a natural-looking full face of makeup. But the minute I come home, I change into something comfortable for lounging around the house in. I try not to think about what it means that Sasha and Stella were the first people I've let into my small circle of trust in years. I hung out with them at home, in PJ's, with no makeup, just doing normal family-like things. And I loved it. I loved the coziness, the comfort of having people around who I didn't feel like I was performing for.

"What are you thinking about?" she asks.

"If I wanted you to know, I'd be talking."

"That's not how this whole confiding in a friend thing works. You share what's going on, and then I'm either supportive if you're making good decisions, or I tell you you're an idiot and you need to stop fucking up your life."

I laugh like she'd intended for me to. "I don't know how to do this," I tell her.

"Do what?"

"Be the one asking for advice."

"It's simple, really. You let go of the need to control everything, and instead tell me what's happening so we can talk through it and you can get impartial advice from a friend." She sounds so confident, which is wholly unlike the Sierra who wasn't sure what to do about her relationship with Beau only a few short months ago. I like this new, empowered version of her.

"You're going to be sorry you asked," I say as I take two piles of underwear from a drawer and add them to my suitcase.

"I doubt that."

I tell her everything.

"So you're telling me that the queen of noncommitment, the one who won't let anyone get close to her, who never wants to settle down—is actually *married* and now trying to help her *husband* adopt a kid?" Her cackle is totally uncalled for, except I'm sure I'd be reacting the same way if I were in her shoes.

I think about all the times I've given my girlfriends shit about "settling down" and talked about how I never would. And now here I am, trying to decide how I can settle down without "settling"—without giving up everything I've worked so hard for.

"I really appreciate your understanding," I grumble.

"Oh, honey," she says when she finally stops laughing, "you are so screwed."

"Thanks." I roll my eyes even though she can't see them.

"Okay," she says, the word rolling out on a sigh. "Seriously though, do you want my real thoughts on the situation?"

"Would I have told you if I didn't?"

I think about how my relationship with Sierra has changed over the past year and a half, how we went from two people with a friend in common to two people who were actually friends. I miss Jackson every day, but I'm also glad that she and Nate getting back together allowed Sierra and me to become closer. If only Sierra hadn't then moved away, too, leaving me in Park City with just one close friend, Lauren, and a bunch of work friends who are more like acquaintances I see all the time.

"Here's the only thing that matters," Sierra says. "Do you love him?"

"I mean . . ." I hedge.

"Petra," she says, her voice serious. "Do. You. Love. Him?"

"Yeah." My voice sounds small and quiet and distant, even to my own ears. "I always have."

"But do you feel differently about him now? Not the infatuation of the unobtainable best friend that you felt during your teenage years . . ."

"That's not what that was."

"Wasn't it?" she asks. "Regardless of how he felt about you then, wasn't he your unobtainable best friend? The older guy you had a crush on?"

"He wasn't unobtainable, I mean."

"Based on how things turned out back then, I beg to differ."

"Ouch."

"But," she says, "it doesn't matter because your story doesn't end there."

Her words make me realize that Aleksandr still hasn't told me what happened that night, why he pushed me away so abruptly. *Why haven't I asked him about that?* He has definitely said that he had feelings for me then, so why did he end things like he did? Suddenly that information feels so crucial to understanding my own feelings, to knowing whether we can ever have something meaningful and lasting.

"So," she continues, "do you feel differently about him now than you did back then? Or is this just you finally getting what you wanted?"

I consider what she's asking as I fold another shirt. "It's hard to separate how I felt back then and how I feel now. It feels like I've always loved him, but yes, what I feel now is different than what I felt back then."

"How so?" Her question feels like a test where I need to prove to her and to myself that I've grown up.

"Back then, my feelings for him were based on two things, need and want. Like he was the one person who was always there for me when I *needed* him, and I loved him unequivocally in return. I was also stupidly attracted to him, and I *wanted* him to feel the same way about me."

"How is that different now?"

"Now, I guess . . ." I pause to think this through before speaking. "Now I don't *need* him in my life. In fact, in most ways, my life is easier without him in it. Yet I still want him. Not just sexually, but I actually want his company. I enjoy spending time with him."

"I feel like love is a lot stronger when you want someone without needing them," Sierra says.

"Please explain." I like this phrase Aleksandr used the other night, and I think I'm going to employ it often.

"Well," she says slowly before pausing. "When you love someone because you need them, it's hard to tell what that love is based on—is it really love or is it codependency? But when you love someone that you don't need in your life, when you're already whole and you love someone because they make you happier, better, more fulfilled—that's a much stronger kind of love."

I sit on my ottoman next to my almost-full suitcase. Was the love I felt for him back then based on codependency? A lot of times it felt like we were all each other had. Sure, he had his father and a ton of friends, but Niko was already away at college. I had my emotionally distant dad and basically no friends. Aleksandr wasn't just my person, he was my *only* person. Was the love I felt for him related to needing him in my life and being thankful he was there?

"I feel like I want to know him better, to understand him more, to know what makes him who he is now."

"You don't feel like you know who he is now?" Sierra asks this question like she's considering her words carefully.

"I do know who he is now, in all the important ways. I know that he's a great surrogate father to Stella, a loyal brother who'd do anything for his family, a dedicated teammate. He's a good man. Do I love who he is now? Yes. But do I know enough about his past to know how he'll act in the future? To understand what makes him tick? What makes him act and react how he does? No."

"It's okay to love him and still feel like you need to know him better before you can commit, you know?" Her words are the assurance I need about the conflicted feelings I'm having.

"I know. But I don't know where to go from here."

"Yes, you do," Sierra says. "You need more time to get to know him, to learn about all those years you were separated, to understand him. You need time to build up that trust you lost when he walked out on you before."

"Yeah, but . . ." Time feels like the one commodity we don't have.

"Relationships take time and constant work, Petra," she assures me, "even with me and Beau. Yeah, we started out as an explosion and I took a *huge* leap, leaving my job to follow him after only a few weeks, but we didn't stop working on our relationship then and we haven't stopped yet. We're *still* getting to know each other, figuring out how to argue without fighting, how to work through big, scary feelings without pushing each other away, and loving each other despite our flaws. It's work, and it's always going to be work, but it's worth it."

In every relationship I've ever been in, I've felt like I was the only one doing the work. But for the first time, I feel like maybe we could be in this together—equally, as partners. We've only ever talked about our marriage from the perspective of him adopting Stella. Even though I know we both have real feelings for each other, we've never talked about what happens *after* he adopts her. Does he still want to get divorced and go on his way, or does he want this to last?

I take a deep breath, because before I talk to him about what he wants, what he sees in our future, I need to figure out what I want. Could I really settle down with one person? Am I ready to be a mom? Can I put my heart on the line, loving not only Aleksandr but also Stella?

This relationship is the antithesis of everything I've ever wanted, but somehow it still feels like it could be exactly right just the same.

Chapter Twenty-Two

PETRA

As I navigate the twisting mountain roads leading up to the house Lauren and Josh built overlooking the valley, I try not to worry about how much more I have to do before I drive down to LA tomorrow.

I've been so busy that I don't think I've slept more than four or five hours a night since coming home, but that means I also haven't had time to dwell on the situation with Aleksandr. I haven't had time to cry since getting off the phone with Sierra on Sunday afternoon and launching into work mode. And it's better this way. It's better to be busy.

Morgan found me a great house on Airbnb, so I've rented that for the next couple months. I'd thought I'd wait until I got down there to find a place, but this is less taxing on me at a time when I don't feel like I could take one more thing. I've spent the last two days getting everything set up at work: assigning different members of my team to be the official point person for each of the events we've taken on, getting Morgan up to speed with all the finance-related parts of the business so she can take care of some of that for me while I'm gone. It still feels like I'm juggling a hundred more balls, and I'm worried I'll drop one of them and they'll break. But I'm sure once I'm settled in LA, this will all feel more doable.

I pull up the driveway to the beautiful wooden mountain house Josh designed, marveling at the huge windows and their view of the valley, and park in front of the three-car garage.

The second my car is in park, my phone buzzes with a text message. It's from CeCe, which is funny because I didn't even realize that I had her number in my phone. It must have been from years ago, back when we had the same circle of friends in New York.

CECE

> Hey Petra! Tony and I miss Stella. Alex is so unaccommodating about us visiting her. Think you could talk to him about that?

A shudder of revulsion runs through me. The way we left things after their last visit, I can't believe she'd dare ask. There is something just not right about Tony. The way he looks at Stella gives me the creeps, and the thought of her having to see them again, much less ever ending up with them, is almost enough to make me hop on the first flight back to New York just to protect her myself.

I don't respond. Instead, I start a text to my favorite private investigator friend.

PETRA

> I know you haven't heard from me in a while, but how would you feel about helping an old friend out?

308

ALICIA

Girl, you're my favorite person to help out. What do you need?

PETRA

Are you opposed to getting dirt on high-profile assholes?

ALICIA

Last name, please?

PETRA

Gionetti.

ALICIA

Like shipping tycoon Gionetti?

PETRA

His son, Tony. He's married to a friend's deceased sister-in-law's sister (long story). I need you to find a reason he would not be a suitable guardian for the deceased sister-in-law's young daughter. Or find something on Tony's wife, Cecelia. Anything that could be used to prevent them from seeing her or ever getting guardianship.

ALICIA

Happy to help. I have a few other priority cases right now. On a scale of one to life and death, where does this fall?

PETRA

Not life and death, but ASAP?

ALICIA

On it. I'll get back to you when I have something.

> **PETRA**
>
> You really are the best, and the best at what you do.

> **ALICIA**
>
> I know. You take care of yourself.

> **PETRA**
>
> You too, thanks!

I throw my phone in my purse, relieved to know Alicia is looking into this for me. After what she was able to find on Ryan back when he was stealing from me and others, I'm confident that if there is something to find here, she'll dig it up. And I will have something that can help Aleksandr even if I can't be there in person to help.

"You're here!" Lauren says when she flings open the front door and meets me on the wide front porch. Her red hair hangs well past her shoulders and with her flat riding boots on, she barely comes up to my shoulders. I wrap her in a hug and she says, "I missed you. First, you desert me for three weeks, and now you're moving to LA?"

"It's just for a couple months," I tell her as I pull back and look down at her. She's wearing a lightweight black sweater dress with a deep V-neck and it shows off her creamy skin and motherly curves perfectly. "Also," I tell her, "that dress is sexy as hell on you. Motherhood gave you a great rack."

A laugh bursts out of her, and in Lauren-like fashion it sounds like it came from the mouth of a fairy. "I can confidently tell you that big boobs are the only physical perk of having grown two tiny humans in my body. This dress"—she points to the part that wraps around her waist like a belt—"hides many of the flaws."

"Well, personally, I think you're even sexier now that you've had kids." I think back to the month the girls spent in the NICU after they were born, and now they are healthy and strong and already crawling. "And it was all worth it for the girls."

I don't miss her side-eye. A few months ago, I told her that watching her pregnancy convinced me I never wanted to have children. I was trying to sympathize with what a terrible pregnancy she'd had, but I'd already decided I didn't want kids, and even I can admit it was a shitty thing to say. Especially now that I've spent the last few weeks around Stella, and could easily imagine what a mother-daughter relationship would be like if it were with her. Maybe kids aren't so bad after all?

"What's gotten into you? Is this because of that little girl you were holding at that hockey game?"

I roll my head back and look at the beadboard ceiling of the porch. *Fuck.* Sometimes it feels impossible to keep secrets with my girlfriends.

"I saw the video of you and Alex Ivanov locking eyes," Lauren says when I don't respond, "and when I texted Jackson and Sierra to see if one of them knew what was going on, Sierra told us that you didn't want to talk about it yet. So neither Jackson nor I pushed."

Even after I told Sierra what was going on the other day, she didn't run back and tell Jackson or Lauren. Interesting.

"Well, we've got some stuff to catch up on then," I tell her as I follow her through the entryway.

"Good," she says, and it's then that I notice the voices coming from her kitchen. Obviously, it's not just Josh in there. "Because, even though I know how you hate surprises, I invited some friends."

We round the corner and Jackson and Sierra are squealing and rushing toward me. "What are you doing here?" I ask as they envelop me and Lauren in a group hug. Over their shoulders, I see Nate, Beau, and Josh watching us closely.

"You didn't think you were moving to LA without saying goodbye, did you?" Jackson asks.

"But you don't even live here anymore," I say, looking between her and Sierra.

"It doesn't matter where we live," Sierra says. "No way we're letting a huge milestone like this go by without being here to celebrate with you."

"But I thought you were in Europe or something?"

"Nope, Beau and I are in Blackstone, staying with Jackson and Nate for a while before we head down to Costa Rica." I marvel at the one-eighty Sierra's done over the past couple months, going from an uptight planner who had to stick to the path she'd set for herself, to someone who can travel the globe with her snowboarding boyfriend, making up their itinerary as they go. "Surf season's starting for Beau and I want to learn to scuba dive."

"And we haven't all been together since Sierra's birthday," Jackson says. "Three months feels like forever to not see all your best friends." She wraps her arms around us for another squeeze, and I'm caught off guard at how uncharacteristically emotional Jackson's being.

"You okay?" I ask her quietly.

"I'm great," she says, "it's just that everything is changing so fast for everyone."

Josh lures us further into the kitchen with the offer of drinks, and we stand around the large kitchen island grazing on the appetizers Lauren's set up on the counter. She's not big on cooking, but she can put together a mean predinner spread and she's the queen of interesting salads.

I add more dip to a cracker and take in the scene around me. It's interesting watching the energy in the room—it's all happiness and love.

Nate has his arm wrapped around Jackson's lower back and is absently stroking her hip with his thumb. The newlywed period is treating them well. I have known them since they were barely twenty, back when their love and their tempers both burned equally bright. And now, a decade later, I'm confident their seasoned love is the real deal. They're going to be the ones we watch to see how it's done.

Next to them, Beau is feeding Sierra a piece of chicken and as she sucks the barbecue sauce off his fingers, he dips his head toward her ear. Given how his body is pressed up against her hip, I don't need much imagination to guess what he's saying. I've never seen a guy so whipped over a girl as Beau is with Sierra, and I've never known anyone who deserved that adoration more than she does.

Josh and Lauren had a whirlwind romance and were married only a few months after they met, but that was years ago, before I knew them. Since then, they suffered through miscarriages and infertility treatments together. I don't know Josh nearly as well as I know Lauren, but I see the protective way he hovers around her, always wanting to make sure she's safe and cared for.

I wonder what that would feel like to know you were loved? To have someone who wanted to build the kind of partnership Jackson and Nate have built, or to receive the kind of adoration that Beau reserves for Sierra, or to have the deep trust that Josh and Lauren share? Is that what Sasha and I started—something that could develop into a lasting love? Did I make a mistake in refusing to stay?

Suddenly I have such a longing for him that my response is physical, a shudder that runs through my whole body like the feelings are refusing to stay inside me.

Nate's the one to notice, and he dips his eyebrows. "You okay?" he asks, and five other pairs of eyes turn toward me.

Oh yeah, just the only single girl here and, for the first time in my life, I'm not okay with that. I want Sasha here with me. I want his hand resting possessively on my lower back, I want him mixing up a drink he knows I like, I want him growing close with my friends and their significant others, and I want to know that at the end of the night I'll be going home with him—to have him to talk to on the drive home, to feel the sexual tension building as we approach my apartment, and then being able to rip his clothes off the minute we walk through the door. I wonder if he's still up? Should I call him?

"Petra," Sierra says, "you're scaring me." Then to our friends: "Look how she's just staring off into space like that."

"Sorry, just lost in thought," I say, shaking my head to clear away the mental images of Sasha and me naked in my apartment.

I exhale and attempt to relax my whole body as I set the glass down. It sort of works, until Jackson says, "This wouldn't have anything to do with that super hot hockey player you were eye-fucking on national television, would it?"

I'm not sure if the heat I feel flooding into my face is embarrassment or anger. It's unlike Jackson to call me out like this, but to be fair, I'd never think twice about saying something like that to one of my friends. It's a taste of my own medicine, for sure.

"It's probably time for us to start grilling that steak, right guys?" Nate is all smoothness as he steps back, cuing Josh and Beau to do the same.

The three of them are at the back door so quickly they almost forget the meat. While I glare at Jackson, Lauren takes the foil-wrapped serving platter from the fridge and brings it over to them.

"That was an asshole move," I tell Jackson once the guys escape to the huge stone patio out back.

She smiles sweetly at me. "Sorry, but we don't keep secrets from each other."

"Like hell we don't. One word—Marco."

Sierra's laugh bursts out of her mouth so quickly it surprises even her.

"Touché," Jackson says with a small eye roll.

"Can we go back to you eye-fucking Alex Ivanov on national TV, please?" Lauren says. "Because it sure as hell didn't look like you just happened to catch his eye. He was flat out staring at you, and who was that child you were holding? And why were you wearing his jersey?"

I share the same details I'd given Sierra over the phone two days ago. When I finish, there's a moment where Lauren and Jackson are speechless, and Sierra looks nervously between them.

"Who even are you?" Lauren asks when I'm done. "What happened to hating kids?"

"And never spending more than one night with a guy? Now you're married," Sierra mutters.

I expect Jackson to chime in too, but when I glance at her, she's just got this lost look like she's sad or disappointed. "I guess we all have secrets," she said. "I just didn't expect that you'd have this person who was so important, so pivotal to your life, and never mention him once in all the years we've been friends."

"It was such a long time ago," I say, trying not to think about the fact that Aleksandr is hardly the only secret I've kept from her and from everyone else. "I guess I didn't feel like sharing the parts of me that were devastated when he left like that."

"Why did he?" Lauren asks. "It sounds like you two were so close, and obviously attracted to each other, and you loved each other . . ." She trails off, trying to interpret his motivations. I've never been able to make sense of that, no matter how many times I thought it through.

"I don't really know."

"You didn't ask?" Jackson asks. Her voice is incredulous. "That's not like you either."

"I feel unlike myself in a lot of ways lately," I say, glancing over her head and out the kitchen window. All I see is the inky blue outline of the coniferous trees, barely lit by the light of the moon, lining the furthest extent of the patio.

"There has to be a reason," Sierra says.

"You need to find out, obviously," Jackson says, "because you can't move forward with this relationship without knowing the truth." Her words echo my own conclusions from my conversation with Sierra. "Maybe that's what's holding you back?"

Maybe. "What's holding me back is the impossibility of it all. I'm moving to LA. He has to stay in New York. And the only way I can help him adopt Stella is to give up my dreams and move back to New York."

"Would that really be giving up your dreams, though?" Jackson asks. "I mean, you didn't even want this TV gig in the first place. You had to be convinced by your producer, and when we talked about it a few weeks ago, you still seemed kind of hesitant. Is this opportunity really worth giving up on a relationship that could be forever?"

"Why does she have to give up on it?" Sierra asks Jackson. "Obviously the show is important to her *now*, even if she was hesitant to start with." She turns toward me. "Why can't you just take these couple months to film your show, see where the relationship goes, and figure out where to go once filming is done?"

"How in the world would I make a long-distance relationship work in the meantime?" I ask.

"Jackson and Nate did it," Lauren reminds me. "After they got back together, he was still in Europe for a few months before he came back to Blackstone."

"It was hard," Jackson says, "but it wasn't impossible. When you have something worth fighting for, Petra, you fight. You don't walk away. Is this worth fighting for?"

I chew my lips between my teeth to hold in the *Yes!* that wants to burst out. "I think so," I finally say.

"Then fight, girl," Sierra says. "Be unapologetically you. Be a badass *and* in love. The two aren't mutually exclusive."

"To being a badass in love," Jackson says, raising her glass. We all follow suit, and I smile, relief flooding through me because it all feels more possible now.

———

Dinner is delicious and over too quickly. Because Sierra and Beau's relationship is so new, and Jackson and Nate didn't live here when Sierra and Beau got together, this is the first time my girlfriends and I have hung out with their significant others all together as a group. That sense of hope that was ignited with our toast earlier has me wishing even more that someday Sasha can be a part of this. I think he'd like my friends and get along with their men.

"I'm headed to Mammoth next month," Josh says in response to a question Nate asks him about skiing. The two have never known each other very well since Josh's departure from the National Ski Team is what opened a spot for Nate. Like nearly all the relationships stitched together around this table, Jackson is the common thread.

Lauren pushes her chair back so abruptly that all six pairs of eyes swing toward her. "I'm going to grab some more wine," she says, and she turns to head into the kitchen.

I'm not quite sure what I saw in her eyes as she turned away, but it has me worried. "I'll help her," I tell my friends before following Lauren into the kitchen.

I find her squatting so she's sitting on her heels, staring at the unopened wine fridge. Her forehead is resting against the glass door, and I watch as her ribcage expands and contracts with a few deep breaths.

Her head whips up to look over her shoulder as I approach, then she sighs with visible relief before saying, "Oh, it's you."

"Who did you think it would be?" I ask.

"I don't know, but I'm glad it's you." Her words are a shock. Out of all my friends, I have the least in common with

Lauren and I don't know her quite as well as I know Jackson and Sierra. We're friends, but I don't know that we would ever have been close if it hadn't been for Jackson.

"What's going on?" I ask as I reach my hand out and pull her up to a standing position.

"Nothing." She pauses. "I mean, it just gets lonely, you know? I'm home *all the time* with the twins. Josh is retired from skiing but still acts like it's his job to travel to every ski resort on the planet. He's gone on some big trip at least once a month, and I'm stuck here. I don't have any family here, and even though Josh's parents are here, his mom is like the queen of the ice queens, you know?"

I nod, even though I've never met Josh's mom. This is not the first time Lauren has mentioned her, and she sounds quite difficult. Instead of being the doting grandmother Lauren had hoped for, her mother-in-law is hypercritical of Lauren as a mom.

"And now that Jackson and Sierra have both moved away," she continues, "and you're going to LA for a few months . . . I just don't have anyone now except for Josh."

"I'm sorry, Lauren," I say.

"No, please don't feel bad about chasing your dreams. And don't feel bad for me about this situation. I'm the one who jumped into this marriage after knowing Josh for what, a few weeks? I left my whole world behind for him. And I didn't regret it one bit, at first. But now that we have kids . . ." she says, "it's like I can feel him pulling away and I don't know what I can do about it. He's gone a lot, and I have no idea who any of these people are that he travels with. I want to hold on tightly, make him stay here and spend time with his family. But I feel like the more tightly I hold on, the more he pulls away."

"Lauren, I had no idea." I wrap my arms around her, and I can tell how hard she's trying not to cry by the way she holds her breath through our hug.

"This is all so new," she says. "Having kids. Feeling my heart grow larger to accommodate how much I love them, and Josh, and our life together. Watching him grow distant while all this is happening . . . we should be enjoying this time together, watching our girls grow and hit their milestones, reveling in the family we've created. Having my expectations be so out of line with my reality is hard."

"Have you talked to him? Told him how you're feeling?"

"Every time I try to bring it up," she says, her voice dropping even lower to make sure they can't hear us in the other room, "he makes it seem like this is about me being insecure and clingy. He thinks that me not wanting him to go on these ski trips every few weeks is ridiculous. He reminds me that he used to be gone for months at a time when he was competing on the National Ski Team, and he clearly doesn't understand why this is different. But that was his *job*, and we didn't have kids."

I can't argue the second point, but the first is kind of wrong. Josh is a ski pro. These trips he takes are him traveling with other pros, representing the brands that sponsor him. As someone who used to be in sports marketing, I know Lauren understands that this is what pays their bills. I'm sure Josh has a decent amount of savings, but this huge house they built had to have cost a fortune, and bills still need to be paid.

"Now he's *choosing* to leave his family like twenty-five

percent of the time just for fun, and when he is here . . ." She pauses. "Sometimes it seems like his head is somewhere else."

I am both shocked by this revelation, and shocked she's telling *me*. I have no experience in this area, no advice to offer.

"Have you talked to anyone else about how you're feeling?"

"Like a therapist?" she asks, then lets out a bitter laugh. "When would I have time to do that? Even when he's home, Josh is useless with the girls."

I think about the way he was hovering near her earlier. "Josh has always seemed so protective of you, like he just wants to make sure you're happy."

"Yeah, it always felt that way to me too. I'm not sure what's changed, but now it feels like he's becoming controlling and absent at the same time."

"Lauren," I say, bowing my head so she won't see the frown. How has she been going through this and hasn't told any of us? "What can I do?"

"There's nothing you can do, really. He's the one who should be doing something differently, and until I figure out how to have a talk with him about this that doesn't result in him telling me I'm being clingy and desperate, or me telling him he's being controlling . . . there isn't much anyone can do."

"I really think you should talk to someone. I'd offer to watch the girls for you, but since I'm going to be gone the next couple months, I'm useless. But," I say, an idea forming in my mind as it comes out my mouth, "Morgan used to nanny during the summers in college, didn't she? And hasn't she babysat for you before?"

"She has," Lauren says, but I can tell by her voice that she doesn't like asking for help, even if it's from her cousin.

"Why don't you see if she could watch the girls while you talk to someone? Her work schedule is totally flexible, so it doesn't matter if it has to be during the day."

Lauren gives me a small smile that doesn't touch her sad eyes, but it's a start.

"If that doesn't work out, I'll help you think up another plan, okay? I really want to make sure you get the help you need to navigate this in a way that's going to be good for you, Josh, and the girls."

Lauren folds into me and I wrap my arms around her small frame, trying really hard not to imagine this same situation playing out between me and Aleksandr if we tried to make things work between us. *Things already work, even with a child in the mix*, I remind myself.

But I can't shake the niggly feeling that what Lauren is experiencing is, if not the norm, still totally normal. Once the newness and the lust fade, is this what you're left with—chasing your husband's affections, begging for his spare moments, hoping he'll be the father you thought he'd be?

I promised myself a long time ago that I'd never put a man and his needs before my own, that I'd always be first string in my own life. I can't go through the kind of hurt I've been through before, or the kind I'm seeing Lauren go through right now.

I just can't.

———

I've never known the kind of bone-weary exhaustion that I'm experiencing. Even back in my modeling days, when it felt like all I ever did was go from photoshoots to runways to parties, over and over again—running on caffeine and too little food—I wasn't this tired. *You were also almost a decade younger,* I remind myself, *you had more energy then.*

I collapse onto my couch, wondering how I can simultaneously feel so fulfilled and so empty at the same time. The show is amazing. The crew, the guests, the whole experience —it has completely blown away my expectations. It's so much better than I could have even imagined. And my company is doing well. Morgan has really stepped up in my absence, the junior event planners are doing amazing. Finding the time to fit in meetings and calls, and making sure that no balls get dropped has been a challenge, but things could not be going better. And yet . . .

I'm running on empty.

I'm lonely.

I'm missing Sasha and Stella more than I thought possible.

Even so, I'm holding him at a distance, afraid to trust him with my heart. I know we need to have some important conversations: about why he cut me out of his life when we were teenagers, about how to move forward from here. But I can't seem to bring myself to talk to him about these things over the phone, especially not when I'm this tired all the time.

I pull up our text thread and rewatch the video Stella sent me earlier.

I miss you so much, Petra. Look what Dada and I made.

The camera flips, and it shows me a calendar on her wall. There are three weeks' worth of red X's on it, and on the last day it says in big red letters: PETRA! She flips the camera back to herself. *I can't wait to see you. How long will you stay?*

I open the camera on my phone to record a video reply and am appalled at the dark circles under my eyes, the way my skin looks sallow and my eyelids look droopy—all the things my "TV makeup" hides are so obvious now that I've washed my face. Ugh. I don't want to document myself looking like this. Even though I know Stella won't care, I don't really want Sasha to see me like this either. It's vain and stupid, this hesitance I'm feeling, but I hate being vulnerable in any way.

I'll film a reply to her tomorrow, after the hair and makeup people on set have had their way with me. I'm sure I can find a few moments alone in my dressing room to record and send it. I pull up the Reminders on my phone and set it for tomorrow so I don't forget. No matter how good my intentions are , I'm juggling too many balls and liable to drop them all if I rely on my memory.

I scroll back to Sasha's last text above Stella's video.

ALEKSANDR

Call me tonight if you have a minute.

My finger hovers over the call button on the screen, but I hesitate to touch it. I'm not sure I have the energy for a conversation. Especially not if it's as tense as the last conversation we had. How have I only talked to him once in the last week and a half? I feel simultaneously awed that the time is passing so quickly, and ashamed that I haven't made time for him. But where would I find the time, exactly? Right now, when I can barely keep my eyes open and it's almost midnight his time?

I hit the button to initiate the call, then put the phone on speaker and set it next to me on the cushion as I stretch out on the couch.

"'Lo?" Aleksandr's voice is groggy when he answers his phone with a half-word.

"Hey there. I'm sorry I'm calling so late."

"'S fine," he says.

"No, it's not. I'm sorry I woke you."

"I said to call me tonight when you have a minute," he says, his voice functioning appropriately now that he's waking up. "I wanted to talk to you, I don't care what time it is."

"Being in different time zones sucks. It makes it even harder to talk to you and impossible to talk to Stella." When I get up in the morning, she's already at school. When I get home from work, she's already long asleep.

"Hey," he says, "what's wrong? You sound like you're tearing up."

I use the back of my hand to wipe away the tears that are streaming down my face.

"I'm just exhausted, so everything seems like an insurmountable problem. I'm fine, really."

"Why are you so exhausted? Are you sleeping poorly?"

"No, I'm sleeping fine." In fact, I don't think I've ever slept so much in my life, but I still wake up feeling exhausted.

"Petra," he purrs. "You shouldn't be feeling exhausted like that if you're sleeping enough. Are you sure you're not sick?" The concern in his voice is endearing.

"I don't feel sick. Just tired. Like hard to even get out of bed in the morning tired."

"You're not pregnant, are you?" His voice is suddenly incredibly alert, and . . . what is that tone? Hopeful?

I think back to the incredibly painful period I had the first week I was here. They seem to be getting worse as I get older. "No, I'm definitely not."

"You're sure?"

"Positive. I got my period right after I arrived in LA."

"Then you need to see a doctor. Get to the bottom of why you're feeling like this."

"I'm feeling like this because I have a grueling schedule that consists of like eight hours of hair, makeup, and filming a day, plus I'm still running my business too."

"That shouldn't make you feel like you can't get out of bed after a good night's sleep."

I know he's right. "I don't even have a doctor here."

"Then go to Urgent Care. This isn't rocket science, Petra." He apparently doesn't like my *Hmm* response because he asks, "Do I need to come out there and take you to the doctor myself?"

The thought of seeing him again, feeling his arms around me, has more tears streaming down my face. I want him so badly. But also, I feel like I *need* him. And isn't that exactly what Sierra warned me about? That I should want him in my life, not because I need him, but because I *don't* need him and my life is better with him in it anyway?

These emotions and this confusion, this *is why you don't do relationships,* I tell myself. Too much angst. My happiness should never be tied to another person's presence.

"You don't need to take me to the doctor. If I don't feel better soon, I'll go. I promise."

He clears his throat. "What if I want to come out there just to see you?"

My heart does a little flip. "You know I want to see you," I tell him. "But there's no time. It would be a wasted trip for you. Even when I'm not filming, I'm still working. My only day off is Sunday."

"You know I'd fly across the country even if it was to see you just for one day, right?"

Cue my heart melting, my breath frozen in my lungs. "Sasha," my voice warns. This is too much. "I'll be back there in a few weeks. It's not worth wasting your whole weekend for a day together."

"I'm sorry you think that would be a waste," he says, but I can't tell how he's feeling. Disappointed? Sad? Angry?

"That's not what I meant."

He lets out a long sigh, and the sound carries through my phone speaker like a big *whoosh*. "When you left, we said we weren't going to say goodbye to this relationship. And yet this is the second week you've been gone and only the second time I've talked to you."

"I'm sorry," I say, burrowing my head into the pillow and wishing I could close my eyes and succumb to sleep. But he deserves to have this conversation. *We* deserve it. "I am not trying to ignore you," I say, and wince a bit at the tiny white lie. I have definitely held him at arm's length since I left, because I know how many balls I can juggle and I'm already maxed out. "I can't over-emphasize how busy I've been. And I do want to see you, I really do. But I think that only having a day to spend with you while you're here would make this harder. I'd rather wait until I can really focus on you, devote more than twenty-four hours to being together. This past week and a half has been hard, but it has also flown by. Only a couple more weeks until I'm back in New York."

His silence gives me hope that he understands. "I'd be thrilled to have even one day with you right now. But I don't want to make things harder for you."

"We can revisit all of this when I'm back for your party."

"That feels like forever from now."

"It will pass quickly," I say, hoping I sound persuasive. "You're about to start your next round of playoff games. You'll be so busy you won't even have time to miss me." I try to laugh to pass that statement off as a joke, but it falls flat.

"I've missed you for fourteen years," he says. "I hardly think I'm going to stop now."

And suddenly I can't breathe. The part of me that wants to demand he tell me why he told me he didn't see me "like that" and then cut me out of his life, wars with the part of me that isn't sure I can even form a coherent sentence right now. This moment, when I'm too exhausted to keep my eyes open for even a second longer, feels like the wrong time to start a crucially important conversation like this one.

Instead, I say, "Good. Don't stop."

"Petra, I couldn't stop thinking about you and missing you if my life depended on it. Is that what you wanted to hear?"

That certainly wasn't what I was expecting to hear, but it's what I needed to know.

"Yes." The word is a whisper escaping my lips. I don't know what the future holds for us, but I need to know he's in this as much, or maybe even more than I am. "I have to go now. I can't stay awake any longer."

"Are you in bed already?" He sounds so much more alert than me, even though I woke him up from a dead sleep only minutes ago.

"I'm on the couch."

"I wish I was there to carry you to your bedroom and tuck you in." His voice is so gentle and I'm so worn out that his words have my eyes stinging as tears threaten to fall again.

"Me too."

"You're not going to get off that couch tonight, are you?" He chuckles.

"So comfy," I tell him.

"Set your alarm on your phone right now," he says, "so you don't oversleep in the morning."

"So bossy," I say, even though he's right. I set the alarm, then put the phone back down next to my face.

After a moment's pause, he asks, "Did you do it?"

"Yes."

"Okay. Good night."

"Night." I don't even disconnect the call, I just assume he's going to do that, and I close my eyes, relieved when everything fades to black.

Chapter Twenty Three

ALEKSANDR

It's been almost three weeks since Petra left and I've only talked to her three fucking times. Her lack of availability is driving me crazy. Every conversation is the same: *I'm so busy, I don't know when things are going to let up, I miss you but I don't have time for you.*

At least she figured out the exhaustion issue. After collapsing at work, they sent her straight to the ER, where she was diagnosed with severe anemia. They gave her iron intravenously and prescribed iron supplements which she promises she's taking regularly. The doctor said it might take as long as a month or two for her to start feeling back to normal, but she insists that just a few days later, she's already feeling much better.

Even though I know she's truly busy, and even though I know her exhaustion was a real thing, I can't help but wonder if she's holding me at a distance because her feelings are changing.

As the driver navigates his way through Hollywood, I check my phone again for my instructions and hope she's going to be excited to see me. I know how she feels about surprises, and I just hope she's not pissed off at my presence here. But after we won our second round of playoffs in Game 5, I found myself with a free weekend. I'd already scheduled Raina to stay with Stella for the weekend because I thought I'd still be in St. Louis and so instead of flying home to New York, I flew to LA.

God, I hope she isn't mad. It's too late now, because the driver is pulling up to the studio gate and giving them my information. She's going to have no clue this is coming, no clue it would even be possible for me to visit her on set. I had to be backdoor sneaky to make this happen.

I watch the nearly identical white buildings pass as we drive through the lot, thinking back to the first conversation we had after she'd arrived in LA. She'd been telling me about her first day on set, where she jokingly said she'd met the president of my fan club—a girl named Jolene—who'd recognized Petra from our playoff game against Philadelphia where the cameras had caught us with our eyes locked on each other. Apparently Jolene was gushing with effusive praise about me as a hockey player, and was a bit star struck that Petra knew me.

Jolene was an uncommon enough name that when I asked Tom to have his people find her, he was able to get back to me with a name and phone number in about fifteen minutes. From there, it was easy enough to call and convince her to help me surprise Petra. She got my name on whatever lists were necessary, and is meeting me to take me backstage so I can watch the show as it's filmed. I could not have emphasized the need for secrecy more than I did, so I just hope she's kept her mouth shut. She insisted that all she wanted in exchange for helping me was an autograph, so I pray that she's holding true to her word and isn't going to sell the story of my surprise visit to some gossip rag.

Each building we pass is marked with a large black painted number and a sign that indicates which show is currently filming on that set. Finally we arrive at Petra's show, *And Yet We Rise*, and a woman with long auburn hair is standing outside looking at her phone. When the car door shuts behind me, her head snaps up and a huge smile spreads across her face.

"You made it," she calls out as she takes a few steps toward me.

"You must be Jolene," I hold my hand out and when she places her hand in mine, I worry for a moment that she's going to pull me in for a hug, but she steps back, keeping it professional.

"Indeed. Here," she says as she reaches into the bag slung over her shoulder, "would you mind signing this before we go in?" She hands me a New York jersey and a Sharpie.

"Where'd you find this on such short notice?" I ask. I mean, I only called her yesterday.

She looks up at me with a distinct eye roll. "I already owned it."

Ah, that's right, president of my fan club and all that. I flip the jersey over and find my name and number on the back, scrawl my signature across the number, and hand it back to her, along with her pen. Then she's leading me and my suitcase through the door.

"So, how long have you and Petra known each other?" Jolene asks casually as she leads me down a long hallway.

"We're childhood friends." I keep my response brief, so I

don't say anything Petra might not want people to know. I'm not in the business of sharing my personal life with strangers anyway—too easy for something to be taken out of context.

"Are you in town for long?" she asks, clearly attempting to make polite conversation as we take a left and head down another hallway.

"Just a couple days." Luckily we arrive at a door labeled with Petra's name, and my stomach flips because holy shit, I wasn't quite ready to see her yet.

"She's on set," Jolene says, "but you can leave your suitcase here."

"Okay," I say, opening the door. The room is tiny, lit mostly by the twenty or so bulbs that frame the large mirror above a counter on one wall. There's a chair in front of it, and a couch on the opposite wall. The third wall, across from the doorway, is taken up by a rack stuffed full of clothes.

I set my suitcase to the side of the door and tell my body to calm the hell down. The realization that I'm going to see her shortly has the adrenaline running through my system. I don't even get this nervous when I'm on the ice, facing five 200-pound players who want to body-slam me into the wall or knock my ass over onto the ice. The potential damage from physical threats doesn't hold a candle to the kind of damage Petra could do to my heart. But I'm tired of treading carefully, waiting for her to come around. Three weeks is too fucking long to go without seeing her. Even if she doesn't know she needs to see me, I know it.

I shut the door behind me and follow Jolene down two more hallways. "Oh good," she says when we come to the end. "They're not filming yet." She points to a light by the door that's not illuminated. "Let's slip in and watch from the back."

I follow her through the door, which she only half opens, and we slink along the back wall. The lights are off in this back section of the studio, and there are cameras and about eight or nine people between us and the stage.

The first thing I see, as if all the equipment and people are invisible, is Petra. She's sitting on the edge of a beige high-backed chair reviewing some flash cards. She's wearing a black dress with a bustier top and spaghetti straps. The dress itself is fitted down past her thighs and the hem has a four-inch row of pleats that comes just to the bottom of her knees, revealing the curve of her muscular calves.

"What's your role in all this?" I whisper to Jolene as people continue moving around us, checking equipment, moving things into place, nodding to Jolene as they pass.

"I'm her stylist," she whispers back. "I decide what her aesthetic will be for each show: what she wears, and what her hair and makeup will be. Today she's interviewing one of the first female billionaires, a rocket scientist who funded the development of a life-saving technology for kids with heart problems. So we're going for high-powered sexy today. Like they're meeting for drinks."

"Nailed it," I mutter under my breath, and out of the corner of my eye I see a slow smile spread across Jolene's face.

"Man, you've got it bad." Her laugh is a low chuckle, quiet enough to not attract attention to us.

My eyes swing over to her, and I'm sure the look of alarm is written all over my face.

"Don't worry," she says, and pats my arm. "Your secret is safe with me."

"Is it, though?"

"I signed the same NDA that everyone else here did. We can't talk about anything that happens on set, or about anyone who works on this show, to anyone outside of the show. In fact, I will probably get my ass canned if you don't sign one too. I'll have legal bring the paperwork down when filming is done, okay?"

"Sure."

She looks down at her phone, shooting off a quick text. "All set."

I'm about to respond when the action starts. I've been a guest on late-night shows in New York before, but the format of this show is so different. Instead of the host interviewing several guests, playing some silly games, and interacting with the live audience, the entire show is just one interview. And all the pressure is on Petra to lead this dance. Watching her onstage is a next-level turn-on.

As the cameras roll, she takes on a variety of different personas: she's curious and hard-hitting with her questions, but also comes across as an understanding friend you can share anything with. The questions she asks are so far below the surface-level fluff that TV shows tend to ask celebrities and athletes, like Petra wants to not only get to know the person she's interviewing, but wants to drill down to the essence of what makes that woman who she is. It's like she's trying to draw out all the life lessons that could be learned and she manages to cast her guest as sympathetic without leaving you feeling sympathy, makes her guest relatable even though her life is so completely unlike anyone else's, and fashions the woman as an inspiration for other women.

An hour and a half later, as Petra is thanking her guest

and shaking her hand, my feet are rooted to the spot. I've been utterly transfixed the entire time. So much so that I didn't even notice that Jolene wasn't next to me anymore. I glance around and see that she's hovering by the door we came in. When the lights come back up, Jolene opens the door, grabs a piece of paper and pen, and is heading back toward me.

I don't even read the NDA, just sign it and ask that she have legal send me a copy of it. Then I'm looking back up, hoping Petra's still onstage. She is. She's reaching down to her chair, collecting her flash cards as she chats with the woman she just interviewed, and when she stands and turns toward the back of the room, we lock eyes.

I know she sees me because the look of recognition is there—the way her eyes widen and her lips part for a split second before she turns her attention back to the woman she's speaking with. They exchange a few more words and a hug, and then Petra is making a beeline toward me. Other people around the studio are starting to notice me too. There's a low murmur as people look at me and then at Petra as she walks toward me.

Her face is stony as she approaches. Knowing how much she hates surprises, I didn't expect her to jump into my arms, but I also didn't expect her to look like she's on a warpath. She walks right by me and shoots a "follow me" over her shoulder. Jolene looks at me and shrugs, and I take off after Petra.

We wind through the same long white hallways back to her dressing room. She holds the door open for me, and when I follow her through into the dressing room, she turns and shuts the door with an eerie silence. The only sound I hear as she turns slowly toward me is her breath, she's inhaling and exhaling like she's trying to calm herself down.

"What are you doing here?"

"I found myself with a free weekend and an intense need to see you."

The hard lines of her face soften and she rubs her palms against her thighs. "I thought I told you not to come."

"You did, and I know you hate to be surprised. But Petra, it's been too fucking long." I cross the room in two steps and stop right in front of her. "I couldn't wait until you came back to New York to see you."

She leans forward, resting her forehead against my sternum and looking at the ground. "I missed you, too, but I'll be in New York in a couple weeks. I needed this time to focus on this new phase of my career."

"I don't want to take away from that by being here. I just want to see you. Even if it's only to have dinner with you and hold you while you fall asleep."

The hot breath of her exhale is a balm across my chest. Then she tilts her head up and looks at me as I slide my hand around her neck, reveling in the feel of her hot skin on my palm. "You're in luck, then. Tomorrow's filming is canceled. Without saying too much, because I can't tell you who she is, my guest had to fly to the Middle East to negotiate some sort of *situation*."

"Does this mean you now have the day free?"

"It does."

"And what were you planning to do with your extra day off?"

"Sleep?"

"Hmm." I nod, as I trace the line of her jaw with my

thumb. "I'm sure we can negotiate some sleep in there somewhere."

Her eyes dance and her lips curl into a predatory smile. "I don't negotiate."

I take a small step closer to her, so our bodies are touching. "Is this like when you told me you don't ask, yet you ended up *begging*?" My voice is so low I almost don't recognize it, but the longing flowing through my veins and what it's doing to my body is achingly familiar.

"I *let* you make me beg, remember?"

"Like you're going to let me win these sleep negotiations?" I dip my head and slide my lips across her forehead.

"Exactly," she says as she tilts her face up, her lips begging for a kiss. And who am I to deny her?

From the top of the hill, Los Angeles spreads out before us in all her hazy glory. It's clear enough to see the tops of the skyscrapers downtown, but the sun hasn't quite burned through the smog.

"I don't hate this view," Petra says, taking a sip of her drink, then leaning back on her elbows. Her long legs stretch out across the blanket and her smooth shoulders shine at the edges of her tank top.

"Just the climb to get to it?" I tease.

"I did hate that climb. It reminded me so much of the conditioning we used to do before the snow fell to get in shape for ski season."

"Except you were walking up a gentle path in the hills of LA, not climbing the Alps." Petra's body is all slim, graceful lines now and she clearly is not in the same athletic shape she used to be. This hike wasn't hard, even for someone carrying around as much muscle mass as me. It should have been easy for her.

"Yes, but it's been a week since I was taken to the ER for exhaustion, remember?"

Oops. "Okay, I'll stop teasing you about it. I'm sure once your energy levels are back to normal . . ." Her energy levels were just fine last night in her bedroom and this morning in her shower.

"I think my legs are just tired from last night." She winks and a laugh bursts out of me so quickly I don't even have time to consider holding it in. And then my body reacts to the memory of her riding me in the cool darkness of her bedroom with the moonlight flooding in through the windows.

"You can tell me if this is too personal," I say, not sure where the question comes from but desperately wanting to know the answer, "but who was your first?" Given that she was still a virgin when I left her in Austria, I'm expecting her to say that it's someone she met at boarding school, or even later while she was skiing on the World Cup circuit.

"You don't want to know," she says and glances away, gazing into the distance like I'm going to forget I asked the question.

"What if I *do* want to know?" I ask. I lean back on my elbow so I'm resting next to her, but she still hasn't looked at me. It doesn't matter, with those movie star sunglasses, I wouldn't be able to see her eyes anyway. All her emotion lies in her eyes.

"Trust me," she says. Her voice is as flat and cold as a

sheet of ice as she turns her head back toward me. "You really don't."

I turn on my hip so I'm facing her. "Why don't I want to know, exactly?"

"Too close to home," she says.

What the hell? I furrow my brow as I try to think about what she could mean. Who the hell would be too close to home? "Not Niko?"

She laughs. "Oh God no. Definitely not Niko. I never so much as looked at your brother."

"Good. I was too old for you back then, so he was *really* too old for you."

I can't read the look that passes over her face. "Petra"—my voice is soft but insistent—"tell me."

"No."

"Why not."

"Because once you know, you can't un-know it." She looks away again, as if downtown LA is the most interesting sight on the planet. Meanwhile, I can't take my eyes off her in that maroon spandex tank top that's barely containing her cleavage.

"You can't say shit like that and expect me not to be even more curious." I reach over and tilt her chin back toward me. "Tell me."

"Fine. But don't say I didn't warn you." She pauses and waits for me to nod in agreement. "Felix."

"Who the hell is Felix?" I ask, but she doesn't say anything. Then it hits me. "Not the fucking gardener?"

A slight nod of her head is all the response I get.

"Are you kidding me?"

Her forehead wrinkles above the top rim of her sunglasses. "See, this is why I didn't want to tell you."

"He was ten years older than you!" A shiver runs up my spine at the thought of sixteen-year-old Petra being mauled by the attractive but creepy gardener.

She gives me a curt nod and takes another drink from the can she's holding with a look of utter indifference. Does she really not see why this is such a big deal?

"Was it that summer before you went to boarding school?" I ask.

Another nod. "After you left."

"Did you sleep with him *because* I left?" My voice is loud, even to my own ears. I need to get a fucking grip. This was over a decade ago. Why am I so upset by it?

"In a way, yes. I was just so sad, and he was there and paying attention to me. It felt like . . ." she says, then trails off for a few seconds. "Like it would help me get over you leaving."

"And did it?"

Her derisive snort is her answer.

If I'd have known that my breaking off our friendship like that would lead her straight into the arms of that perverted asshole, I never would have done it, even though my father demanded it. In trying to protect her from a truth and a marriage she didn't want, I led her to seek comfort from someone with the power to hurt her. As much as I've thought about it over the years, I don't know what I could have done differently—but I really wish I'd tried harder to figure out a different solution.

"Was it any good?" I don't know what makes me ask this.

341

Maybe a morbid sense of curiosity, or an instinct to make sure she wasn't hurt.

"It should have been. *He* should have been." Her nostrils flare, but I can't tell how she's feeling because of those damn reflective sunglasses covering her eyes.

"Petra, look at me," I say, and she moves her head a quarter-turn so she's facing me. "Without the sunglasses."

She shakes her head, a tiny movement back and forth.

"Did he hurt you?" I ask, reaching my hand over and resting it on her forearm. Her skin is soft, but the muscles beneath them ripple with tension.

"What do you want me to say?" she asks, her voice thin and sad.

"What happened?" In my mind, I'm calculating how long it'll take me to track him down, and how I can kill him with the least chance of getting caught.

"He didn't hurt me physically." Her sigh is enormous, and the part of me that wants to tell her she doesn't have to tell me anything she doesn't want to is eclipsed by the part of me that needs to know what happened to her. In the end, I stay silent and she continues. "Except that it was my first time, and I really wasn't ready, but he was incredibly persistent and persuasive. And in the end, he wasn't exactly gentle —with my body or my feelings."

"Bastard," I spit out. "Wait, you had feelings for him?"

"No. But I had feelings about him being the first person I had sex with. And it didn't mean anything to him. He'd pull me into the potting shed for a quick fuck, then push me out the door and tell me I had to stop distracting him from work. That kind of thing."

I can tell by the way she studies me that she doesn't like

the reaction she sees on my face. Then she tilts her head down, focusing on my hand and the vice-like grip I have on her. I exhale, trying to let the tension out and loosen my grip. I slide my thumb along her skin, caressing the red mark I left behind. "I'm sorry."

"Don't be. This is why I didn't want to tell you."

"He wasn't good enough for you," I growl.

"*Even now* you're jealous?" she teases. She has no idea how I watched him watching her that summer. How I saw that predatory look in his eyes. I almost insisted Petra's father fire him, I even went to him to make the demand, but I lost my nerve. How would I have explained it? *I don't like that he looks at your daughter the same way I do?*

"*Even now* I feel responsible."

"Don't." She sits up, her back ramrod straight as she crosses her legs under her. She looks like she's doing yoga, if pissed-off yoga was a thing.

"I can't help it. I should have been there to protect you."

"No, you should have been there so it could have been you."

Her words slay me. She's right, it should have been me. But also, how much could she really have cared if she turned to someone else, gave herself to him just because I wasn't around?

"You shouldn't have gone running to him when I left, Petra. If I really meant something to you back then—"

"You shouldn't have broken my heart," she spits out.

I don't think I look down quickly enough for the brim of my hat to cover the way I wince at that statement. I can't go back and make it right. There's only now.

"I shouldn't have, you're right." I look up at her. "Can you forgive me?"

"Sasha," she says, her voice so low it's practically a whisper. "You haven't even told me why you cut me out of your life like that. This isn't about forgiving you. It's about figuring out how I could ever trust you again."

This is your chance. Tell her the truth. I watch the way the warm breeze blows a few strands of her ponytail against her neck and shoulder. I want to reach out and brush them away. I want to curl my hand around her neck, brush my lips across hers. I want to hold her and be with her, and I don't want to do anything to jeopardize the possibility of a future between us. *She's not ready for the truth.*

I don't stop to ask myself when she could ever be ready, I just plow ahead with a flimsy, minuscule piece of the truth. "I had to. I can't explain it, except that there was so much pressure. I needed a clean break from everything and everyone in Austria, so I could fully commit myself to hockey in Russia. I couldn't be thinking about you all the time. I swear I spent more time that first year trying to find you that book you wanted than I spent practicing hockey. I would have done anything to make you happy, and it was jeopardizing my hockey career. I needed distance and clarity. I needed to focus. I would never have gotten where I am now if I hadn't left like that."

Do I believe my own words? I don't know. There's a kernel of truth in there. I've thought many times over the years that breaking things off like that with her allowed me to make hockey my obsession instead of her, and so in a way, it led me to the NHL.

"You thought about me all the time, huh?" Her lips curve into a small smile.

"Every. Single. Minute."

"I wish I'd known that then."

"You were my best friend's baby sister. You were too young. And most importantly, you were just about to launch your skiing career. I couldn't get in the way of that."

She gives me a small nod of understanding. Both of us, at the beginning of promising athletic careers, headed to different countries. It's a plausible reason to have pulled the brake, even if it wasn't my *only* reason.

"I didn't want to hurt you," I tell her. "In fact, I was trying to make sure you didn't get hurt."

An acerbic laugh slips out. "Trying to make sure I didn't get hurt by hurting me?" Her eyeroll is legendary. "Men are always trying to make decisions about me, for me. No thanks. If this"—she gestures between us—"is going to be something, you have to know that about me. I make my own decisions, and I always do what's best for *me*. I spent too many years getting hurt, taken advantage of, and left. I don't even do relationships, Sasha."

"Why not?"

Her swallow is convulsive and for a minute I think no words will follow. Finally, she says, "The best way I know to protect myself is to always be the one leaving."

"Before someone else can leave you, you mean?"

"Exactly."

She's so strong and independent and fiercely protective of the people she loves. I didn't realize that front hid so much damage.

"I would never leave you. I would never hurt you." She

has to know that. If she didn't already know it back in New York, she has to know it now that I'm here in LA. Now that I came out here even when she told me not to, because I literally could not conceive of not seeing her for even a few more days.

I soft hiss escapes her lips. "Really? Because you were the first one to do both."

"Petra, we were *teenagers*. We are not the same people now that we were back then."

"I hope not," she sighs, then she leans over and lays her back against my chest. "I *really* hope not."

———

"At some point," I say as I pull her foot into my lap and slip her heel off, "we are going to need to talk about this relationship."

Her eyes roll back in her head as my thumb runs across the ball of her foot and then down the arch. She makes a soft, indistinct sound of contentment, a rumbling deep in her throat that is distinctly sexual.

"That is amazing," she says.

"Imagine what I could do if you were naked."

She glances around the small but crowded outdoor seating area of the restaurant, taking in the tables of other diners scattered amid the brick patio and surrounded by ivy-covered walls. String lights hang above us and hurricane candles sit on the tables, giving the space an ethereal glow. I want to recreate this ambiance on my terrace, so Petra and I can eat out there every night and be reminded of this dinner.

Our teak table is against one of the courtyard walls and

the nearest table is a good six feet away, but still, she looks nervous that someone will hear me. So what if they do?

"Just keep doing that, and we'll get to the rest later," she says, keeping her voice low. It's the huskiness of it that turns me on more than anything. As it always does for her and only her, my body reacts.

"Your calves still sore from the hike?" I ask as I slide my hands up her leg and massage her calf gently. The heat of the LA day is abating, and it's comfortably cool out tonight. I still can't get over how amazing the weather is here. Sunny and dry and perfect almost all the time.

"Yes. Even those amazing views weren't worth this soreness."

"Maybe you shouldn't be wearing those heels, then?" Her heeled sandals make her legs look sexy as hell, but I don't understand why she'd wear them if her calves are sore.

The way she rolls her eyes suggests she'd never be caught dead in anything else. But even though I appreciate how she looks tonight, all dolled up in a strapless sundress and these gorgeous sandals, I prefer her completely natural—just out of the shower, makeup-free and hair wet, in her pajamas, settling into my couch for the evening.

I want her permanently back in my apartment.

"Don't think that your legs are going to distract me from talking about this relationship."

"You're the one who started talking about my legs." She bats those impossibly long eyelashes at me.

"I need to know what you're thinking, Petra. Before you left, you said you didn't want to go. But once you were gone, you cut me out of your life. What happened? And how do we make sure that doesn't happen again when I leave tomorrow?"

I'm not dumb enough to think that just because things have been relatively normal while I've been here—that just because the sex has been amazing and the company has been easy, that just because we finally talked about our past—she won't try to remove herself from my life again once I'm gone. I think one of the keys to her success is her ability to hyper-focus on what's in front of her, whatever challenge or opportunity that might be. The by-product of that is pushing away everything else.

"I don't know what to say, Aleksandr," she says, and I try not to visibly cringe at the use of my full name. She seems to be using it more than my nickname now. "I am filming an entire season of a show in less than two months and also running a company from seven hundred miles away. Even though I'm not facing medically diagnosed exhaustion anymore, it's still exhausting. It's two full-time jobs. I don't have anything left to give." She leans back in her seat and crosses her arms. "The only reason we're even having this dinner, the only reason we had a great day today, is because of a freak coincidence that you happened to be in town right as my schedule cleared."

"Would this be a bad time to tell you that I manufactured a crisis to get her out of the country?" I give her a small smile, hoping that some humor can lighten her mood.

She leans forward, her face serious. "I want to be with you, Sasha. I love how things are between us, how easy and good everything is when we're together. But I just can't make that commitment right now. I don't know what my life is going to look like in two months when we finish this show.

Maybe it'll flop and I'll go back to my life in Park City. Maybe it'll do well and I'll need to be in Los Angeles full time."

It doesn't escape my notice that she doesn't mention an option that involves her being in New York. "So, what are you saying?" I don't know if this means she doesn't see a future for us.

"I . . ." She sighs. "I can't make any promises right now. I thought maybe I could, back when I was in New York, before I knew how crazy my life was going to get. It's not that I don't *want* to be with you. I really do. And it's not that I don't want to help you adopt Stella. It's just that right now, I don't think I can commit to anything more than trying this long-distance thing and seeing how it goes."

"Like I told you before, I don't want to pressure you into anything you're not ready for. Just because I know what I want this to be, what I've always wanted it to be between us, doesn't mean that I expect you to be in the same place mentally or emotionally. I understand why work has to come first right now," I tell her, because hockey has always had to come first for me. Even when Stella first came to live with me, I couldn't just not show up for games or practices. I had to learn both balance and compromise, and she will too, eventually. "I'm okay with long-distance, if that's what you're comfortable with. But Petra, I have to know that you see the possibility of *some* future between us. Even if you have no idea what that could look like or how it could work out, I need to know that's what you want, or there's no point in us moving forward."

She slides her foot up my thigh and sucks her lower lip between her teeth. "Yes, I see a future. Even though I have no idea what it will look like, and even though it scares the shit out of me to trust you."

"I swear to you," I say, leaning forward and taking her hand, "I will do everything in my power to protect your heart. I know I screwed up once. I will *not* make that mistake again."

Her breath hitches and she opens her mouth to say something but the waitress arrives with my credit card slip right then. There's so much heat in Petra's eyes, I can't wait to get her home. My signature at the bottom of the slip is an illegible scrawl, and I slide her sandal back onto her foot and usher her out of there as quickly as possible.

Chapter Twenty Four

PETRA

I'm not sure my front door is even fully shut before my back is slammed against it. Aleksandr's knee is between my legs as he trails hungry kisses down my neck to my collarbone, leaving a fresh burst of lust in his wake. His impatience thrills me. Everything I did from the moment we walked out of that restaurant was meant to torture him. The way I turned and pressed my breasts into him when I kissed him on the sidewalk. The way I brushed the back of my hand across his crotch as I reached for the car door. The way my fingers trailed up and down the inside of his thigh in the back seat on the way to my place.

I roll my hips forward, sliding my center along the ridge of his thigh. His huge legs are insanely built, thick bands of muscle that reflect how hard he works his body every day. He presses into me, the hard line of his erection pushing into me.

I move to slide my hand in between us, eager to feel him again. But in response, he grasps each of my wrists in his hands and brings them up, pinning them over my head against the door with one of his enormous hands.

He steps back half a foot and looks at me, naked lust making his eyes into a twisting riot of steel. *I will never tire of seeing him look at me like this.* The thought makes my stomach flip over angrily. I don't do forever. And yet . . .

"This is better," he says as he appraises my position trapped against the door. "But maybe it would be better without the dress, no?"

Yes, my body screams, but I just raise my eyebrow, daring him to undress me. He slips one hand behind me and gently works the zipper down, and the strapless dress falls away, landing in a puddle at my feet. His sharp intake of breath is his only visible reaction, but as his eyes slide down my body, taking in my nakedness, I glance down below his buckle and sure enough, his dick is straining toward me even bigger and harder than before.

"Could you possibly be any sexier?" he asks approvingly when his eyes finally meet mine.

"I'd be even sexier without my thong," I say. He uses the tips of his fingers to move the straps of my underwear over each hip, where they fall down my legs. I step out of both the thong and the dress and kick them to the side so I'm standing in front of him in nothing but my heels.

He steps closer to me and trails the tip of his nose down the ridge of mine before tilting his head and capturing my lips with his. The kiss is gentle, like he has all the time in the world to appreciate my body. As he parts my lips with his tongue, his free hand slides up my hip and along my ribcage until he cups my breast in his palm. When his thumb finds my pebbled, aching nipple, I moan into his mouth and that small sound seems to unleash a beast.

His kisses turn hard and insistent, his thumb slides over

my nipple again and again until I'm wrapping my leg around his lower back to bring him closer to me. My hips tilt up to meet his, thrust for thrust, but I don't want the stiff fabric of his jeans, I want the silky smoothness of his body.

I turn away from the kiss, mumbling "Take your pants off." His lips are already kissing that sensitive spot behind my earlobe and I can feel myself getting even wetter in response. I need him inside me now.

He trails his hand from my breast down my sternum, the rough pads of his fingers leaving a trail of fire as he slides them over my stomach and down to my center. He slides a finger along my crease, but even as my hips move toward him, he doesn't enter me. He brings a finger, slick with my juices, up between our faces. "How long have you been like this?"

"It started when you were rubbing my feet in the restaurant," I tell him, though our serious conversation was a bit of a buzz kill for my arousal. "And then it really kicked up a notch in the car. I wanted to climb on top of you and fuck you right there in the back seat. I bet the driver wouldn't have cared."

"Jesus, Petra," he hisses between clenched teeth. He's working hard to maintain his self-control, and I'd do just about anything to break him down, including telling him a story.

"Could you imagine?" I ask. "I could have just swung my leg over your hip and slid my underwear aside." He plunges two fingers into me, stroking deep and hard, how he knows I like it. "I was already so wet, I could have slid down your cock, taking you inside me easily." I rock my hips toward him to meet the rhythm his fingers are setting. "My breasts would have been at the same level as your face, you could have just slid the top of my dress down and taken my nipple in your mouth."

He's panting, soft breaths meeting my neck, and they turn to a groan as he pushes his erection against my hip as he plunges his fingers into me over and over. "And what would the driver have thought?"

"I mean honestly," I say, imagining the scene, "he'd probably have been jerking off to the sounds I'd have made."

"Why does the thought of having sex with you in front of someone else turn me on?" he muses.

I don't actually know. I've never before thought of having sex in front of an audience, but for some reason, this is turning me on as well. "Because it's hot."

"You're fucking unreal," he says as he pushes his fingers deeper into me, stroking the spot he knows will send me over the edge. The heel of his hand is pressed against my clit and I am so close. His lips crash into mine again, his tongue plunging inside and dominating my mouth. With each stroke of his tongue against mine and his fingers against the walls of my core, he brings me closer and closer to release. And then it's there, an explosion of sensation that ricochets through my body. I'm seeing stars behind my eyelids and I'm moaning, almost screaming, into his mouth, but he doesn't let up one bit. He milks that orgasm out of me until my legs hardly work and it feels like the only thing holding me up is his hand between my legs.

"I need you to stand by yourself," he whispers into my ear. I laugh at the thought, certain I'm about to collapse. "Just for five seconds," he says.

I nod, my eyes still closed, and lean back against the door to support myself. With one of his hands still holding mine above my head, I know I won't fall. But then he lets them go, and I bring them down to my sides, rolling my shoulders. Already there's an aching need inside me that only he can fill.

I hear him undo his belt, followed by the sound of his zipper. I open my eyes halfway to watch him slide his pants and briefs down his legs in one smooth motion. He unbuttons his shirt and tosses it to the side where he's kicked his pants. And then he takes his erection in his hand, sliding his fist over himself twice. I didn't think he could get any harder or larger than he was, but I was wrong. I lick my lips as I watch the scene, and my nipples tingle with anticipation. I want this man like I've never wanted anything in my life. It's the same feeling every single time we're together, like I will never be able to get enough of him.

He steps back to me and lifts one of my legs up so my knee is at his hip. I wrap my arms around his neck and bring his head to me so I can kiss him, and when I do, he lifts my other leg and slides himself into me in one smooth motion. With my legs wrapped around his hips and one of his forearms under my ass, he pulls out and then careens into me. I've never felt stretched open this wide and I've never been so deliciously full. I rock my hips to meet him thrust for thrust and he dips his head, trailing his tongue around one nipple before taking the other in his mouth and sucking hard. Long, pulling kisses brings my nipple deep into his mouth and it's like there's a lightning rod connecting my nipple and my core as both begin to pulse.

Oh my God, am I going to come again already? "Yes," I say, resting my head and shoulders against the wooden door. "Yes, keep doing that."

His hum of agreement reverberates through my body as I

lean my shoulders back against the door, chasing my second orgasm only minutes after the first. The feel of him, long and rigid, sliding along my already sensitive walls has my muscles quaking in response. He switches to my other breast and the minute he sucks that nipple into his mouth, my core muscles begin clenching around him. He pounds into me, lifting his head from my breast to look me in the eye. "Yes," he coaxes, "give it to me."

I climax with his name on my lips, and my body goes limp against him. I'm spent, but he's not done. He sets me down gently, then turns me so I'm facing the door. I'd forgotten that there's a circular window in the arched door until I'm looking out at my quiet street. He uses his feet to spread my legs so they're shoulder width apart, then he takes each of my hands in his and places them above the window. Gripping my hips, he tilts them back and pushes into me from behind. I'm so sensitive that just having him inside me again is making my muscles clench around him.

"Is this okay?" he asks, his mouth next to my ear.

"Yes. I'm just so sensitive. Be gentle."

"Like this?" He slides a hand down to my clit, running his finger over and around it, but so light he's barely touching me.

"Oh no," I pant as I push my hips back to meet his thrusts. "No, Sasha. I can't."

"Can't come again a third time?" His voice is deliciously low and seductive. "I beg to differ."

"I'm too tender," I tell him, afraid I'm so sensitive it will hurt.

"Really?" He continues running his finger over my clit featherlight, and it doesn't hurt at all. It's so gentle and loving, and I'm so keyed up and it's bringing on another kind of orgasm.

"No." The word is a whisper as it escapes my lips, and in the window I watch the reflection of his face. He's all concentration right now. His eyebrows dip low as he focuses on bringing me even more pleasure, but the tight pull of his lips between his teeth lets me know how hard he's working to control his own orgasm.

He slows down, his hips meeting mine with less speed, but he drives even deeper into me, if that's possible. As his finger works its magic, my legs start to shake, and he wraps his other arm around my waist, holding me to him. "I've got you."

Within seconds my entire body is tensing up, my back arches, and I feel him swell inside me as he can't hold his own orgasm back any longer. "Yes Petra, *now*," he growls into my ear. It's as if his words trigger the breaking of the dam, and heat floods through me as my white-hot release triggers a full-body orgasm. I feel him pulsing against my inner walls as he pumps his release into me, but it's the words spilling out of his mouth that turn me on the most.

"I've never felt this way about anyone else. It's always been you, love. Always, only you."

My orgasm hits me full-force with those words, and I may or may not scream in agreement, I really can't be sure because suddenly there are tears leaking out of my eyes and it's like I've lost control of all my emotions. I've never felt this way about anyone but him, either. Nothing in my life has come close—the ease I feel around him when we hang out, the undercurrent of sexual tension that has me constantly wanting to rip my clothes off and offer myself up to him, the trust we're building slowly but surely. *I could get used to this.*

"Hey," he says softly, his cheek pressed against mine as he holds me against him. "What are these tears about?"

"I'm just . . ." I search for the words. "Overcome with feelings is all. Nothing bad."

"You have feelings?" he jokes, and it's exactly the mood lightener I need. We laugh together.

"I assure you, it comes as a shock to both of us." I turn my head and kiss him on the cheek.

"Let's get us cleaned up," he says as he pulls out of me. "I'll get the shower going."

"Sasha, I can't have shower sex right now."

"Who said anything about sex? But I do want those lips on my dick as soon as possible." He has the freaking nerve to smirk at me.

"Always the romantic," I say, rolling my eyes, even though the thought of being on my knees in front of him, taking him in my mouth with water raining down on us, actually does turn me on. Again. Already.

"It's been weeks since I've had your mouth on me, and I just gave you three orgasms," he reminds me. "A man has needs too, you know."

———

"A girl could get used to this treatment," I say as he hands me a plate with half a bagel and an egg, and sets a glass with a smoothie in front of me. He's packed it full of raw spinach in an attempt to get more iron in me. The iron supplement sitting next to it already gives me plenty, but I appreciate the effort. "Do you really have to leave?"

He takes a seat across from me. "You know I'd stay if I could, right?"

"I feel a little guilty that I've taken you away from Stella this weekend."

"Don't. I was supposed to be away this weekend for Game 6. Raina was already planning to stay at my place, and she and Stella had some fun things planned anyway."

"Did you tell her you're here?" I take a sip of my smoothie and swallow down my supplement so he can't read anything into my facial expression. I don't want him to feel like he has to hide this relationship, but at the same time, it's too complicated to explain to her.

"No. Raina knows I'm here, but I don't want Stella to get any ideas, or be upset that I didn't bring her too."

"What kind of ideas?" I ask.

"The forever kind." He pauses and takes a long gulp of the enormous smoothie he's drinking. "We had a long talk your last night in New York, when I took her to the park for ice cream."

"Oh yeah?" I hold my breath, hoping he'll say more.

"Yeah. She . . ." He pauses again. "She had certain ideas about you staying in New York."

"What kind of ideas?" I ask again, and take a bite of my bagel to distract from the way my heart is racing and my stomach is flipping over. This feels like the relationship talk I didn't want to have. But Stella *is* an important piece of our relationship, and I have to think of her too. I'd promised myself I wouldn't get too close to her so that I didn't hurt her in the end when I left. My leaving was inevitable, but I'm still here, holding on.

Like I told Aleksandr last night, I've spent years walking

away to protect myself. And now, suddenly this isn't only about me. I have to do what I can to protect Stella from getting hurt too.

"You're not ready for this conversation," he says and gets up, turning his back to me. I watch him select a glass from the open shelving on the kitchen wall and walk over to the refrigerator, where he stands at the door, filling the glass at the water dispenser. I hold my tongue, waiting for him to say more. He returns to the table without another word, but his disappointment is written across his face.

"Sasha." I wait for him to look up at me. "What did she say?"

His eyes bore holes into my face in a way that makes me feel like he's trying to determine whether I'm worthy of knowing this private piece of info about Stella. By the look on his face, I know what he's going to say before he says it, but I need to hear it just the same.

"She—" He stops and takes a breath. "She wants you to be her mom."

My eyes widen, but my vocal cords are paralyzed. Motherhood, my greatest fear and my most secret desire, wrapped into one. I'd set up my "no attachments life" so that a situation like this never happened. And yet something has shifted since Aleksandr walked back into my life with Stella in tow.

My feelings for him are entirely separate from her. I'd love him with or without her. I never really stopped loving him, I suppose, despite how badly he hurt me. That's the funny thing about love, I guess—it doesn't always make sense.

But Stella. I'd do just about anything to make sure she doesn't get hurt again. And is my relationship with Sasha more likely to hurt than help her? What if we try this relationship out, what if we tell her about it, and then things don't work out between us? She would be absolutely crushed.

I realized I've spent too much time in my head when Aleksandr looks out the window to try to hide the disappointment in his eyes.

"Hey," I say as I reach across the small table and take his hand. He looks up, startled. "I'm just taking this all in. I'm not running away, okay?"

He nods. "I didn't want to spring this on you."

"It's not exactly a surprise." I give him a small smile. "I love the hell out of that kid, and it's not like I don't know she feels the same way. I'm just so afraid that us—our relationship —could hurt her in the end."

"Only if we let it," he says.

"There are no guarantees," I say sadly. I've had too many relationships, including one with him, not work out.

"Sure there are." He shrugs and squeezes my hand. "Petra, we're legally married. If we choose to honor that, we're committing ourselves to each other and to Stella. That's as close to a guarantee as you can get."

My heartbeat is pounding in my throat, making it hard to swallow. "Sasha, what are you saying?"

"Why not try to make this marriage work?"

The question is asked so casually I'm actually taken aback. "Well, that's a casual proposal if I've ever heard one," I tease.

"I'm serious," he says as his thumb strokes the back of my hand. "And I'm being pragmatic. There is no one else I've *ever* wanted to spend every minute with. There's no one else my body has craved the way it craves yours. We are so good together, Petra. And you and Stella have this special bond too. I'm so cautious with her, maybe too cautious. Very few people in my life even know I'm her guardian. I don't want to put her in the spotlight. I want to do everything I can to protect her. And I know you feel the same way, about her at least."

Does he not know if I feel the same way about him?

"Sasha, even though I feel the same way about you and even though I adore Stella, right now I am married to my job."

"So am I. Our relationship may not look like anyone else's, but with a little give-and-take from both of us, we can make this work."

I kind of feel like he's talking about forever, as if it's a business transaction with some feelings involved. Is that what it is? Maybe the reason I've gotten hurt in the past is that I let the feelings lead? Maybe it does make more sense to approach this like balancing a math equation?

What he's saying right now makes a lot of sense from a logical standpoint. We *are* good together. We enjoy each other's company and we have a serious sexual connection. We both adore Stella and want what's best for her. But is that the foundation of a good marriage?

"I think we need to see where this goes. See if we can make it work. I don't want to tell Stella about us until we're one hundred percent sure, and there are still a lot of unknowns."

He presses his lips between his teeth for a brief moment, then says, "We'll have more time to talk about this and to see where things stand when you're back in New York."

Chapter Twenty Five

PETRA

"So tell me," I say as I hold up a hardcover copy of A-list actress Maritza Delaney's memoir at the perfect angle for the camera to zoom in, "what prompted you to write *Anything, Not Everything*?"

She shifts in the white chair that's angled toward mine and her red wrap dress clings to her perfect body. "When I was younger, my mom was always encouraging me to dream big and set these lofty goals for myself. One of her favorite sayings was 'You can have anything you want, you just can't have everything.' She taught me to prioritize what was most important to me and let go of the superfluous crap that didn't help me achieve what was most important. More than anything else, that was the life lesson that stuck with me. *Anything, Not Everything*. I wanted to pass that wisdom on to other women, with some concrete real-life examples."

"One of the things I liked most about your book," I tell her, trying not to think of how much it affected me when I read it right after Aleksandr headed back to New York, "is how you talk about personalizing your goals. Can you tell our audience a little more about that philosophy?"

She flips her long, dark hair over her shoulder and looks me straight in the eye like she's about to unload a huge secret. "Oh, I could talk for days about this. But essentially, my philosophy is that your goals are only worth working for if they are *your* goals. Your goals don't have to look like anyone else's, and they don't have to make sense to others. They say that comparison is the thief of joy, but I'd argue that it also leads lots of people into lives that aren't what they really want. They take promotions at work so they can use a fancy new title and enjoy a higher salary even though what they really want is more time to spend with the people they love. Or they buy a bigger house in the suburbs so they can show it off to their family and friends, even though they really miss the vibrancy and diversity of living in the city. When we let society's expectations or even the expectations of our closest friends and family members too heavily influence our decisions, it becomes more and more difficult to stay true to ourselves. And I don't see how we can ever achieve true happiness if we don't stay true to what we value most."

That thought has me going off script, asking a question I wasn't planning. "What would you say to someone who isn't sure what they want? Who maybe thought they knew, but whose values and goals seem to be shifting in an unexpected direction?"

She nods once, like she knows the right answer without even having to think about the question. "I would say to listen to your gut. Most of the time when we make decisions that take us in the wrong direction in life, it's because our gut instincts told us one thing, but we listened to societal expectations instead. I'll give you an example about listening to your gut from my own life."

Maritza goes on to describe a time five years earlier when she was offered a role in a blockbuster film that not only won Best Picture that year, but the actress who took the role also won Best Actress.

"I knew that film, and that role, were going to be huge. Everyone criticized me for turning it down, especially after Eva won Best Actress for it. But she absolutely *owned* that role in a way I wouldn't have at the time. I was suffering through some depression related to infertility issues before we conceived my first daughter, and things between Marcel and me were getting a little rocky. I needed that time to focus on my family, to go to counseling, to listen to what my body needed. What good would it have done me to have turned all my attention toward that film, and have my marriage break down as a result? I knew what my goals and my priorities were, and if I hadn't, maybe I'd have won an Oscar but lost my marriage. Maybe I wouldn't have my two beautiful daughters with my amazing husband. You have to take the time and put in the work on what's *most* important."

I can't afford to get distracted, so I try not to think about how much that story resonates with my own life. I'm here filming this show, and it's amazing. More amazing even than I'd dreamed it would be. But I feel like my heart is still in New York. I want to be with Sasha and Stella so much it's a physical ache in my chest. Even though he's been traveling again for the semifinals and now the finals, we've managed multiple video calls in the two and a half weeks since he left —some while he's on the road, and some while he's home with Stella. But those hurt. Every single time we talk, it's a reminder of all that I'm missing out on. Even though he keeps saying that this long-distance situation isn't forever and even though I know this show is going to be amazing when it airs, there is this pervasive, underlying ache that doesn't go away even when I remind myself that I currently have everything I ever wanted in life.

"That's an interesting example," I say with a slight tilt of my head. I'm hoping she can't see how close to home that scenario hit, as I sit here in LA while the people I love are in New York.

Holy shit. The people I love are in New York. What am I even doing here?

"So many people are calling *Anything, Not Everything* the 'New Feminist Manifesto,'" I say. "But when most people think about feminists, they don't think of a happily married mother of two. Can you say a little more about that dichotomy?"

"Absolutely. I don't see feminism and motherhood as a dichotomy at all. What is feminism if it's not a woman unapologetically going after what she wants? A lot of people claim I'm not a feminist because I'm married and have two kids, and because I've made sacrifices in my career in order to make sure my family situation works. I'm here to say what every woman needs to hear: you can have *anything* you want, you just can't have *everything*. Could I have been more successful as an actress, taken on more movies or earned even more awards if I hadn't had two kids? Probably. But what would I have given up? A husband that supports me in every-thing I do, and kids that bring me immense love and joy? So I'd have been more successful in my career, but how mean-ingful would that be if I didn't have people that love me unconditionally to support me and celebrate with me? For me, having a family isn't *sacrificing* the work, it's what makes the work *worthwhile*. There is no such thing as 'having it all.' Not for women, and not for men either. We always hear that you should surround yourself with people who love you and will lift you up. Who better to do that than family? In fact, I would say that having a family has made me into the ultimate feminist: someone who has *chosen* to live life on her own terms, *regardless* of what people expect of her. I'm a woman who has chosen my own happiness over anyone else's expectations and that, I believe, is what makes me a feminist."

Her words hit me like one of those huge weights that falls from the sky and land on a cartoon character and I stumble, missing my cue for the next question. When she looks at me expectantly, I'm sure my shock-widened eyes stare back at her.

"I'm sorry," I say, trying to recover gracefully, "I'm just taking a moment, as I'm sure all our viewers are, to absorb what you just said. The ultimate feminist," I repeat her sentiment, "is someone who unapologetically goes after the life she wants, someone who has chosen her own happiness over anyone else's expectations."

Maritza nods sagely, and even though we're roughly the same age, she somehow feels like a wise old teacher to me in this moment.

"And what would you say to someone who realizes their happiness might require them to totally shift course? To actually give up on the goals they'd been working hard on for years, the goals they thought were what they really wanted?" I ask, praying that Charley isn't standing somewhere behind the cameras and judging me. She knows what questions I was planning to ask. Does she know that the ones I'm ad-libbing are selfishly personal?

"I'd say that if you come to a crossroads like that and you don't listen to your heart, if you don't shift course, then you're back to what we were talking about at the beginning of this conversation—working toward someone else's goals. People change, they evolve, and their goals do too. If you're someone" —she looks off past my left shoulder, directly at the camera— "who is stuck working toward goals some previous version of you wanted, when what you now want is actually something else, then you're not being true to yourself."

This woman keeps dropping bombs right and left, and I need time to think about what she's said.

"So important," I say, nodding decisively. "So tell me, what's next for Maritza Delaney?"

She throws her head back slightly and laughs, then looks at me with a big smile. "Whatever. Makes. Me. Happy."

———

I step into a dark corner of the crowded room and pull my phone out of my clutch. It's been buzzing like crazy, but I'm surrounded by the who's who of the television industry and I haven't had a second to check it until just now. When I see seventeen missed texts from Morgan, my stomach flips over. We have a massive wedding tomorrow in Salt Lake City —a relatively famous "influencer" who is getting married in a small, private ceremony at the Salt Lake Temple with a lavish, huge reception in Temple Square. Almost everyone on my staff has been working crazy hours in my absence to make sure everything goes off without a hitch. And that red circle with a seventeen inside it glares at me like a big warning sign.

But when I open the texts, it's just a series of details and confirmations about Aleksandr's event next weekend. The first message is an apology that she's sending them by text, but she's having some sort of problem with our email and for me not to worry, she's already working with tech support on it. Which is probably why she's sending these messages after 8:00 p.m. her time. I send off a quick, grateful reply and then put the phone back in my clutch just as Charley walks up.

"It's about to start," she says. "Let's grab our seats."

A waiter passes with champagne, and Charley tries to hand me one, but I decline. Adding champagne to my nervous stomach would be like lighting a dumpster on fire.

One hour later my stomach has settled itself, the knots of unease slowly untangled as each minute passed. The episode was fucking brilliant. My guest was an amazing woman who, as a child, had escaped the genocide in Rwanda in the backpack of a South African journalist who hiked through the central plateau with that little child hidden in his camera bag for three days. He not only saved her from death, but he gave her a life. He died shortly after she graduated from college, and she dedicated her life to helping others as he'd helped her. The international relief organization she'd founded is now the fourth largest in the world, and I'm pretty sure I'll never meet a more inspiring person.

Personally, I've never looked better or sounded smarter than in this interview and somehow, watching it, everything looked so natural. No hint of the exhaustion I was experiencing at the time we filmed. Any mistakes or awkwardness were edited out. It was one hour of TV perfection. Exactly the kind of show I'd watch. The kind I'd want my daughters to see. *I wonder what Aleksandr and Stella thought of it?*

My phone has been vibrating silently in my bag throughout the entire show. I can only imagine I have a slew of texts on the group chat with Lauren, Jackson, and Sierra, and probably a few from Aleksandr too. I'd rather be watching this episode with any of them than stuck here in this fancy party. So ironic, since this is very much my scene. Or was. Now I want to be surrounded by people who truly love me, not just people who adore me.

Charley puts her hand on my forearm as Dave, one of the network executives, stands with a champagne glass in hand. All chatter that's been buzzing around the room in the sixty seconds since the show ended comes to a grinding halt.

"Petra," he calls out, and waves me over to him.

I leave my clutch behind and cross to the front of the room. A passing waitress discreetly hands me a champagne flute and I smile at her gratefully.

"Darling," Dave says to me as I approach, "you've done it." The room erupts in cheers and applause. "This show is smart and interesting and compelling, and it was a delight to watch." More applause. "*You* were a delight to watch."

I glance at him, then at Charley in her seat next to my empty one. "I think most of the credit goes to Charley, actually. This show is her baby. The vision, the concept, the guests, that was all her." I raise my glass to her, and she smiles, tilting her chin down in a thoughtful nod. I stretch my arm out to her and cup my hand toward myself a few times until she gets up and crosses over to us. Next to me, I get the feeling that Dave is bristling at the interruption to his speech, but I don't even look at him because I don't really care. I take

Charley's hand in mine when she reaches me and whisper, "Feminism is a team effort." Then I turn to Dave and give him my most winning smile.

"To Petra *and* to Charley," he says as he holds up his champagne flute, and the room is on their feet, clapping and cheering.

I want to bask in the moment. I want to think about my career. I want to absorb the energy and excitement that's surrounding me. But I can't.

Even with everyone rushing up to us and congratulating me, all I feel is an aching emptiness. I want Sasha here to share in this success. I've sacrificed everything for this show, to meet this goal that I thought was going to make me feel so powerful and fulfilled. But Maritza Delaney's words from a few days ago are ringing through my head: "I'm a woman who has chosen my own happiness over anyone else's expectations and that, I believe, is what makes me a feminist."

But I've done the opposite, haven't I? I didn't want to leave Aleksandr and Stella behind in New York. I left because I'd agreed to film this show, and because I was scared to admit the depth of my feelings. I was scared to give up the show—it was my opportunity to promote the valuable work women are doing in this world. Leaving to come do this show felt like I was living out my feminist ideals, fighting for women everywhere rather than giving everything up for a man. But what did I really give up? My own happiness?

I think back to how Maritza rhetorically asked, "What is feminism if it's not unapologetically going after what you want?"

When I was in New York, it was easy to wonder if what I was feeling was just "in the moment" feelings that would pass when I left. But this time away from them has made me more confident than ever that those feelings are real. That it could actually work between Aleksandr and me, and that I could—even already *do*—love Stella like a daughter.

What am I even doing here in LA?

What feels like hours later, the party is winding down and I make it back to my chair, anxious to grab my stuff and head home. I want to read my messages from my friends. I'm hoping that Aleksandr and Stella sent me a video message after watching the show. I know I won't be able to call them because it's almost three in the morning on the East Coast, but I'm aching to see their faces, hear their voices.

I open my clutch and slip my phone out, anxious to read my messages as I walk out to the car I know is waiting to take me home. But the most recent one, the one that came through only minutes ago, has my breath escaping my lips in a low hiss.

ALICIA

Girl, I have BIG questions.

Chapter Twenty Six

ALEKSANDR

"You need to find something, some *concrete reason*, that Tony and CeCe aren't fit to be Stella's guardians," Tom says. His voice is ominous as he slides a copy of their newest petition to get custody of Stella into his gym bag.

I glance past him and take in the players on the squash court beyond the glass wall. "How the hell am I supposed to do that?" I say quietly, even though there is no one else waiting for a court. "All I know is that Tony creeps me out and CeCe is a relentless social climber. My brother and sister-in-law were insistent they didn't want them to be Stella's guardian. Why isn't that enough?"

"I don't know. What do they stand to gain by getting guardianship of her?"

"Hell if I know," I sigh. "It can't be Niko's money, unless Tony's not actually a billionaire and they're strapped for cash. I guess it's possible. Maybe that whole shipping company is a big sham that's about to collapse?"

"If that's the case," Tom says, "he's doing a good job

hiding it. Anyway, you've already been granted guardianship, but they aren't going to stop with these petitions unless you give the court a reason that the two of them aren't fit. On paper, they look pretty damn good. Married and rich as fuck. Blood relations."

"You kind of just described me, you know?"

Tom rolls his eyes, then turns his attention to the players on the court who are currently shaking hands after wrapping up their game. "The judge has no idea you're married, since *you* didn't even know when you got guardianship. And you're no billionaire." He's right, I'm not. But he also has no idea about my trust because I've never had to touch it. "Plus, you're a professional athlete who travels a lot. According to their argument in this petition, that leaves Stella in someone else's care too often."

"I'd retire from hockey before I'd let her go live with them."

Tom's face gets serious. "That may need to be an option, unless you have a good reason that she's better off with you and a nanny than she is with CeCe and Tony."

"I can't just make up something about the two of them out of thin air."

"Listen," Tom says as he picks up his racket that's resting against the wall. "Look into Tony's business practices, or CeCe's social connections. Find something, anything, that makes them seem sketchy."

We nod to the players leaving the court and head through the glass door.

"How am I supposed to do that?" I ask him, thankful for the privacy of the enclosed court. It's not soundproof though, so we keep our voices low.

"I know a woman. She's a private investigator. I'll put you in touch with her. If anyone can find dirt on them, it's her."

"Okay," I say uncertainly. "I'll give that a shot. In the meantime, do I need to talk to my agent? With my contract ending, he's actively negotiating with New York and also looking at other opportunities. I'm eyeing LA."

Tom's eyebrows dip. "Why LA?"

He knows why, but he's going to make me say it. "Because Petra's in LA. That might be the answer to these problems, actually. If we can make this marriage work, even if it's in LA, it takes away their main argument against my guardianship. And then we can pursue adoption too."

Tom clears his throat as he bounces the small ball against the floor, then catches it in his hand a few times in rapid succession. "Petra's on board with this plan?"

"I haven't told her yet. I need to make sure LA is a possibility before I bring it up."

"Or," Tom hedges, as he walks to the service box on his preferred side of the court, "maybe you should talk to her before making a potentially life-altering decision?"

"I'm not going to make any decisions without talking to her. But I don't see the point in bringing up the possibility until I know it's actually a possibility."

"I won't pretend to know Petra well," he says, bouncing the ball again several times to warm it up, "but I get the sense that she likes to have some level of control over things. She doesn't strike me as the type who would like to be surprised."

A laugh bursts out of me as I gaze down at my racket. "No, she doesn't like surprises."

"So don't surprise her then," he warns. "Don't come to her with this big plan for your future that you've concocted without her. Let her be a part of the decision-making from the outset."

"Avery has made you both soft and wise, hasn't she?"

"Something like that." His voice is gruff, like it always is when he talks about her. It's been fun watching my ruthlessly emotionless squash opponent fall in love.

Tom hits the ball against the front wall gently, and we volley it back and forth for a few minutes to warm up. "I'll talk to her when she's back for our end of season party," I tell him.

"This weekend?"

I grunt out a "yes" and I dig down deep to return the ball he just hit.

"How are you having your end of season party before your season is over?"

"Scheduled it before we knew we'd make the finals." We've just won Game 7 of the semifinals, so now we're headed to the Stanley Cup finals in just over a week.

"I'm sure Avery'd like to see Petra while she's here," Tom says.

"Tell Avery to get in touch with her, then," I tell him, wondering if Petra hasn't told Avery she'll be back. I suspect that she's been too busy to do a good job keeping in touch. "I'm sure Petra would love to see her."

"All right," Tom says, catching the ball in his hand and setting himself up for a real serve. "Let's play."

———

I towel-dry my hair and then wrap the damp towel around my waist. I normally shower at the club after we play, but since it was lunch hour, there were too many professionals like Tom waiting for the showers, and I decided it was easier to just come home.

I make my way through my room and into the hall, heading toward the kitchen. I'm so hungry after that workout that my stomach is making all kinds of sounds.

As I cross through the entryway toward the dining room, the elevator dings. That's weird. Only two people have access here, and one of them is in LA. I turn, expecting to find Raina and preparing to apologize for walking around in my towel. But instead, the doors open and Petra is standing there with her suitcase.

I know my jaw drops open at the sight of her. Hers does the same.

"You're here." I can't quite contain my smile.

She looks nervous. "I hope you don't mind me showing up a day early with no warning?"

"I guess that depends on your reason for coming early." I'm frozen in place as the thought crosses my mind that she could be here to break things off.

"I missed you." Her reason is so simply stated, so raw. She shrugs nonchalantly, but I see some sort of fear or pain flash across her eyes before she gives me a small smile.

I open my arms and she rushes into them, curling her limbs around my back, pulling me tight to her. I do the same, and kiss her forehead gently, considering how precious she is to me. She stays cradled against me for a few minutes and then pulls her upper body away, glances down at where our bodies are connected at the waist, and laughs out a "Really?"

"You're pressed up against my naked body, and I haven't seen you in weeks. What do you expect?"

"Don't look at me like that," she warns.

I lift one eyebrow slightly. "Like what?"

"Like you're undressing me in your mind. I can always tell by the way your eyes change." She plants her hands and forearms against my bare chest.

"If you want me to stop undressing you in my mind, you're going to need to stop touching me like that." My lip curves into a smile. Whether we have sex right now or not, it's just so fucking good to have her back in my place.

"Fine," she says as she steps back out of my arms. "Not because I don't want to be naked with you, but because I come with a shit ton of information I need you to look at."

"Information?"

"About Tony Gionetti."

My stomach sinks. If that name isn't a mood killer, I don't know what is. "Why do you have 'information' on Tony?"

"Because he's skeevy as hell and so I had a friend of mine who's a private investigator look into him."

"Funny," I say. "Just this morning, Tom gave me this woman Alicia's number and told me to give her a call about this very thing."

Petra just stares at me like she's dumbstruck. "Alicia?"

"Yeah, he didn't give me a last name, but he said she's the best."

"She is," Petra confirms. "That's who I had look into Tony. And you're going to be completely disgusted at what she found."

What are the chances?

"Let me get dressed," I say. "I'll be right back."

"Okay." She pushes her suitcase against the wall of the entryway and takes her over-the-shoulder bag and heads into the living room.

I get dressed as quickly as possible, wondering if I should tell Tom that Petra has dirt on Tony? It only makes sense to wait until I know more—until I know if it's significant enough to keep him away from Stella for good.

She's not in the living room when I come back from my room in sweatpants and a T-shirt, so I head into the den and find her curled into the corner of the couch.

"This is my favorite room." She lets out a contented sigh.

"The den?" I ask, glancing around.

She laughs. "This whole time I've been calling it the 'sitting room' in my mind."

"Like we're in a British period drama?" I can't hide my amusement.

She shrugs. "I guess. I love the light, and the view, and the fireplace." She looks me up and down as I cross the room to sit on the couch. I tuck one leg under me as I turn to face her.

Her lips curl up on one side and there's laughter in her eyes. Not what I expected, given the conversation we're about to have. "What?"

"Remind me sometime to tell you about my friend Sierra and her thoughts on gray sweatpants."

What? "Will do. Now, about Tony?"

She clears her throat. "He's into some bad shit, Sasha. I have literally felt sick for the last twelve hours since I found out."

379

I look at her expectantly. "Are you going to tell me?"

Petra looks like she might throw up, and the way she swallows makes me think she might actually be choking back bile. She hands me her phone and says, "Start reading from the top."

The name at the top of the text message is Alicia. No last name.

ALICIA

Holy shit. I hope you're sitting down, cupcake. Because this is not what I expected to find when you asked me to look into TG. I should have known a rich shit like him would have skeletons in his closet.

PETRA

The rich ones always do.

ALICIA

Truth! Unfortunately his skeletons are of the underage variety.

PETRA

???

ALICIA

It seems he's really into sleeping with underage women. Particularly coked-up underage victims of sex trafficking.

PETRA

No. Full stop, no!

ALICIA

There's a woman in the East Village who runs a sex trafficking ring. He has regular payments that get sent to her every month from an offshore account.

That's sickening. How do you know about payments from an offshore account? And that those payments are for underage girls?

You don't want to know the answer to either of those questions. The thing that matters is that I have evidence, and I need to know what you want me to do with it.

Give me a day to figure that out.

I lift my eyes from the screen and look at Petra. "What the hell is she talking about?"

"Which part do you need me to explain?" Petra asks flippantly. "The part where Stella's uncle is a pedophile or the part where he's regularly cheating on his wife with underage victims of sex trafficking?"

"When they were here for dinner that night, you knew, didn't you?" I ask her. I knew Tony was making Stella uncomfortable, but my brain didn't jump to something like this, whereas hers clearly did.

"I knew something was off," she says as she tucks a dark curl behind her ear and looks up at me with those big, beautiful eyes. "It felt like he was conditioning Stella to accept unwanted sexual attention, which is a big trigger for me."

"Why?" I try to phrase the question as gently as I can. What has happened to her in the past that makes her able to recognize this behavior so easily?

She takes a deep breath through her nose and raises her chin. Her lips are pressed together tightly. "Tony reminds me of a lot of my dad's friends back in Austria, the creepy ones who always liked to refer to themselves as *Dyadya So-and-so.* They weren't my uncles, they weren't related to me. But they used their friendship with my dad as an excuse to touch me, to tickle me, to give me attention I didn't want. It started happening when I was a little older than Stella, maybe around nine or so. And my parents would always be like 'Oh, just give your uncle a kiss,' and I felt so helpless, like I didn't have control over my own body."

"Shit, Petra, I'm so sorry." I didn't know that was happening, but I feel like I should have been there to protect her. Or Viktor, or her dad, or her mom should have stood up for her. It eats at me that she felt so alone even before her mom and Viktor died.

"There was this one friend of my dad's," she continues, "who always had his hands on me. He'd come up behind me and rub my back or give my shoulders a massage. I was thirteen when we passed through a doorway in my house going opposite directions and he openly groped me. He slid his palm right across my nipple, then squeezed my breast, leaning down to whisper some creepy term of endearment into my ear. My mom had died a few months earlier, and while she was alive, no one had tried anything that blatantly inappropriate. I remember thinking 'I'm the only one who can save me now.' So I put syrup of ipecac in his drink that night. He started vomiting, and when he rushed to our front door to leave, I handed him his coat and said, 'Don't ever touch me again.' I used that strategy more than once, and pretty soon my dad's friends stopped spending time at our house."

I gaze at her across the couch, noting how her face is triumphant, as it should be, but her eyes are sad. "I'm really sorry that you had to go through that alone. I wish you'd told me back then."

"So what? You could come over every time my father had friends over and be my bodyguard?" Her laugh carries the notes of bitterness.

"If that's what it took. I would have done anything to protect you," I tell her. She shakes her head slightly and her lips curve into a frown. "What is that look?"

"Nothing."

"Petra, I said I'd have done anything to protect you, and you shook your head and frowned. What. Was. That. Look?" I ask, drawing each word out.

She raises her eyebrows and smiles brightly. "Honestly, it was nothing. I don't know what you're talking about."

She's blatantly lying to me, and an uneasy feeling is wrapping itself around my intestines, snaking its way up to my stomach, clawing at my esophagus. "Petra," I draw out her name slowly, a low warning. "Don't lie to me."

"What do you want me to say, Sasha?" She looks away, glancing out the windows at the terrace.

"I want you to explain."

She straightens her back, sitting up to her full height, and squares her shoulders. Then she slowly turns her head toward me. "Because no one—nothing—ever hurt me more than your leaving did."

Oh shit. "I thought we talked about this when I was in LA. I thought we were okay?"

"You explained, yes. That doesn't make it hurt less."

I wish I could tell her how much it hurt *me*, to know how she felt about me and to have felt the same way, and to have had to walk away from her to save her. I want to tell her the truth, but mostly because I want her to see that I was trying to protect her. I didn't want her to know that her father had essentially sold her off.

She deserves to know the truth.

But the truth would only hurt her *more*, it wouldn't make her feel better. And it would bring up so many more questions and issues, and there'd be no real resolution because both our fathers are dead now. No, telling her would make things worse, not better.

"I'm sorry," I say. "I really am. I did what I thought we both needed me to do at the time."

"I would have done anything for you, you know?" Her husky voice has that sentence coming out low, like a promise or a threat.

"I know," I assure her. "And that's partly why I needed to leave. You needed to go to Switzerland, Petra. You needed to chase your dreams. And I needed to chase mine. We made our way back to each other as adults," I remind her.

"Yeah, because we were secretly married, and we didn't know it," she gives a sad, sarcastic laugh and a knife of guilt twists in my stomach because, in a way, I did know. "We didn't come back to each other by choice, necessarily."

"However it happened," I tell her, "I'm glad it did."

She waits a beat too long before she says, "Yeah, me too."

———

"Where is she?" Stella asks me for at least the fifth time in the last fifteen minutes. She's swinging her feet under the table and fidgeting with a french fry that now resembles a lump of smashed potato between her fingers.

"She's on her way," I assure her. "Traffic is terrible at this time because everyone's leaving work. And she has to come from Brooklyn, which is farther away than the Upper East Side." Stella has no sense of the city yet, so I arrange our basket of fries, the ketchup, and the salt and pepper shakers to try to explain to her where Times Square is relative to other parts of the city.

Clearly bored by my explanation, Stella says, "I've hardly seen Petra since she's been back."

"It hasn't even been two days yet, and you had school today. You saw her last night, and you'll see her tonight. She'll be here for the whole weekend."

"Yeah, but you have that party tomorrow night so you'll both be gone and I have to stay behind with Raina."

"I thought you liked Raina?" I'm careful to ask, not to insist, because I want to make sure she's telling me how she really feels, not saying what she thinks I want to hear.

"I *do.*" She sighs, then looks at the ceiling in frustration. And we're officially to the eye rolling years. I had expected we'd at least get to nine or ten before she started in with that. "I just like Petra better. Besides you, she's my favorite person."

"Want to know a secret?" I ask, leaning toward her conspiratorially. She nods. "Besides you, she's my favorite person too."

Stella's smile is huge. Petra and I haven't tried to hide our feelings for each other since she's been back, and Stella has certainly noticed that there's something going on between us that she didn't see when Petra was here before.

Last night when I was sitting on the couch watching a cartoon with Stella before she went to bed, Petra ambled into the den and sat down on my other side. I wrapped my arm around her and pulled her into me. I run so hot that I don't normally like having people and their body heat pressed up against me. But with one arm around Stella and the other around Petra, and both of them curled into my opposite sides, I realized maybe I didn't mind when the people pressed up against me are my two favorite people.

"Is that why she's sleeping in your room now?" Stella asks, and the feeling of my stomach dropping almost makes me choke on my drink. I probably should have thought about how I'd answer this question when it came up, since we aren't trying to hide it this time around. It seems stupid to put her in the guest room and then for us to sneak around after Stella goes to sleep.

"Yes, because I want to spend as much time with her as possible."

"Even while you're sleeping?"

"Yes, I like having her close by even while we're sleeping."

Stella nods and I can practically see the wheels turning in her mind. "Can she sleep in my room one night?"

"Probably not on this trip, but maybe another time." I don't want to commit Petra to anything, but she's a sucker for making Stella feel safe and loved, so I can only imagine she'll probably agree.

Stella's face lights up right as I hear, "Maybe another time, what?" The words are a low, husky caress across my neck and I turn my head to find Petra standing right over my shoulder. I reach behind me and run my hand up the back of her leg and her breath hitches even though her face doesn't give away that I've even touched her.

"Dada said that maybe sometime you'd sleep in my room for a night instead of his," Stella beams and I can tell Petra's trying not to laugh.

Instead, she reaches past me and plucks a french fry out of the basket on our table. "He did?"

"I said *maybe*," I remind Stella.

"That's what I said. I said *maybe*," Stella insists.

"She did say maybe," Petra says, her voice taking on a sort of singsong quality as she winks at Stella.

I have a few teammates who have girls, and they're always complaining about how their wives and daughters gang up on them. It feels a bit like that's what's happening here, and I'm okay with it. I'm okay with Stella getting the love and attention she wants, and I'm more than okay with Petra being the one to give it to her. Petra, who told me she never wanted kids, who didn't do committed relationships.

feel like we're on the right track.

I slide my hand further up Petra's leg, letting my fingertips trail along her impossibly smooth skin and squeezing her thigh gently. She gives me a quick kiss on the cheek, then moves away to walk around the table and give Stella a big hug. "Of course I'll stay with you one night. How about next time I'm out here?"

"When will that be?" Stella asks, and then without waiting for Petra's answer she says, "I don't want you to go." She's not whining, but it's damned close.

Petra shrugs. "I'm not sure. I have to be back in LA for filming next week, but then we do have Memorial Day weekend coming up. We will figure it out before I leave, how's that?" She taps the tip of Stella's nose.

Stella wraps her arms around Petra's waist and pulls her

in for another hug. Across the table, my eyes meet hers. Those cool blue eyes soften in a way I haven't seen before; it's like watching winter ice thaw into a sea of pale blue water. She's a lot of things, but soft isn't one of them. Only Stella brings out that side of her, and watching it happen loosens something in my chest, making me feel like I can breathe more deeply than normal. Maybe this will all work out. Maybe we can keep Stella safe, while loving her and each other. Maybe our past won't screw up our future.

You have to tell her, I tell myself. *There is no path forward if it's built on a lie.*

Even though I know that's true, fear makes the hair on the back of my neck stand up. I don't want to lose her again. I don't want Stella to lose her now that Petra's such an important part of both our lives. But I don't know how Petra will react to the truth, and that terrifies me.

She must see something flash across my face, because she dips her eyebrows in confusion. I just shake my head slightly in response. I don't know when the right time to tell her is, but it's certainly not now.

"So, are we bowling or what?" Petra asks when Stella finally lets go of her.

"We're just waiting for a lane to open up," I tell her, nodding toward the pager sitting on the table next to the basket of fries. I glance at my watch. "It should be ready any minute now."

"I'm starving," she says. "Did you guys already eat?"

"Yeah, but I figured you'd want something when you got here." It's closing in on seven o'clock, and with Stella's bedtime fast approaching, there's no way I could have held her dinner off any longer. "Want me to flag down the waitress for you?"

"That'd be great," Petra says to me as she pulls her phone from her bag. "Want to see some pictures from today?" she asks Stella.

Stella leans in with an enthusiastic "Yes!" and Petra opens her photos on her phone. I glance around but don't see our waitress, so I watch as Petra and Stella lean their heads together.

"This is the view from where we're having the party tomorrow night," Petra says, and Stella sighs.

"I really can't come?" She looks at me when she asks this.

"Sorry, it's adults only," I remind her. We've had this conversation already.

"But can't you make an exception for me?" she whines.

I'm about to give her a look because we're working on her understanding that whining isn't an acceptable way to get what you want, but Petra beats me to it. "I don't think anyone gets what they want by whining."

Stella clears her throat. "Could I please come? I just want to see everything all decorated. I don't have to stay."

Petra glances at me, then back at Stella. "I have an idea." She makes eye contact with Stella and says, "This is only an idea, not a definite yes, okay?" When Stella agrees, Petra looks up at me and continues, "Since Raina is going to be watching Stella tomorrow night, couldn't we have them come with us since we're arriving early? Then they could leave right before the guests arrive? That way Stella can see the space, and maybe have a Shirley Temple with us or something, and then Raina can take her home."

In her seat, Stella is bouncing with barely contained enthusiasm.

"I don't see why not, as long as Raina doesn't mind."

She won't mind, I already know. Raina's great about doing whatever I ask of her, and I appreciate that as well as how much she seems to enjoy spending time with Stella.

"So it's a maybe then," Petra tells Stella. "We'll talk to Raina and see if we can set it up. You have to be flexible though," she says, "because there's still a chance that it might not work out."

Stella's eyes are so wide and hopeful, and she takes a deep breath. "Okay," she agrees.

Just then the waitress passes behind them, so I flag her down and no sooner has Petra ordered her burger than the pager goes off. We take our drinks with us as we make our way over to get our bowling shoes.

We're settled into our lane and Petra's devouring her burger when Stella heads over to get her ball from the ball rack.

"I missed you today," I tell Petra, leaning over and planting a kiss on top of her hair. The sweet and tangy scent of her shampoo overwhelms my nostrils, a welcome relief from the musty smell of floor polish, fried food, and beer. Even though this bowling alley is sparkly and new, and right in Times Square, it still smells like any other bowling alley I've ever been in, minus the smoky air.

She swallows her bite and tilts her chin up toward me. "I missed you too." Then she leans into me, resting her head on my shoulder as I curl my arm around her.

I take a deep breath as I push away my thoughts, because since I've been back from LA my brain has been arguing with itself—screaming at me that I need to have a serious talk with her about our past, and simultaneously insisting that I not ruin what we have with the bullshit of our parents' misdeeds.

None of that was us. That was our parents and their stupid choices. Don't make Petra suffer because your father was an asshole, her mother was conflicted, and her father was emotionally stunted. Everything is so good right now, don't you dare ruin it, half my brain argues. But the other half reminds me, *You can't build a future on a lie, even if it's a lie of omission.*

"Everything okay?" Petra asks. I'm so busy trying to relax that I forget to respond, so she says, "Your whole body just went rigid."

I watch Stella roll her ball down the lane with two hands as I say, "Did it? I guess I just have a lot on my mind."

"Want to tell me about it?" Petra asks, her husky voice so low it unleashes emotions inside me, making me want to both strip her out of her clothes and also spill my secrets.

Stella's on the tips of her toes, leaning forward as she watches her ball s-l-o-w-l-y roll to the end of the lane, where it knocks over three pins on the right side. She jumps up and down, and Petra springs up off my shoulder, her hands held high as she cheers for Stella.

Then, as Stella rushes back toward us, Petra looks at me and whispers, "Later."

"Your turn, Petra," Stella says as she slides onto the bench next to me.

Petra rises, and I can't take my eyes off her hips as she walks to the ball return. There she slides her hand over and around several of the balls before sticking her fingers into one and picking it up, testing out the weight in both hands. I don't know if she intends for watching her to be an erotic experience, but I find myself growing hard nonetheless.

"Do you think she knows what she's doing?" Stella asks me, and because I'm so focused on whether Petra's intending to turn me on, it takes a second for me to realize that Stella means does Petra actually know how to bowl or is she just making a show of feeling all the balls to compensate for not knowing what she's doing. I laugh because Stella has excellent bullshit radar.

And then I remind myself to mentally rein it in—I'm with my kid, I don't need to be picturing all the things I want to do to Petra right this moment.

"I guess we'll see," I tell her as Petra walks toward the lane with her ball cradled in both hands in front of her chest.

She stands lined up with the center of the lane, swings her arm back, takes a few steps forward and releases the ball in front of her. It rolls off her fingers like she's an expert, none of that dropping that happens with an awkward release. But it spins oddly and hits the gutter before it makes it to the end of the lane.

Stella looks at me like we're conspirators about to take Petra down. While neither of us is great at bowling, it looks like we're both better than Petra.

The woman in question turns toward us, rolls her eyes, and shrugs. She takes off the jean jacket she's wearing over a lightweight black sweater dress. It's fitted with sleeves that go to her elbow and a deep neckline that starts right at the edges of her neck and descends well into her cleavage. The slit is only a few inches wide, but the visible crease between her breasts has me moving to adjust myself because it's getting tight in these jeans.

I pull my hat down a little lower over my eyes, hoping that nobody here recognizes me, or her. Now that her show has aired, it's more likely she'll start getting recognized in public too.

"Can't bowl when my arms are restricted like that," she says as she tosses the jacket on the bench next to me, turns, and walks back to the ball return with her hips swaying seductively. How does she manage to make even bowling shoes look sexy?

She grabs the same ball before approaching the lane. Then, with the grace of an expert bowler, she winds up and sends the ball straight down the lane, knocking every single pin over with a clattering so loud that everyone in the bowling alley seems to be staring at her now. She turns, and gives Stella and me a huge smile before hollering, "That's better," while brushing her hands together.

"Shit," I mutter.

Stella turns toward me and says, "Maybe we need a swear jar like they have at Harper's?"

"Maybe we need to find a way to stop Petra from kicking our butts," I suggest instead.

"Hmm," Stella says. "I'm not so sure that's possible."

Is there anything this woman can't do?

———

As it turns out, I think as I watch Petra's face twist in pleasure as the orgasm rips through her hours later, *no . . . in my eyes, there is nothing this woman can't do.*

"This feeling," I say through gritted teeth, "is a fucking

miracle." I grip her hips tightly as I slam her down on me a final time and give in to my own release.

She gazes down at me like I've said something funny, and then quirks an eyebrow. "How so?"

It's a moment before I can speak again. "I've never felt like this," I tell her as I wrap my arm around her lower back and pull her down so she's hovering just above my chest. "You and me together. It's amazing."

"I always knew it would be," she says. It's the opening to the talk I know we need to have. It would be so easy to return to the conversation she said we'd have 'later,' but then Petra rolls her hips, and I slide out and back into her, and I feel myself already starting to grow hard again.

"If you don't stop that," I say as I reach up and run my thumb along her cheekbone, "round two will start immediately."

"Already?"

"You do amazing things to my body," I say, because how the hell am I already ready to take her again? I have no control here, she's in charge of my body now.

"I like that." She smiles a wicked, private smile as she rolls her hips again. "I like that a lot."

She leans down a bit more, letting her breasts slide along my chest as her mouth meets mine. The kiss is slow and sensual, matching the way she's moving her pelvis. And there's no way in hell I'm stopping the direction this is heading in to have a conversation I don't even want to have. Talking can wait.

Chapter Twenty Seven

ALEKSANDR

I'm rolling up the sleeves of my custom tailored shirt—they don't make dress shirts that fit guys with shoulders and arms the size of mine—as I walk out of my closet. Petra's in Stella's room helping her get ready, and I have butterflies in my stomach that I haven't felt since my first time on the ice in the NHL. The three of us have done many things together, but somehow this feels different. This feels like a *family* thing.

I grab my phone to slip it into my pocket and see a message from my agent on the screen.

> **JAMESON**
> LA is interested. Let's talk.

> **ALEKSANDR**
> I need a few more days to sort some stuff out in my personal life.

> **JAMESON**
> I can give you a day. We can't wait longer than that if you want this to happen.

Well, shit. I guess Petra and I are having this conversation tonight, after all. I would have talked to her earlier today, but she was at the party location with her team finalizing everything, and when she got home, she was stressing about getting showered and ready in time. There is no way I am adding to her stress, or even having what's sure to be a highly emotional conversation right before the party. So it'll have to wait until later tonight, when everything else is wrapped up.

ALEKSANDR

Okay. We'll talk tomorrow.

My bedroom door cracks open and I slip my phone into the front pocket of my dress pants. Petra slips through and looks relieved to see me. "Oh good, you're dressed. Stella's going to the bathroom. Her hair is done, she just needs help getting her dress on. Can you take care of that while I get myself dressed?"

"You're not wearing that?" I eye the *Go ahead and underestimate me, that'll be fun!* T-shirt she's wearing with a pair of booty shorts.

"I mean, I can if you want." She shrugs as if she'd be willing to step out of the house like that if I dared her.

"No." A laugh rumbles out of my throat. "I want to be the only one to see you like this."

I plant a kiss on the top of her head as she walks up and wraps her arms around my waist.

"You look . . . really nice," she says. "I've never seen you this dressed up." She tilts her head up and traces the length of my tie with the tip of her finger. "You look hot in a tie."

"I have all kinds of plans for you and this tie later

tonight," I say as I give her ass a little smack with the palm of my hand.

She presses forward into my body, leans up on her toes, and whispers in my ear, "I. Can't. Wait." And just like that, I'm so turned on I know I'll think of nothing else tonight except getting her home and naked. It should probably scare me that someone has this much influence over my thoughts, my body, and my soul, but it doesn't. It feels right. It feels like it should always have been this way between us, and I hate that we wasted half our lives being apart.

Regret is my own form of punishment, I suppose. But after tonight, we can move forward without regret or fear clouding our vision. And whether we're in LA or New York, I just want the three of us to be together.

With a kiss on my cheek, Petra turns wordlessly and heads into my closet to get dressed, and I head to Stella's room. I find her standing in her underwear taking the dress she's chosen for tonight off the hanger. It's short sleeved with a knit scoop neck top, and a few rows of pleated fabric between the waist and hem. "Where'd this dress come from?" I ask.

"Petra got it for me today. Isn't it perfect for your party? I mean, I know I'm not going to be there when the party is going on, but if I were, this dress would be perfect."

"It is."

Stella could easily have worn her pajamas since she's leaving before the party starts, but the fact that Petra wanted her to feel included and to have the opportunity to dress up too . . . it's so thoughtful. How did Petra find time today to go pick out a dress? Even if she sent her assistant out to find it, the fact that she prioritized that with everything else going on has a lump rising in my throat. "Can I help you get it over your head without messing up your hair?"

We've just gotten the dress on when I hear Petra's voice behind me. "Wow, Stella, you look beautiful."

I turn from where I'm kneeling next to Stella getting her dress straightened. Petra's standing in the doorway with her hair slicked back, wearing a white formfitting dress that ends right at her knees. The dress skims across the tops of her breasts with nothing but thin spaghetti straps holding it up.

"*You* look beautiful," Stella tells Petra. "Spin around, I want to see the back!"

Petra does as she's instructed, spinning slowly in a circle. The spaghetti straps skim over her shoulders and meet the sides of the dress. The dress has no back, there's nothing but skin from the low bun at the top of her neck to the curve of her lower back. Her feet are adorned with strappy gold sandals that wrap around her ankles and up her calves. She's a Greek goddess come to enchant me with her beauty. *Holy shit*. Sixteen-year-old me would have had to excuse himself to the bathroom to take care of the erection that's sprung up in my dress pants. I have *slightly* more control of my body and emotions now, especially with Stella standing right next to me.

Petra's eyes meet mine and the heat flares. I notice immediately how her nipples pucker beneath the fabric of her dress. I can't imagine that she's able to wear underwear with how low-cut that is in back, so I'm guessing she's totally naked beneath the dress.

"I love that dress," Stella says. "Can I wear it when I'm older?"

Petra laughs and says "Of course" at the same time I grind out "No way in hell" through my gritted teeth.

Petra ignores me and looks directly at Stella. "When you're an adult, you can wear whatever you want. Your body, your choice. Don't ever let anyone"—here she glances from Stella to me—"especially a man, tell you what you can and can't wear."

"Okay," Stella says softly beside me.

I consider what Petra's telling her. "Petra's right," I tell Stella, even though it pains me to think of my six-year-old ever being as grown-up and sexy as Petra.

"You guys ready to go?" Petra asks.

Stella springs forward to take Petra's hand. "Yes, let's go!" She looks over her shoulder at me, where I'm still on my knees on the floor. "Come on, Dada," she says and drags Petra forward through the door. Petra glances over her shoulder at me as I stand and adjust myself, and the way her eyes are dark orbs of black pupil surrounded only by a thin ring of her blue irises, I know she's forgiven me my earlier comment and is already thinking the same thoughts I am right about now.

The night is winding down, one player after another coming over to thank me for hosting this party. Some, like my coaches, are heading home because it's late. Others, because they have a tipsy wife or girlfriend hanging on their arm and whispering too-loud dirty thoughts into their ear.

In a moment of quiet reprieve between goodbyes, I tip the beer bottle back, then take in the scene Petra has created for the party. It really is amazing. A big awning covers the outdoor roof deck, and rows of string lights hang from the highest part of the brick building down to the low point of the awning opposite it. The long length of the roof deck is a low glass wall, and beyond it are spectacular views of the river and the Brooklyn Bridge, with the Manhattan skyline lit up beyond them. A few people are still curled up, their drinks on the gold and glass coffee tables between several sets of velvet sofas facing each other. Along the glass wall, leather-backed barstools sit tucked under the glass countertops that adjoin the wall—those too are littered with drink glasses being left behind faster than the waitstaff can clean them up. There are plants everywhere, especially in the corners like the one I'm standing in, and around the bar at the opposite end of the deck.

My eyes land on Petra. She's talking to her assistant, Morgan. In that tight white dress, she's sexier than she has any right to be while working and I've been taking tonight to observe, so I know I'm not the only one who has noticed. The guys have all eyed her with interest, the wives and girlfriends with a little bit of jealousy. I want to slap a sign on her that reads "She's mine," but maybe a ring on that finger would be slightly less caveman and more socially acceptable.

"Is that the girl from the game?"

The question shocks me out of my stupor and I turn my head to find Thompson standing right next to me.

I don't have to ask what girl, or which game. "Yep."

"I've been trying all night to figure out why she looks so familiar. You couldn't take your eyes off her then either, even while we were playing."

I think about how he held my ass up when I almost got knocked over because I was so busy staring at her after I scored my goal. "We won, didn't we?" I give him the side-eye when I say it.

"She's got a kid?"

I furrow my brow at the question, wondering why he thinks she's a mom until I realize that last time he saw her she was holding Stella. I don't know how to respond to that, but I'm starting to feel like a bit more honesty might be beneficial to my teammates realizing I'm not a hockey-playing robot.

"That was my niece she was holding."

Thompson makes a sound in the back of his throat like this clears something up, even though I imagine he still has some questions about that.

"You're into her?" he asks.

"What gives you that idea?" My voice is so sarcastic he actually snorts.

"So you're saying I shouldn't give her my number?"

"Not if you know what's good for you." He probably assumes I'll beat his ass if he tries, but really, I'm just saving him from Petra's response.

"You going home with her tonight?"

"You ask a lot of questions," I respond instead.

"So yes, then," he says.

I'm not going home with her, actually. She lives with me. The words float through my brain, but I trap them there and take another long swallow of my beer instead. She doesn't technically live with me. She stays with me when she's in New York. We need to figure out a more permanent solution, and I'm not talking to my teammates about our relationship until it's more settled.

Tonight. We have to figure things out tonight.

"All right, I'm heading out," Thompson says. "Just

wanted to say goodnight. And good party. Mystery woman over there did a nice job."

"I'll let her know," I say, and we clasp each other on the shoulder in farewell.

The last few people leave and we're down to only me and Petra, her staff, and the waitstaff. She ambles over to me in those sexy heels, leans into my shoulder, and sighs. "My feet are killing me," she groans.

"Want me to massage them?" I ask, and nod toward the empty couches. "Plenty of space."

"I would feel guilty if everyone were cleaning up around us while I sat here with you rubbing my feet."

"I'll wait until cleanup is done." This seems like a good place to have the conversation we need to have tonight. If we go home, we'll end up naked in bed. We need to talk first.

"Okay, you've got a deal."

I set my beer on the edge of the balcony to my right. "Okay, what do we need to do?"

"You're paying for this," she says, looking around the space, "you're not working."

"I'd feel guilty if everyone was cleaning up around me while I stood here having a beer."

"Touché." She rolls her eyes at me. "Fine, we need to move these couches and tables inside." She points toward the glass wall to the inside space where food was served. The waitstaff is already in there, breaking down tables and pulling the spindle chairs to the side of the room.

It doesn't take long for me and Petra's staff to move the couches and coffee tables inside, then I head out to start grabbing the leather barstools and bringing them in too. "How's this all work?" I ask Petra when she steps up beside me. "You rent the furniture and they deliver it for the event?"

"Pretty much, yes. The hard thing is finding enough of the same items for a coherent look. Sometimes for events like this, where I want eight matching couches, I have to buy the furniture. Then Morgan turns around and sells it online, but that adds a whole layer of complexity when you're only in town for a few days. Back in Park City, I have a whole storage unit with stuff we keep to reuse at events."

I pull out one of the last two barstools for her. "Here, sit for a minute. Let me rub your aching feet."

Petra glances into the interior loft space where her team is chatting as they grab a few remaining items and head toward the elevator. "You good, Petra?" Morgan calls.

"Yeah, we'll lock everything up," she calls out. "Thanks everyone!"

They call out their goodbyes and Morgan says, "Okay, see you at the airport tomorrow."

I see Petra's shoulders reflexively stiffen, and I hope it means she hates the idea of leaving as much as I hate the thought of her going.

"See you then," she says.

"Are you flying back to Park City with them?" I ask as we watch them all get into the elevator.

"No, but my flight to LA leaves at the same time as their flight through Denver, and apparently our gates are really close. Morgan had mentioned that earlier, which is"—she shrugs—"whatever. I just wasn't planning on being in work mode tomorrow morning."

"You seem like a pretty close-knit team."

"We are. It's been hard on them with me being in LA."

"I can sympathize with that feeling," I tell her as I reach down and pull her foot into my lap.

"Hmm." She lets the sound out slowly as I untie the gold straps that wind around her calf and slide her sandal from her foot.

"What does 'hmm' mean?" I ask as I scoop up her other foot and repeat the process of removing her other heeled sandal.

"I'm just trying to figure out what you mean by that."

"What's to figure out? I've missed you while you've been in LA and it's been hard on me being separated like that. I want you back here in New York," I say and she shakes her head back and forth slowly. "Or I want to be in LA, if that's what it takes."

Her eyes shoot up to mine, huge and wide and questioning. "What are you saying?"

"I want us to be together wherever it works. And with my contract up in New York after the finals, I'm free to either renegotiate with New York or try to move to another team."

"You would leave New York?" Her voice is quiet and unsure.

"To be with you? Yes." My thumbs are making small circles on the ball of one of her feet, and I slide one thumb down along the arch of her foot. Her eyes roll back until they're closed and a small sigh escapes her lips.

"This . . ." she says. "This feels very sudden."

"Petra." Her name comes out rough with my Russian accent. I hold the long *e* and roll the *r* deliberately, and no other words follow until she opens her eyes and looks at me. "Is this the direction you see our relationship heading in?"

She pauses, then says, "Yes, eventually."

"But not now?"

Her lips part, but no words come out. I think back to what my dad said about her and her mom: *She knew how I felt about her and she used every available opportunity to manipulate me, sharing little pieces of herself here and there when it was convenient for her, then denying there was anything between us and telling me I was a jealous fool. And I've watched Petra do the same to you . . .*

No, that's not Petra. She's not denying there's anything between us.

"I don't know," Petra says, and I've almost forgotten what I asked.

"What would be different if we waited longer, aside from having to figure out how to make this work long-distance which, let's be honest, is not working all that well." Aside from the couple days I spent with her in LA, it's been over a month since Stella and I had seen her before this weekend. The FaceTime calls we fit in only made it harder because we got to see her without really seeing her.

"Sasha," she says, as she reaches over and her hand strokes down the side of my face. "I don't know what my life even *is* right now. I don't know if my show will get picked up for a second season—"

"It will," I say emphatically. I saw the season premier, I read the reviews, I saw the ratings. If the other episodes are as good as the premier, there's no way she's not getting a second season. And I've seen another episode while she was filming it, so I know how good they're going to be.

"But what if it doesn't? What if you move yourself and Stella to LA, and I don't get a second season and then I go back to Park City?"

405

I think about this for a second before I ask, "You'd go back to Park City even if I'd moved to LA?"

Her eyes are wide as she lifts her shoulders in a questioning motion, like she's pleading with me to understand. "I don't know. My whole life is in Park City."

"Your whole life? What about me and Stella?"

"You know what I mean." She looks away, out at the Manhattan skyline, like the answer to my question might be somewhere over there.

"No," I say as I switch to massaging her other foot. "I don't."

"I mean that everything I've built, my business, my employees, my circle of friends . . . it's all in Park City." The look on her face is so conflicted.

I think about how both Jackson and Sierra have moved away, and how hard Petra's told me that's been on her to only have Lauren in Park City.

"Is that something you could be flexible about?" The knot in my stomach is growing tighter by the moment. "There's no NHL team near Park City. It's not even an option for me."

She takes a deep, steadying breath. "I think I'd rather come back to New York than have you move out to Los Angeles."

"Okay, we can work with that."

"It's just, I have contacts here. I can much more easily move my business here than I can start over in LA. And whether the show gets picked up for a second season or not . . ." She pauses, closes her eyes and takes a deep breath, then says, "I think I'd rather be here with you and Stella, even if it means I can't do the show."

My stomach flips over. "You'd walk away from the

show?" I'm stunned. I didn't expect this at all. I know how much the message of that show means to her, how privileged she feels to get to tell these women's stories.

"There's an interview that will air later this season, I think it's episode thirteen. In it, a super famous actress said something to me that just . . . resonated. She told me: 'If you're someone who is stuck working toward goals some previous version of you wanted, when what you now want is actually something else, then you're not being true to yourself.' I've heard those words over and over in my head since she said them, and it's like she knew exactly what I needed to hear in that moment. This show, the platform it gives me, it *is* something I wanted. But what I want now is you. You and Stella. And I think we can make that happen more easily here in New York than anywhere else."

I drop her feet and stand, spreading her legs in her seat so I can get as close to her as possible. Her arms come around my waist, pulling me to her. I tip my head down and our foreheads rest against each other.

"Thank God," I say. "For a few minutes there, I thought maybe we were becoming our parents."

I feel her pull back with a sharp inhale of her breath. "What do you mean by that?"

Shit. I should have thought more about those words. I should have planned out how I would tell her.

"Sasha," she says when I don't respond instantly. "What do you mean, you thought maybe we were becoming our parents?"

I take a deep breath. "I've been feeling like I should talk to you about something, but also feeling like nothing good can come of talking about this part of our past."

407

She sits back in her chair, leaning against the seat back. She's officially as far away as she can get without getting up and walking away, which I don't take as a good sign.

"If there's something you're keeping from me, I need to know about it right fucking now." The hard edge in her voice matches the icy glint in her eyes. "Don't you dare ask me to make a life-altering choice about our relationship if you're hiding something big."

"I'm not hiding anything," I say and hold my hands up in what I hope is a gesture of peace. "But I do know things about our parents, and things about our past, that I wish I didn't."

"Go on," she says, her voice deadly low.

"There was something happening between my father and your mother. I'm not sure how far it ever went, but my father said she wrecked him, always giving little pieces of herself but never willing to completely give herself over."

"Did they date before she met my father? In college or something?"

"I don't know. I know they knew each other in college, so maybe? But I'm talking about when we were older."

She narrows her eyes at me. "How much older?"

I tell her about the day I stayed home from school, and what I overheard before her mother left to pick Viktor up.

"So they both died because she was rushing home to prevent your father from talking to mine?" Her voice is ice.

"I think it's likely that's why she was driving so fast, yes."

"Why didn't you tell me back then?"

"I didn't know for sure if there was any truth to my father's accusations. And I didn't want you or your father to think your mom had been cheating if it weren't true."

"But it was true?"

"I think there was *something* going on between them. I'm not sure how far it went."

"When did you figure it out?"

I reach out to pull her hand into mine but she pulls away, folding her hands in her lap so tightly her knuckles are white.

"I know this is hard to hear, which is why I didn't want to tell you."

"When did you figure it out, Sasha?"

"My father confirmed it the night we signed the marriage license."

"But you didn't know it was a marriage license the night we signed that paperwork, *right*?" she clarifies, like she's trying to trap me in a today lie instead of a years-old lie.

"Not when we signed it, no. I found out later that night." Her eyes snap to mine, anger flashing in them, and now it's my turn to look away.

"You told me . . . what, like two months ago, sitting in Tom's office . . . that you didn't know what we were signing back then. You told me that you thought it was just paperwork for your father to give my father the money for my boarding school."

"That wasn't a lie, Petra. I *didn't* know what we were signing when we signed it." I explain how I found out later that night in my dad's office.

"Wait, so the money for my schooling was actually from *you*?" She's sounding angrier by the second.

"*That's* what you're focused on here?"

"That's the first thing, yes. You had no right to sign over part of your trust to me like that, without asking me first."

"You needed to go to that school, and I would have done anything to see you happy. I still would."

She purses her red lips. "You knew I wouldn't take the money from you if you offered it, so you had your dad lie to me?"

It sounds worse than it was when she says it like that.

"I did what I had to do to make sure you had the opportunities you deserved." There's a finality in my voice because she can't argue with that point.

"Okay, second then. You found out about the marriage license and contract that night, after we signed them?"

I nod.

"And again, you didn't tell me?" It's a rhetorical question.

"I made sure he wouldn't file them, so there was no need to tell you. Or so I thought."

"So, given the choice of either marrying me, or walking away forever, you took the latter option." There's no life in her voice. It's just flat. Dead.

"You were *sixteen years old*. You were not ready to be married. And neither was I, not even at nineteen. And there was no way I was beginning forever with you as my 'reward' for paying for your schooling. I wasn't going to *buy* you, Petra. And I didn't want you to know that your dad had agreed to that plan. I just wanted you to have every opportunity you deserved."

"But you stayed away for *fourteen years*," she reminds me. "You could have come back at any time. You could have told me about your father. You could have told me when I still had a chance to talk to my dad"—her voice cracks—"and find out why he agreed to this plan."

"I didn't think you'd forgive me for leaving in the first place," I tell her.

"I would have," she says, and the use of the past tense

doesn't escape my notice. "I would have if you'd just told me the truth. Instead, you continued to lie to me. You knew all this stuff about my past, about my family, and you didn't tell me. You made it seem like you found out about the marriage contract when your dad died, not later the night we signed it." She gasps in a breath like she needs the fortitude to keep going. "You made decisions about my life without including me in the decision-making process. You patronized me without me even knowing it."

"Petra, it wasn't like that."

She schools her face into a steely expression, perfect and porcelain-like. "Like hell it wasn't. I don't even know you at all."

"You're the *only* one who knows me!" My voice is raised and I'm glad no one else is still up here with us—they'd have heard that even inside. Though at some point we've switched to yelling at each other in Russian, so it's not like they'd understand. "You're the only one I can be open and honest with, the only one who knows my past, the only one I want to spend my future with."

"How pathetic is that?" she says with a sad laugh as she hops off the side of her chair. "I'm the only one who knows you, and I can't even know you because you can't be honest with me."

"I kept *one thing* from you," I emphasize, but even I realize it's a paltry defense.

"Even if it had only been one thing—hiding what you knew about our parents' relationship, or what you knew about my mom and Viktor's death, or that you'd been the one to give me the money for school, or that you'd cut me out of your life to 'save' me from a marriage to you—even *one* of

411

those would have been too much to lie about. But instead, the lies just built on each other." She pauses as she bends down and sweeps up her heels from where I left them on the ground at the base of our chairs. "I don't *know* you." The emphasis on the word *know* hurts even more because Petra is the only person who actually knows me. "And you don't know me at all if you think keeping everything from me was something I could ever be okay with."

She takes her shoes and storms into the loft. I watch as she grabs her purse and calls back to me, "You need to leave so I can lock this place up."

I rush into the loft, desperation quickening my steps. I cannot lose her like this. "Petra, please be reasonable. We can work through this."

Her laugh is acerbic. "You're delusional. Take the stairs down so I can lock that door behind you."

"I'll wait for you in the lobby," I tell her and she lets out a cruel little laugh.

"Sure, you do that," she says as she pushes me out the door into the stairwell and locks it behind me.

I'm halfway down the twelve flights of stairs before it occurs to me that she might take the elevator down, beat me to the bottom, and disappear. And that's exactly what she does.

Chapter Twenty Eight

PETRA

"You're going to get through this," Jackson assures me as she hands me a fresh cup of coffee.

When I dip my nostrils over it to inhale the scent, it feels like my nose hairs are singed off. "Holy shit." I draw back. "What's in this?"

"It's Irish Coffee. Seemed like the right kind of drink for today."

I glance out at the mist that hangs over the tree tops. We've taken the chairlift up to the top of Blackstone Mountain and are planning to hike down.

"You're getting me day drunk? I don't know if flying up here last night was the best or worst idea I've ever had."

She holds her mug in two hands as she sits in the Adirondack chair on the deck outside the upper lodge. The view will be spectacular if the sun burns off this mist. "Tell me everything," she says.

My flight out of New York last night was much like my last one—full of nonstop tears. But this time I wasn't crying because of what I was leaving behind, I was crying through the frustration of having been taken advantage of and lied to once again. I was crying for the life I thought Aleksandr and I were going to have together, only to find that it was all built on lies.

I tell her his side of the story and end with, "Lying is a deal breaker for me."

"Shit, Petra. I don't know what to say. On the one hand, it's horrible that he knew details about your mom and his father, and about your mom and brother's death that he didn't tell you. It's horrible that he deserted you the way he did, especially knowing how you felt about him. But on the other hand, he made sure you got to go to the boarding school you wanted, for the ski training you needed. He made sure your life didn't get signed away in a marriage you weren't ready for. And he did it because he loved you and wanted what was best for you."

I take a big gulp of the Irish Coffee, expecting the whiskey to burn but it's tempered by the sugar and the whipped cream. It goes down far too easy. "You can't possibly be taking his side here."

"I'm *always* on your side," she assures me. "I just want to make sure you're looking at this from all angles."

"Are there really multiple angles here?" I glance down at my lap and am alarmed for a second to find myself in unfamiliar clothes. Everything I'm wearing is Jackson's: her hiking boots, socks, leggings, and sweatshirt. Even the underwear and sports bra.

Because that's what happens when you leave a party in a fancy dress and strappy heels and head to the airport, unsure of your destination. It might have made more sense to call Emily or Avery, but the thought of staying with someone who knew Aleksandr, who knew us together as a couple, had my stomach in too many knots. Instead, I called Jackson, who suggested I come up for a day or two.

I'm supposed to be back at the studio tomorrow. I still have to figure out what to do about that. And how to get all my stuff from Aleksandr's back to LA. But these are future-Petra's problems and more than I can handle right now.

"There are always multiple angles. Sometimes it's just hard to see things from a different perspective when you're standing at a fixed point. You and Aleksandr have a past together, like Nate and me. That's part of what makes your current relationship so strong but it's also something that can cause friction because when you've loved someone since you were a teenager there are bound to be dozens of mistakes and missteps—big and small—along the way."

I take another gulp of coffee, draining it and setting it on the arm of the chair. "I'm going to need another one of these if you want me to start looking at this situation from Aleksandr's perspective, my wise friend."

Jackson whips her phone out of the pocket of her tunic-length, full-zip wool hoodie and taps her screen a few times. I take the moment to marvel at her in her element: dressed like she's in an Athleta ad, building her dream ski resort one step at a time with the love of her life. I'm so happy for her I could burst. "Done," she says triumphantly.

"Is Blackstone so fancy now that you can order food and drinks on an app and have it delivered on the deck?" I mean, I know she and Nate are working hard to make Blackstone a destination ski resort, but that feels next-level.

Her face lights up. "No, but that's a brilliant idea. I'm going to talk to Nate about that possibility."

"So . . ." I lead, "what just happened then?"

"I texted Lori, a friend of mine who runs this lodge, and asked if she could have someone bring another drink out for each of us."

"Must be nice," I tease.

"This life does have its perks." She gives me a small smile. "But you know it wasn't all wonderful getting here. Nate and I struggled a lot to make things right, and I pushed him away because he'd hurt me so badly when we were younger. I wonder if maybe that's what you're doing with Aleksandr too."

"Jackson, when I look back at all the pain in my life . . . he's responsible for a lot of it. And he lied about it all."

Just then, a woman comes out of the lodge in a forest-green long sleeve polo with the Blackstone emblem embroidered on the chest. She's holding two steaming to-go cups. Jackson thanks her and slips her a tip as she hands over our drinks.

"I fully understand that intent and impact are not the same thing," Jackson says, her voice placating as she hands me a drink and nods her chin toward the trail we'll take to hike down the mountain. I stand and follow her as she continues, "And I know how he's made you feel, so I understand the impact. But don't you think the intent matters too? He was trying to help you, all along he was shielding you from further pain and trying to make sure you got opportunities you badly wanted. Does that count for something?"

"He lied to me," I say, hating how much I sound like a broken record player. I want her to be as angry at him as I am, and I hate that she doesn't see this as something fatal to our relationship. "Even if I could get over that, how could I ever trust him again?"

"Do you trust me?" she asks before taking a sip of her drink.

"Of course I trust you." I follow her around a boulder and onto the dirt bike path that will be open in summer. I'm hoping this is an easy walk down because these drinks are strong.

"But I lied to you. I lied about me and Marco, and I definitely lied about Nate . . ."

"You lied to me about your own life. Marco—protecting a friend. Nate—lying to yourself. Either way, zero impact on me."

"Aleksandr's lies were not only about things that had happened to you, they were lies about things that had happened to *him* as well. And they were lies that were meant to protect and help you."

I'm quiet as I let the truth of those words sink in.

"Are you sure you aren't lying to yourself here a little too?" she asks. "I think he means a lot more to you than you're telling me. And I think the reason you're holding onto this lie, *these lies*, of his is because you're looking for a reason to run. Feelings scare you, Petra. Especially the big kind of forever feelings."

I step up next to her when we hit the switchback in the cluster of trees. "I told him I would give up the show and move back to New York to be with him."

Jackson breathes in sharply, then coughs and clears her throat. She looks over at me. "You—what now?"

"Yeah, and *that's* when he told me he'd been lying to me basically since I was thirteen."

I think I'm pretty strong, but there are only so many times you can be screwed over by a man before you lose faith in the entire gender. And I think I've hit that low point I swore I'd never sink to, the point where I'm ready to give up on men altogether.

The worst part is, I can hear my own advice here—I know exactly the kind of things I'd say to a friend in the same situation. *The best way to get over one guy is to get under the next one. You need some no-strings-attached sex.* Or, *If you're truly over men, I know some incredible women I could set you up with.*

Why didn't I ever stop to think that people need time to grieve in a breakup situation like this? Nope, I was always ready to throw my friends into the arms of the next man they came across. Now that I'm in that situation, I can see how dismissive I was of people's very real and very hurt feelings. Luckily, Jackson is a better friend than me in this situation.

"Okay, now I'm floored," she says. "And even more pissed at him. But also, I'm still hopeful that you'll go back to New York . . . talk it out with him. Figure out a way forward. You deserve to be happy, Petra. Even though I don't think you believe that, it's true."

"I deserve to be happy, yes. I don't think I need a man to make me happy, though. That's the part I don't believe."

She glances over at me and says, "Yeah, and I think you have put so much stock in that belief that maybe you're sabotaging your own happiness here because it's linked to a man."

I think about that as we descend the mountain, my legs and glutes burning with the effort of walking downhill over a 1,500-foot elevation drop. I think about that as we drive back to Jackson and Nate's house, and as I text Avery pleading with her to arrange to get my bags from Aleksandr's and to meet me at JFK with them tomorrow when I fly through on my way to LAX. I think about them all night, when I can't sleep because of the anger and the longing that are fighting against each other in my heart and mind. And in the morning, I know the truth of the matter is: I'm not sure. I'm not sure if Jackson is right, and I'm not sure how to figure it out.

———

It's been six days since I left New York and I haven't heard from him, nor have I contacted him. I guess it's up to me to make this decision. There's no way in hell I want Tony Gionetti anywhere near Stella, so I'll do whatever I can to prevent that—whether Aleksandr and I are together or not.

I slip my phone from my pocketbook as I make my way through the crowded Laguna Beach restaurant. I pause in the bar area to send Alicia a message.

PETRA

What is the most discreet way to turn the information you found over to law enforcement?

ALICIA

I thought you'd never ask! I've got a guy.

PETRA

What does that mean?

ALICIA

> It means I know and have worked with several officers. If someone walks by them on the street and hands them a package and says "Please deliver this to your supervisor," they know it's from me.

PETRA

> If this evidence wasn't legally obtained, it'll be useless though, won't it?

ALICIA

> Girl! What makes you think it wasn't legally obtained? No laws were broken in the process of gathering this evidence. There was no entrapment. Just a good, upstanding citizen—that's me—turning in non-law-abiding folk.

PETRA

> Okay, good. Do you need me to do anything else?

ALICIA

> Just pay me for my time, beautiful.

PETRA

> Transfer coming at you.

The bubble pops up on the screen to let me know she's typing, and then they disappear. Over and over.

I glance up while I wait and am surprised to find New York playing Anaheim above my head. It's not that I didn't know the first two games of the Stanley Cup finals were this week, it's that I forgot they were in Anaheim, a city I have to drive through to get back to my place in Los Angeles. The camera zooms in on Number 4, with Ivanov clearly written across his back. He approaches an Anaheim player from behind and checks him right into the boards. Several Anaheim players surround him and punches are thrown before his New York teammates show up to protect him. It's a huge brawl and by the time the referees break it up, Aleksandr is sporting a bloody nose and the most pissed-off look I've ever seen.

When the penalty is called and he's sent to the penalty box, he doesn't even try to pretend like he didn't start that. That complete lack of sportsmanship is not like him at all. The programming cuts over to the two sportscasters who each take up their third of the screen with a big picture of Aleksandr in between them. I glance at the bartender, ready to ask him to turn up the volume quickly, but he's halfway down the bar and not even looking in my directions. *Shit.* I don't want to miss whatever they're saying.

The remote is sitting about a foot away, so without thinking, I grab it. The volume rises so quickly everyone looks at the TV as if it must be some sort of national emergency. I drop the remote in my pocketbook as the bartender starts looking around to find it and turn the volume down.

"After two major penalties two nights ago, I thought Ivanov would be a bit more controlled," one of the sportscasters says.

"Ivanov's on some sort of rampage in this series. It's like he's a totally different player," the other announcer says.

"Yeah, he's known for his emotional control, and as a steady presence on the ice for his teammates. The only other time we've seen anything even approaching this was in that first playoff series against Philadelphia."

"That was child's play compared to this," the other announcer adds. "We're still waiting on word for whether he's going to sign with New York again or with Los Angeles. I wonder if either team is having second thoughts after seeing him play like this these past two games?"

Wait, he's still considering Los Angeles? That can't be right. I'm sure he's already told them no, especially given how we left things between us. There'd be no reason for him to move here at this point.

"I expect we'll learn very soon where Ivanov is landing for the next few years . . . if this series and his poor sportsmanship don't cost him his career." The words carry out of the TV and circle around me, making my head spin.

"Yeah, depending on how this game and this series go, he could be looking at an early retirement."

Above me, the camera zooms in on Aleksandr sitting in the penalty box. His helmet is on his knee, sweat drips off his hair and down his face. He's looking down, but when the game starts again, he looks up to watch his team, and I've never seen a look like that on his beautiful, stoic face. It's pure and utter rage. He looks like he's ready to kill someone out there on the ice.

Shit.

I dash toward the front of the bar as quickly as I can, my phone to my ear, willing Avery to pick up. "Hey, Petra," she half yells as I dig in my purse for the TV remote and throw it to the host on my way out. "Are you at the game?"

"No," I tell her, realizing that she's probably at a bar in New York watching the game, "are you watching it?"

"Yeah, me and half of NYC." A cheer goes up in the background, then a collective groan. A missed shot on goal, I suspect.

"Avery, I need your help. Is Tom with you?" I say as I

burst onto the sidewalk and look around for the town car the studio sent me down here in. Perks of the president of the studio insisting I come down to meet with him in Laguna Beach where he lives. Apparently, his daughter has a violin recital tonight that he couldn't miss. The exciting Friday nights of people married with kids.

"Yeah"—her voice gets serious and lower—"he's right here. What's wrong?"

"Nothing's wrong with me, but as you can see, Aleksandr is . . . not doing well."

"Yeah." Her voice is grim.

"Can I talk to Tom, please?"

There's a pause, then, "What?" The word is barked through the phone and it surprises me so much that I pull it away from my face and look at it for a second before I open the door to the town car that's just pulled up to the curb in front of me.

"Tom, it's Petra." I settle into the back seat as the car pulls away from the curb.

"I know."

Oh. Okay. "I need your help."

"Why in the world would I help the woman who wrecked my best friend? Have you seen him out there these last two games? YOU DID THAT." I don't know if he's yelling at me because he can't hear himself over the crowd, or if he's just yelling at me.

Maybe I deserve that. I left. I made Avery go get my stuff. I didn't call. I didn't come back. I didn't reach out to him, even though he was right outside of LA for the first two games of the series. *He's the one who should have reached out with an apology*, I tell myself.

"I want to make it right. Can you help me get in to see him?"

Tom's laugh is bitter and hysterical at the same time. "Into the Honda Center? Oh, that's funny. I'm his lawyer, not his agent."

"Right," I say, feeling less desperate as the pieces of a plan start to emerge in my mind. "Can you give me his agent's info?"

"Why would I do that?" he asks and behind him there's another big groan from the crowd. "Oh good, Anaheim just scored a goal because we're playing with five players on the ice for the next . . . three and a half minutes, thanks to Alex's penalty."

"*That's why*, Tom. That's why you need to give me his agent's info—because I'm the only one who can keep him out of the penalty box. If you don't let me help him now, he's going to wreck his career, and it's going to be on *both* our consciences."

"Fine," Tom bites out. "I'll text you his info."

"Thank you, Tom. Really."

He disconnects the call with no response, and I'm not even sure if he heard me. More fences to mend later.

The contact comes through via text immediately.

"Excuse me," I say to the driver. "I'm going to need you to drop me off at the Honda Center on your way back to LA."

He glances at me quickly in the rearview mirror before his eyes shift back to the road. "You want me to . . . drop you off?" Is that skepticism or confusion making his question come out so slowly?

"Um," I say as I glance down at the contact info on my phone.

"You don't want me to wait for you?"

"No, but thank you. You get back to LA and go on with your night."

"But . . ." He glances at me in the rearview mirror again, the lines at the corner of his eyes wrinkling as he tries to make sense of my request. "I was told to bring you back to LA."

"Change of plans." I shrug as I call Jameson Flynn, who, according to the contact info Tom sent me, is apparently Aleksandr's agent. The phone rings four times, then goes to voice mail. I don't leave a message. He's probably screening his calls and doesn't recognize my number. Instead, I send him a text message.

PETRA

> Hi Jameson, my name is Petra Volkova.
> Tom Sheppard, Alex Ivanov's lawyer, gave
> me your number.

I pause for a moment to think of what I can say to get Jameson to help me get into that game. Is he even there? It's the Stanley Cup finals—of course he's there. I glance at the clock. It's after 8:00 p.m. so I'm sure I've just missed the first intermission. I have to make it there in time for the second intermission, or this is all for naught.

"Can you go just a bit faster?" I ask the driver. "I really need to make it to this game before the end of the second period."

"There's no traffic. We'll be there in about fifteen minutes," he says as we cruise along the highway. Around us, the hills boast the green grass that's only present in the winter and spring.

PETRA

I know the way he's playing tonight is . . .
less than desirable. I need to talk to him
before the next period begins. Can you
please get me in to see him? It's an
emergency.

The bubbles pop up on the screen and at least I know he's seen my text. I hold my breath while I wait for his response.

JAMESON

I'm sorry, I don't know you or how you
know Alex . . . and you believe I would "get
you in to see him" because . . .?

Suddenly, our relationship is not only a risk I want to take, it's something I'm committing myself to fixing. But I don't know how he'd feel about me telling his agent. I just have to hope that he'll be understanding once I explain why I shared this information.

PETRA

I'm his wife.

JAMESON

Bullshit.

PETRA

I'm not sure what I can tell you that will
make you believe me. But I'm the only
person who might be able to turn his game
around. I assume you want him to sign a
new contract when this one is up?

I glance out the window as we head into Anaheim, and

there's nothing but sprawl. The sameness is killing me slowly. The same weather every day, the same low buildings everywhere I look, the same golden hillsides, the same clogged freeways, the same people drinking their green juice on their way home from yoga. We're an hour out of LA and the sprawl just keeps going on and on, different cities and it all feels the same.

An hour outside of New York, I could be lounging on the beaches of Long Island, or visiting farms in quaint small towns upstate. I could be watching horse racing, or exploring outdoor gardens and art installations in the Hudson Valley. I miss the variety of landscape and people, as well as the fast-paced life of New York City—almost as much as I miss Sasha and Stella.

My phone buzzes in my hand, the repeated vibrations signaling an incoming phone call. It's Jameson.

"Who's the most important person in his life?"

Without even a moment of hesitation, I respond. "Stella."

"Okay. I'll meet you at the main entrance. How soon will you be here?"

I glance at my watch. Based on what the driver said about timing, I tell him, "Less than ten minutes."

"How will I know who you are?"

"I'll send you a picture," I say, and he gives me a gruff *Okay* before he disconnects the call.

I open up the photos on my phone and pull up a photo I took of me and Aleksandr before the event last weekend. My smile is huge, my eyes are crinkling at the corners and you can barely see my baby blues through my lashes because I'm glancing sideways at the love of my life. I send the picture to Jameson but even after it's been sent on its way, I can't stop staring at the two of us. We were so happy. I almost told him I loved him that night, was just on my way to saying it when he dropped the bombshell about our parents and then all the other lies came tumbling out in its wake.

My heart aches, physically, when I consider how I'd walked out on him later that night. I needed time and space to think about why he'd lied to me and if I could forgive him for it. And once I realized I could forgive him, I needed time and space to plan how I'd make my way back to him.

Maybe I should have reached out sooner, let him know where my heart and mind were, but I wanted to be certain. I wanted to have my plan in place with no option to back down. I wanted to be one hundred percent committed so he'd know how serious I am, before saying anything.

After watching him self-destruct on the ice tonight, I pray I didn't wait too long.

Chapter Twenty Nine

ALEKSANDR

My time in the penalty box is up with three minutes still left before the buzzer sounds to end the second period. To no one's surprise, Coach doesn't put me back on the ice. He also doesn't even look at me when I get back to the bench, so I know how pissed off he is. I'm the steady one, the player he can always depend on, the one who's a role model for the other players. Until these last two games.

After this last penalty, I can't afford to let my temper get the best of me. With a new contract on the line, I also can't afford to make these kinds of mistakes.

I keep my head down as we march through the hallway toward the locker room. No one speaks to me, and I don't blame them. Anaheim scored two more goals during the power play, so we're down three to one right now. I can't even convince myself it isn't my fault, and my own guilt and my teammates' silent accusations hang heavy in the stale air outside the locker room.

There's a holdup at the locker room entrance as we enter

single file, each player's shoulder pads taking up the full width of the doorway. At the end of the line, I'm a couple players away from the door when Thompson steps out of the way and Coach steps through the door. He's followed by my agent, Jameson Flynn, who was apparently in the locker room. *Shit, this is not good.*

Jameson has never once come to see me *during* a game. I can't imagine why he's even down here unless it's to rip me a new asshole and remind me that I'm costing him a lot of money right now by not getting my shit together. At this moment, that's the last thing I need.

"Ivanov," Coach barks. "Go with Flynn." My agent turns to head down the hallway.

"Wait, what?" I ask, glancing between my agent and my coach, and eyeing the locker room behind him. "I need to know what the plan of attack is, I need to come back into this game with my head on straight."

Coach reaches up and puts his hand on my shoulder. "There's a family emergency, son. Go with Flynn."

My stomach roils and I feel like I could throw up on the spot. Stella. What's wrong with Stella?

I turn toward Jameson, the question poised on my lips.

"It's not Stella," he says, his voice level and firm. "Let's go."

I dip my head toward his as we walk down the hall together. "What the hell is going on? I don't have any family aside from Stella."

He stops in front of a conference room. There's a window, but the shades are down so I can't see inside. "This is about you getting your shit together. You've got five minutes." He opens the door and with a strength I wasn't expecting, he pushes me inside.

I stumble as my skate slides along the carpeted floor, but I right myself with my hand on the back of an office chair that's sitting at a table. I toss my helmet and gloves on the table and turn back toward the door to demand Jameson explain himself, and that's when I catch sight of her.

Petra, my heart screams. *She came back!*

She fucking left you, my brain argues.

I'm so dumbfounded with the fight that's happening inside me—the tangible need to grab her and hold her is at odds with the instinct to protect myself—that I just stare at her stupidly.

"What the actual hell do you think you're doing out there?" she asks as she pushes her chair back and stands.

"I'm having a crappy game." It's a struggle to keep the emotions I'm feeling—the anger, the sadness, the hopelessness—out of my voice. I'm good at being unreadable, so I school my face into the neutral mask I usually wear and make sure there's a solid layer of armor around my broken heart.

"This is not a *crappy game.* This is a career ending performance when it should be the pinnacle of your year: another Stanley Cup championship and your choice of where you want to go when your contract is up." Why the fuck does *she* sound mad? "Instead, you're showing all these clubs that you're not serious about your game, that you can't keep it together when the pressure's on."

"And why do you think that is? Why do you think I'm struggling to keep my shit together right now, Petra?" I prop my stick up against the corner of the walls nearest me.

"I assume that you're trying to blame your utterly piss-poor performance"—she shakes her head—"on me leaving you last weekend."

My eyes rake over her. She said she wanted to make this marriage work, then she left me and Stella. Of course I'm pissed and my performance is suffering—Stella and I are both heartbroken and I'm still trying to figure out how long it will be before she stops crying herself to sleep every night.

A scoff bubbles up out of the back of my throat. "And now what? You think showing up at my game and yelling at me about my game is somehow going to make things better?"

I notice Petra is wearing a black form-fitting dress that hits at her knee. She's got black heels with those red soles that I know matter to lots of women. She's sexy and sophisticated and looks like she came straight here from a business meeting. Meanwhile, my hockey uniform is practically stiff with dried sweat and my beard is damp.

"No, I think that *you* accepting that I needed a few days to sort out my emotions is what's going to make things better. Yes, I left last weekend. But what did you expect me to do when you told me that you'd lied to me, repeatedly, basically as long as we've been friends? That's an almost impossible piece of news to get over, Aleksandr."

My heart sinks. She's not wrong. "Yes, I kept something huge from you, and I should have come clean much earlier. I *own* that, and I am *deeply* sorry. I should have told you from the beginning, or at least when we reconnected in Tom's office. I know it will take time to rebuild that trust. I've been committed to rebuilding that trust, Petra—everything I've done since you've been back is geared toward that. But you didn't even give me a chance to explain my reasons. You just left."

"You can't be committed to rebuilding trust while continuing to lie."

I let that sobering thought sink in. As usual, she's right.

"I had been planning on telling you, I was just trying to find the right time. I didn't know how to say that my own father might be responsible for the death of your mom and brother. Or explain your dad's role in this arranged marriage. I just wanted to save you the pain of having to deal with those facts, because they've been eating me alive for a decade and a half."

"Sasha," she says, stepping forward. "You are *not* responsible for your father's actions—"

"But if I hadn't stayed home sick that day—"

"You are *not* responsible for what happened to my mom and Victor, just like you are not responsible for our fathers' choices. And I already know why my dad made that decision."

"You do?" This whole time, I've been trying to protect her from the truth of her father's involvement, and she's known why he did this? How is that possible?

"The last thing he said to me when I left to go to boarding school in Switzerland was, 'I would do anything to make sure you have the life you deserve.'" She takes a deep breath. "In hindsight, I think he did what he thought he needed to do in order to help me have the life I wanted."

Her eyes are watering, and I close the distance between us with one large step so I can cup her face in my hand.

"Petra, I am so sorry that I lied. I swear on all that's holy—it won't happen again. Everything I've ever done is to protect you, to make sure you have the life you deserved."

"You have to trust that you can tell me hard things, and that I will be able to deal with them," she says.

"You are the strongest person I know," I admit. "I didn't keep this from you because I thought you couldn't handle it. I kept it from you because I didn't want you to have *another* terrible truth to deal with."

Her voice is firm when she says, "I can handle the hard truths, Sasha. I can't handle lies."

I rest my lips against the top of her head, then mumble, "I know, and I'm so, so sorry," into her hair. Then I pull back, drop my hand from her face, and look her in the eye. "I am one hundred percent committed to this relationship, and I will do whatever it takes to make this—to make us—work. I know it will take time for you to trust me again, and I'm willing to work for that. But also, I need to know you aren't going to run the moment things get hard."

"You don't get to be mad that I needed a few days to think things through. *You* left, and *you* didn't come back for fourteen years. I just needed a little time to work things out in my head. I didn't wait fourteen years."

"The two situations are *not* the same, Petra. We were children back then. We're adults now, and there's a *child* involved. How do you think Stella took it when I had to explain to her that you left? And then when Avery came to get your bags and Stella began to understand that you weren't coming back?"

"But I *was* coming back."

"Well, how were we supposed to know that? You leaving broke Stella's heart...and mine." Of course my voice has to go and crack on the word *mine*. Now there's a lump in my throat, and I'm having trouble swallowing it down.

She looks up at me, her face as open and unguarded as I've ever seen it. And all I see there is hope. "I was in Laguna Beach tonight when I saw the game on the TV at a restaurant as I was leaving," she says, her voice low, and soft, and husky.

I just stare at her, then raise my eyebrows in question, because what the hell does this have to do with breaking my and Stella's hearts?

"I was in Laguna Beach because that's where the president of the studio lives," she says. "I met him there for dinner because we needed to talk about the show. He let me know it was being picked up for a second season, and I let him know the only way I would sign on for Season 2 is if we can move the show to New York."

My intake of breath is so sharp it feels like I've sucked all the air out of this tiny meeting room. "Are you serious?"

"Yes," she says, reaching up and running her fingers along my cheek. "So tell Jameson to stop talking to LA and go back out there and make sure New York signs you for a few more years."

I drop my head down and rest my forehead on the crown of hers. "Petra, we're married. If we're going to make this work, we're going to make good on that commitment we didn't know we'd made so long ago. I can't do 'we'll figure it out.'" My voice is barely above a whisper, but I keep my words firm. "I need you to be all in."

She lifts her head so I have to pull mine up as well, and she tilts hers back so she's looking up at me. She locks her eyes on mine and cups my jaw in her hands.

"I'm in. All in—with the marriage and with raising Stella. I'm ready for this." She pauses. "But first, you have to go out there and kick some ass and remind New York why they've kept you around for the past eight years. Okay?"

"Okay." I lean down and take her mouth with mine, gently sucking on her lower lip until she opens for me. I keep the kiss short, then I wrap her in my arms and hold her to me. I have to get back to work, but I'm not ready to let her go yet.

"Sasha," she murmurs against my chest.

"Yeah, love?"

"You stink."

My chest rumbles with laughter. I'm sure I do. I pull back and as I slide my hands down her shoulders, my finger catches in her bra strap. It's lavender lace.

"You wore sexy undergarments to go to your meeting?"

"Do you think I have any other kind?" she purrs with that sexy-as-fuck voice of hers. "I'm looking forward to showing them to you after you win your game tonight."

That's a bribe if I ever heard one. "And if I don't win?"

"You will," she says decisively. Then she runs a thumb over my lip, hands me my helmet and gloves from the table and my stick from the corner, turns and opens the door, and ushers me out. "He's ready," she tells Jameson.

"Coach is expecting you in the locker room," he tells me. I head down the hall and when I look over my shoulder, he's leading her out of the conference room and toward an elevator that will take them back up to the stands.

When I open the door to the locker room, Coach is standing there waiting for me. "You good?" he asks. I nod. "Your head on straight?" I nod again. "Good. Don't ever again let me see you play like you've been playing these last two games."

"Understood," I say.

He reaches across the short space between us and grasps my forearm. "You're too valuable a player to waste your time and talent in the penalty box. Go out there and show us what you're made of."

"I will, sir."

And then I do.

———

"Stella's going to be up any minute," I tell Petra as I rub my nose against the back of her head, inhaling the intoxicating smell of her hair. These last few days since I saw her in Anaheim have been excruciating without her, and I'm so glad she's back in New York.

The light is already filtering through the curtains at the edge of my bedroom, the rays of sunshine reminding us that even though Petra's flight arrived in the early hours of the morning, we still have a six-year-old who will be bouncing off the walls to see her the minute she wakes up.

"Let me sleep until she wakes up, then. You already kept me up all night. I only closed my eyes five minutes ago."

My chest shakes with easy laughter. "You're so dramatic. We got at least four hours of sleep."

"Four hours . . ." she half mumbles, half groans.

With the arm that's already wrapped around her waist, I pull her even closer. I love having her pressed up against me when I sleep, but somehow in the early hours of the morning she managed to scoot away from me half a foot. I know she thinks my body temperature runs too hot and that she needs her space, but I hate the distance between us.

I'm okay being the clingy one—she needs to know she can trust me, that I'd never leave her, or lie to her, ever again.

She curls into me. "More sleep."

I bury my face in her hair and smile—something I seem to be doing a lot these days now that my contract in New York has been renewed and there are only four more weeks until Petra is back here permanently. She's here in New York this weekend for our games, and unless we lose both, I'm bringing Stella with me when we head back to Anaheim next week for the end of the series.

I'm actually surprised Stella slept at all last night. I fully expected her to come out of her room, still wide awake, when Petra arrived. But I guess one in the morning is later than she can keep herself awake, even with all the excitement of the surprise we've planned for this morning.

I'm pretty sure Stella is as in love with Petra as I am.

I lie there for probably twenty or thirty minutes, listening to Petra's rhythmic breathing as she sleeps in my arms. Ending up here, together for real—forever—is like having all my dreams come true.

When Stella finally cracks the door to the bedroom open, I raise my arm and wave her in, careful not to wake Petra. She tiptoes across the room and around to Petra's side of the bed, where she climbs up on top of the comforter.

"Hey," I whisper into Petra's ear. "You've got to wake up now."

Across from us, Stella's practically shaking with excitement, her smile almost splitting her face in half as she holds our gift out in front of Petra's face.

"Hmm," Petra murmurs, but I can tell she hasn't opened

her eyes yet because she'd be having a much different reaction if she had.

"Open your eyes, sweetheart," I coax.

"Too early." The words are a mumbled whisper, and as much as I want to let Petra go back to sleep, I can't deny Stella this opportunity. I never pictured myself balancing the needs of two high-maintenance women in my life, and yet these moments are the ones I now live for.

"Petra," Stella says softly. "Open your eyes."

Petra stiffens against me as she jolts awake, her breath swallowed up by a gasp. "What the hell, Stella?"

My chest is shaking with laughter. How did I not anticipate that response?

Stella laughs, too, holding the open ring box out so Petra can see it better. I prop myself up on my elbow so I can watch this scene play out, and Petra turns her head to look up at me, her eyebrows knit together.

"Are you proposing to me?" she asks.

"We're already married," I remind her. "But I figure my wife ought to have a ring. And a wedding, if you want one. And whatever else you want, as long as it's in my power to give it to you."

She pulls me down and gives me a quick kiss, then turns back to Stella. "This is what you want, too?" Petra asks her, because of course she does. She's never not thinking about what's best for Stella.

"More than anything," Stella says and launches herself at Petra. They wrap their arms around each other, and I fold them both into mine. I take a moment to send a heartbroken prayer of thanks up to my brother and sister-in-law. I will never not feel guilty that their death gave me Stella and led me back to Petra. I will also never stop trying to prove myself worthy of this life.

Stella pulls away first and then hands Petra the ring box. My wife gazes down at it like she's paralyzed over what to do next.

"Stella and I picked it out together."

"It's beautiful."

"Are you ready to be wearing my ring?" I ask. "I won't be offended if you want to wait."

She looks up at me with so much love in her eyes. "I appreciate that you asked, and didn't assume. And yes, I'm ready. I don't want to wait anymore—for anything. I'm ready to accept all these blessings—you," she says to me, then looks over at Stella and taps her on the nose, "and you, and this amazing life we get to live together."

I pluck the ring out of the box and slip it on her finger.

Epilogue

PETRA

Fifteen Months Later
St. John, US Virgin Islands

"I got it!" Jackson gasps as she comes running through the open doors of the house to the pool out back.

Sierra, Lauren, and I look up from the lounge chairs we're relaxing on under umbrellas. For the past twenty minutes we've been the judges for our significant others' diving competition, where each dive has gotten more ridiculous because they're nothing if not competitive.

"Got what?" Sierra asks, then groans as she pushes herself up to a full sitting position. She folds her legs under her so she's sitting crisscross with her adorable baby belly resting on her thighs. The girl is glowing, her skin radiant and her long blond hair piled into a messy bun on top of her head; she looks like she's going to have this baby any minute, even though she's not due for another two and a half months.

Jackson pulls a rolled-up magazine out from behind her

back and walks around the pool to bring it over to us. I'm splayed across the cover in a white pantsuit with the black letters of the Vogue masthead above me. I'm sitting with my knees spread out, the heels of nude Louboutins pegged over the rungs of a black stool. One of my hands is resting on the stool between my legs and the other on my hip as I lean forward. The low-cut blazer shows a tasteful amount of cleavage, and my dark curls fan out over my shoulders. My lips match the red soles of my shoes.

Even though I've seen the photo before, and knew this was coming, it still takes me by surprise. "How . . .?"

"I only had to go to two stores to find it," Jackson says excitedly.

"Three," Nate coughs out from behind her, "but who's counting?"

She rolls her eyes before turning toward him. "Obviously not you."

Nate's got two six-packs in his hands and heads toward the built-in cooler of the outdoor bar area on the opposite side of the pool.

Jackson sits down on the foot of my lounge chair, her ankles crossed and knees pressed together. Her white empire waist dress falls around her baby bump. Jackson's only a month behind Sierra, but she barely looks pregnant. She was so sick for the first four months of her pregnancy that she actually lost weight, and now she just has the perfect little belly—enough that you can tell she's pregnant, but you'd never guess she's so far along.

"What's that say over the photo?" Lauren asks. She sets her margarita on the table beside her lounge chair and leans over toward Sierra so she can see the magazine better.

"Unstoppable Power, Meet Sex Appeal," Jackson says.

I roll my eyes. "I begged them not to go with that," I tell my friends. I hate the way it makes it seem like the two things are exclusive, like it's an anomaly to be powerful *and* have sex appeal.

When water drips over my head, I look up in time to see Sasha's lips descending toward my forehead.

"It's out," he says, a bit of awe in his voice, as he rains wet kisses across my hairline. We knew the magazine was releasing this weekend, but I'd honestly hoped to avoid it, and the spotlight, given that we would be away on our vacation.

Besides, this article is coming out on the heels of news that Tony Gionetti is going to prison for the next twenty-five years, and that's the news I really care about. CeCe claims she's absolutely appalled at her soon-to-be ex-husband's crimes, and is begging us to let her be a part of Stella's life. Sasha and I are still considering whether that would be good for Stella or not.

I reach up and run my fingers through his longer locks. Every member of his team refused to cut their hair this entire season, and even though they lost in the semifinals over a month ago, he still hasn't cut it. Half the time he's got it up in a man bun, which isn't a look I thought I liked until I saw it on him.

Jackson makes a dramatic show of flipping to the article, then clears her throat.

"Petra Ivanova has a face that you just *know* you've seen somewhere, even if you can't quite place her. But these days, the number of people who aren't sure how they know her is dwindling. With an Emmy award-winning talk show under her belt, the former Olympic skier, model, and event planner opened up to Vogue about some of the challenges her newfound fame has brought. 'I really value my privacy, and privacy for my family,' Ivanova tells me when we meet for coffee on the terrace of the penthouse apartment overlooking Central Park that she shares with her husband, hockey player Alex Ivanov, and their seven-year-old daughter. 'I know that with my career and my husband's career, it's not realistic to believe we can remain out of the public eye, but we used to at least be able to walk down the street without being recognized.'"

Sierra runs her hand up and down my leg like she's soothing me. "Don't worry," I tell her. "I know that famous people problems are not *real* problems."

"Petra, acknowledging that you wish you had more privacy in life doesn't make you a bad person, or ungrateful," Lauren says. "You didn't agree to do the show because you were looking to become a household name."

"Yeah, but what did she think would happen after everyone found out how fabulous she is?" Jackson teases as she swats my knee with the magazine.

Behind me, Sasha chuckles. "Right? That's what I've been telling her all along." He rests his hands on my shoulders and gives me a supportive squeeze.

I already know I'm awesome, but for those moments when the doubt or anxiety creep in, or on days like today where it starts to feel like maybe it's too much—too invasive, too taxing, too overwhelming—it's good to have a support group who believes in me as much as, or more than, I believe in myself.

"Oh, wow." Jackson sighs as she holds the magazine back up. "They reference 'The Kiss.'"

"Oh God," I groan, rolling my eyes back as I tilt my head up to look at Sasha. It may have been one of the best moments of my life, but I've been forced to live it on repeat, nonstop for the last year. Everyone remembers it. Everyone brings it up. It's the romantic grand gesture that will not die. "You made the whole freaking world fall in love with you that day, you know?"

He raises his eyebrows and gives me a small shrug.

"Let's hear it," Sierra says, leaning toward Jackson so she can see the print. "Ooh, they included a photo of it too."

Lauren reaches across the space between our lounge chairs and takes my fingertips in hers as Jackson reads, "Maybe it's true that there was a time that the two could walk down the street together incognito, but that all changed a year ago when New York clinched the Stanley Cup in game seven of the finals. The team celebrated on the ice as each player took his turn skating a lap around New York's home rink with the Cup hoisted high above his head. Quietly and without ceremony, Alex Ivanov skated away from his teammates, over to the side of the rink. There, he kissed his hand and pressed it up against the glass in front of a beautiful woman wearing his jersey. On the other side, she kissed her fingers in return, and held them up against his. Fans near her caught the moment on video and everyone realized she was wearing a wedding ring. *His* wedding ring, as it turns out.

"Despite his long tenure on the team and his role as team captain, Ivanov mostly stayed out of the public eye, preferring to lead quietly by example. That all changed the night he skated over to his wife instead of basking in winning the Stanley Cup. But the two are secretive about their marriage. Ask them how long they've been married and they'll tell you 'a while' . . ." Jackson trails off and looks up at me. "Do they only care about your marriage? What about your career?"

"Calm your outrage," Sierra says. "I'm sure it's all in there. They're just starting out with how everyone first learned who Petra was."

"That's bullshit," Jackson says. "Her show had already aired and been picked up for a second season before that even happened."

Sasha is running his thumb up and down my neck—our secret signal that one of us is ready to leave.

"It's all in there. Aleksandr and I have both read it," I say, nodding up at my husband, "so while this is all new and fun for you, I'm getting bored of hearing about myself. I think we'll go get ready for dinner."

"We don't need to leave for"—Lauren looks at her phone —"almost two hours."

"Yeah, but I'm hot and sweaty and you know how long it takes for me to wash this hair," I point to the rat's nest of curls currently pulled back into a ponytail as I stand.

"Uh huh," Sierra nods, her lips between her teeth like she's trying not to laugh. "You go have fun 'getting ready.'"

We turn to walk back into the house at the same time they all burst out laughing.

"They definitely know we're leaving to have sex," he says as he clasps my hand in his, "and I couldn't care less."

———

"**F**inally alone," Sasha breathes into my neck as he pulls me up against him. We've only made it three steps into our bedroom.

"If I'd known you were trying to get me alone, I'd have made an excuse to come inside much sooner." *Thank goodness for our sign*, I think as I run my hand through his hair. I can't believe how sexy I find him with this shoulder-length hair.

"I'm *always* trying to get you alone." He nips at my neck, grazing his teeth along the length of my skin until his lips are at my earlobe.

"Does that mean you don't like hanging out with my friends?" I ask. This isn't the first time we've all hung out together, and every time I'm thankful for how at ease he seems with my friends' husbands. But this is the first time we've gone away on vacation together.

"You know I like your friends," he says, then trails his tongue across my earlobe. "But this is the first time we've been away without Stella, and I want as much time with you as possible before we go back to being parents."

"You have no idea how much things are about to change," I tell him, but I can't keep the affection out of my voice. "When we get back, shit's about to get real."

He steps back and drops his hands to the concave curve of my belly. "Shit's already real. But I can't wait for it to get even real-er." He drops to his knees and unties the long white kimono where the belt is strategically tied around my waist, hiding the still-small bump that we're told is a girl. "You really don't want to tell your friends yet?"

"This is Jackson and Sierra's joint babymoon. It's lovely that they wanted to include us, but we don't need to steal their thunder. We can tell them once we're back."

"Earlier you didn't want to tell them because you wanted them to enjoy being pregnant at the same time, and didn't

447

want to pull the attention away from that and onto you. Don't you think they'll be thrilled that we're having a baby too?"

"I do," I assure him. "But right now, this is *their* thing."

He kisses my belly button, then looks up at me from his knees. "You. Are. Beautiful." The words are reverent. His lips meet my belly again, and this time they are hungry. He trails his tongue down to the triangle of fabric that makes up the front of my bikini bottoms as he slides his hands over to my hips. With one tug on either side, he has them untied and falling to the floor.

"God, I've missed this," he says as he leans forward.

"It's only been since lunch—" I'm about to remind him of our quickie in the pool house bathroom a few hours ago, but my words die in my mouth as his tongue flicks out and the warm smoothness of it slides across that sensitive ball of nerves at the junction between my legs. I can't help the moan that escapes my throat and shoots right past my lips. Pregnancy has given me an insatiable appetite for sex—there's no limit to the number of times I want him to make me come every day. I'm told this is normal, and luckily he's happy to serve my every need while I grow this child of ours inside me.

His fingertips run up my calf to the sensitive flesh behind my knee and his touch is a current that sends shockwaves throughout my body. He lifts my knee and places it over his shoulder, then rains kisses up my inner thigh until his mouth is back between my legs. He's so close, but he doesn't touch me like I want him to. Instead, the heat of his soft breath washes over me. My entire core clenches with desire, white-hot need running through me.

"Take your bathing suit top off," he says as he gazes up at me. "I want to see you."

I reach up with both hands, untying the bow behind my neck and then behind my back, before pulling the suit away from me and dropping it on the floor.

"Holy shit," he says, his eyes focused on the undersides of my breasts. "Have they gotten bigger in the last few hours?"

I cup one breast in each palm, testing the weight of them as they spill over my hands. Then I run my thumbs up and over each nipple just to tease him. His breath is a hiss as it escapes his lips. "They may have," I tell him. It does feel like it's possible, given the rate at which they're enlarging now that I'm pregnant. I run my thumbs over my nipples again and my thighs clench in response. I bring my hands down to his head, run my fingers through his hair, letting my nails drag against his scalp in the way I know drives him crazy.

"Sasha, please. Please touch me."

"Shit, I love it when you beg," he says, then buries his mouth into my folds, licking the length of my opening and then circling my clit several times. His thumbs spread me open over his mouth and his tongue laps me up like I'm an ice cream cone and he doesn't want to lose a single drip. I groan because I'm so close already, and he takes that as his signal to intensify his assault. Suddenly, his tongue is gliding over me with a fast but controlled energy.

"I'm so close," I whisper, reaching out and gripping the side of the armoire to hold myself up. I glance down and see the huge length of him jutting out against his swim shorts, and I'm filled with an aching need to be joined with him. "I need you inside me."

His eyes flick up to mine and I can read his meaning clearly—soon enough. This is just the warm-up act, and he wants to leave me wanting more.

There's a gaping emptiness where he's not filling me, and it edges out the pleasure of his tongue. But then he clamps his lips around the bundle of nerves and sucks hard, pulling me into his mouth and running his tongue over me. The pleasure is so intense I start to come undone and I drag my fingernails along his scalp and he repeats the motion over and over until the white-hot sensation is flooding my core and sending waves of pleasure through the rest of my body, making every single cell stand at attention. I come down from my orgasm, immediately wanting him again.

"Now, Aleksandr," I insist, as I pull him to his feet and immediately untie his swim trunks. He pushes them down to the floor and I take a moment to marvel at the monstrosity that is his erection—thick and hard, so smooth and long and perfectly made for my body.

He reaches to my shoulders and pushes my open kimono down my arms, then sweeps me into his arms and walks toward the bathroom.

"What are you doing?" I ask. What the hell? We were standing two feet away from the bed.

"We're supposed to be showering and getting ready for dinner. We're going to have to make this a two-for-one."

I understand his meaning perfectly. "We haven't had shower sex in a while," I note.

"Exactly." When we get to the shower, he opens the glass door and turns the water on, and while we wait for it to warm up, I press myself up against the back of him. I reach my arm around and grip him tightly at his base, then slide my hand up and down his shaft. "Petra," he groans as he grows even harder in my hand.

I turn him around and drop to my knees to take him in my mouth, letting him slide through my tight lips and cupping him between my tongue and the roof of my mouth as I suck the length of him into me repeatedly. Then I let him slide out, and slowly stand so that his cock runs along the length of my throat, through my cleavage, and along my stomach as I rise.

I step away from him, into the shower, and can feel him on my heels as the water sprays over me. Before I have time to turn around, he takes my hands and places them against the wall in front of me. He runs his hands from mine, slowly down my arms until he cups my breasts in his hands, which has me pushing my ass back into his erection. I'm so ready for him to be inside me. He pinches my nipples between his fingers gently, and my hips move back against him in a rhythmic motion.

With one foot he spreads my feet, then his hands trail down my sides and are on my ass, pulling me open and pushing me forward. He brings his cock up and slides it along my seam until he is slick with my juices. One of his hands comes above my head and plants itself next to my hand, then he's pushing into me achingly slow until he fills every last bit of space inside me, stretching me until I feel impossibly full. He wraps his free arm around my lower belly to keep my hips at the exact angle he wants, then he pulls out a bit and slides back into me over and over again. His movements are small and precise, because he knows the exact spot deep inside of me that he needs to hit to get me to orgasm. I can feel the pressure building and hiss out a "yessss," but instead of continuing, he pulls out slowly. I'm pretty sure I whimper, but I don't even care—he's prolonging this when he knows how much I need this release.

He spins me around and his mouth crashes into mine as he backs me up until my spine rests against the tile. The water cascades over our bodies, but I don't even need its heat. I'm burning up with my need for him. He pulls one of my legs up to wrap around his lower back, then he's sliding himself along my wet seam again. He bends his knees slightly and then enters me so quickly my back arches in response, pressing my breasts up against him. With one hand under my knee and the other cupping one of my breasts, he picks up the pace sliding into me and out again so quick and deep it almost takes my breath away. When his mouth latches onto my nipple, I'm pretty sure I stop breathing entirely. The pressure's building in my core and every time he rolls his tongue over my hardened nipple or sucks me further into his mouth, I climb closer to the peak of that orgasm.

He brings his mouth to meet my lips, then his hand moves between us and his thumb finds the ball of nerves above our joined bodies and with that additional pressure, the sensation builds until I feel like I might actually explode. I groan into his mouth as the orgasm rips through me and as I convulse around him, I can feel him spasming inside me too as he finds his release.

"Holy shit," he whispers into my hair, his body still connected to mine. "How does it just keep getting better?"

"I don't know," I tell him, "but I'm sure glad it does."

He pulls out of me, then turns me toward the shower head as he reaches for the body wash. "Here, let me clean you up."

———

"I don't understand how you just slept for an hour and you're still tired," Sierra says. "Only I'm allowed to be that tired right now." She rubs her hand over her belly.

I can hardly keep my eyes open in the back of the car as it bumps along the road outside the city we're headed to for dinner. "I think the sun just took it out of me today. After my shower, I felt like I had no energy left." Sasha glances at me in the rearview mirror and I can see the laughter he's holding in dancing in the gleam of his eyes. He knows why I'm tired, and how he wore me out. Twice. "I don't even remember lying down, and next thing I know, Aleksandr is waking me up and telling me I have fifteen minutes until we leave."

In the front seat, Beau glances over at Sasha and I can tell he wants to say something but is holding it in. I'm half afraid he knows. There's a lot more going on behind the party-boy image he's shown the world for so long. I'm glad he's found Sierra and that they've settled down in Blackstone with Jackson and Nate. Both my friends are getting the happily ever after they wanted, and the fact that they get it together is amazing.

"What's wrong?" Sierra asks. "You look like you're going to cry."

Oh God, my eyes are all watery as I think about how happy I am for my friends. And for myself. I got the happily ever after I didn't think I wanted, and it's better than I ever expected.

"Nothing's wrong. I'm just thinking about how lucky we all are. And how happy I am for you and Jackson that you're both going to be mamas soon."

"And that got you all teary eyed?" Sierra's skepticism is clear in her voice. I don't get sentimental like this. These fucking pregnancy hormones are messing with me. *Rein it in, Petra,* I tell myself.

"Probably just PMS," I say.

In the driver's seat, Sasha snorts, then says, "Sorry. Hormones really are the one thing that makes my wife emotional."

"Well, that got awkward fast," Beau says. We drive in silence for the remaining few minutes until we arrive at the restaurant.

Jackson and Lauren are already at our outdoor table with their men when we arrive. The seating is built into the corner of the deck, with two sides of bench seating covered in cushions and pillows leaning up against the solid deck wall. This part of the restaurant is built out over the rocky coastline of the Caribbean Sea, with waves crashing directly beneath us on this beautifully warm night. A palm tree growing on the shore overhangs our table, and string lights are strung between its tall trunk and the roofline of the restaurant. It's a magical setting, and I think again about how great Nate is at finding places like this. He has a knack for ambiance, whether it's finding the right property to add to his vacation rental empire, or finding the right restaurant for dinner on his wife's babymoon.

Jackson and Nate are sitting on the benches, and Lauren and her man are sitting in two of the four chairs. "Do you want the bench seating or the chairs?" I ask Sierra.

"I'll take the bench," she says. "I can probably get more comfortable there." Beau helps her get situated and then takes his seat next to her on one edge of the table while Sasha and I take the seats along the other open edge.

The waitress arrives to take our drink orders and I ask for a club soda with lime. "Hold up," Jackson says. "You can drink all of us under the table and you're not drinking? At least let me drink vicariously through you. I can't tell you what I'd give for a margarita right now."

"We make a really great virgin pineapple margarita," the waitress says, eyeing Jackson's maternity dress. "You won't even miss the tequila."

"The hell I won't," Jackson says, but she's laughing. "All right, fine, I'll take a virgin pineapple margarita."

"Me too," Sierra says.

When she's done taking drink orders, the waitress heads off with a promise of returning with chips, salsa, and guacamole. Meanwhile, I try to pretend like I don't notice Jackson staring at me like she's trying to figure out if telepathy is real and if she can use it on me.

The guys are asking Aleksandr about the coming season and I laugh, reminding them that the current season *just* ended a couple weeks ago. I can't help but think about how different this year is going to be.

At least I know Stella will be the best big sister ever. That girl may be my mini-me, but her heart is bigger and more open, and she wants a little sister more than anything. We're going to have so much fun bringing another little girl into our family.

On my left, Lauren leans toward me. "Are you really not going to tell them?" she whispers and I close my eyes, focusing on keeping my face as serene and unaffected as possible. "I'm pretty sure they already know," she continues. "And they're going to be mad if it comes out before you tell them."

I lean my head even closer to hers. "How did you know?"

"Besides that adorable belly you are trying to hide under your kimonos and loose-fitting dresses? You also haven't been drinking even though you are pretending to."

"What are you two whispering about?" Sierra asks from my other side. "You better not be telling Lauren you're pregnant and not telling us too."

Her words are a record screech that brings all conversation and movement to a halt. Mouths hang open, water glasses are suspended in hands midair. I don't think the entire table could go silent more quickly if I said I was dying.

"Um, what?" I ask, my voice small and high-pitched. I feel Aleksandr bring his hand up to the small of my back, rubbing a circle there.

"I *knew* it!" Beau says, his face triumphant. "PMS my ass."

"I don't even want to know what that means," Nate says, glancing at his brother-in-law.

When it's clear I've lost the ability to speak, Sasha says, "This isn't exactly how we wanted to tell you all."

"I'm sorry," I mumble. "We weren't trying to lie about it, but this is your babymoon," I say, looking from Jackson to Sierra, "and I didn't want to co-opt that with my news."

No one speaks, we all just look at each other, our eyes roaming around the table making eye contact with every person there. And in those moments, we're having silent conversations of excitement and apology.

"I can't believe you're having a baby," Sierra finally says, and she sounds breathless. "Like, I *really* can't believe it."

"So eloquent, babe," Beau teases, then leans over and kisses Sierra's temple.

"I think this is just a bit of a shock, you know," Lauren says, "since you were always pretty against having kids."

"Well, she was always against getting married too, yet she's been married longer than any of us," Jackson smiles. "I knew you'd come around."

"I'm glad someone did," Nate says, and I shoot him a look in response. "Hey, I've known you since you were what, eighteen? You were always a rebel. You always wanted to blaze your own trail—"

"She *is* blazing her own trail," Sasha interrupts, and though his tone is supportive, there's a note of warning there for anyone who'd disagree.

I take his hand and squeeze. "I'm just not doing it alone."

"Tell us more about this baby," Sierra says. "How far along are you?"

"Just passed the eighteen week mark. We're having a girl!"

"What are the chances?" Lauren murmurs. "All of us with little girls. My girls will be so excited to have *three* little girl cousins." She beams at the love of her life, and I have this moment of gratitude that after the horrendous year she's had, things are better for her now than they've ever been.

"And now that you're in Boston," Jackson says to her, "we're all finally at least in the same region again."

The waitress arrives then with our drinks and sets several baskets of chips, along with salsa and guacamole, on our table.

I hold my glass up. "To new beginnings and growing families, and to all being together-ish again!"

There's a chorus of "yeah" and "hear, hear" and "finally" as we all raise our glasses in a toast. When Jackson says, "This should be an annual trip, next time with kids," my agreement could not come any quicker or be more adamant. I settle into Sasha's side, his arm wrapped around my shoulders as I gaze at the happy, slightly sunburned faces of my family—the one I built for myself—and feel nothing but utter contentment.

If the last couple years have taught me anything, it's that there will be ups and downs for all of us. But we'll get through it like we always have: together.

THE END

———

Not ready for Petra and Aleksandr's story to end? Get their bonus epilogue to see them as parents when Stella graduates from high school.

Scan here for
Petra & Aleksandr's
Bonus Epilogue

Curious how Avery and Tom ended up together? You can read their story in the Christmas novella, One Little Favor.

Keep reading for a sneak peak from Lauren's story, On the Line.

On the Line

My marriage wasn't perfect, but my husband's unexpected death yanks away my sense of security and leaves me floundering.

Enter Jameson Flynn, former NHL star and my late husband's sports agent, who's back in my life as the executor of the will. Things between us are as contentious as when we worked together five years ago, except now we're working together to navigate all of the secrets and deceptions my husband left behind.

I remember Jameson as arrogant, condescending, and heartless. And yet, he repeatedly shows up for me and my daughters – helping me pick up the broken pieces and put my life back together.

Now I'm seeing a side of him he only reveals to people he truly cares about. He's protective in a way I didn't know I'd like, caring in a way I didn't know he was capable of, and still sexy as hell.

The problem is, he broke my heart a long time ago. But the closer I get to Jameson, the more I see that the only thing easier than hating him might actually be loving him.

Read on for an excerpt from Lauren's book . . .

———

LAUREN

Park City, Utah

Today is going to be a great day. I can feel it in my bones. Things are starting to come together, to line up in just the way I need them to.

I pull out into downtown Salt Lake City traffic, and the office where I just verbally accepted a job offer fades away in my rearview mirror. After several years staying at home, first as a newly married wife and then as a new mom, I've finally made my way back into the world of sports marketing.

And I've done it on my own: no handouts, no nepotism,

no connections. I got this job solely based on my own merit, and it's the best feeling.

"So you haven't even told Josh yet?" Petra's voice carries through the speaker in my SUV as I approach a stoplight. Petra's one of my three best friends, but she's the only one who knows the struggles Josh and I have had over the past year and a half as we adjust to being the parents of twin girls.

Well, I've adjusted. He's slowly pulled away.

"He hasn't exactly been reachable these past few days," I tell her.

"Where is he this time?" she asks.

In the couple years since Josh retired, he's made his living skiing—traveling to ski resorts all over to promote different brands that sponsor him, filming videos and ads, and generally relishing the fact that he still gets paid to ski even though he's no longer competing.

"Somewhere in Washington. They were at Stevens Pass, then I think they headed somewhere near Spokane a couple days ago. He'll be home tonight, but I texted him earlier and haven't heard back yet. At least after this trip, he'll be home until Christmas."

"Well, that's a good thing," she says encouragingly.

"I don't know how you handle everything when Aleksandr is away," I say. Her husband plays in the NHL, so he's gone a fair amount during the season and together they have a seven-year-old adopted daughter.

"I just do." I can practically hear her shrug over the phone as I change lanes to head toward the on-ramp for I-80, the road that will take me into the mountains and back to my home in Park City. "He was already traveling when we got together, so it's all I've known."

Josh was also already skiing professionally when we met and got married. He traveled a lot then, but since I'd quit my sports marketing job in Boston in order to move out to Park City with him after we got engaged, I was able to travel with him to his races that first year.

And I'd made some great girl friends in Park City, starting with his physical therapist, Jackson, and her best friends Sierra and Petra. They brought me into their group and we were all so close, but all three of them have moved away and gotten married over the past two years, right as Josh and I were starting our family. With him traveling a lot, I'm now often on my own with the kids, so his travel is hitting me harder than it used to.

But that's on me, because I don't have anything else in my life except for him and the kids—which is why the job is going to be such a big deal for me.

Having something to focus on besides my family will help me feel like a more well-rounded person, able to bring more to our relationship and our family than just my role as a mother. I'll finally have things to talk to my husband about again—things besides nap schedules and the infinite minutiae of what our girls did each day. Plus, with my background in sports marketing and my general passion for hockey, getting to work for one of the NHL farm teams is a perfect mix of my interests and abilities.

But I thought the interview and offer process would take longer than it did, so I assumed I'd have more time to figure out how to tell Josh.

"Soo," Petra says when I'm so lost in my own thoughts I forget to respond, "how are you going to tell him?"

"It's like you're reading my mind right now," I say.

"I'd hardly have to be a mind reader to know that's what you're thinking about. I know how he feels about you working."

I didn't know he was so old-fashioned about the role of wife and mother before I married him. I guess that's what happens when you have a whirlwind romance and marry someone you've known for six months. At the time, it was all so romantic, and he was so attentive and passionate and protective. Completely unlike any of the guys I'd dated up until that point.

I used to joke that I was going to marry the first nice guy I dated, and I held true to that—I just wish that the Josh I'd dated and the Josh I'd started a family with were the same person.

"He's going to have to adjust," I say. "We'll work out childcare. Morgan mentioned that one of her friends might be looking for a part-time nanny position, so I'm going to talk to her as soon as possible."

"That's great," Petra says. My cousin Morgan has been immensely helpful in watching the girls when Josh is out of town and I need to be somewhere else, like at today's final interview when they offered me the job.

"When it comes to talking to Josh," she continues in that husky voice she's literally famous for, "I've found that a good meal and good sex can convince a man of just about anything."

"I must finally be learning," I say with a laugh, "because that's pretty much exactly what I have planned for tonight."

"Yes." The word is a low hiss. "I've taught you my ways and you're going to have Josh eating out of your hand before the night is over."

My smile spreads. "I mean, the man's been gone for a week and a half, so there's a good chance you're right."

Petra's the only woman I know who is as unabashedly driven by sex as most men. She's also straightforward to a fault, strikingly beautiful, powerful in her own right, and intimidating as hell. If you'd told me years ago when I met her that we'd end up being incredibly close, I'd have laughed.

She intimidated the shit out of me when we first met. But love, marriage, and an adorable daughter have softened her hard edges just enough, without dulling the intense, passionate aspects of her personality.

"When are you going to tell Jackson and Sierra about this new job?" she asks.

"Probably tomorrow. I just want to talk to Josh first."

Not knowing how Josh is going to feel about me going back to work is taking a bit of the shine off this victory, but I remind myself not to let that dull my joy in this moment.

"Lauren," she says, and there's a warning in her voice. "Do not back down. Don't let him talk you out of this. Don't let him convince you that you're not a good wife or a good mom if you go back to work part-time. It's only three days a week. Everything will be fine."

I take a deep breath through my nose. "I know. And don't worry, it's going to be fine. He knows I need this. I really do believe that me going back to work is going to bring Josh and I closer, and I'm positive I can make him see it that way too."

"Good. But if the conversation doesn't go well, or if you need anything," she says, "just call. I don't care about the time difference."

"Thanks, Petra. I really couldn't have taken these steps without your encouragement."

"You one hundred percent could have," she says, her voice emphatic. "You're a badass, and you're doing the right thing taking this job."

Her confidence in me is often the boost I need to believe in myself. "You're right. This is the perfect job, at the perfect time. Things are going to be great."

———

I toss the bottle of balsamic glaze into my cart on top of the flank steak and come around the end of that aisle into the produce section. Josh always eats like crap when he's on the road and loves to come back to a good home-cooked meal. I hate cooking and don't do it often, but tonight I'm making his favorite: seared flank steak stuffed with spinach, garlic, butter, and Parmesan, along with creamy mashed potatoes, and green beans sautéed with garlic and topped with a balsamic glaze.

I still haven't heard from him, which is a little odd. Normally, he texts me when he gets on the road to head home. Maybe he lost his charger again, like on his last trip. Sometimes he's a little scattered like that.

It's a long drive from Washington, so I figure I still have time to get home and spend a little time with the girls, get the food prepped, put the girls to bed, and have dinner waiting when Josh walks in that door.

I'm pushing my cart through the produce section toward the front of the store when it happens—it feels like the floor drops out from under me, and I have the sensation of falling.

The moment replays in my mind, so vividly that I'm forced to relive it.

The music is pumping and the crowd is clapping in sync with the beat as I finish a sequence of artistic moves and then go through a series of backward crossovers to gather the speed that will take me into the most difficult jump in my routine: a triple axel.

I've landed it in competition before, but never on a national stage—this is going to make me a household name. That's what I'm thinking about as I turn forward, push off the outside edge of my left skate, kick through with my right leg to get the height I need for the three and a half rotations of the jump, hug my arms to my body and spin through the air on the perfect axis. And when the blade of my right skate hits the ice and I'm about to kick my left leg out behind me, I know I've executed a textbook perfect jump.

Then the ice is coming at me with alarming speed, and I don't know what happens after that. Dozens of experts have analyzed the footage and no one can quite say why, instead of sticking that landing and clinching my first national championship, I end up on the ice, the side of my head connecting with the rink hard enough that I'm completely knocked out.

I come to a full stop in the middle of the aisle, relieved that the store is so empty. I've broken out in a full-body sweat, and I bend at the waist, resting my forehead on the bar of the grocery cart and taking a few deep breaths to get my bearings.

I don't know what it means when I relive that moment like this. It's only happened a few times since I recovered—and each time it has felt like a terrible omen.

That's when Josh's name lights up my phone screen.

"Hey." I take a breath, ready to launch into the story of what just happened.

"Is this Lauren Emerson?"

The unfamiliar voice has me standing up, gripping the phone so hard I'm surprised I don't bend the metal and glass in my hand.

"Yes. Who's this?"

"Ma'am," he replies with a steady, deep voice, "this is Lieutenant George Marshall from the Blaine County Sheriff's Office in Sun Valley, Idaho."

I'm pretty sure my heart stops. Josh isn't in Sun Valley, Idaho. He's in eastern Washington. This has to be a mistake. Except, he's calling from my husband's cell phone.

"Is everything okay?" Even as I ask it, I know how ridiculous the question is. The Sheriff's Office doesn't call because everything's okay.

"Are you somewhere where you can sit down?"

"I'm in the grocery store right now." I glance around self-consciously, but the only other person in the produce section is an employee stocking apples along the far wall.

"Do you want to go somewhere more private so we can talk?"

"No!" My voice is shrill even to my own ears. "I want to know why you're calling from my husband's phone!"

My words are verging on hysteria. I need to talk to Josh. I'm going to tell him about this new job, and he's going to be proud of me. We'll get back to everything being good between us again.

I can hear the concern in his voice when he responds, "Okay, ma'am. Your husband was skiing out of bounds at Sun Valley Resort with a small group of people. We've had heavy snowfall over the past five days and the avalanche threat was considerable. Their group triggered a substantial slide earlier this morning."

An avalanche is a skier's worst nightmare, especially if you're skiing in the backcountry. Josh was a ski racer—he's best on smoothly groomed trails where he can go as fast as he likes. He's not a backcountry skier. What the hell was he doing out of bounds? And why was he in Sun Valley?

A sob bursts out of me as I consider my husband buried under all that snow, like being trapped in frozen concrete, injured and in pain. "Is he going to be okay?"

On the other end of the line, he pauses, and let's out a shaky breath. "I'm sorry ma'am. He didn't make it."

I sink to my knees still clutching my phone to my ear. "What?" This doesn't make any sense. Josh is too smart to ski out of bounds when there's an avalanche threat. Isn't he?

"Rescue crews got to them as quickly as possible, but they were buried under too much debris. No one survived."

My body feels frozen in shock and my chest heaves as I try to draw a breath. Everything around me seems to be spinning. I think I'm hyperventilating, but I have no idea how to calm myself down.

"Ma'am?"

"I'm here," I squeak out, then take a few ragged, gasping breaths.

"I'm going to have someone in my office call local law enforcement and get them to come to you and make sure you get home safely. Please stay on the line with me until they arrive." He asks the name of the grocery store I'm at and where in the store I'm located, and, while he keeps me on the phone, he answers my questions to the best of his ability given that "the investigation is ongoing." All he's able to tell me is what time the avalanche happened, and how long Josh and his fellow skiers were buried before rescue crews were able to dig them out.

There were no survivors. That sobering piece of information is winding itself around my brain. I have so many questions—about why they were in Sun Valley and why they skied out of bounds when there was an avalanche threat—but anyone who could answer them is dead.

I feel like I'm trapped, suffocating, as I sit on the floor shaking uncontrollably. It feels like an hour, but is probably only a few minutes, before two police officers are walking up the aisle to me. The older one helps me up while the younger one takes the phone and speaks to the officer in Sun Valley.

"We're going to get you home," he says as he puts his arm around my waist to support me. The wrinkles around his eyes crinkle as he smiles a sad smile. The younger officer says something to him, but while his lips are moving, it sounds like he's talking to me underwater. I feel like I might pass out. "It's going to be okay."

And in that moment, looking up at him, I'm certain nothing is ever going to be okay again.

Books by Julia Connors

FROZEN HEARTS SERIES

On the Edge

(Jackson & Nate's Story)

Out of Bounds

(Sierra & Beau's Story)

One Last Shot

(Petra & Aleksandr's Story)

One Little Favor

(Avery & Tom's Novella)

On the Line

(Lauren & Jameson's Story)

BOSTON REBELS SERIES

Center Ice

(Audrey & Drew's Story)

Acknowledgments

Petra. This side character, who I wrote into On the Edge with absolutely no intention of ever giving her her own story, really took on a life of her own. In the back of my mind, I guess I always knew that her bravado hid past loss, but it wasn't until I started writing Sierra's story that I really thought about how Petra got to where she is when we meet her in the first two books of the series.

A self-made woman who easily separates sex and feelings, who loves her friends fiercely but eschews romantic love, who never talks about her past and always looks to the future, who isn't afraid to reinvent herself over and over.

I thought that writing her was going to be fun. And then she nearly killed me. Seriously. One Last Shot was the most difficult writing experience I've ever had. Intensely private Petra just did not seem to want her story told—but, bit by bit, her story unfolded in my mind. Petra was at times more fun than I'd imagined, and also more complex and more damaged. In the end, I hope I've done her justice in this story!

I have so many people to thank for their support and feedback on this book, but most especially:

My readers, knowing how many of you wanted Petra's book kept me going when the writing got tough. Your messages of support about my earlier books, your questions about this world I created, and your enthusiasm for my characters has lifted me up. This story is for you!

Anna, this book is for you, girl! Thank you for being the inspiration for Petra's character. Every beautiful thing about Petra is based on you! Thanks also for being my go-to girl for all my questions about Russian culture and language.

Danielle, I honestly could not have written Jackson, Sierra, and Petra's books without your feedback. Our conversations about writing and cover design and graphics and business have sustained me. I wouldn't want to do this without you!

Laura and Marti, for all the feedback on Petra's story, especially the last-minute rewrite of the beginning, right before this went to the editor—thank you! And *Keri,* thank you for always being my go-to person to bounce plot and character ideas off of. I'm so glad we all found our way to our little writing group years ago.

Jane, we've been meeting to talk about writing for over a decade. I so value our coffee dates and all the advice we share with each other (though let's face it, I'm mostly the beneficiary there). Keep writing amazing books—you're such an inspiration!

My fellow indie romance authors, who are getting too numerous to name—this publishing journey has been so much less lonely because of you! Seriously, indie romance authors are the best, most generous people on the planet. The number of people who have provided business suggestions and tips, offered to promote my books to their readers, given me publishing and marketing advice, and generally just been awesome, keeps growing and growing.

Mr. Connors, who continues to encourage me and to do everything within his power to help me fulfill this lifelong dream of becoming a writer. Every trip to the grocery store, every load of laundry, every meal you've prepped, every time you take our kids to and from their activities—I see how you create the time and the space for me to write by taking so much off my plate. I love you!

Afterword

Thank you so much for reading! If you enjoyed the book, please consider leaving an honest review. Reader reviews mean so much to authors, and your time and feedback are appreciated.

Sign up for Julia's newsletter to stay up to date on the latest news and be the first to know about sales, audiobooks, and new releases!

www.juliaconnors.com/newsletter

About the Author

Julia Connors grew up on the warm and sunny West Coast, but her first decision as an adult was to trade her flip-flops for snow boots and move to Boston. She's been enjoying everything that New England has to offer for over two decades, and now that she's acclimated to the snowy winters and finally found all the places to get good sushi and tacos, she has zero regrets. You can usually find her in front of her computer, but when she stops writing she's most likely to be found outdoors, preferably with a pair of skis or snowshoes strapped to her feet in winter, or on a paddleboard in the summer.

goodreads.com/julia_connors

amazon.com/author/juliaconnors

instagram.com/juliaconnorsauthor

tiktok.com/@juliaconnorsauthor?

facebook.com/juliaconnorsauthor

pinterest.com/juliaconnorsauthor